TOKYONIGHTS

JIM DOUGLAS

Tokyo Nights
Jim Douglas
© Jim Douglas 2016
The author asserts the moral right to be identified
as the author of the work in accordance with the
Copyright, Designs and Patents Act, 1988

Cover illustration: Graeme Clarke
Lyrics of Puff the Magic Dragon reproduced by kind permiddion of
Lenny Lipton and Peter Yarrow

Published by:
Fledgling Press Ltd,

www.fledglingpress.co.uk

Printed and bound by:
Charlesworth Press, Wakefield

ISBN 9781905916191

Acknowledgements

Firstly, and especially, we would like to thank our publisher Clare at Fledging Press for her patience and fortitude that provided wings for this book to fly and Sally Homer for making the flight path possible. Thanks to Sue Ellis who was our first reader and was invaluable in tightening up what was then a loose snarl. In addition, thanks are due to friends who read the book at the initial stages of production – Michael Bickett, Andrew Robinson, Pete Gisborne, my sister, Jane Hickey, Mike Foley, Jennifer Owens, John Pugh and Phil Beadle – for their incisive and varied comments that helped to strengthen the book.

An appreciation is more than due to the writers of *Puff the Magic Dragon* – Leonard Lipton and Pete Yarrow – who, with marvelous generosity, allowed us to use this seminal and outstanding song in a chapter of our book.

Personal thanks are owed to Phil whose encouragement and help throughout our long friendship has bolstered the journey and whose dogged friendship keeps me at large.

And to Sally, too, for everything. The book is an ode to Japan and we wish to thank all our friends here who brought the scenery to it, inspired us and were with us in the neon nights of the drink, laughter and gaiety that stirred this book into existence.

Thanks also to Charlie Cubbit, Helen Greensides, Tommy Saunders, Katz, Tomo, Yuka, Emichan and Tomochan.

Gratitude also to Barry Eisler, author of The Rain series of crime novels. We read his advice on how to publish this genre of fiction and found it down to earth,
salient and to the point.

Finally, I wish to thank my friend and co-author Douglas Forrester who sadly and tragically died before seeing his work and dream become a published novel.

Thankfully, his loved ones, Victor and Moira, his parents, and his wife, Shoko, will.

This brings me some solace. Without Doug I would still be writing poems to birds and demons in a Spinoza trance inside my urban cell to which he came with beers from Belgium and French cheeses that we consumed before getting our heads together and down to work.

For Douglas.
With Gratitude and Memory

PART 1-TOKYO

STREETS BROAD AND NARROW

Charlie Davis adjusted his cap, tilted it, and grinned. He wasn't unhappy with the man in the mirror nor with the light spring in his heels. It was his first day off in a long time and he had slept most of it to ready himself for the coming night. Thus far the new life had been all work and getting acquainted. Twilly had aged and done what is called 'well for himself' here, putting together quite an enterprise.

"Just the surface is all you're getting now, mate. But there's candy and lots of it. Play it right, Charlie boy, and some of it's for you."

The quarters were spick and span and he had the evening in front of him. He felt grounded but not entrenched. The basics had been laid down and from here it was all about living. From a second-hand bookshop in Kanda he had picked up some Japanese verse by Basho, who he had heard of, and Santoka, who he hadn't. He liked it. The elements at work in the words weren't literary, more ordinary – or what he thought the ordinary should be. Ideas formed; he would travel through Japan as they had done – with little – find out and be found out. It would be exhilarating.

He gathered up his cards from the *tatami* flooring and wrapped them in a handkerchief. Twilly had apologized about the place, "Get you something better later pal. Not like you ain't use to slumming it, though."

He was and he liked it. He owned little and had brought less. The mind was the best carrier for anything of worth and the rest was just baggage. Putting the final touches to his raiment he slipped on a light silk scarf and, leaving the door unlocked, headed for the station and the big city.

✄

The force of the night dazzled him as he stepped from the kerb into the fray of the street.

Not knowing where he was going, he just walked – staggering and stalling, feeling like a Gulliver among these people, not because of his size but because of his difference. He bumped into a crush of drunken *salarymen* and apologized. They laughed, said, "Hello to you," bowed and swayed away. Rail-thin flame-headed boys in pipe-slim suits flickered around like fireflies. As always he took particular notice of the talent. The birds of big cities come in all varieties, none of which he had seen in finer plumage or with a better scent and promised flavor than these.

Spying a kiosk, he went to buy cigarettes. The girl smiled and tipped her head to one side like a marionette and pointed to the wrong pack. He noticed that her nails were long and adorned with some enamel embossed pattern. 'Okay,' he motioned, as she finally located the right pack. At a smoking corner he lit up to watch the street life and feel the nicotine calm his pulsing being.

Many of the women were deeply daubed and the glister of the artificial excited him. They had been worked by some great god to fall down here and were garbed in outfits that sparkled and shone, perching themselves on heels of scimitar sharpness, painting themselves to absolute perfection. But then look: a piggy *geisha* with huge thighs thumping past provided an alternative narrative. There were ladies of the office too, with a porcelain and delicate attractiveness, dressed less extremely but still sumptuous. He was humming and basking in this wonderland, the new reality that had entered him, filling up the emptiness with unfathomable and dimensionless possibilities. He could be something again here; perhaps better, perhaps worse, a fabric newly spun and tailored. He felt a new kind of estrangement and a curious dissolving of self, as if the lights that sparkled and the hieroglyphs that gleamed and burned catered as an erasing force. Looking up at the sky he could see no sign that he was on the Earth. The stars had vanished and there was no moon, no orientation or way for man to steer his craft, or himself, home. 'Suits me, man,' he thought as he took a final drag. Here he was cast naked into the blinding lights of the unknown, adrift in the music and sights of an everyday carnival, one quite normal for them, but not for him. It was a second life and he would embrace it.

He weaved through a stream of bodies so dense as to be discomforting, then turned into an alleyway full of cafés and bars. Climbing a flight of stairs, he entered one of them and was greeted with silence. The place was tiny, just barstools and a counter, an older lady with a chalk face and two young dolled-up women staring vacantly at him. Men in suits sat in front of them, some red-faced. Smoke hit him as it passed through the bar lights in blue rivulets. He smiled but the chalk face motioned 'No entry' with an X made by her two index fingers and a stern visage.

Davis continued further down the alley and came to a

place that hailed him better, as a lady held up a finger and pointed to a seat in the corner. He took it and was given a menu in Japanese, but without looking at it he made a gesture, raising his arms and pushing out his palms.

"Please, *sake*, *nihonshu*?"

The lady gave a slight bow and soon returned with a small jug and a tiny cup along with a dish that contained what looked like miniature whole baby fish. He poured out a measure and took a hit then refilled. This bar was also small but the clientele more varied. In here nobody looked his way and he felt almost betrayed, but soon the potion kicked in, and with it a mood of reflection. He finished the small flagon, then another, and retraced his steps, heading for the main drag, walking on neon. The *sake* lifted him like an ichor of the gods: the fish had been rank but he had devoured them out of propriety.

Weaving through a litter of young, happy drunk people he found himself back at the station and decided to head for a different part of the city. The seats on the train were mostly taken and he found himself standing near the doors, sipping the can of lager he'd bought and casting his eyes around the carriage. A young girl in office clothes was crashed out comatose, head forward, resting on her chest, face curtained by the fall of her hair.

Two men in matching suits boarded in a hurry, nodding in some rite of affirmation. An announcement came across the tannoy that he guessed signaled departure. He closed his eyes and felt a shudder as the train began to move. He didn't really know where he was going and the lightness of that pleased him.

■

She was hard to miss, parting the people like an infernal Moses, gazing into her sparkling mobile phone, fingering the screen as she swayed down the lurching carriage. Her hair was ash blonde streaked with purple and her skin as smooth and brown as milky coffee. She advanced slowly and stopped at the corner opposite Davis, then turned her back to the carriage, facing the window and her own reflection.

Davis shifted his position to best view her profile and thought about making a move but he was frozen, unable to act, too mesmerized to do anything. Then the train halted and as the passengers shifted position she turned and their eyes met. He glanced away momentarily but when he looked back she was in front of him. He gazed into her glittering blue eyes and they stared back and held his. People got on the train and pushed forward and Davis found himself crushed against her. She was smiling playfully and holding her phone against her chest.

"What number?"

Davis shrugged against her shoulder. "I don't have a number."

She tutted at him, "No good. Okay. Take with me."

"Take?"

"Me."

The train jerked over points and he felt his body push against her breasts, partly shielded by a black lacy bikini top. He nodded and grasped her hand. "Where?" She stared back at him through her mask of cerulean eyelids and spider-legged lashes like he was stupid, and said again, "You take me."

He nodded and passed her the can of Malts he was drinking from.

This was Davis's odyssey and it was a far better one than what had been before. He knew only illumination could come of it, here in waves of light made by the forces of men. All and every element was at play here and at grief, buzzing and shaking with doomed but celebrating wings, like a giant cicada in the dark light of a Tokyo night.

THE CONCRETE HAYSTACK

The speeding train took Colin McCann and all the other red-eyed, tired and crumpled travellers from Narita International Airport – a concrete slab deposited in the countryside of Chiba – to Shinjuku in northwest central Tokyo. He rubbed the three-day stubble on his chin and pulled the rumpled trousers from his crotch. 'Long journey', he thought. 'Long journey, for what?'

It was his third visit to Harold Philips' big Victorian house in Altrincham that did it. Philips didn't smile much but when he saw the look on McCann's face, he chuckled. It wasn't a pleasant sight. "Don't look so shocked Mr. McCann. Next logical step."

"That's… a long way Mr. Philips. And no guarantee I can actually find him. And even if I do, no guarantee I'll get any useful information from him either. A needle in a haystack, and it might not even be the right needle. Jesus, it might not even be the right haystack!"

"But it is something. And it's not taken you long to find out some strange inconsistencies regarding our daughter's death already. I knew I was right … I could feel it. Even a cynic like yourself must admit it's worth chasing up, Mr. McCann. Even if it is all the way to Japan."

He held his hands out, palms open. His eyebrows were raised. It was almost a Gallic shrug. "I am not ungenerous when I see results; of course all your expenses to Japan will be paid, and for the unexpected trouble this causes you, I'm willing to recompense considerably more than the original sum agreed. You said yourself the information you received from that little prick you talked to seems to hold up."

For a few seconds Philips had seemed almost in a good mood but his face darkened, the jowls shook and the eyes were fierce. "I do not give up, McCann. Not in business, and certainly not when my family are involved. I saw that Davis scum once with my Natasha, and I should have ripped his fucking head off right then and there. He doesn't touch my daughter and walk away scot-free."

Philips breathed in and out deeply. The darkness subsided slightly. "It seems that your business and mine are not quite as far removed as I had first supposed. Money talks. And your little squealer has furnished enough information to merit... shall we call it an unexpected business trip?"

McCann's turn to shrug, "All we've got is the name of the guy who is friends with Davis and runs a private language school in Japan. I've run his name past my sources and it's good. And I've looked up the language school. It checks out as well, and the owner's name and face match. Personally, I think you'd have to be insane to think that alone is enough information to merit a trip half way across the world. But it's your money, Mr. Philips. Let's be clear though – I can't guarantee anything."

"It is a lead. In two weeks you have come up with a better lead than the police have in four months. Put yourself in my shoes. How could you live with yourself, knowing that you hadn't done everything possible to determine what caused the death of your daughter?"

McCann thought about that for a few seconds. Out the window behind Philips he could see leaves spiraling off the trees towards the ground, dropping one by one.

An announcement, first in gobbledygook and then in

a clear, robotic American English, pulled him back to the present. 'Serves you right for taking this on in the first place', he thought. 'Should have stuck with the regular work.'

He considered the phone messages he had received in the two days before leaving for Japan – two simple, regular jobs. One low-level fraud, and a suspected adultery – a tasty divorce case from Hillary, Moss, Weston and Partners, his best clients. He had had to turn both of them down to follow up this lost cause. He ran his hands through his dishevelled hair. After twenty hours of non-stop travelling it needed a wash.

"Why the hell did I get myself into this?" he muttered, a little too loudly. The man in the seat across glanced up from his newspaper at him. An Asian face in a slim, dark grey suit.

As sharp as the folds of his paper. Unruffled.

江

McCann staggered off the train at Shinjuku Station into a cacophony of movement and noise. He travelled light, and wheeled his small Samsonite suitcase through the blur of people as he tried to get out onto the street. It was a huge, confusing maelstrom of shops, noise, escalators and passageways leading off in all conceivable directions. Everything gleamed in the fluorescent light. He struggled out the station into the grey twilight. It had stopped raining.

Though dog-tired and desperate for a shower and a sleep, he couldn't resist a short walk around before heading to his hotel. It was a sensory overload of sights, sounds, smells and above all energy, the energy of fourteen million people in perpetual motion, unwilling, unable to slow down or stop.

Buildings everywhere: massive business skyscrapers; smaller concrete office blocks covered in pipes and air conditioner units like barnacles stuck to a ship's hull; quirky designs at odd angles; tiny noodle shops slipped in between crazed-looking square block buildings spewing noise and flashing epileptic lights with huge neon signs saying 'Happy Pachinko' beside ten foot tall green-haired cartoon girls dressed in leather hot pants and blue thigh-high boots.

Signs all over the place, lit up in red, yellow, blue and white; some on gigantic billboards atop the skyscrapers, others on massive digital screens clinging to the sides. In English he read: MMC, Sony, Takashimaya Times Square, Hitachi. At ground level, a mishmash of digital displays and lighted signs advertised stationery shops, bars, a myriad of restaurants, bookshops, and coffee shops, the occasional English word peppering the Japanese hieroglyphics and catching his attention. There was plastic food in windows – so realistic McCann had to double-take to check it wasn't real – showing everything from noodles suspended in mid-air on chopsticks held by invisible hands, to large glasses of beer, complete with frothy head and simulated frosting on the glass, looking so tasty they made McCann's mouth water.

Rows and rows of taxis, almost identical four-door box saloon Toyotas and Nissans – some black, some apple green and banana yellow – picked up a dark blue and grey stream of *salarymen*, the monotones punctuated by the occasional older lady or backpack-wielding Western couple, and whisked them off into the flow of trucks, buses, private cars and motorbikes roaring round the main arteries of Shinjuku Dori and Yasukuni Dori. On McCann's left, a chemist's shop, its wares spilling onto the street: energy drinks made from the alchemy of ginseng and nicotine placed beside hand cream and shampoo. The owner was engaged in aural mortal combat with a staff member from a mobile phone shop on his right. Each was screeching ear-splitting slogans at the passing stream of commuters through megaphones. The two voices melded with each other and with the Euro-beat techno music being blasted out from another nearby shop into a jumble of white noise that almost physically knocked McCann reeling. The commuters seemed not to even hear, pushing relentlessly towards or away from Shinjuku station.

He decided to eat something before attempting the daunting task of making his way through the crazy maze of streets and people to wherever his hotel was, and settled on a cheery looking burger shop. The comforting familiarity of an English menu set out on a large easel by the window, with pictures of western fast food reassured his jet-lagged mind and already travel-sick belly.

Inside, the decor was what he supposed to be a Japanese take on a 1950's American diner. The stereo seemed to be playing the entire Beatles back catalogue, which was annoying when it was *Twist and Shout* but cheered McCann up when replaced by *Helter Skelter*. He moved to the counter, where a lovely girl of about eighteen greeted him with a dazzling smile and something in Japanese. McCann responded back with the best face he could muster. He was delighted; how could he not be? At this the girl's grin broadened to Cheshire cat proportions and she said to him, "Are you English menu?"

"Yeah, please." Things had started well, he felt like a teenager at the school disco who has just been asked to dance by the hottest girl in the year. 'How could anyone look so happy to be working in a burger joint,' he wondered.

In an attempt to show some sense of recognition of his

new surroundings, he chose the teriyaki chicken burger. Amazingly lager was also on the menu, so he asked for a glass and she beamed at him some more. Confused but massively cheered up, he found a place to sit. The meal was brought to him a few minutes later. It was good and he ate ravenously.

Wiping his mouth and hands with a paper napkin, he took a glug of lager, rummaged around in his travel bag for his iPhone, and pulled up the digital notepad filled with names, memos, dates and staccato comments; his memory jogger.

Scrolling through the file, he stopped at Carl Pounder. A psychic pain shot through his left leg. No danger of forgetting that bastard in a hurry.

TIANANMEN TANKMAN

The lock clicked and the chain unzipped. The door opened with a stench of occupancy and Mr. Carl Pounder – laughing about something – grabbed his dog by its nail-studded collar and hauled it back into the house. The tenant had the shadow mark about him, something that hid there and waited. A hand was offered and McCann shook it. It was calloused and gripped hard and for too long. McCann looked at the man's eyes and they were insensate too: a grey blue. Pounder was not tall and had the look of a shaved weasel about him. A wall of heat hit McCann as he entered; the central heating gasped. Pounder indicated that McCann should sit at the kitchen table.

"Me name's Carl. Want a brew?"

"Bit early, isn't it?"

"A cuppa, mate."

"Oh. Sure."

Pounder was shirtless and barefooted and moved well, as if in a semi-glide, cat-like.

"That's Marvin, by the way. The most useless fuckin' pit bull in England."

"He a pedigree?"

"Not exactly but his old man was a ripper. Game as they come. Christ knows how he begat that piece of shit."

McCann patted the dog's head and sat back down. It was time for work.

"Why you leaving, Carl?"

"Cash flow, mate. Lost me job and that."

True enough. Since the incident the police, anxious to be seen doing something useful, had busted some dealers and Pounder was one. His main job had been to launder stuff; pick it up from meeting points on the hill and redirect it, bagged and ready, to the metropolis. The police had caught him in the act and he was on bail, likely to go down for a spot of hibernation. There was a silence as the gas hissed under the kettle in the other room. McCann blankly considered Pounder's shifty-looking face.

"Hard times right enough."

"Well you must be doing alright, mate. Wot you do, like? Just a sec, kettle mad for it." McCann let the seconds tick and waited as Pounder went back to the kitchenette, turned off the heat and opened the cupboard for cups. It struck McCann that Pounder had one eye on him all the while. When he looked up with a furrowed brow from the tea cups,

McCann answered.

"I am a private investigator."

If Pounder was spooked he didn't show it. He continued dipping the teabags in the cups and came towards the table with the tea and a bag of sugar.

"I don't take sugar, Carl. You do, I presume."

Pounder slid gracefully into the chair opposite McCann. "What the fuck you want?"

"To help you Carl, and for you to help me. A deal shared, a negotiation agreed on, a win-win situation for both the gents involved."

He took a wad of notes from his pocket and keeping his eyes on Pounder placed them on the table. Pounder remained silent, calmly rolling a cigarette and giving McCann the cold glacial eye.

"How's Charlie, mate?"

Pounder blew nicely spun rings of smoke at McCann.

"There's a lot of Charlies pal. You're a bit of a one your fuckin' self."

McCann picked up the notes that were new and clean and almost gleaming with greed and strummed them. "Fresh, Carl. Your name written on them, except for these two." McCann took two fifties from the bunch. "Fly away Peter, fly away Paul. You know that game, Carl? It's for kids. Sometimes the birdies fly away and some of them come back. Other times all the birds fly away and don't ever come back. Which game does little Carl want to play?"

Pounder's gaze had stirred and a look approaching curiosity had entered into it. Perhaps the predator had scented blood.

"Look Carl, let's have a real brew. You get the glasses. I've got the hooch."

Pounder watched McCann extract a bottle of Macallan from his bag. He let out his breath and grinned. "Alright, could do with a nip of that. Ain't got no glasses like. Bottle alright?"

Bottle it would have to be then. McCann watched him empty the whisky bottle to below the neck and wondered how well Pounder could handle the booze, and if the drink would work in his favour or not. Pounder had pushed the chair back from the table and had moved to the edge of it, shoulders hunched but loose and elbows at rest on his knees; a stance coiled for adversity. He looked hard, and he was. It wasn't a pose.

"I fought middle, Carl. Read about you. Welter, wasn't it?"

"Still fuckin' is."

Pounder handed the bottle to McCann, held onto it briefly and then released it. "Don't like your type but the money looks aright. So what the fuck you want?"

"I told you. Where's Charlie?"

The room would have been silent if not for the dog that was pacing back and forth in excitement, as if it felt the tension filling the darkening room and the murmur of coming violence. Pounder slowly stood up, moved to the side and twisted fast, punting the dog with a hard right kick. Marvin snarled but backed off, whimpering, into a corner.

"You should leave Marvin alone lad. It's another mongrel we're interested in. Charlie Davis. Where is he? Where's he run off to?"

McCann took another nip of whisky. Careful son, he was thinking, just enough to relax the nerves. You'll need them supple, for here is a contender and you never were. The afternoon light was dimming and given the circumstances of the undercurrent present, it was with some gentility that McCann handed back the bottle. Pounder breathed, sat back down, took another hearty slug then slammed down the bottle in the centre of the table. He was a man marked by the look of never getting ahead beyond anything but a few steps in front of him. He spoke slowly and made his accent more pronounced, as if mocking the gap between the classes. "Charlie fucked off after the trouble at the hippy do. Owed me money and that, but he done a runner."

McCann smiled and raised his eyebrows. "You were best mates. Where did he run to?"

"No idea, man. London maybe. The cunt grassed me up."

McCann stretched his arms and laughed. "Closing time, Carl." He hoped he looked hard but knew he was just heavy. All the same he had to appear dangerous, intimidating and real, no matter how he felt. Part of the job. He took the notes and halved them. "Don't mind if I smoke as well, do you Carl?" In the silence McCann lit up and blew blue smoke into Pounder's face. "Camel Lights, on the doc's advice. A shite smoke, but a smoke.

You've got until the end of this smoke."

Pounder played with a pinkie ring and first lowered his head then raised it up like a marlin, sword first, jaw hooked.

"Okay. I got names for you."

McCann picked up his coat. "You got fairytales Carl. I want one name, Charlie Davis', and a place, and it better be the right one."

Pounder's restless vibe varied like the clouds rumbling across Pendle Hill outside. Now he faked indifference, made to ignore McCann, began to roll another cigarette, his head bent over the job, frame taut like steel or glass in the dark blue light cast by the window. The dog was also quiet, still waiting. It was almost dark. Pounder was lighting up and focused on his first drag.

Time to act. McCann threw his coat over Pounder's head and dropped onto him, knocking him to the floor and hammer-thumping him to the head. Pounder twisted and slipped but McCann had him smothered and hurt. He kept the coat over Pounder's face with his left hand and thumped him with the right. "Submit time, Carl?" He was trying to sound more convincing than he felt. No answer. He hit him again and just managed to avoid Pounder's attempt to leg-grip his neck. But Pounder wriggled out of his clasp and let him have two ferocious but uncontrolled swings, catching him on the neck and the back of the head. McCann gasped and heaved the smaller man down onto the floor again, using his big body to pin Pounder down; it was like trying to wrestle with an octopus. They smacked into the table; something fell off it and there was a breaking sound. McCann's legs scrambled for leverage but could only uselessly kick something behind him. A crisp, hard kidney punch almost winded him but gave him the boost of adrenalin he needed for five quickfire hits, and then he knew the other was really hurt. He forced his whole weight down on Pounder, who finally grunted a submission. McCann released him. Pounder got up slowly. His face was bruised and reddened, his eyes outraged. "Put the fucking money on the table."

"Yes, Carl. As you say. Now where is he?" McCann tried to get his breathing under control and eyed a bemused-looking Marvin, who had strangely sat throughout the dramatics without a sound or motion.

Pounder paused, rubbed his aching body, retrieved his cool and his cigarette from the ashtray, drew, exhaled, and through the smoke said, "Japan. He's in Japan."

Dripping with sweat McCann backed out and slowly took the stairs. Pounder had scared him. He was shaken alright, but it was done now and he had what he wanted. He was looking forward to the drive home, and the view of the dales of Yorkshire looming above the ground mist. One down. He hit the bottom floor and stepped out.

The dog came at him like a torpedo but from a distance. Pounder was a hazy figure in the dimming smoky light and McCann could hear him laughing. The animal moved fast for a creature of such bulk and McCann backed into the building, keeping the door slightly ajar and readying himself for the dog's attack. It was a heavy steel fire door and if he timed it right the brute would go for the gap and he would crush its head with repeated slams. The dog's speed increased and McCann braced himself for the canine tank to fly, but nothing impacted. Marvin screeched to a halt before the door, raising dust and barking, then just sat down, turning his head to the side, and looking at McCann with a kindly, 'What's next?' expression.

What's next was Pounder, who was on his way hissing curses and spitting. McCann turned and went for Pounder again, stepping over the dog and slamming the door behind him, throwing his extra weight into the offensive, knowing the other's skill would overcome him if he didn't use the next seconds to his advantage. The contact first went McCann's way and Pounder was stopped in his tracks with a hard right, but he danced back with stealth and started bobbing. McCann had never faced a kick boxer before and Pounder seemed to know it as he kept his distance, circling and throwing kicks to the shins and calves. McCann knew how to avoid punches but not kicks and he could quickly feel his legs weakening. He went forward and at Pounder, throwing hooks, and caught him hard again, but not hard enough. Pounder backpedalled once more, composed himself and resumed kicking, then switched styles and moved in punching, fast steady punches flying at angles into McCann's body and face.

In return McCann let go two lefts that glanced, threw a right that missed and was clocked by an uppercut. Two straight rights followed, jabs, but hard as only a southpaw can throw them. Then came a huge right. He saw it and his nose was saved but the impact put him down as it connected to his ducking skull.

McCann had little left and Pounder was howling, "Get up you cunt! Sometimes birds fly back and sometimes they…" The boot caught McCann in the chest, direct to the sternum. He was helpless, panting and spitting blood. McCann's lungs had given up; all he had left was willpower but he felt himself sliding downwards. He tried to balance himself and grab Pounder by the balls when he felt the horror of the dog move in. Its hind leg scraped his face and he could feel its breath in his nostrils as he brought his hands up to protect his face. Then he waited for the fangs to strike and fix and begin ripping his hands to shreds. Somehow he had to protect his throat; it was the waiting game now. But all he could feel was the softness of the dog's tongue and all he could hear was a concerned whimpering coming from the dog's throat. But then the dog yelped and the voice of Pounder screamed at it and he laid in with hard kicks, "Out of the way you fuckin' useless hound!" Sensing a space McCann removed his hands and saw that Marvin had Pounder by the calf and was biting deep into his flesh. Pounder went down and tried to grab the dog by its back legs but failed as the dog used its instincts to protect the tender parts and twist beyond the reach of the man. McCann stood up to a spinning world and knew he had to act fast. He smacked Pounder hard then took the boot to him. Again and again he kicked, even once losing his footing as Pounder caught his leg. But he kept kicking and Pounder got weaker and McCann went down hammer punching Pounder's face until he felt the other lose consciousness. The dog still held fast to his master's ankle and McCann could see blood around the trouser hem. Struggling for breath and in considerable pain, McCann carried out a brief damage assessment. The prognosis was – he'd live.

Lurching towards his car, he got in, scrabbled around for his keys and started the engine. He could see the inert figure of Pounder as he twisted the mirror. He put his foot down and almost didn't see the dog. Marvin was in front of the car. And Marvin was smiling, through bloodied fangs and with the look of one pleased with himself. McCann pressed the horn and edged forward but the dog wouldn't budge. Marvin just repositioned himself like the tank man in Tiananmen Square. McCann swore at the stupidity of it. He opened the passenger door and the dog hopped in, looking at McCann with a satisfied smile.

McCann looked back in a daze.

He stopped the car some way out of Pendle, retrieved a water bottle from the back seat and splashed it on his face, trying to clean the cuts and make himself less noticeable. The whole time the dog was watching him. McCann looked at Marvin, cupped his palm and poured a little water out for it to drink. The dog seemed grateful and gave a little bark.

"Thanks Marvin."

The dog boomed out a bigger response. They drove off towards home and neither of them noticed the rolling hills of the dales or much else for that matter. But a sense of good future communications had perhaps been established.

GUINEA PIG

McCann absent-mindedly looked out at the darkening evening and massaged his temples with his right hand. His brain was fuzzy and the heaving mass of people outside was not enticing him to leave his temporary haven, but he needed to find his hotel and rest. He sighed, stood up and glanced once more towards the girl at the serving counter. For a second their eyes met and she smiled briefly; so natural it stopped his heart for a beat and he felt a pang of sadness for all the things that weren't going to happen in this life, or any other.

He had booked himself into the Happy Sunshine Hotel Shinjuku – stupidly cheerful and compared to the other options, cheap enough. He pulled up the map on his iPhone, trying to equate the icon marking the hotel with his current location. He followed the crowds back towards the monolithic Shinjuku station and walked for a few minutes in a vaguely northeastern direction. The hotel was somewhere between Shinjuku Sanchome station and the main road, Yasukuni Dori, but incredibly most of the streets were unnamed and although fairly sure he was in the correct area, he walked round and round the labyrinth of narrow, bustling alleys with a gradually increasing sense of fatigue and frustration. Even the map on his smartphone seemed to be playing games with his mind. Three times he wheeled his seemingly heavier and more cumbersome travel case from the station along Yasukuni Dori, bumped into people, turned down one of the multitude of side streets to his right, got hopelessly lost, and ended up back at the station. Passing the same jewellery shop again and again was starting to piss him off. He would have to ask for help.

Approaching the man closest to him, who was wearing a business suit and carrying a briefcase, McCann pointed vaguely at his phone map. "Emm, excuse me…"

The man bustled straight past him, head down, appearing to not even hear him. He cursed himself, thinking he should have asked the girl in the burger shop. Next up, a woman of about thirty-five . Smile, Colin… "Excuse me…"

The woman, startled, looked up at him quickly, gave him a body swerve worthy of an American football wide receiver in full flow, and disappeared into the crowd. McCann shook his head and giggled to himself exhaustedly. Back near the East exit of the station again, comparing his online map with the large tourist one, he heard a sing-song female voice behind him. "Hello. Can we help you?" It was sweet and slightly shy, like a talking baby chipmunk in a Disney cartoon. He turned round and saw a young couple, perhaps university students, standing arm in arm, smiling at him. Their heads were cocked to one side, interested. Trainee scientists in lab coats with clipboards observing an experiment? McCann was starting to get the floating feeling: dislocation of time and space.

He blinked, smiled, spoke. "Actually, yes. I'm looking for a hotel and I'm having a terrible time finding it."

"Hotel? Can you show map?" It was the young man who spoke. The chipmunk girl was looking at her boyfriend, obviously delighted that he was taking on the Good Samaritan role.

"Umm, this one, 'Happy Sunshine Hotel Shinjuku'."

The couple briefly discussed it together, comparing the map with the phone and pointing.

More big smiles. "It is okay! No problem! *Achi desu ne. Sugu soko desu yo.*"

They walked back towards Yasukuni Dori.

"You are American?"

"No, English."

"Oh! England! I like The Beatles."

"Yeah, they seem to be very popular here. They were playing Beatles stuff in the burger shop."

Blank looks. Empathetic, almost apologetic smiles. "Sorry. English, no." The couple talked quickly together then laughed. The Good Samaritan tried again.

"England. Soccer?"

"Yeah, I suppose I like football."

"Manchester United?"

"Ha! Actually I live very near Manchester. Near. Close."

"Manchester," the young man nodded his head thoughtfully. "David Beckham – now *ojisan*, no more soccer, but still very cool!" Thumbs up.

McCann's turn to laugh. "Yeah, but my Dad took me to watch Aston Villa. He wasn't a Man United fan. Aston Villa. Charlie Aitken, Gordon Cowans, Paul McGrath ... you probably don't know any of those lads, eh?"

"*Nan te iutteta?*"

"*Mattaku wakkanai!* Do you like Japan?"

"Well, I just got here, but so far yes. Good!" McCann's turn to give the thumbs up.

The girl spoke, "You are cool!" then laughed and playfully slapped her boyfriend on the arm. He laughed too. "This street, hotel. Look."

He followed the pointing arm. Sure enough, in front of him the bland concrete block of the 'Happy Sunshine

Hotel Shinjuku' and the name clear in English. He'd probably walked right past it three times. More smiles, handshakes, small bows.

"You are okay now?"

"Yes! Thanks so much for your help. *Arigato! Sayonara.*"

"Oh! You speak Japanese. Great! *Ja, gambatte.* Goodbye."

The automatic doors slid open and McCann made his way to the front desk, where a man and a woman looked industriously busy typing on computers and moving bits of paper around. "*Irashaimase,*" they said in unison, straightening behind the desk like junior officers ready for inspection by a visiting general. McCann responded by mumbling his third and final Japanese word; "*Konnichiwa.*" Smiling uncertainly at them, he pulled the crumpled internet reservation printout from his jacket pocket. "Ummm…"

"Good evening, sir. Do you have a reservation?" The man's English was smooth but seemed unnecessarily grave.

"Oh, yes. McCann, for three nights."

He was shown to his room, put his case down beside the cheap desk and chair in the corner and flopped onto the bed, exhausted. Then he opened the fridge, took out a can of Asahi Super Dry and drank it as he lay there, propped up on pillows, flicking through TV channels that offered noise and colour but meant nothing to him.

He thought about mailing Philips just to let him know he had arrived, so he pulled out his phone again, but his mind was wandering and the room was swaying vaguely, like a pleasure boat on a tiny pond. One of Japan's infamous earthquakes already? His eyes rolled in his head and he felt a strange static buzz somewhere at the back of the optic nerves and in his ears. Not an earthquake, he guessed. Exhaustion, disorientation and jetlag. He needed to shed his travel skin, both the metaphorical and the literal dust of the road. The moulded plastic shower room was cramped and utilitarian, but the hot water running over him made him feel human again. Then he had a second Asahi, crawled into bed and was asleep in seconds.

☕

McCann was falling into the bed, or perhaps the bed was falling through the floors of the hotel. The sheets were clingy and crumpled and sticking to him, trapping him, twisting around his body. His head was roasting hot, his throat desert-dry. His tongue was stuck to the upper palette of his mouth. Pounder was a huge Jolly Green Giant, hands on hips, throwing his head back and laughing like a demon, and Marvin was roaring towards him, jumping at his neck, fangs bared, and he was turning to run, turning in treacle, so slowly he was never going to get away, turning in a dream…

He opened his eyes. Something had awoken him but it was no longer there. He rolled onto his side. The blue-green glow of the digital clock said 21:44. The room was like a furnace and the air was dry and stale. The window refused to open so he snapped on the air con and exhaled. He needed a glass of water desperately; took the two steps to the bathroom, gulped down a glass from the tap, tepid and chemical-tinged, and returned to the bed, puffing the pillow and sitting up.

Now he was wide awake. There were some miniatures and more beers in the mini bar, so he grabbed one of each, and seeing with pleasure the ashtray that adorned the table, took a pew on the edge of the bed.

His head was empty at first, then thoughts and images drifted in – he remembered observing Japanese women on the plane as the craft had risen into the blue stillness and transported him beyond what he knew, towards what he didn't.

They were a group of four, about forty-five years old and all dressed with ladylike elegance and economy. He understood not a word of their conversation but paid attention instead to nuance, pitch and timbre. The language rattled on sing-songy, but was punctuated by pauses of "*ano*" and full-stopped by a snapping sound he heard as "*neigh!*" He watched the posterior of one who made for the toilet and it was flat and lean below slim but shapely hips. The others kept talking and neighing and incongruously sipping beer. They reminded him of puffins, with their large pale heads, striking outlined eyes and trim, neat little bodies. They kept smiling and bobbing their heads in jovial agreement with each other. All of them were carefully and tastefully made up but their demeanors seemed fixed and somehow fake. Fake – was that it? Or excessively mannered? Or was it something different?

Thoughts drifted on with the airliner; he was talking with the passenger beside him, a lean, older businessman from South Wales.

"So it's your first time in Japan? Oh, you'll love it. I lived there for years. Going back to visit a friend in Osaka. Worked together in a trading company in Kobe for twenty years. Great guy. He has some really marvelous stories about all sorts of stuff: a hilarious one about when he used to be a celebrant, back in the nineties. He almost managed to marry the wrong people by mistake."

McCann turned away from the puffins and looked at his fellow passenger.

"Celebrant? What's that?"

"Wedding celebrant. Pseudo-Christian weddings. They need a Westerner to dress up in the robes and act like a man of the cloth. Wave a Bible, do the, 'I now declare you man and wife,' kind of thing. Don't need to be religious. Only two requirements for that job: One, speak some Japanese. Two, don't look Japanese. White face good, black face good – any face good except an Asian face. Doesn't fit the exotic image. So that was his weekend job, acting as a Christian priest – he made quite a lot of money at it, I believe."

McCann smiled, incredulous. He mumbled to himself, "Fake…"

"But that's Japan for you. It's … different."

"I don't get it. Why would anyone want to do that – a fake Christian wedding?"

"They like the idea of it. Western is cool. White wedding dress in a church, girl feels like a princess. Maybe that's the 'dream wedding', I don't know. But it's not so strange when you think about it. They already mix up Shinto and Buddhist ceremonies anyway. One for a birth, different one for a death, throw in another for a marriage – not such a leap of faith, is it?"

McCann smiled again at the turn of phrase. "Well … I can't imagine people in the West going for a Protestant baptism, a Catholic wedding, and an Islamic funeral, put it that way."

"Mmmm. Because for us, doing that would be blasphemous. As you say, fake. But it's not to them."

McCann looked over again at the happily chattering, beer glugging puffins. The man followed his gaze.

"If I could say one thing to you about Japan that you won't read in the guidebooks, it would be this – in Japan, what appears to be, is. The appearance is the reality. It might not sound like much, but it makes for a big difference from the West. You might even say that hypocrisy is a slippery concept to understand in Japan. I mean, if you appear to be taking part in a Christian wedding, then you are, whether it's a 'real' Christian wedding or not. If you appear to be praying to a Buddhist god, you are, whether you 'believe' in Buddhism or not. And if you appear to be in a loving relationship with your partner, you are. Whether you actually are or not."

McCann looked skeptical. He asked a passing flight attendant for a beer. The man continued.

"I told you I worked in a trading company, right? We had a big scandal in the early nineties, a real peach. A couple of the directors were diddling the books to screw the taxman. Totally deliberate, of course. Lots of money involved. When they were found out, they only got a slap on the wrist, but the catch was they had to hold a big press conference, do the whole apology on national TV, the bowing, the 'sorry we made a big mistake, brought shame on the company' stuff. They didn't look very sorry to me – seemed like they were just sorry they got caught, that's all. It seemed so insincere. But none of my colleagues said anything about it, just, 'They've made a public apology, that's what they had to do.' Appearance is reality. So a public apology means they were publicly sorry for their actions. And publicly shamed." McCann made one of his non-committal faces; it could have meant anything, but demonstrated that the other's speech had been heard and acknowledged; he was good at expressions that were simultaneously non-judgmental and supportive. The man relaxed further into his chair.

"Now, that might sound trite. But if your reality is what it looks like – and remember this is not a self-deception trick, it is the actual reality of what people feel – then that means… for example, if you *appear* to be happy, you actually *are* happy. It's a thought, isn't it? Like controlling your reality with your willpower. And if you take it a bit further, it means that if you're in a relationship in Japan, then cheating on your partner isn't the worst thing you can do. The worst thing you can do is *tell* your partner that you cheated on them, because that *becomes* reality. But if you don't tell, and your partner doesn't ask, then... what is real?"

The man's eyes gleamed; he was jovial. McCann looked over at the ladies on the other side of the aisle, who appeared now to be sharing some kind of beer snacks along with their drinks and apparently never-ending happy stories. McCann didn't think anything at all. The plane flew on over Siberia.

Rising from his reverie, he made his way to the window. The artificial light beyond was dazzling and the city hummed with voices and clacked with the sound of heels on concrete: a calling he couldn't escape.

YIN OR YANG

McCann walked past the closed but still illuminated department stores, past Comme Ca du Mode and Muji, marveling at the volume of people still walking around at that time of night.

An elaborately designed chalk signboard read:

Real Irish Pub, in Tokyo since 1999. Guinness, Murphy's, a wide range of draft beers, live music, happy hour 6-8 weeknights (all drinks 600 yen), live Premier league football. Come and enjoy the craic!'

He climbed the nondescript flight of stairs to the second floor, pushed open the door and walked into the ersatz pub. It looked like a bar in an international airport lounge.

He ordered a pint of Murphy's and sat on a high stool. About twenty people, a mixture of Westerners and Japanese, were drinking in groups of two or three. It was relaxing, letting the background music and the mixed up snatches of English and Japanese and Janglish wash over him.

"Yeah, yeah, yeah, I know ... it's fuckin' ridiculous, I told him there's no money in English schools unless you teach kids..."

"... so where did you say you live? *Doko ni sundeimasuka?*"

"… more of a football fan, y'know? … yeah, American football, not soccer…"

"… up to the ski resorts in Nagano…"

"*… kare wa itsumo so nano. Dakara tsukareru noyo…*"

"… then I buy lunch for you. Do you understand? *Wakaru?*"

McCann sipped his pint, looking into space, mulling over some of the reactions that the name 'Charlie Davis' had elicited so far.

Harold Philips was saying how pleasantly surprised he was with the progress McCann had already made in just a week, and how poorly it reflected on the police that they had achieved so little. Somewhere in the house a phone started ringing. Irritated, Philips glanced at his wife. She had already put her Wedgwood cup and saucer down and was halfway out of the room. In a few seconds she was back.

"Mr. Russell, dear. He says it can't wait, I'm afraid."

Philips rose from his chair, "Please excuse me, a business call. I will keep it as short as I possibly can," and left the room, muttering under his breath.

McCann glanced at Barbara Philips. She smiled and he thought she had a kind face, one untouched by spite. With a bit of luck, Mr. Russell and Mr. Philips will have quite a lot to say to each other, he thought.

"Your coffee is excellent, Mrs. Philips. It really is."

"Well thank you, Mr. McCann."

"You … met this Charlie Davis. What was your impression of him?" Gentle emphasis on the 'your'.

A few seconds of reflective silence.

"He was charming. And I could see why Natasha fell for him."

"Not an ordinary bloke then?"

"Heavens no, there's nothing ordinary about Davis. He's a very charismatic young man. Almost like…" her brow knitted in thought, "like a cult leader or something."

"How many times did you meet him?"

"Just once. He seemed like a nice boy, well-mannered and well-spoken. Of course, I could tell he wasn't … maybe wasn't what you would call our usual kind of company. I was prepared to overlook that, certainly for the time being. But my husband hated him on sight."

"Why was that?"

"Instinct. I think Harold once described the boy as a virus. He said he was a rotten smell, a cad."

A cad. Years since McCann had heard that word.

Mrs. Philips went on and McCann listened, enjoying the coffee.

"Harold said that Davis was a dyed-in-the-wool pariah and not a kid dressing up as one. As far as he was concerned, Davis was a real danger. Natasha was easily influenced, trying to assert her independence, I suppose, and she would go against her father just to rile him. Harold is used to staring everyone down but he couldn't do that with Charlie Davis. I mean he literally couldn't do it. When they met, Davis stared at him until Harold broke into a blink. He thought it the height of insolence. It outraged him."

"Did he look at you like that?"

"No, on the whole his manners were … I don't know. I couldn't say good or bad, really. But not rude. Apart from the stare, that is."

"What kind of a stare was it? If you'll forgive the oddness of the question."

"Well, I couldn't say it was really aggressive. Not impudent either. More … mischievous."

"Can you tell me a bit more about that meeting between you and your husband and
Davis?"

"Well, we had a house party – nothing too grand – but Natasha said she had plans for that evening already. As our son was travelling in Europe at that time and she was our only other child…" She broke off for a second, sighed and dabbed her eyes. "I'm sorry… As I said, we really hoped she could be at the party, so she said yes, but asked if it was okay if one of her friends could join us. Of course we agreed it would be fine. I don't think either Harold or I would have said so if we had known who Charlie Davis was. He arrived fairly late on, when everyone was relaxed after a few bottles of wine. But as I say, as soon as he came in the door, the atmosphere between him and Harold was tense. For a while it was okay because they didn't have much to say to each other, though I could see Harold was seething. The conversation turned to literature. As you can see we have quite a collection here. Davis said nothing at first, but there was a quiet moment and he pointed to the bookcase and said something about what a cultured man Mr. Philips must be. A lover of the bard, nonetheless."

"Uh-huh."

"Now everybody knows Harold has no taste for books. The only things he reads are golf magazines."

"Davis was mocking him?"

"I'm not sure. They'd never met before, so I don't know if Davis knew that. Maybe Natasha had talked to him about us. I suppose it's possible that he didn't know this would be a sensitive topic, I really don't know. It struck me as a strange thing to say at the time, I must say. Anyway he said directly to Harold, 'You must recite us your favourite soliloquy.' My husband was very angry of course, and said, 'Why don't you recite yours?'"

"And did he?"

"Yes, and did so beautifully, like a real actor. Quite a performance. At the end our guests applauded."

"One-upmanship."

"Yes, perhaps. Making a show of Harold. And nobody makes a show of my husband."

"What did Davis recite?"

"Macbeth. It was … the lines about killing King Duncan."

McCann mentally flipped through his misty memories of Mr. Lyons' English class. "Is this a dagger I see before me…"

"Yes."

"Interesting choice. Sounds like he's read a book or two, at least."

"Yes, Natasha thought him awfully clever. She said he was an autodidact. I didn't even know what the word meant. Anyway, that was the only time we saw him."

She paled as she remembered something and her coffee cup shook a little in her hand.

"Are you okay to go on Mrs. Philips? I don't mean to upset you."

"I am fine." Composing herself, she looked down at her hands and straightened her skirt.

"Davis didn't stay long after that. The atmosphere improved immeasurably after he left. But at the end of the night after everyone had gone home, Harold said his piece about never wanting to see the Davis boy in this house again. There was a bit of an argument. Natasha was acting quite strangely at that time, but I thought it was because of this Davis situation. Harold went to bed and I was tidying up. That was when Natasha came to see me. I think she was having some kind of panic attack. Then she collapsed. We called an ambulance and she was taken to hospital. She had taken drugs. Since we could see that this was the kind of influence Davis was having on Natasha, after that incident Harold put a curfew on her."

McCann shifted in his seat. "Could I use your toilet, Mrs. Philips?"

"Of course. Down the hallway on the right." He walked down a polished hallway, past more bookcases and a set of golf clubs. The toilet was clean enough to perform minor surgery in. He looked in the mirror and mouthed to himself, "You need more on the relationship from a mother's point of view." He shook carefully and zipped up, then returned to the living room. She was sitting as before, very still, very genteel, like a small bird. Without the presence of her husband to dominate it the room seemed too big, too bold.

"Did you like Davis, Mrs. Philips?"

"Well, no, but I didn't hate him. I didn't know what to think. I usually trust Harold in these matters but Davis was hard to hate then. He was quite charming."

"Why were Davis and Natasha together?"

"Heavens, I don't know. Natasha was a lovely girl and she had a lot of admirers. But she said all the boys were the same – and all the girls too. Then Charlie came along and he wasn't the same as anything. Perhaps she wanted adventure."

"Common enough."

"Yes, but from the time of that incident she started acting strangely. She told me that she was going to quit university and go away on a quest."

McCann couldn't hide the surprise on his face and in his voice. "A quest?"

"Yes, with Davis. She told me she would run away with him anyway even if I didn't agree."

"Did you speak to Harold about that?"

"No. Not at the time. I didn't know how to react, to be honest. I was very confused, and very angry. When I heard her say that, I felt a kind of helplessness and a... an anger that I'd never experienced before. She seemed to want to throw away everything that we had strived to give her. How could she say that, when our purpose as parents was to make her happy, give her all life has to offer? How could she be so unhappy when she had all there is to have?" Mrs. Philips began to sob quietly. McCann remained silent waiting for the unhappy woman to regain her composure.

"I'm sorry Mrs. Philips, but could I ask you one more question?"

"Please, go ahead."

"Had Natasha taken drugs before she met Davis?"

Mrs. Philips looked blankly out the window for a few seconds. "She overdosed once on sleeping pills."

"How did she get them?"

"They were mine."

McCann nodded as Harold Philips' unmistakably purposeful footsteps approached from the hall.

⚓

He ordered a second Murphy's and started to consider just how wild this goose chase was. The name given to him by Pounder was Oliver Twilly, owner of a small private language school in a place called Yamato in Kanagawa, to the west of Tokyo. Apparently, in the past Twilly had been linked by the police to Davis' suspected drug dealing activities. It seemed they had been operating as a pair but about three years previously Twilly had disappeared off the radar. He was originally from somewhere in Essex and when he dropped out of the scene it was assumed he had gone back south. McCann had crosschecked all this with his police contact, Inspector Brough, and sure enough, the name was known to him, and to a number of other officers who had been trying without success to pin something on the two of them. Slick mover – who would have thought he'd turn up in Japan running an English school? It was easy enough to find the website for the language school, 'Hunky Dory English Club', complete with a picture of smiling Japanese kids, a couple of Westerners behind them grinning under the school slogan, 'For ALL Your International Needs'. Brough, tapping his pen on the computer screen, had confirmed that the one with the more crooked leer did indeed bear an undeniable resemblance to Oliver Twilly, suspected of small to medium scale dealing of everything from marijuana to smack, and anything in between. "Yep, that sure looks like Olly Twilly to me. A bit older, a bit fatter round the chops, but that's the fucker all right."

Was Charlie Davis really with him? On an extended holiday visiting his old partner in crime, or working? Lying low or in the open? If he really was here in Japan was it just coincidental that he seemed to leave Manchester very soon after Natasha Philips' death, or was there something more to it? McCann had plenty of questions, and a pretty low chance of getting concrete answers.

THE GREATEST HAPPINESS PRINCIPLE

A group of three people, a Western man, a Japanese man and a Japanese girl, were having an animated discussion at a table nearby, voices rising but laughing at the same time. "… I'm telling you! Come on, I'll ask this guy over here and see if he knows."

The Western man, by his accent an American, ambled towards McCann, eyes sparkling with alcohol but a big friendly smile on his face. "Hey, buddy, I don't want to interrupt or anything, but do you mind if I ask you a question? See, we're having an argument, my friends and I, and the internet reception in here sucks, so I thought we could just ask someone to see if they can help us, ya know?"

McCann turned his body half around on the bar stool. "Sure, fire away. Don't expect me to know the answer though."

"Okay, okay, so … umm, we're all a little drunk, so this might be a bit stupid … or maybe it's just me that's drunk, but anyway, we're talking about the, like, the fastest thing in the human body, and I said, well, it's got to be ejaculation, right? I mean, I'm not trying to be funny or anything. It's pretty fast, right? Here it comes, *orgasm*, whooooosh!" His arm followed the trajectory of a fighter jet taking off from an aircraft carrier. "It just jumps right out there! You know what I mean? But my girlfriend, Toshiko," he leaned over the bar conspiratorially, pointing to the girl at the table who was smiling amiably,

"Typical woman, you know? She's like, naw, that ain't it. It's a sneeze, says she. A sneeze! And I'm like, no way, that is just so *tedious* an answer! And Jun, there," he pointed again, this time at the man sitting with them, "he's smart, he's being all political, not taking either side. So I figured, well, let's ask someone, see if they know."

McCann couldn't help but smile as he raised his eyebrows and took a sip of stout. "Well, don't quote me on this, and I don't want to disappoint you or anything, but I think your girlfriend's got it right. I think the average sneeze travels at something like ninety miles an hour and is the fastest thing in the human body."

"You serious?" He turned back to his companions at the table. "Did you hear that?" They heard it. "Ninety miles an hour? How do you know that stuff, man? You should be in a pub quiz team. They teach you that shit at school or something?"

McCann smiled. "I have no idea why I know that. Must have heard it somewhere, I suppose."

The American's face took on a mock-serious look. He wagged his finger at McCann. "Just think of what kind of useful, important, fundamental knowledge you could be excluding from your brain because of that piece of information! You gotta be careful not to learn too much!"

"Yeah, you're right. Wasn't it Sherlock Holmes who said his brain is like a loft, and you need to keep only the important stuff in it, because if you clutter it up with too much junk you lose space for the information you really need? I think he said that."

The man's eyes widened to golf ball size. He had a very expressive face. "There you go again! Isn't knowing that, like, a Catch 22, another example of what you're talking about? Who needs to know that Sherlock Holmes said that we don't need to know that stuff?"

"Who needs to know that knowing that is a Catch 22? You have useless information cluttering up your brain too!"

The man roared with laughter. He was big, certainly over six feet tall, and broad with it. McCann guessed he was in about his mid-thirties.

"Dude, that is some funny shit right there! Hey, you want to come over and join us for a beer? C'mon on over an' have a chat with us."

Kyle liked to talk, and being a private investigator, much of McCann's job was to listen, so in less than ten minutes he knew all about Kyle's upbringing in North and South Carolina – "raised in both Carolinas. That'd give you a split personality right there, man." – and his parents' horror at finding their white, European-stock son more interested in hip hop than AOR – "my mom used to listen to The Eagles an' shit. I was like thirteen an' I said to her, 'Yo mom, the seventies are over! Try listening to this', and I'd give her a Public Enemy tape or an NWA tape and she'd put it on and be like, 'Kyle! Don't you dare bring that foul language trash into this house!'"

Then all about his arrival in Japan, a few years as teaching assistant in a junior high school in the sticks, his change of career, and his current incarnation as co-owner of a headhunting business in central Tokyo. When Kyle got round to asking McCann some questions he was in for a shock.

"First night in Japan? Are you serious? We gotta get a drink and celebrate this. What ya doin' here? Gotta job lined up?"

"Actually I'm here on business. For a business meeting, you might say."

"What is that, like import-export or something?"

McCann made a non-committal face. "More like a … business personnel matter." Kyle became conspiratorial again. "Personnel? Personal? Oh, I get it. Human trafficking, right?" and he laughed his big booming inclusive laugh, "I'm just joking!"

Toshiko and Jun had been chatting to each other in Japanese. Now they joined in. "Hey, if it's your first night in Japan, you should go somewhere really Japanese, not like this Western-style pub, right?"

"Absolutely!" Kyle agreed.

The girl, Toshiko, spoke for the first time. "We should take you to an *izakaya*. It's like a Japanese bar where people eat and drink." Her English was good, and had a North American twang.

"Let us take him to one of the little *izakaya* in Shomben Yokocho, then." suggested Jun.

"That is a fine idea my friend. You wanna do that? Want to see something really Japanese, Colin? First night an' all…"

"Lead me to it. I'm jet-lagged out my head and ready for anything."

Back slap. "You're my kinda guy, Colin. My kinda guy!"

Jun led the four of them out of the pub and, after a five minute walk, into a lane so narrow that a long-limbed man could almost simultaneously touch both sides of it with outstretched arms. McCann had entered another world.

The lane was jammed full of tiny restaurants adorned with red paper lanterns hanging outside the entrances. Customers sat on wooden benches and stools at long counters, or huddled together in tiny, cramped spaces at makeshift tables of plywood stacked on Sapporo or Kirin beer crates. Chefs, owners and bar staff, towels tied round their heads like bandanas and sleeves rolled up exposing thick, muscular forearms, were constantly in motion, cutting onions, mushrooms, cabbage, and tofu, turning the sticks of skewered chicken and pork they cooked on charcoal grills, pouring glass mugs of beer from little kegs squeezed into impossible corners, and all the time shouting to entice those walking down the lane, welcoming new customers as they slipped sideways into their *izakaya*, or thanking customers who edged past on their way out. A warm golden glow emanated from the lamps of each eatery. The smell of cigarettes mingled with the smoky aroma of the charcoal and the grilling meat.

Every available piece of wall space was covered with strips of parchment paper advertising the menu or with posters of raven-haired girls in bikinis advertising beer. "This is old-school Shinjuku. *Salarymen* come here for cheap beer and food. Imaginative tourists come to suck up the atmosphere."

While Kyle was talking, Jun led the four of them into one of the tiny izakaya. They crushed into a corner, and were soon drinking ice-cold lager and eating delicious morsels of meat, fish and vegetables. They talked about the food, the beer, their previous trips to this little alley. Time passed.

Toshiko asked McCann, "So what's your first impression of Japan, Colin?"

"Well, I just got here. Pretty difficult to make a judgment after four jet-lagged hours. It seems ... busy. Everyone rushing around. People everywhere. So much energy. Also, everything seems super clean." He looked around. "Well, maybe not right here in this alley, but everywhere else, you could eat your dinner off the streets. Everything looks like it works the way it's supposed to. And most people seem ... I dunno, polite." He thought for a second, looking at his half-full beer mug. "Actually, it's more than that. People genuinely seem nice. One of the first things I noticed walking around here at night is I don't feel like I've got to watch my back. It just doesn't seem like the sort of place where you've always got to have your guard up. A bit different to home."

Kyle nodded enthusiastically. "Absolutely, dude! People here are so nice! Nobody tries to rip you off, no-one gives you stress or a hard time. No-one tries to fight you or steal your shit. Man, first year I was here, I lost my wallet on the train one night. Aw, I was drunk as a skunk. No idea where I had been. I was in a bad way. Lost everything – my credit cards, my Japanese ID, about 50,000 yen. Next morning I went back to the station, reported it missing. Three hours later I had the wallet back, cards, money – the lot. Someone had found it on the train, handed it in, bingo! I couldn't believe it. I love that about Japan, man. When I go back home ... aw, I don't even wanna think about that shit, man. Everyone's on the make, tryin' to get somethin' from you. Here, I swear you could leave a bag fulla stuff on the street, walk away, and come back two hours later and it'd still be there. Seriously. No exaggeration." Toshiko smiled. "Kyle is always talking about leaving bags on the street, like it's some kind of obsession of his..."

McCann grinned, "Well, so far I certainly haven't got the feeling that I've got to watch myself or worry about getting into trouble. So it's a perfect society? Everyone's nice all the time?" He was still smiling, looking round the table. "What's the secret?"

Jun laughed. "I think this is your … gentle joke, correct?"

"Well, it sounds pretty ideal, the way Kyle describes it."

"Of course there are many problems as well as the good things in Japanese society, just like in others. It is maybe for you an … interesting society, I think. Here most people are similar in their way of thinking. And our system has … *eto* … maybe you can say a kind of omnipotent power? Our society is built around a … utilitarian system, maybe?"

"There he goes again, man, talkin' big words I don't even know. An' he asks *me* to correct *his* English! I'm a man of action, Jun. You read too many books…" Jun continued with a mischievous smile, "Kyle-san is maybe too busy trying to catch girls to read books. Do you say the 'chasing skirt'"?

Everyone laughed.

"Hey, don't you be sayin' that in front of my lady here! She'll be getting ideas that ain't true. The days of that kinda action are over for me, man." Toshiko gave him an exaggeratedly suspicious look.

Jun prodded on. "So now you are just chasing the yen?"

"Yeah! Now you're talkin' my language!"

Kyle ordered another round of drinks.

McCann looked back to Jun. "Utilitarianism. You were saying?"

"Yes. The Jeremy Bentham? I think you know him?"

McCann nodded.

"If he were alive today I think he would be interested in observing this country. Japan is I think maybe a kind of practical application of utilitarianism. Of course we do not need such special words or … eto… social theories of the philosophy, because for us it simply is the way our society operates."

Kyle daintily popped a piece of grilled chicken and onion into his mouth. "Seriously, what you talkin' about now?"

"'The greatest good for the most people is the ultimate moral law.' It is very simplified, but maybe Mr. Jeremy Bentham says something like this?"

McCann nodded trying to get his jet-lagged brain to think. "That sounds about right. Moral decisions and laws should be made based on whether they are good for the majority of people in the society or not. If they benefit most people, they're basically good, if they don't benefit most people, they're basically bad. With exceptions, of course. Anyway, something like that."

"Well, as you describe it, this is Japan. We sacrifice a great deal of our personal freedoms for the ... *eto* ... communal good. This is how our society operates. That is why people can work such long hours, attend so many meetings, do so many community activities together. It is more or less natural for us. The general society benefits the most, at the cost of individual freedom?"

Kyle drank more Kirin lager and looked at McCann. "Yeah? Communal? Or communist? The local community – it's a caring sharing communist collective, man. Everyone works together for the benefit of all. It sounds great, huh? I'll give you a practical example of what that means, rather than all this nice theoretical barroom philosophy. When I first came to Japan I stayed in a big old apartment block up in rural Chiba. People used to knock on my door at seven am on a Sunday morning, sayin' stuff I couldn't understand. I was like, 'Fuck this shit man, it's Sunday morning and I gotta hangover from hell!' Of course, I never answered my door.

Then one day this obasan who could speak a bit of English told me – once a month someone from every apartment in the block has to get together and do cleaning. At seven am on a Sunday! I was like 'What? Whaddayamean, cleaning?' and she was like, 'It is the

Japanese way. Do you prefer gardening or washing the stairwells?' I'm tellin' ya, after workin' all week, and drinkin' all weekend, the last thing I needed was to get together with a hundred people I didn't even know and weed the communal sidewalk! And they'd have meetings to organise local festivals, an' meetings about meetings, and all kinds of other shit, everyone together, on the only day of the week I could get some time to myself! Like I said, communist, not communal!"

"*Yaa*, Kyle-san! It is sometimes difficult for the individual like you to be part of the Japanese community, yes? But you can be right. I think maybe it is possible to describe Japan as a kind of communist society. Not perhaps the way Marx-san expected, but it is possible, sure. Many people used to say Japan is the only successful communist country in the world."

"Yeah, man! Everyone's in, nobody's out. Unless you're a foreigner, in which case you're *out* whether you like it or not." Toshiko rolled her eyes at her boyfriend, who continued, "It's true! If you're a foreigner who's married with kids, you might be in, 'cos when you put your kids through the system, you put yourself through it too. All those stages of educating kids how to be Japanese. That's what education's for here. But if you're not married with kids, forget it. You're just a tourist passin' through – no matter how long you live here."

Jun looked mildly hurt. "We are friends, are we not, Kyle? You are not 'out' in my eyes."

"You're weird, Jun, that's why you're friends with me, man."

Everyone laughed again. Jun giggled and glugged a mouthful of lager then scratched his head and continued. "Of course, you can say in some ways Japan has a kind of communist social philosophy, but there still exists an

… umm … *nandaro*, underclass here too, like anywhere. Unemployed people. Working poor, who have a job but not enough income for anything more than today's meal. But perhaps I think this group is smaller than in western countries."

"It's getting bigger, though," commented Toshiko.

"Yes, but the gap with the rich people and the poor people, this is not so big here. Sure there is also the – I do not know if this word exists – can you say an 'overclass'? Of the politicians, the business executives, of … I try to remember this word … yes … conglomerate. Okay, conglomerate monopolies. And utilities and construction company bosses. And maybe the *yakuza*. It is they who make the decisions in Japan. They rule Japan. They are untouchable, answer to no-one. These people are strong in Japan, and they are bad for Japan, because they are corrupt. Of course we do not think they do a good job for Japan. Especially the politicians. Maybe they are the worst of all."

Kyle snorted, "That's the same all over. But that's what you've got a democracy for. Why don't you vote those corrupt politicians out?"

Jun shrugged his shoulders. "How are your American politicians? Do you like them? Are they honest? Are their favours not bought by donations, like the prostitute? Anyway, it is not so easy as you say. Japan is not a democratic country like you imagine in Western countries."

McCann looked at Jun. "In what way?"

"It is difficult to explain. You are not Japanese. But I think you can understand if I say that we have been a … umm … feudal society until quite recently. And only since after World War Two a democracy. That is a very short time. Your countries have had the democracy for much longer, I think." He smiled. "I do not even know if it is possible to call Japan a democracy. Japan, we lost the war, and then the new political system is forced on us by the winning country, America. Like the boss ordering to the workers, the workers have no choice. Can you call this making a democracy? If you create the democracy by … what do you say … a not democratic way, is this still a democracy? Is this what you call the oxymoron?"

Everyone thought about that for a few seconds as they drank some more lager. "So you're saying that there is a group of powerful politicians and businessmen at the top in Japan who answer to no-one, do what they like, and rule the country, and nobody can control them because there's no effective check in the system, right?"

"Yes, Mr. Colin. This is the idea nutshell."

Kyle sighed. "Look man, all I know is I didn't come to the pub for a goddamn endless political debate. I'm a workin' man, and this tired workin' man wants a beer and a few laughs. So cool the sociology lecture okay?"

Toshiko pouted. "Poor Kyle-chan's getting tired. His brain is melting down. Let's change the subject."

Kyle grinned goofily, crossed his eyes and made a face akin to brain overload. "Fanksh, honey."

Toshiko turned again to McCann. "Are you staying in Shinjuku the whole time you're here?"

"Well, actually the guy I'm here to see is in a place called Yamato. You know it?" She thought for a few seconds. "Umm, yeah, it's in the middle of Kanagawa I guess. Kind of near Machida." She looked at McCann. "You're going to Yamato?" Her voice suggested mild surprise.

"I will be, yeah, for my business meeting. Why, what's it like?"

She shrugged. "Like anywhere, I guess. I've only been

there once. Around the station, it's a little bit … dirty? Not dirty like unclean, dirty like…" She looked at Kyle and said something in Japanese. He beamed back at her.

"Sleazy. She said it's a bit sleazy."

"Yeah?" McCann nodded thoughtfully. "Sounds like I've got the right place then…"

Kyle winked exaggeratedly. "If you like sleazy, look no further than good ol' Shinjuku, man! Right here, we got it all! Let's eat, drink, enjoy. Then we can show our new man in town something of the other side of Shinjuku."

AFTERMATH

McCann opened his right eye, then closed it again. Then the left. The clock said 9:35am. He groaned, wrapped the duvet tighter round himself and curled into the foetal position. He needed water but the pull of inertia was temporarily stronger than the need to hydrate. Immobile, he could feel the blood pounding through his body, could imagine his liver and kidneys cursing him as they worked overtime to cleanse his body of the alcoholic poison. Eventually he crawled to the bathroom, gulped down three cups of water and went back to bed.

Two hours later he was sipping his third coffee and nibbling miserably at a crustless tuna sandwich. It was as limp as he was. The night came back to him in a jumble of faces, places, Jagermeister and endless beers. He closed his eyes again and felt a wave of nausea.

A snapshot came back to him, a short conversation with a nasty-looking, burly Aussie in a hippie hat and designer clothes, about an area of Tokyo called Roppongi; the man had leered at McCann, expelling tiny sparks of spittle as he spoke, "It's great, man, most of the girls are lookin' for Western cock and'll put out after a few drinks and plenty of platitudes."

Then he recalled a long, entertaining conversation in pidgin English, sign language and laughter with a group of young Japanese guys and girls that had revolved around *nihonshu*, seafood and cigarettes. There were long chunks of blank darkness through the evening, but he remembered it had been after three am and only Kyle and himself had remained, staggering through the still busy streets, when they had been accosted by a talking mirage, an Englishman in a tweed hunting jacket who had addressed them heartily in a dissolute Etonian voice as 'gentlemen', made some comments about the latest reality TV star's indiscretions, and offered access to "The best whores in Shinjuku, all Japanese. No Filipinos, no Chinese, no Thais." They had thanked the man for his kind offer and moved on. McCann had no recollection of getting back to the hotel, but somehow he had managed to return and so had his wallet.

He finished the coffee. Time to get on the phone to the Hunky Dory English Club in Yamato and tell them he was looking for a job as an English teacher. The website stated that the company was always looking for part-time instructors, with on-the-job training offered. On-the-job training; he was going to need a bit of that. The working visa could also be a bit of a problem, but he could cross that bridge when he came to it. Right now the only thing that mattered was to make contact and confirm whether Charlie Davis was there or not.

A few rings, then, "*Hai, moshi moshi,* Hunky Dory English Club *de gozaimasu.*"

"Umm … sorry, do you speak English?"

"Oh … yes, this is Hunky Dory English Club. Can I help you?"

"Yes. I saw your website is advertising for English teachers. I'm looking for work and wondered if I could come in for an interview sometime?"

"Oh … *eto,* hold the line please."

He waited. In the background he could hear people's voices, kids shouting. Then, "Can I 'elp you?" English, with an edge. He couldn't place the accent exactly but certainly from the south. Perhaps Essex?

"Hi, my name's George Peters. I saw your website is advertising for teachers. I'm looking for work and would like to apply for an interview."

Pause. More kids' noises in the background. A hand cupped over the receiver muffled a brief conversation, then, "Alright, when can you come in?"

"Well, I'm free pretty much all this week, so whenever suits you. Earlier is better, though."

"How about this afternoon, two o'clock? Bring your CV and a photo of yourself."

"Eh? This afternoon? Umm … that's a bit, emm…"

"You want an interview or not?"

"Yeah, yeah … okay I'll get there for two."

Stepping into the café bathroom, he took a piss and splashed water over his face for the fourth time that morning. Time to straighten up a bit. The coffee and sandwich had helped but his head was still raging and logical thought hard to come by. Bit of a wild start to this 'business trip', but before leaving the café he fired off a quick email to Philips letting him know he'd arrived in Japan safely and that he had made contact with the language school. Important to keep him up to speed. Right from the off it had been obvious that Harold Philips was the kind of employer who looked for concrete results in a short time, no fucking about.

"Do you have children of your own, Mr. McCann?"

"No, it never seemed to fit into my game plan, somehow."

"Uumh." Phillips grunted, nodded, appraising McCann

53

with his eyes, and probably coming up with about fifteen reasons why the other had failed in that most fundamental of genetic responsibilities. A clock ticked smoothly in the corner; Philips had the window behind him and a huge mahogany desk in front; McCann, feeling somewhat exposed, was sitting almost in the middle of the room in a studded red leather easy chair. It felt very expensive indeed.

Philips went on, "Perhaps for some people it's the best thing, not having kids," but it was not a reflective tone. These were the words of a mind made up, not the musings of an open one. He spoke in clipped, barbed wire phrases. Obviously used to giving the orders. "Strange. Comes down to it, you can do everything for them. Set things up perfectly. And yet you're powerless, really. Life has a way of getting to them, somehow. Just got to hope that what you've done for them will be enough…". His voice trailed off, he looked away briefly.

McCann followed his glance to the family photos. They looked nice on the antique bureau over in the corner. Arranged generationally, it seemed. A moustachioed man in a military uniform; a woman in a hat with a bob and a pearl necklace; a couple that looked, as all photos of a certain era do, like George Orwell and his wife. Then a large black and white of a wedding couple in a simple silver frame, sometime in the late seventies perhaps. In front of that, a family portrait: Mum and Dad, still clearly recognisable all these years later, and two kids about eight and six, scrubbed up neatly for the picture. Boy and girl. Healthy-looking kids, smiling, with newly-washed hair and those big white teeth that tell as much as a bankbook does about the family finances. Two more pictures, each child's individual portrait. Here they must be in their mid-teens. Perfect skin, and those teeth again.

54

McCann turned back. Philips had a detached, hard look to him.

"I suppose you know something of why we would like to engage you, Mr. McCann? It's hardly normal behaviour for people like us to employ a private investigator…" He spat out the syllables of the last two words like you might the name of a serial child rapist.

McCann shifted in his chair, moved the weight from one side to the other. He cleared his throat and spoke.

"Well, Mrs. Philips gave me a brief outline on the phone of what has happened, if that's what you mean."

"Then go ahead and tell me what you think you know. And just remember I do not suffer fools gladly, so be brief and to the point."

McCann raised his eyebrows. A real charmer, this one. "Well, when Mrs. Philips told me the basics on the phone, of course I remembered the incident. It was reported in the papers a few months ago, 'Manchester Girl in Festival Drowning Tragedy – Drugs Suspected' or something like that…" Philips' face tightened. McCann noted that but carried on, "The papers followed it for a couple of weeks. There were some editorials about the amount of drugs in modern society. Then I suppose they moved on to their next story."

McCann was aware of the effect his words were having on the man. Philips didn't speak loudly, but there was great effort in the control and precision with which he spoke.

"The 'story', as you call it, Mr. McCann … we are living that tragedy every day of our lives. You will respect us with a little more sensitivity. I do not expect someone like you to understand what effect the death of our daughter has had on us. But you might try a shred of civility in this house. What happened is not something we will forget easily … Or forgive."

The door to the study opened and Mrs. Philips entered the room carrying a silver tray with chinaware: a plate with fancy cakes and dainty French biscuits, a cafetiere of coffee and a jug of milk, a bowl of sugar. It looked like the sort of deal rich old ladies order in overpriced hotel restaurants.

There was silence in the room while Mrs. Philips poured the drinks, handed them to McCann and her husband, took one for herself and sat on an armless dining chair by the far side of her husband's huge desk. Only the sound of the clock ticking in the corner remained, smooth as a metronome. The cadence of each second seemed to hang in the air just long enough for the next one to slide into the rhythm. Very smooth.

No-one spoke for a few minutes, then McCann continued. "Well, as I was saying, as far as I understand it, the situation is that your daughter Natasha went away to a weekend festival, a kind of outdoor club party, called 'Sublime' I think, on June 12th, took ecstasy and also cocaine at the party, disappeared sometime around three am and was found next morning having fallen from a bridge and drowned in the river. Am I right so far?"

It was Mrs. Philips who spoke, barely whispering, "Yes, that's correct."

Harold stood up and looked out the window with his back to the room. He had broad shoulders, broad back, broad everything. Hands crossed behind him, his voice was far away with his thoughts when he spoke. "It's her birthday in two weeks. She would have been twenty."

He turned round and snapped back to the present.

When is this bomb going to go off, McCann wondered to himself.

"We are not satisfied with the results of the police investigation, Mr. McCann. Not satisfied at all. It is inconceivable that our daughter would have behaved in the manner the police have suggested. She was not the kind of girl to take those kinds of drugs then wander away from her friends to 'drown'. Someone has done this to her.

Something happened. I feel sure that someone compelled her to take those drugs. Whoever it was that forced those drugs on our daughter is a killer. I simply do not believe that her life would have ended this way without the involvement of someone else, or of other people. I know this but I can't prove it." He looked at his wife, but she was staring transfixed at the Persian rug three feet in front of her. Harold reiterated, "We know it but we can't prove it…"

His wife said nothing.

McCann cleared his throat again; ticklish cough today. Autumn was really drawing in. "Well, what exactly is it that makes you think the police are wrong? I mean do you have any specific reason for thinking…?"

A huge fleshy fist thumped on the table. "The only reason I need is the knowledge that my daughter would not do this!! I know my daughter, goddammit! Do not tell me what I know and do not know!"

Silence.

McCann drank some of his coffee. It was exceedingly good. He savoured the taste, rolled it around inside his mouth.

"Well, you know, Mr. Philips; this isn't exactly my line of work. I help out with divorce cases, insurance scams, that kind of thing. Manslaughter, if you want to call it that, if that's what you think it is, is a little out of my regular line of business."

The big man sat again. Suddenly, briefly, McCann could see the huge psychological weight Philips was carrying, suffocating him like an Old Testament burden from a vengeful God that he had no hope of understanding.

"I am tired, Mr. McCann. I am tired of excuses, tired of waiting, tired of watching incompetent people fail to do their jobs. I am not a time waster. You were recommended to us by friends of ours – probably you remember Mr. and Mrs. Wilcock – you were very discreet and professional, they told us. But I'm sure I can find another private detective as equally capable as you. So let's cut to the chase, shall we? You investigate the case. You talk to her friends, the people she was at that party with. Find out what really happened. Find the man, or the men, or the women or whoever it was responsible, get the evidence and get this case reopened. Ten thousand pounds. Take it or leave it, no negotiating under any circumstances."

McCann clicked his tongue. Another silence. "Expenses?"

Philips let out a guttural, mirthless noise. "You keep a record of what you need, what you use, and I will see you recompensed. I don't make offers twice. Your choice. As I said, take it or leave it."

McCann thought about it. He thought about the small flat he had bought nine months ago and the twenty-year mortgage that went with it, about the grotty puke-green kitchen units he had inherited from the previous owner, about the back windows that needed to be double-glazed. He didn't think for very long. "I'll take it."

HARD TIMES

It wasn't difficult to get to Yamato from Shinjuku on the Odakyu train. McCann had a map and directions from the Hunky Dory English Club website, and some tips on how to get there from Kyle and Toshiko as well. Gradually the huge skyscrapers and big city bustle gave way to more monotonous suburban sprawl: concrete blocks of flats, small privately owned companies, school sports grounds where kids played baseball and dodgeball, oblivious to the drab repetitiveness that surrounded them on all sides, as are all children from Bangladesh to Brittany when immersed in playing games. The journey took about an hour. The train car was a big solid box of space. It made the trains back home seem more like cheap plastic kids' toys.

Stopped at a station on the way to Yamato, he looked out the window and saw a cleaner on his hands and knees scraping off a piece of chewing gum from the concrete. It was quiet at midday; there weren't the crazy scenes of Tokyo commuters he remembered from photos in school geography textbooks, men in white gloves pushing people onto already jammed trains like cattle being sent to the slaughterhouse. There was space on this train to sit down, even. Most of the people around him slept. Next to him the head of a somnolent, suited man bobbed gently back and forward, then occasionally sideways towards McCann. Eventually it slid more and more towards him, resting inevitably on his shoulder. McCann shifted his weight;

the head lifted without a word, without opening its eyes, and continued its front-to-back bobbing movement. The train rocked its passengers like that all the way to Yamato.

☒

Following the map, he walked up from the station through still, narrow streets that were obviously made for the nighttime, not the light of the day. The signs that had English words were like a roll call of lasciviousness, sordid in the unhooded daylight:

Party Time!; Filipino Girls; For Your Delight – Nurses ... Secretaries ... Hot Tomato; Club Supreme; Seventh Heaven – Special Massage 5000yen. All the lights were off, nothing moved, no people were here.

McCann quickly needed to get used to orienting himself without street names. Left turn at the Family Mart convenience store, past the Kitten Snack Bar and there it was the sign for the Hunky Dory English Club. Check of the watch; twenty minutes early. He walked past the front of the school, looking in through the window at the reception desk where a pouty Japanese woman was talking on the phone, and where a couple of people were sitting in the waiting area. The building next door seemed to be connected to it, but the lights were off there.

He turned around, cleared his mind, walked back to the door, opened it and gave his false name to the woman at reception. Her eyelashes were as long as her brightly painted fingernails; ink-black hair tumbled over her shoulders in loose waves, and her full lips were expertly made up. He couldn't say she was beautiful, but she was a sexual woman and she wore it well. Her eyes were hard and the mask that she had put on that morning registered nothing.

"You are early, Mr. Peters. Mr. Twilly is teaching a class now. Please wait."

So he did.

At five past two, a door behind the reception desk opened and a man came out and spoke with the receptionist. His face was pale and shiny and his tousled hair was almost as black as the woman's. McCann guessed he was in his early thirties. Cheap shirt and tie, shapeless chinos, gold chain on one wrist, watch loosely worn on the other. He came to McCann with a crooked smile and a brief handshake.

"Alright? You George Peters then? Come for an interview to teach, right?"

"Yes. You must be … Mr. Twilly?"

"Olly Twilly. Come in 'ere an we'll 'ave a chat then." The head motioned to a door and they walked through it into a room with a whiteboard, a large table and five cheap looking chairs. Olly Twilly sat down heavily in one of them, stretched, and put his hands behind his head, ruffling his hair as he did so. There were patches of sweat under each armpit. "So … you wanna job, right?"

"That's about the size of it, yeah."

Twilly had a sly look, like one of Dickens' less savoury characters. McCann could well imagine that inside the head, cogs were turning, with the express and singular purpose of personal gain. Shifty.

Twilly sniffed. "Can't place your accent. Where you from, mate?"

"I lived in Birmingham for a bit, all around the Midlands, and Manchester as well."

A yawn. "If you don't mind me sayin', yer a bit old to be lookin' for part time jobs teachin' English here in sunny Yamato, ain't cha?" That brought out the crooked leer again.

McCann registered it. He made a non-committal gesture. "Things don't always pan out the way you expect…"

Twilly snorted through his nose and scratched his ear. "Got a CV and a picture?" He leafed through the CV McCann gave him. Most of it was half-truths and plausible lies, and they chatted around it for ten minutes.

"Alright, so here's the deal, George. I don't really care that much about what you done or you didn't do in the past, or about your visa, or if you got the bits of paper that prove you can do what you say you can. Like I say, them things don't mean much to a … humble businessman like meself."

Smile.

"Here, you work cash in hand so no-one needs to know what you're earnin' or not earnin'. I only need the answers to two questions. One – can you keep my students entertained for a class so they come back for more? An' two – will you turn up for work when I need you to turn up for work? They's the only two things that matter. People say you need to get trained for this kinda job. Way I see it, best trainin' is doin'. So. Here's what we'll do. I got a class of four comin' at six tonight. I'll give ya the files. Show ya what we done last class an' that. You got a few hours to get some tucker, look over the files and make a lesson. You teach it, I'll watch it, an' if it looks like you can do it, I'll take you on. Alright?"

McCann was surprised by the suddenness of this, but allowed no change in his expression. He had arrived in a random town half way across the world on a rich man's whim, but he knew exactly what he was dealing with across the table. He'd dealt with this most of his working life. Olly Twilly was just like the others. Only difference was he was in the role of an English teacher in Yamato,

Kanagawa, not a petty drug dealer in Harlow, Essex.

"Sure, that seems fair. What's the pay, if you don't mind me asking?"

"Pay is the goin' rate. But you get nuttin' for a demo lesson."

"Okay … what *is* the going rate?"

Olly Twilly's dark eyes shone. "1500 yen an hour, mate."

✆

Feeling surprisingly nervous at the prospect of suddenly being thrust into the role of an impromptu English language guru, McCann took the files from the sultry-looking receptionist. She seemed to have perfected the art of doing as little as possible in her job. As soon as she had pulled the student files for him it was back to examining the talons. He wandered into an unused classroom, flipped open the cream cardboard files and glanced over the notes.

Forty-five unproductive minutes later he was squeezed into the miniature bathroom, splashing water over his face and cursing both himself and Harold Philips under his breath for the ridiculous circumstances he was in. He looked into the mirror at the visage before him. Not looking too clever, Colin…

"What the fuck am I doing here? Stupidest job I ever took on … teaching an English class in a two-bit town in some Tokyo suburb just to find a guy who might be mates with a guy who might have something to do a girl who's dead… This is stupid."

He went for a walk to gather himself together and eat something. The receptionist, still apparently busy with her claws, didn't even look up when he walked past her and out the front door. He was tempted to keep on walking and not turn back.

THE TIN DRUM

Olly Twilly was nowhere to be seen but it was six o'clock and the predatory secretary led McCann to the small classroom. She managed a single sentence. "One of the students cancelled."

He stopped, turned around. Just about had enough of this already. "Thanks for the advance warning," he spat back, "care to enlighten me which one?"

She registered mild surprise at the tone, glanced down at the files thrust in her face, and selected one. "This one." She was almost smiling, serpentine. The first response she had given with a hint of human emotion yet. Not nice human emotion, but better than nothing. Perhaps.

He opened the door and walked into the room. Sitting silently round the table were three students. On his left, a woman in her sixties. In the middle, a nondescript man who could have been anything from thirty to fifty. On his right, a high school boy wearing a black school uniform with a standing collar. It looked like a cross between a 19th century military uniform and a Beatle suit.

He wiped his hands on his trousers, forced a smile and stepped over to them. "Hi, my name's George Peters!" He held out his hand to shake.

The woman physically blanched. She seemed confused by this introduction, but managed to scramble out from under the chair and offered a hesitant hand. The two males also looked surprised but nodded their heads and mumbled some kind of words, which McCann took for a greeting.

The secretary, standing behind him in the doorway, gave what he hoped was some kind of explanation of the situation in Japanese, then closed the door. As she did so, through the Perspex window McCann caught a glimpse behind her of another man, carrying Manila student files similar to his own, walking towards the next classroom.

The man wore a cap tilted over his blue-black curls and had that loose rangy gait of the early twenties. Though he wasn't tall, he gave an impression of height. He walked as if he was leading, or expected to be followed. He wasn't smiling and looked somber, but a shift must have occurred as he opened the classroom door next to McCann's and strode in, for he bellowed out, in a voice of mischievous gaiety, "Well, what we got here? Pokemon,

Tinkerbell – flutter, flutter – and a coupla young Ichiros! Mush Mush..."

McCann turned back to his students, rubbing his hands together nervously. He began to sweat as he looked at the three facing him, a creeping triad threatening to engulf him. "So ... let's start with some introductions, okay? I'll tell you about myself first. Ummm ... like I said my name is George Peters, I'm from England." Blank looks, silence. He was aware that he was talking quite quickly, but couldn't stop himself.

"Actually, I just arrived in Japan a few days ago! So everything's new to me here..."

The bland man opposite smiled uncertainly at him and nodded his insecurity. Lacking a response of any kind from the other two students, McCann took this reaction as a positive sign. "You are...", he looked down at his files, "Taro Nagashima, right?"

"Yes. My name is Taro Nagashima. Nice to meet you."

McCann was chuffed. "Can you introduce yourself to us, Taro?"

"My name is Taro Nagashima. Nice to meet you. *Eto, nanni o ieba ii kana* … I like baseball. And drinking beer."

"Right! Beer! Haha! Me too! Good one. Baseball. Is baseball popular in Japan, then?"

The high school kid to McCann's right gave a long, loud sigh. He had been staring at his hands the whole time. He looked exhausted.

"What baseball team do you support then?"

"*Cheem*?"

"Yeah. The team you support. The team you like. What team?"

"My team?"

"Yes. The team you like."

"Ah! Yomiuri Giants."

"Right. Giants? Where are they from, then? Are they a good team?"

"Team?"

"Yes… Are. They. A. Good. Team?"

"Good team? Yes … good team."

McCann felt a trickle of sweat run down the small of his back. Jesus it's hot in here, he was thinking. His mouth was dry. Should have brought a drink with me … gagging for a glass of lemonade…

Meanwhile, in the room next door the volume had been gradually increasing. It sounded almost like a party was breaking out. McCann couldn't be sure exactly what they were doing, but there was chanting, shouting, laughing and hand clapping. He could hear a group of voices bellowing in unison, "That's crazy!! What do you think?" followed by the crackle of uncontrollable laughter, an answer he couldn't hear, then again, louder, joyful voices in synchronicity, "That's *crazy*! What do *you* think?" Judging by the noise and movement, people were jumping up out of their seats, moving around, animated. Then the teacher's voice, full of life and brio, "You must be joking! That's *crazy*!" and howls of laughter from what sounded like twenty people all crushed together, having a party.

Separated only by the thin partition wall, it was difficult for McCann to hear the monosyllabic answers of his timid group of three, difficult to hear himself think, and most difficult of all to ignore the fact that while he was pulling teeth in this room, the comedy event of the decade was taking place in the next class.

He turned to the woman, who seemed to have recovered from the initial shock of the handshake. "I suppose you don't like baseball and beer, eh, Mrs...." he checked the files again, "Mrs. Ida?" Big smile.

Not reciprocated. Confused looks, a worried frown. "*Sumimasen, chotto wakaranai no de mo ijido, onegaishimasu.*"

"Umm, sorry I don't speak Japanese. I, emm, just arrived in the country a couple of days ago, you see?"

"She?"

"... Okay ... can you introduce yourself to me, Mrs. Ida?"

"Iida."

"Sorry?"

"Iida. My name, Iida."

"Yes, I know. Mrs. Ida."

"..."

He looked over at the high school kid, though for what he wasn't sure. Certainly not support. The kid continued to look down. Clearly it would require a titanic effort for him to open his mouth and speak. Back to Mrs. Ida. Or Iida. "Okay, what are your hobbies, then?"

"Oh, hobbies. Is garden. And my dog. Walk my dog every day."

On safe ground here... "You own a dog? I have a dog

too! Mine is a pit-bull. Wanted a basenji, but it didn't quite work out that way. Kinda like life, really, eh? Anyway, what kind of dog do you have, Mrs. Ida?"

"Dog?"

"What kind of dog. Is it an Alsatian? A Dalmatian? A spaniel?"

"My dog? Is Shiba-ken dog. Japanese dog. You know?"

"Shiba-ken? No, I don't know it. What does it look like?"

"Yes! I like very much."

"I mean, the appearance. Is it big? Small? What does it look like?"

"Big? Not big I think. Small, maybe."

"Uh-huh. Good, that's good." Struggling to keep his train of thought, he moved to the last student with a feeling of quiet dread.

"So, you must be Yusuke Hirosaki, yes?"

The boy looked up at McCann without moving his head, hands or any other part of his body. But at least he spoke.

"Yes, I'm Yusuke Hirosaki. I live in Yamato, near here. I am a third grade high school student. Every day I study for university entrance exams."

"University entrance exams, eh? Sounds hard…"

"Yes. Every day, study."

"Well, let's try and all speak some English and have some fun, okay? Let's see now. In your book, you're on page twenty-three, right? Unit four, 'Shopping!' Let's turn to that page and get started…"

But his instructions were drowned out by the class next door bursting into uncontrollable laughter as the teacher yelled, "Of *course* I can't do that, can *you*?", followed by a scrambling and a mocking cry of, "All rise."

McCann looked blankly down at his textbook and

quietly sighed as the next door opened. Through the window of their classroom, they could all see the group of four students from next door as they almost skipped out to the waiting area in the centre of the school. The man in the cap followed at the rear, carrying a small drum. It reminded McCann of one he had bought years before for his sister's young child. The teacher spoke, "Okay, we all know the rules and there'll be no fools!" and then he started drumming and the students began marching.

It was a long hour for McCann. He kept looking at the clock on the wall behind the students, willing the hands to slide faster towards seven. At 7:01 all four of them shuffled out the room, the end of an experience of questionable value for both students and teacher. McCann had never much liked teachers when he had been on the receiving end of their wisdom, and now the tables were turned he didn't much like dishing it out either. 'Loners don't make for great teachers – at least this one doesn't anyway,' he thought miserably.

As the students chatted unenthusiastically with the glammed-up secretary for a few minutes, he decided he'd had about enough of this experiment in a mid-life career change. Since he'd come all the way over here, a couple of days' holiday would just about make the ridiculous trip worthwhile; maybe some late autumn rays down on an Okinawan beach.

The receptionist looked up with a cold smile and said, "Can you drink Japanese tea?"

He nodded. Sipping the tea, he could still hear the giggles and slapstick that accompanied the other teacher's class. He stood up and drew closer to the room. The group was acting out some scenario and the teacher was perched upon a chair set on the table, waving a red stick and grinning. Then the teacher said, "Okay, game over. More next time folks." As the satisfied clientele made their way out the door and into the night McCann backed away and took a seat near the receptionist.

"He is *saiko* isn't he?"

"Psycho…"

"Yes, *saiko*. It means 'the best' in Japanese."

McCann and the secretary looked at each other, sizing up, appraising. He considered her coolly impassive face, her cream blouse, her body-hugging charcoal grey skirt, and down to the shapely legs encased in black tights and framed by high heels, and wondered what she made of him, if anything. The only sound in the school now was the other teacher tidying up his classroom and whistling the theme tune from T*he Great Escape*.

"The, emm, student files," McCann said as he passed them to her.

Another glacial smile response. "Did you write them up?"

"Thought I'd wait for Mr. Twilly to show me how he'd like it done, and seeing as he's not here, think I'll leave it for now, thanks." And not to be outdone, he flashed a bitter smile back.

"Don't worry Mr. Peters, my husband will be back soon."

"Your husband?"

"I'm Mrs. Maki Twilly." She held out a hand. There was a look on her face that McCann could not decipher. Irony?

The psycho made his entrance. He stopped walking, but not moving, when he saw

McCann, who noted it, thinking – a nervy one, a finicky breed. They were introduced by Maki. Charlie Davis' eyes were deep-rooted blue and they flickered and changed hue like the water of the sea in mutating light. He was slim-faced with an aquiline, hawkish nose. He took off his cap and pushed back his mane from his forehead with a ring-fingered hand. There was nothing still about him. He seemed like a raw burst of light, looking for something to burn up, something to ignite. When he spoke, McCann caught the accent, similar to his own but more laddish.

"Alright then, now we're done, let's turn down the sound and turn up the fuckin' vibe. Where's Olly at, Maki? Out fluttering again?"

"Boat race."

"Fuck. A swain of culture he be."

There was a short, uncomfortable silence as Davis and McCann assessed each other. McCann opened his mouth to speak but Maki Twilly beat him to it, saying something to Davis in Japanese which the other seemed not to understand, so she took him by the arm behind the reception desk where they talked in subdued voices. McCann took his cue and went to the toilet. When he came back out Davis was sitting in the office chair and Maki was shifting some papers around the desk.

The front door opened.

"Off me fucking throne!" Oliver Twilly was back.

Davis responded, "Kiss the ring."

"Wot ring, the one on your arse?"

Davis obliged, shifting to one of the plastic chairs.

"Sorry I missed the class, pal. Had a boat race to go to. Sort of business. Lost *san man* an' all, puts in a geezer in a right mood. Maki love, get us a drink together, would ya? What you havin'?"

GREETINGS FROM TORQUAY

As the drinks were poured and the banter started McCann got into objective mode, casting a trained eye over the pair of them. Olly Twilly, face gleaming with oily sweat, tie askew and belly hanging over his belt like a bag of money; he was running things here and doing so loudly. Charlie Davis, who had whipped off both tie and shirt, was now sitting on the floor swaying back and forth, cradling his Canadian Club and drawing on a chain of cigarettes with a Bogart intensity, releasing enough plumes of smoke to gas the hamsters that Maki had introduced as Peco and Pilto, housed in a single-tier cage with one wheel between them for entertainment.

There was a laddy rapport between Davis and Twilly but there was competitiveness too and they duelled well. They were clear opposites. Twilly was all weight and gluttony, chewing on something called an American Dog while necking a beer. He relished company and his position in it as a voice to be heard, envied and maybe, he probably hoped, a little feared. Now he was pontificating loudly at McCann and Davis, "Fuckin' getting kippered in 'ere. You lads wanna lay off them cancer sticks, it ain't 1950 you know. Apart from anything else," he sniffed and pulled up his trousers, settling them just below the blubbery waistline, "dulls the performance in the sack, dunnit? No wonder I'm the only one who gets any good pussy round ere, eh Maki? Haha!"

Davis was all lightness and nerves, with darting eyes

72

and moving hands, fiddling and fidgeting. McCann noticed a kind of disdain enter his expression any time Twilly looked away, at least he read it as that, but there was something of the bluffer in the body language, something of a man playing big stakes he might not be able to afford.

Davis rose from the floor. "You want owt from shop?"

Twilly put in an order and Davis turned around and looked at McCann. "How about you, man? Any beer you recommend, George?" He put emphasis on the name and looked hard at McCann, all youth and braggadocio. McCann thought of Harold Philips. Davis had a strange stare right enough. A challenge, but a quizzical look also.

"Sure. The whole lot of them." McCann watched Davis as he slid through the school exit.

Twilly poured himself a Bells, added Coke and sank further back into his padded office chair. "He's a good lad, is Charlie." His eyes gleamed. "Isn't 'e?"

"I don't know him."

"Well, you better get to, pal." He smiled unpleasantly, paused and looked at McCann.

"This school is like a family and I am the dad, and she," he motioned at Maki who was coating her face with even more goo before a hand held mirror, "is Mum. You are an adoption on trial. Tell you what, Maki and me got some business in town. Why don't you let Charlie show you the sights and you can get to know each other? He might be able to drop you a few hints on teaching. According to the missus you were a bit limp in there, know what I mean?"

McCann didn't like the insinuation. He could feel his face reddening as Twilly continued. "This ain't a school, pal, more of an entertainment factory. Fun sells, so lighten up, old man. You're on the afternoon shift tomorrow. I'll chuck in a few cuties an' see if that lights up your pipe. Remember: smile, laugh, roll your fuckin' eyes, just don't sit there like a bleedin' copper. Think Bruce Forsyth, Jimmy Tarbuck, or any other clown that lit up your black-and-white evening TV after you got the homework done."

"Alright. Let the games begin. You got a drum-kit I can use?"

"No, but Charlie has. Ask him nice." Olly stood up. "Catch ya later in the Pong. Charlie's off to pick up his Panda and get some readies."

With that, Twilly knotted his tie, beckoned to his other half and was gone with a bang of the door. McCann heard laughter and the click of high heels fading away followed by a silence, and realised with amazement that he'd been temporarily left alone in the school.

A cursory glance around the ceiling confirmed there were no security cameras, and no alarms that he could see. Not that he had expected any. Standing, he took a look around. It was a shit-hole really. Cubicles stacked together to maximize punters, cheap plastic drawers, a Dell desktop. He made the rounds of the building in less than a minute. There was an exit to the basement but nothing below there except a heating system and cleaning equipment. There was a locked door at the end of the building that perhaps indicated secrets. He thought about picking the lock but now wasn't the time, and instead he went through the unlocked drawers in the reception desk. Little there at first but then he found the account book. There was a lot of money coming in but nothing was clear as to how; just figures, calculations and results. He started taking pictures with his phone in case he needed them for future cross-checking or reference. He found various letters, some addressed to The Hunky-Dory English Club, one or two to 'Oliver Twilly-san' and still others that were written entirely in Japanese, as incomprehensible and exotically beguiling as hieroglyphics on a Rosetta stone.

He snapped pictures of them all, then caught sight of a postcard on the notice board, a seafront with the words *Greetings from Torquay* in red. He unpinned it from the cork board and turned it over. Postmarked only two months before, 'from Mum and William' to Oliver Twilly, an address in a place called Shonandai. He remembered seeing that name a few stops further along the train line. He made sure he got a good photo of the address; it was the only one written in English he could find. When he was done he forwarded all the pictures to his work email account as a backup.

Then instinctively, he froze. Something moved, a noise like the turning of a lock. He stuck the postcard back on the wall, slid the drawers shut and moved back to the chair. Silence. Again there was a sound of something turning. He took his drink and lit a cigarette, then noticed one of the hamsters quietly fluttering round the wheel in the cage; moving without going anywhere, just like him. He took a deep breath, sat back, drank and started thinking.

"I really don't feel comfortable going over all this again, Mr. McCann. Tasha was my best friend, and she's gone. The police talked with me. I told them everything I know. I'm still in shock about the whole thing, y'know? I want to remember Tasha, but I also need to get on with my life. It's been four months and I haven't been able to do anything since it happened. Can't sleep, can't think straight. I just feel so guilty, like there was something I could have done, or should have done…"

Annabel Hollis glanced out the window of her father's plush living room. McCann admired the perfect line of her nose, the sprinkling of freckles, the auburn hair pulled into a ponytail, exposing the neck and the fine hairs that had slipped loose there. She looked even better than in the photo Inspector Brough had shown him. The purple bags under her eyes looked uncharacteristic, and suggested that she had indeed been awake through those summer nights. 'Or she's just recovering after a big night out,' the imaginary cynical bastard on McCann's shoulder whispered.

"You went to school together, right?"

She nodded. "All the way from eleven. Boarding school. We were best friends." They talked briefly about school life, mutual friends, Natasha's personality, boys, and weekend horse riding. From her manner it was obvious that she wanted to get McCann out of the house as quickly as possible. For a private investigator, this was not an uncommon reaction; most of the time he was about as popular round the doors as the Jehovah's Witnesses. Gradually, perhaps realising that telling her side of the story was the best way to get rid of McCann as quickly as possible, the ice thawed slightly.

"You said you started going out on the town when you were about seventeen?"

"Yah. I mean we went out younger than that, but we started getting into it about seventeen."

"Take a lot of drugs?"

"No. We smoked some pot and had some fun, like everyone else. We took our first 'E' at a DJ night at The Castle. It was brilliant. We didn't do it much, once every six months or so. For a special event or someone's birthday or something. That was what happened with the Sublime party." She slipped some of those beguiling strands of hair away from her face and tucked them behind her ear. Even in the loose sweater and jeans she was wearing, guys would do a double take. Girls like this are used to a lot of attention, reflected McCann to himself. He didn't say anything, waited for her to continue with the story.

"We had all more or less finished our exams at uni and decided to get together for this outdoor party. There was a great lineup of DJs and some bands; it was in a beautiful spot. We just thought it would be a great chance to have fun together and party… Celebrate the start of summer." She looked away.

"Let's talk about the people you were with, and the people you met. And of course, the people you got the drugs from." He smiled thinly.

She sighed, and then started her story in the monotone of someone who was clearly tired of repeating it over and over. McCann felt as if he could stop her at any point and she wouldn't know what she had already said and what she hadn't.

"There were five of us. Tasha and me, a guy called Conrad Malthorpe who was her friend from uni and who I'd met a couple of times, our friend Haley who we knew from school, and Haley's boyfriend Ivor. We met on the Friday in Manchester, bought some hash and some E's, and had a few drinks. We drove up to the party on Saturday morning: Conrad had his car and he was taking us all. We talked the whole way. We were so excited about it." Then her voice changed, the monotone dropped: it was a real memory, a moment of recollection not repetition. She laughed to herself and her face lit up. "Haley was psyched 'cos she wanted to see this guy play, Mana Chua or something. Some French or Spanish guy with a band playing I don't know what, like a gypsy acoustic set. None of us had heard of him so we were pretty skeptical. Even Ivor just, like, made fun of her and she went in a huff…" She smiled. "He played early on, as the sun was going down and the clouds were turning pink. He was just brilliant. So, so good. Tasha hugged Haley and told her, 'You were so right, Hales, we love you!'…"

McCann left the silence to its own peace as she sniffled and wiped her nose. He wanted her to continue but no more was forthcoming, so he sledgehammered the moment.

"Who did you get the drugs from? And where?"

Her face closed and she looked down at her hands. "A guy called Swanny, in the Shakespeare Bar on York Lane. We were introduced to him about a year ago and when we wanted something, he could get it for us."

"What does he look like, this Swanny? Got a real name, has he?"

Her head lifted. She scowled at McCann with distain. "He looks like a guy who sells some drugs in a pub. His name's Swanny. At least that's what we knew him by, okay?"

Tetchy. "Okay. Tell me about the party, then."

"It started in the late afternoon. We had some drinks, smoked some joints. Some guys tried to chat me and Tasha up but we weren't interested at all. We weren't there looking for guys. In the evening we watched some bands, the sun went down and then at about nine thirty we took our pills. We were all dancing, laughing, having fun. Tasha was fine, she was high and peaking but she was having a great time. We went into the big tent to catch a DJ that we really wanted to see, but to be honest I really don't know what time it was. I was really high. We hugged each other lots, and we were dancing, dancing away. That was the last time I saw her. I suppose it must have been about two thirty. I think she said she wanted to go to the toilet, but I'm not absolutely sure. It was noisy and, well, we were both a bit wasted. She kissed me on the cheek then turned to go. It was the last time I saw her."

"Did you see her go with anyone?"

"No."

"Was she talking with anyone before that, during the rest of the night?" Hollis looked at McCann with distaste. "We had taken pills. So had lots of other people. People were talking to people they'd never met before. They were enjoying the party, the vibe. Everyone talks to everyone else at that kind of party."

McCann couldn't suppress a smirk. "Sounds lovely … but nothing out of the ordinary? I mean, no-one … stalking her or hassling her, for example?"

She shook her head, looking beyond McCann, beyond the Ligne Roset sofa, into nothingness.

"What about the cocaine?"

Annabel Hollis' eyes shot back into focus. She darted a look at McCann. "We didn't buy any of that."

"It's a bit strange, then, that there was cocaine in her body in the post-mortem, don't you think?"

She put her head in her hands. "Mr. McCain…"

"McCann."

"… McCann. I wasn't her chaperone, you know. God knows, I wish I had been. But there were times when we weren't together. We went to watch different bands or DJs, then met up again later. I lost track of the time, I didn't know where I was myself half the time. I must admit I was really surprised when I found out about that, though. She never once mentioned coke. I know for sure that until that night she had never taken it. I guess she just wanted to try it. We were all having such a great time…"

PUNCHY DRUNK

The door opened and Davis walked in, clutching a carrier bag and trailed by what looked at first glance like a banshee. "Got black beer, gold beer, shit beer and some fags. What you got?"

"Just watching the hamsters."

Davis smirked. He seemed more buoyant now, less edgy. "This is Yukari, me bird. What you called again?"

"George."

The banshee bowed and said, "Hello! Yap, yap!" in a throaty but childish voice, totally avoiding eye contact.

McCann replied, "Nice to meet you, dear."

"Aw-rite, let's get stuck into a few bevvies here. No harm in keepin' the boss waitin' a bit, eh?"

He poured a beer into a pint glass for himself and added ice, then filled a smaller glass with something that looked like toilet cleaner, for Yukari. "*Super chuhi*. Fuckin' swill. Avoid at all costs. Teaching gives you enough brain damage without this. What you drinkin'?"

"I'll have one of those. I've never drunk toilet cleaner before."

Davis held his eye for a second. "You want a hamster with that? Fuckin' rodents. Stinky and Shitty. Yukari, *hamusta suki desu ka?*"

Yukari yelled something in Japanese without looking up.

McCann looked at Davis, "What's her verdict then?"

"Dunno. Probably cute but smelly. The aesthetics

of girl-land here in Japan can be easily summed up."
Davis was helping himself to another Canadian Club
and studying the bottle as if he had never seen the drink
before. "They are cute or scary, clean or stinky, interesting
or strange. A philosophy of … singular antonyms."

"How would she classify me?"

"Dunno. Why you want to know? You goin' to fuckin'
hit on my missus, like?"

"Nah, just askin'. Go on."

They eyeballed each other for a second. Davis shrugged
and turned to Yukari. The exchange was a bit longer, a
mish-mash of English and Japanese words. Davis grinned
and waved his thumb from side to side. "She said you are
a bit suspicious but not a bad-looking old lad."

With a sharp and ironical glance at McCann, Davis
adroitly switched the subject. "What's your take on Japan?
Quite a head-fuck, ain't it?"

McCann took a look across the table where Yukari
had perched herself on the school throne and appeared to
be using a white board marker to touch up her dramatic
eye makeup even further, and had to agree. "Yeah, it's a
culture shock alright. Pretty schizophrenic. Extremes all
over the place." He was looking at a couple right now.
"Does your girl speak English?" he asked Davis quietly.

Davis grinned at him, "Not really. But then the birds
back home don't really either do they? At least not the
ones I know. And them that do, the poshies, do your head
in with their fuckin' theories and rights. Ain't a problem
here, like."

There was a beckoning from the reception table,
"More, Charlie, please."

"Comin' right up, love." Davis arose from the floor
with a spring and almost danced over to the fridge door.
The alcohol had kicked in and he was laid back now.

"Judging from your dulcet tones I take it that you are one of our friends from the north. Ish. I'd put me money on somewhere in the north west."

"Aye? Round about. And I'd put you just around the corner in Manchester." Something passed across Davis's face. Not enough to be called anger, but something, nonetheless. "Spot on. I'm a Manc, born and bred, splayed and raised. Fucked and duffed, dyed and spied ... fuck this stuff's good. How d'you like the super shit juice?"

McCann was on his second one and was rather enjoying it. "Good. Light and punchy."

At that moment Yukari stood up and as she passed, looked at McCann deeply, nodding, "*Umai. Nomiyasui deshou!*"

McCann noticed for the first time that her eyes were sapphire blue.

"She said it's easy to drink, mate. It's easy to shit too."

McCann wasn't sure what to make of the kid. He seemed sharp and good at covering up what lay beneath. He was good at playing the jester and playing down or up his obvious charisma. "You enjoy the teaching then, Charlie?"

"Piece a piss really. Gives us a few bob to enjoy the life, and this place is kicking. You? This your first shot at it?"

"Yeah. Few problems back home. Time to take off."

"With the law?"

"Is a wife the law?"

"Maybe, man. Your fault for locking yourself up like that. Holding your finger out for the padlock. Don't do it again. The girls man, when they want fun, nowt better, when they want owt else, nowt worse."

McCann was about to ask him just what exactly had brought him here but Yukari came clattering out from

82

some hidden den and latched onto Davis's arm like a child does a daddy's, and said in a smoky cute rasp, "Let's going!"

"Y'right! Drink up, then. We're off to scale the neon lights."

McCann finished up his lemon *chuhi*, took a leak, gave himself a onceover and realized he was half-cut.

The trio headed through the evening to the station, Yukari's heeled boots cracking the asphalt, the couple hand in hand and the single man wearing an expression of amused puzzlement. It was an odd group that took the train that night: Ziggy Stardust's moll, Charlie the psycho and McCann the private dick. His police mate Brough would love this, McCann thought – if he saw it on television. He wouldn't believe it otherwise.

THE MANDRAKE AND THE
MANNEQUIN

The last train back to Yamato left Shinjuku at just after midnight. It was another swaying, blurry recollection of people all talking at once, laughing, endlessly hanging dog-tired from hand straps, shifting weight from one listless leg to the other and back again, falling asleep standing up. Most of the lucky ones who had seats sprawled twisted, mouths open like dead carp in an aquatic St Valentine's Day Massacre.

Although well after midnight the throng of people was tenacious, a jumble of men and women clattering on and off at every stop on the way. The hum and crackle of conversation, so noticeably absent from the afternoon train, was ubiquitous now. Some girls wearing matching J-Pop t-shirts were gabbing excitedly, drinking bottled green tea. A group of older people were sitting across from them, the red-faced men wearing black suits with white ties and supping cans of beer, the ladies wrapped in gold and cerulean *kimono* like exclusive Belgian chocolates. A young man in a suit was slumped on the floor by the train doors, oblivious to the world. He seemed to have lost his shoes somewhere.

McCann viewed this multitude through a stupid smile, which Twilly called the '*shochu* cloud'. Almost every generation from teens to octogenarians was on board, and McCann felt simultaneously an empathy with this communal *joie de vivre* of humanity barreling down the tracks but also a distance from it, as if looking in on a party from an outside window with only the Ghost of Christmas Past for company.

At Yamato Twilly and Maki said their goodbyes and Davis invited McCann to join him and the banshee-Panda for drinks at his. McCann had forgotten that he was a man in his late forties with a mortgage and grey in his stubble. It didn't seem to matter here, or at least it was much easier not to let it matter. He acquiesced.

"Alright! The night ain't young and neither is George, but he's learning!"

❧

The night had been another blur, but one in which he had got to know something of Davis, although it seemed that here 'something' wasn't like something anywhere else. He looked at the Panda. When not gazing into a pink star-studded mobile phone she had spent the night referring to the gaspers or the mirror. She seemed to have little interest in portraying herself as a person and if she was hiding something, the disguise was immaculate. Not that she mattered; it was Davis McCann wanted to see through – and that one had other ways of hiding.

The night had begun with the sort of edgy laddish banter McCann hadn't indulged in for years. With the arrival of Twilly, the tone nose-dived further. When a spectacular dame appeared dressed in a skirt that drew a line labia-height, Twilly shouted, "Give us a flash, luv!" and the girl smiled.

"Where's she going, man, to a whorehouse?"

"Probably. Or a wedding party."

"Same thing," quipped McCann, drawing a laugh.

Twilly was warming to him and McCann was

finding it easy to play the part of a pubby geezer and to get acquainted with the shallowness of the cut and thrust. Davis spoke little at first, seemingly engrossed in the nightscape and looking intensely at what passed before him. He drank quickly and with pleasure and smoked a lot, but he ate little, only paying attention to the food when the *sashimi* arrived. The Panda selected some choice bits and retreated into a corner with Davis and began feeding. McCann found himself shoulder to shoulder with Oliver Twilly; the scent of some over-applied expensive fragrance hit him in the nostrils. He noticed a Western girl in a far corner of the bar talking to herself and lighting up a cigarette even though one still burned in the ashtray.

She had large dark rings under her eyes. She seemed animated and unhinged.

"Looks like she's drugged up mate. Shabu. Amphetamines big here. If I wasn't such a clean operator I'd think about goin' into the market meself." Conspiratorial wink.

"So you just have the one business here then, Olly?"

"Keep me options open, mate. Doin' alright here. Thinking of opening another school in the spring. If you stick around there might be more work for you. Definitely more work for him." He shrugged a nod towards Davis. "Fuckin' star that fella. Mind, I always knew he would be. He was the same back home. Could wind the birds round his little finger. Now, I thought, let's put that to use. Otherwise, bleedin' waste, innit? So, I gets him out here and he's doing well. Could do without that freak mind you. Worry about him sometimes."

"What freak?"

"That Panda."

"Aye, they don't make them like that back at home."

"Ah, the chicks here. Apparently back in the day – that's the late nineties – that kind was everywhere, that silver haired, tanning-salon type. The Flowers of Shibuya me mate called them. All wearin' platform boots like Marc fuckin' Bolan. Woulda been right up your street – about your time, Marc Bolan, eh? Or were you already too old for that?" Twilly cackled, friendly enough but unmistakably tinged with barbed disrespect. He continued, clearly enjoying himself, "Had changed a bit by the time I got here. But that Panda there is a hybrid model. Bit of a throwback, bit of the modern as well. But Charlie's kinda taken with her, and that's not usually his way."

"First love then. Bit old for it ain't he?"

Twilly smirked and knocked back his highball.

"Bit young for it more like. Me and Maki got knotted last year and 'ere I am. Not complaining, like. Had a string of birds before her. You should've seen me when I got here, mate, I was like a fuckin' kid on Christmas Day. Like a fuckin' pop star I was. Christ how my cock hurt! I was beatin' them off with a shitty stick."

Another smirk. He was impossible to believe, but somehow difficult to reel in.

"Old codger like you, you should get a move on. Look at this fuckin' place." He pointed to the human traffic flow beyond the bar, the tottering girls giggling with idiotic exuberance, the repugnant chancers in pursuit, the carnival lit up and the sparkling night carrying them all on a dark river heading downstream.

"But that Panda. He don't even know what she does, like. I mean where she get that bag from? It's a Louis Vuitton. And that shit she puts on her face. Chanel lippy, that's five Jap grand a throw. I reckons she selling her purse to fill her purse, know wot I mean?"

"It doesn't look to me like Charlie was born yesterday."

"He weren't but this place got a way of fuckin' with you and Charlie's always been a bit…"

"Same again, lads? What have I always been then, Olly?" Davis had blindsided Twilly and was giving him a nasty, confrontational look as he leaned against the bar. Olly fashioned a comforting laddish smile and flashed out a calming hand to shake.

"I was just telling George 'ere what a great fuckin' teacher you is. Our future. He can learn from you."

Davis just scowled at him, ordered two beers and a highball for Twilly, and took his own back to the corner.

"Bit temperamental, is Charlie."

"Got a bit of a short fuse, has he?"

"He's a good lad. A good skin. Temper? Yeah, me too. Who ain't? Fairies an' sad cunts, that's who." He groaned orgasmically. "Feel a good shit coming on, mate. Me old teacher in Essex, dead up on biology, he said you need a good shit once a day and two minor ones in-between. Eat me All-Bran everyday and take me cod liver oils, so I got no problem releasing the wastes that come with a business life."

Olly burped and walked out the bar to a toilet somewhere, picking up a *manga* from a small bookcase on the way.

The music in the bar had stopped and McCann could hear the passing noise from the streets and the conversation around him. He glanced to his right. Davis and the Panda were close together and Davis was stroking her forearm. He strained to eavesdrop on the conversation.

"London *ikitai, ikitai!* When?"

Davis was feeding her slices of raw fish and sliding his hand up her sheathed thigh.

"You know, I told you."

"I want shopping at Burberry. Can we buy some?"

"I'll get you some Burberry, honey. A whole set of the stuff. Maybe not from the shop though."

"Net shopping?"

"*Niteiru*. Similar, baby, but cheaper."

They had exchanged roles and this time Yukari was serving Davis.

"Want to see Roma and Paree. Many things I want. With you."

The Panda let fall the slice of white fish she was holding to his lips and her tongue came from her mouth in a long tapered point and entered Davis' waiting mouth. McCann turned his gaze from the snoggers. Youth. It happens once, then forget it. McCann pawed for a fag, found one and lit up absolutely nothing.

In time Twilly returned, looking even more pleased with himself than before.

"Good shit then, Olly?"

"A cracker. Ready to zoom, pal. You look after them two and I'll be back pronto." McCann watched him exit with a waddle and a trot. He looked into his beer and then over to the far corner but the Western girl had left. Perhaps she had found someone other than herself to talk to.

"He's gone then?" It was Davis.

"Yeah. Said it was business. But he'll be back."

Nodding, Davis ordered a drink. When it came he sipped it slowly and gazed through the night as if it wasn't there. McCann looked over at the Panda, who was talking on her smartphone and nodding her head like a mental patient. He was drunk.

"What you think of all this, then? Must seem like a bunch of shit to you. All them temptations you are old enough to still want but too old to get. That's crap, ain't it? Stuff beyond your reach and that."

"Don't know, kidder. Hard to appraise. There's always ways to get what you need."

Two girls walked past in micro mini skirts and one smiled at Davis who smirked back. "We are in the heart of one mad blinking samsara. It's all surface. And what a beautiful, sick veneer it is. Welcome to hell, mate to the neon fires and blazing temptations." Davis smiled and theatrically pointed around him. "By the time I hit your age I hope to be a bit more enlightened than to be here."

"Why? You missing home? A real girlfriend? A future?"

Davis laughed. "Yeah I am missing my future. What kind of knobhead wouldn't? Nah, man, I like it here, in the thick of what we are." He sneered and belted down his drink. "You want another? I do. Got paid yesterday for me circus act."

"Billy Smart's Circus, remember that?"

"Never heard of it. Must be your time. I'm well into all the fun of the fair. Get a couple of Siamese twins and stick 'em in a classroom and the lolly rolls in."

Two beers arrived.

"You don't like your job then, I take it?"

"I like it man. I like the students and I like teaching them something. I like this country."

"You don't like Olly too much though, do you?"

"Olly's a mate. We go back years and I wouldn't be here without him. It's that simple."

"Why are you here?"

Davis ran his hand through his tumbly curls and they flopped back easily, framing his face. He wasn't really handsome but he had a look that demanded attention; eyes glacial blue but the whites bloodshot.

"It was on the cards. I did a reading and the cards told me what was next."

"What was before?"

Davis gave McCann that same appraising look, weighing up the man before him and the meaning of his question. "A cul-de-sac."

"So, a reading of the cards. What's that, like, choosing the ace of spades?"

"A bit." Davis picked up his knapsack and pulled out a grubby-looking green silken wrap that contained the cards he had spoken of. It was a tarot pack. "Don't leave home without them. Better than a library."

"So, you a fucking pikey as well as a teacher, are you? How do you divine the future from the cards then?"

Davis's voice and look suddenly had a hardness similar to when they had first met. Perhaps McCann's questions were putting Davis on edge again. "There isn't really a future, but you can read the present. I'll do yours later and we can find out who you really are." It was probably a joke but made McCann uneasy. Tread lightly, no need to blow this into the open yet.

"So what was the card that brought you here?"

"They work in combos, George, but the central motif in mine was the death card." Davis looked at McCann with a sideways smile, "And that means change. Or rot."

McCann's face puckered up slightly. "How you finding the change?"

Pause. No answer, just that same quizzical, challenging stare that had freaked Harold Philips out so much.

McCann continued, "You look to have landed on your feet, anyway. How you meet your lady friend?"

"She was on the same train as me, got off at the same station and followed me home. When I opened the door she entered."

McCann laughed at the simple absurdity of the story. "She's been there since, then?"

"Nah, she's nomadic. Comes and goes and never stays long enough to stifle the vibe." He heard the familiar clacking; the Panda was slinking back to her perch on those very high-heeled leather boots. She was quite something. Slender as a whip and coffee skinned, hands tipped with darts of painted fire and wearing a tight, short skirt. Her slim upper body was wrapped in a thin, pink fleece and her sensual face was topped by a think mane of streaked silver. She looked like a miniature supermodel seen through acid.

"So when she goes away you keep your rings on and stay a good boy?" McCann pointed to Davis' heavily ringed left hand and for the first time noticed a tattoo on the inner wrist.

It was unusual and depicted a small seabird taking flight.

"I like gals, George, and as a species they don't get any better than here. How about you? Said you left home 'cos of the wife, didn't you? You got owt to stay good to now?" McCann thought for a second and the only answer he could come up with was, "Just to myself."

Davis grinned. "That's the hardest one, innit? Respect that one."

A bulky man – Oliver Twilly – with a small entourage, came into view and it seemed to McCann that Davis' eyes hardened. Twilly was jovial and bedraggled and greeted them with a sneery laugh. "You two look a bit stuffy-iffy. Come on, we're off to Honeys for the last one." Twilly had been joined by Maki and a blonde-haired Japanese man who he introduced as Beef. The Panda arose and Davis put his arm around her protectively.

Beef looked like a cyborg beamed up from the Philip K Dick future. Something about him vaguely unsettled McCann, although he couldn't quite put his finger on what: perhaps nothing more than the feeling of complete alienation from a fellow human. In some ways Beef seemed like the male equivalent of the Panda; all hair, clothes, jewellery and plucked eyebrows. But he possessed a different kind of presence, effortlessly yet excessively calm and cool, which demanded a form of respect. If Twilly had introduced him as a multi-millionaire international fashion designer, McCann would have believed it. In fairly broken English Beef was telling Twilly and Davis about a Halloween party that they all seemed to be going to the next night. McCann was temporarily sidelined from the conversation and was losing focus and drifting into another jet-lagged blur when a nudge and a comment from Twilly pulled him back to the present.

"Got your glad rags ready for a little dance, George?"

"Eh?"

"Tomorrow night. Party time, mate. Fancy dress an' that. But in your case, just your usual clobber will do, eh?" Twilly cackled again and turned to the others. "Right, come on lads an' lassies, drink up, we got ten minutes till the last train…"

KARAOKE NIGHT

They all removed their shoes upon entry and the Panda shrank by several inches. Davis's pad seemed to have two *tatami* rooms containing almost nothing except nicotine-yellow daubed bare walls. There was a door that McCann assumed led to a toilet, and a kitchen off to one side. It was beyond simple, more like tawdry. Through the bedroom doorway he could see two futons on the floor; a cheap Spanish guitar was hanging from a hook on a wall.

The room smelled of tobacco and joss sticks and was lit by a single floor lamp. There was a battered-looking low table in the main room and several cushions around it, and little else. No TV or computer, just a tiny CD player by a window that was uncurtained. The night was surprisingly hot and close and Davis lit a mosquito coil then settled with ease on a cushion, juggling a bottle of liquor with one hand. The Panda had gone straight to the bathroom, from where the sound of falling water emerged.

McCann looked around. "You not a big one for possessions then, Charlie?"

"What you can't fit in a rucksack ain't worth having. Do the honours, mate. Some long glasses with ice and we'll sort out a drink. Kitchen's pretty easy to find."

If you could call it a kitchen. An old fridge gurgled in the corner as McCann walked over a squelchy linoleum floor, noticing that the area by the sink was littered with an array of potted plants: alfalfa, watercress, herbs and a hanging basket of mini tomatoes. He opened the fridge door and found little within; cubes of tofu, beers and several bottles of vinegars.

Not the cooler of a bon vivant. He grabbed a plastic tray of ice cubes and opened the cupboard above the sink: a few glasses inside, and something else above them, accompanied by a faint scratching sound. He peered in to investigate: two large cockroaches mating. Shuddering, he took out three glasses and washed them under the tap in a weak trickle of hot water. Seeing nothing to dry them with, he shook the water off them. There was an electric kettle plugged in by the floor but no cooker. It was a kitchen easy to find and difficult to forget.

The scent of a Drum rollie mingling with the smoke of the mosquito coil hit him as he returned with the three glasses and the ice. Something about the way Davis looked put McCann on edge. Davis was difficult to read; he flitted suddenly from apparent relaxation to intense attentiveness. McCann considered when to lay his cards on the table. The moment wasn't quite right yet. Wait till the kid drinks more, relaxes more.

"That all you brought? More ice, George! We need buckets of the stuff."

They went back to the kitchen. Davis dropped smoothly into a squat, opened the icebox and rose with a bag. "Loads of ice. Takes off the hangover, hydrates your alcohol."

"What's with the greenery? Anything dodgy in there?"

"Nah. All good. I am a raw foodist. This is living food, best of the lot. Grow it myself – in this climate it's a piece of piss."

"In this dark cubby hole?"

"The living room gets a lot of light. Enough in the day. They rest here."

"What's that one?" McCann had seen it before, a tapered pod-like plant, rather pretty, but he couldn't remember the name.

"At home it's called Lady's Finger and only the rich eat it. Here it's known as *okura* and everybody eats it. But I eat it raw. The best food is fresh from the stalk."

"What about your girl Yukari? She a rabbit too?"

Davis grinned. "She's more of a carnivore. Eats her meat live, that one."

They returned to the main room. McCann watched him pour two drinks, change from a squat into a semi-lotus and roll up another Drum with ease and delight. It seemed like there was something adaptable about the guy, something unfaked and measured by experience he didn't have the years to possess. Not the usual pantomime that the young play through with their politics, costumes, poses and idol worship. This kid was relaxed in himself and there was no front, he was just there.

McCann stretched and lowered himself onto a cushion, feeling his knees creak. Time to start prodding, see what reaction he got.

"So, Charlie, you really like living in this shit hole and working in that dead-end job then?"

No response.

"What did you do back home?"

"Wanted to get here."

"What d'you like about here?"

Davis changed his position and adopted a thinker stance, mockingly rubbing a ringed finger over his chin and furrowing his brow.

"Living at floor level is what the Japanese still do and what we have lost. I like being on the ground and not above anything. Nothing too mystical, George. Listen, I got a good whisky here, Hibiki. I was waiting for the chance to open it. It's your 'Welcome to Japan' drink, man."

It tasted good, slightly cooled with ice and water, clean, relaxing. The Panda appeared from her shower and was clad in a bathrobe patterned with emblems from Disneyland.

She padded past them wordlessly and entered the bedroom.

McCann swirled the ice in his glass and Davis filled it up some more.

"Tell me more about the tarot, Charlie. The mystic pictures, the maps of the golden way."

Davis had taken out the tarot pack and was shuffling them intensely, grinning and murmuring some chant to himself. He looked up. "Don't take the piss, mate."

In the other room a mobile phone rang and McCann heard the girl answer. He took a big swig of whisky and looked back at Davis: maybe now's as good a time as any. "Put the cards away, Charlie."

Davis grinned. It was a nice grin, one you would like your child to have.

"Forget about this tarot shit for a second. What really brought you here, Charlie?"

Davis continued to smile and began to lay out the suit of cards in some fancy system. But McCann wasn't here to watch card tricks. He stood and launched a contemptuous kick at the array in front of him, catching Davis' dealing hand at the same time and scattering the remaining cards across the floor. Davis let out an involuntary cry and bounded to his feet, ready for action.

"You see, Charlie, when the wind blows the house falls, if it's made of cards."

Davis wasn't sure how to react at first, and a range of emotions crossed his face.

Eventually he exhaled and settled for a smirk.

McCann heard the sound of more movement from behind. The Panda had appeared and was shouting something, the tone sharp and angular, then she swung wildly at him with a pink stiletto-heeled shoe. McCann, who was out of range anyway, ducked away and Davis, almost giggling, turned to restrain her, enveloping her in his arms, placating her with whispered words and touches. He guided her into a corner; it took some minutes before she calmed down, then she went into the kitchen. Davis returned to the table, looking unflustered by the situation, still in control. He was buoyant, on his toes, and it was McCann's nerves that were becoming frayed.

"You didn't answer my question – why are you here, Charlie?"

"Time enough for questions. Sit down. Things are getting a bit heavy, George, so Yukari is going to make you one for the road and us one for the sack. But before that we are going to listen to a bit of night music. Fucking trouble is we don't have much to choose from – got no iPhone. And no internet connection anyway. Just a mo."

Davis stepped into the bedroom and the Panda returned from the kitchen, sullenly placing the drinks on the low table. She looked up at McCann and her eyes were a dark brown now that she had removed her contacts; there was little tenderness in their gaze. She said something unintelligible under her breath. McCann gruffly thanked her and took a glass, draining half of it in one.

The great hush of the late hour seemed to hiss in McCann's head. He watched as Davis pulled the battered guitar, spattered with peeling stickers, from the wall. Davis gazed pensively at McCann and began to tune up. He heard muffled claps from the Panda and then something else as she emitted a peculiar hum that rose to a high-pitched cicada release. She had removed her necklace and was fiddling with it on her lap as if in the throes of some trance. On the verge of saying something about rosemary or worry beads, McCann found the words failed him. Then a tune emerged from the guitar, one McCann half-recognized as an echo of a time long past. He thought hard and tried to place it as Davis alternated between tuning and finger picking.

McCann looked on blurrily as the Panda moved and began crawling towards him, smiling through snarly teeth. On arrival, she paused, then pushed back the dun-coloured mane that was her hair and leaned over him, switching on a lamp from which a puce green glow emanated. She stood and extinguished the main light. Davis continued to mess with the guitar until he stopped and murmured, "Welcome to our home. It is an empty space for original drama and subtle – or none so subtle – release. Enjoy."

McCann took a gulp from his glass and the sweetish liquor slightly nauseated him. His body felt hot and prickly and he watched the couple side by side. Around them the shapes in the room were beginning to melt. The pair seemed to be encased in a miniature gold frame like the Elizabethan pictorial courtly love tokens called limnings. He needed to piss and to clear his head of all this and as he stood up he found himself asking Davis directions even though he clearly knew where the toilet lay, around a yard to his left. There was a pause and Davis spoke, "Bog, mate? Good idea, George. Just thinking, man, why did you come here? You keep bugging me with questions. How about one from me?"

'Fair point from the kid,' McCann thought. 'But fuck him, they both knew why they were here.'

"I am here on account of a bad ending that needs a closure, son".

Davis tapped himself on the temples, "I get it. Well, I think you are reaching it. Don't forget to flush, pal."

McCann stood up and made his way to the toilet in a state of unpleasant disorientation. The chrome was as damaged as rotten teeth and a smell of endless toilet duties exuded forth from the latrine. In contrast the mirror was tacky new and illuminated the current physical stage where history had parked him: the grey flourishing at his temples, the shrinking skin around his neck and the sprouts of silver in his chest hair. He pissed long and hard and then shook his head as he looked into the mirror one final time. These kids were playing with him. It was time to do something. He ran water into the tiny sink and splashed it on to his face. He then ran more water and drank from the tap.

McCann opened the door to a different sound, something punky and charged with youth. Davis grinned up at McCann and stopped playing. "This one ain't your song, mate. It's crap and crude and rude. Got somethin' a bit more classic for you. Traditional, like. It's an old ballad mummies used to sing to pox-ridden nippers cursed by runaway dads. Lovely tune all the same. It makes Yukari sob.

McCann, feeling momentarily better, took a pew and returned the smirk from Davis with a teasing one of his own. He would let Davis do this and then the tomfoolery would be over. It began with a whoop from the Panda and fast strumming from Davis in bastardised country and western style. Then it stopped and after a brief silence Davis began to play very softly with his head hung over the guitar and his eyes half closed. He sang in an enticing way; neither ferocious nor soft but with force and authority.

"Hush little baby don't you cry
Mummy gonna sing you a lullaby
And if that lullaby don't sing
Daddy gonna give you a golden ring
And if that golden ring turns fake
Mummy gonna take you to Poppa's wake
'Cos when he told you what he knew
The hushed baby was blessed by dew."

McCann tried to speak. For some odd reason he wanted to compliment the singer but couldn't. He was in some kind of rigor mortis. The singing had ceased. Davis was still strumming the guitar whilst nuzzling and whispering to his girl, who locked eyes with McCann and whispered a word that could have been 'weeping'. Davis resumed the song but this time in a duet with the girl, although it wasn't singing she was doing, more a hymnal sobbing. McCann looked out through the window at a moon that curved darkly into a cloud and then into him.

He tried to raise himself from the cushion but his arms and legs were like lead pipes. Davis smiled effortlessly at him. "You believe people can fly, George? Yogis do. It is a kind of meditation."

McCann's voice seemed to come from somewhere underneath himself and he was aware he was speaking very slowly. "No, I don't. But they can fall alright, and that's what you've just done."

"Out of real fags, man. You wanna rollie?"

"Yeah … You ready to talk, then?"

Davis looked at the light in the corner, then picked a sliver of tobacco from the tip of his tongue. "How did you find me?"

McCann tried to scratch his ear but his arm failed to

respond, although he could still speak – just. "Had a ... chat ... with Carl Pounder."

"That gent. How's his face?"

McCann managed a big, stupid, doped grin. "Ugly as ever."

The room had begun to spin like a merry-go-round. McCann looked at his whisky, the source, he realised now, of some kind of anaesthetic influence on his consciousness. Davis and his moll had been a couple of steps ahead all along. A dull fear chilled him and he made a monumental effort to get up, but the power had gone from his body and he fell heavily over, like a collapsing factory tower. As he was veering away from consciousness Davis's face appeared in front of him and he saw the mouth moving but heard no words, then it was black.

HUNKY DORY

He woke up to a spinning room and an exiting footfall. He tried to rise, or thought he did, but then fell back into a sleep and a dream of a Japanese girl, bizarrely dressed, guiding him through Tokyo and laughing, until they were in Paris and people were laughing at her. Then he thought he had awoken properly and the place was empty. He tried to stand but fell back when he did. His legs quivered and he had no idea where he was, if in a dream or in the real world.

He could smell something chemical quickening in his nostrils when he awoke next. He half-opened his eyes. A light dazzled him and in that light there was a nebulous figure, walking barefooted over the *tatami* with a cigarette between her fingers, which she then placed in an ashtray as she squatted down and held a mirror before her eyes. She was clad in purple underwear and her ornaments flashed and jingled as she removed her dazzling array of adornments. She unhooked several gold hair-pieces and took out her earrings. She then removed her bangles and rings and placed them on the table. That finished, she began to remove her make up with wet wipes and her mask of brown came off revealing a pale, light-coloured skin. Next, she bent forward and her hair fell like a waterfall, shining in the light. Then she unclothed herself and her nakedness was before him. She wiped her genitals and covered them with white panties and attached a white bra to her sharp breasts and took a drag from her smoke. He thought he recognized her and tried to speak. No sound came and he wasn't sure if this was a dream or not.

She pulled tan tights over her legs, followed by a formal skirt and blouse, put out the cigarette and made a phone call in broken English. He could only understand "Yes, okay." Then she began to apply a different type of make-up, one for the world, the mask of normality, and put a brush through her hair that he heard crackle in the morning light.

She placed something on the table. Then he felt something shaking him and it was her. "Wake up. Work time." And he awoke to watch her slip away quietly over the matted floor.

At the school Twilly was on sterling form and McCann was still half-drunk and drugged.

Davis was nowhere to be seen. Perhaps he hadn't had a chance to talk with Twilly yet?

Twilly had simply giggled when McCann arrived. "Ready for action, my son?"

"I'll be okay … in a bit. Charlie not here yet?"

"Day off, innit?"

McCann's addled mind started muddling through possibilities of Charlie doing a runner or contacting Twilly and telling him to punt McCann, but he had classes to teach and that was enough to worry about for now, and he staggered towards the classroom with some dread.

He surprised himself by teaching some goodish lessons. In a break between classes Maki made him a coffee, patted him on the head and said, "Good job. Welcome to Japan."

Even with his lack of experience McCann knew that she was right. The students had opened up in the classes, and so had he. Marvin had helped. Instead of talking about him as a dog, McCann turned him into a myth. 'I Miss My Dog' was the theme of all the classes, and the students reacted. They listened and said, "It's like Hachiko's story. Do you know Hachiko? So sad story. But very good dog, waiting for his dead master. He looks *samishii*. Do you know *samishii?*"

"I know *sashimi!*"

The students giggled madly. "No, it is not same!"

They told him the story of the famously faithful Japanese dog and he could see Maki looking through the class window smiling. She held up her thumb and Olly joined her, pressing his against hers. He was in, but into what remained to be seen.

During lunch Twilly handed McCann a curly black wig and a stick-on droopy 70's moustache. "Try that on for size, mate."

"What the fuck's this supposed to be?"

"Halloween party tonight, innit? Up in Tokyo. Gotta wear some kinda costume. This is the only thing we've got handy here at the school."

McCann reluctantly put the wig and 'tache on. "So who am I supposed to be in this? Terry McDermott?"

"Looks great, man. Suits you down to a tee."

Maki was giggling and McCann suspected a set-up of some kind. "So, is Charlie going to this party as well? What are you two going as?"

"I got me James Bond tuxedo, ain't I? Think Charlie's gonna take a white sheet for a toga, stick on a pair of Jesus sandals an' go as one a them Greek philosophers or somethin'. Here, take a look at this."

Twilly grabbed his iPad from the reception table, thrust it into McCann's hands and showed him a picture of his much younger self with a group of five motley-looking friends, all dressed in ill-fitting tuxedos and holding martinis. He bobbed a stubby finger at the screen. "Me an' me mates at a Halloween party back home, donkey's years ago. We all went as different James Bonds. Which one d'you think I was, then?"

"Ummm … Connery?"

"Nah, man, fuckin' Pierce Brosnan. You blind or somethin'? That bloke, me mate Spivvo, he's Connery. So is this twat, Harry Dunford. So he said, anyway. I was like, 'Nah, man, you're that Ozzie bloke, if yer lucky!' Twat."

"George Lazenby. I thought he was really good, actually."

"Yeah, whatever. Anyway, check this out. Love this iPad. Got me thrillers for the train, all me work stuff, all me photeys on this."

He pulled the iPad away from McCann and entertained him with images of Twilly does Disney, Twilly in Kyoto, Twilly with drinking chums. As he showed McCann the endless, pointless pictures he said, "By the way, you're doin' good today. Just as well. After yesterday, thought I might have to give you the boot." He held out a sweaty palm for McCann to shake. Like all wannabe strong men, Twilly tried to break his hand.

BESPOKE COFFEE

That evening, back at his hotel in Shinjuku, McCann tried to rest his exhausted mind and body for a couple of hours before the party. 'Got to be an easier way to get under Davis's skin than this,' he thought. 'At this rate my liver'll be pickled after five days in this country … Still, if Davis turns up tonight that'll be my chance to talk to him about Natasha.' He boiled the kettle and made a cup of green tea, relishing the natural verdant taste that was the epitome of Japanese good health, and lay back on the bed, dozing, drifting in and out of consciousness in a state of pleasant reflection.

⛭

The waiter slinked over. McCann ordered a black coffee, Conrad Malthorpe a caffé breve. The waiter took down the order, nodded conspiratorially with a smug, approving smile, and glided away.

"It's like a latte, but with a steamed milk and cream mixture for extra punch."

Malthorpe looked like a minor character in the royal family pantheon: the son of the Duchess of Somewhere. With a square jaw, tousled brown hair and perfect skin he was amiable enough. He looked like he'd never done a stroke of work in his life.

After brief introductions McCann brought out his MP3 voice recorder and placed it on the table. "You don't mind if I record this, do you? Just for my own personal use, you understand."

A cloud of doubt tumbled over Malthorpe's face. He gave a short, tense laugh. "Haaa, actually I do mind a bit. You know, as I said to you last night on the phone, I told the police all they needed to know when they interviewed me." His eyes narrowed. "I don't think I'm under any obligation to talk to you, Mr…?"

"McCann."

"Yes, Mr. McCann. I'm doing this out of respect for Natasha, and for her family. But that doesn't extend to letting a man I've never met before record my memories of that night. Sorry."

"Sure, I get you." McCann put the recorder away in his bag. He rubbed his chin, pulled out a small notebook, waved his pen at Malthorpe with a smile. "I'll just make notes in the old style then." He knitted his brows together. "You said just now that you told the police all that they *needed* to know. Kind of a strange turn of phrase that, isn't it? Maybe there's more to the story that they don't need to know?"

Malthorpe said nothing, tried a James Dean furrow. It didn't work.

"You were studying with Natasha at university, right?"

"Yah. Law. We met in Freshers' Week, got on well, became really good friends."

"You spent a lot of time together?"

"Yah. We hung out with the same people. Did stuff together."

"What kind of stuff?"

"Haaa … what kind of stuff? I think we were drunk for most of the first month. What do you want to know about? Stealing traffic cones on the way home from a night out? We could be here for a while, Mr. McCann."

A vaguely friendly smile from McCann. Thought: 'twat'.

"Well, how about these for starters – were you in a relationship together? And did you take drugs together?"

Malthorpe pulled a pack of menthol cigarettes from his jacket pocket. "Hope you don't mind. This is why I wanted an outside seat."

McCann snorted and pulled a pack from his own pocket. "In case of emergencies, light one and draw."

Malthorpe grinned, lit up, inhaled, blew the smoke into the air and thought for a while. "No, and yes."

The waiter came back with the drinks.

"Care to expand on that?"

"No, we weren't in a relationship, and yes, we took some stuff together." Malthorpe moved his chair close to the table and leaned across it. "Mr. McCann, as I said, I want to help Mr. and Mrs. Philips if I can, but you know, I have my own life, my own future to think about. Going over and over this story isn't quite how I had envisaged spending this weekend... Look, we were students together. I'm twenty-one years old. We got drunk at the weekends, we smoked some pot. Every now and then we took something a little ... stronger. Anyway that's all by the by. The rest of the time we were studying, reading books. I play squash – we have a really good squash team at the uni, you know. County champions last year." He waved his hand in the air. The smoke from the cigarette coiled into the autumn sky. "We're not angels, we're not devils, we're just people who do things like everyone else, okay?"

McCann glanced at the sparkling silver Audi Malthorpe had parked across the street. 'Not quite like everyone else,' he thought to himself. "Don't worry, I'm not making a list for St Peter ... did you take cocaine much?"

Draw, exhale. "Let's not talk about me. I thought you wanted to ask me about Natasha?"

"True enough…" McCann thought for a minute. They both drank some coffee. "I was looking at some photos the other day. Pretty girl, Natasha. More than pretty. Pretty sexy. If I was twenty-one and her friend, I think I'd be trying to be a bit more than just her friend…"

Malthorpe's face turned bright pink. He couldn't hide it, and he knew it. A look of anger flashed across his face, before he broke out in a laugh. "Hahaha! You got me, Mr. McCann! Yah, she was sexy." His voice dropped. "And I did like her. I liked her a lot. But she … we didn't get together if that's what you mean."

McCann let that go for now and changed tack. "Mr. Philips seems convinced that his daughter would not have done what she did the night she died – take E and cocaine, disappear and end up drowned in a shallow river. I'm guessing you know a little more about Natasha Philips' extra-curricular life than her father does. Do you think it's possible that she died the way the police say she did, or do you think there's more to it?"

"How should I know? I was high as a kite when this all happened. To my knowledge she had never taken cocaine. But is it possible that she would? Of course it's possible. Swanny had some with him, and that little … he would give her anything she wanted, including coke, I suppose. Anything white, hence his name." Conrad Malthorpe was pleased with himself.

"Yeah, funny. Swanny had some with him? So Swanny was there at the party with you."

The smile died on Malthorpe's face. Cogs began turning behind the visage.

McCann continued. Too easy, this. "This is the same Swanny that Natasha bought her drugs from? Swanny, the dealer from the Shakespeare Bar, was with you at the party that night? The guy who sold you the pills in Manchester the night before."

110

McCann paused, but not long enough to allow Malthorpe to recover his poise. "The police don't know that, do they? I've seen the police report, Conrad. There's no mention of anyone called Swanny in it. Zilch. In fact, there's almost no information at all from you lot on Swanny the dealer. No-one seems to want to talk about him." Malthorpe looked down at his coffee and cleared his throat.

It was McCann's turn to lean over the table and speak in a low voice. "Listen, Conrad, I'm not here to get you into trouble. I'm here to help Mr. Philips put to bed the death of his daughter. Now, I'm not the police; there's no reason why your name should come up in connection with this. But I will find out about your Mr. Swanny one way or another and if you don't lift a finger to help me, that will reflect very fucking badly on you indeed. I know how much you want to distance yourself from this affair, so let me tell you right now, the best way to get me the fuck out of your life is to tell me what's what with this Swanny drug dealer. And listen, I know when people are bullshitting me, so I suggest you keep it nice and simple, don't miss anything out and don't try to be too smart. You do that and I promise you, you won't need to hear from me again."

He sat back in his seat with a surprisingly nasty little smile. "So let's go."

SWANNING ABOUT

Malthorpe drew again hard on the cigarette, choked on it, coughed, and stubbed it out. He took a few seconds, looking across the street where a man was walking his dog and a woman carrying shopping was passing by. He drew a deep breath, sighed and rubbed his hand over his face. "Charlie Davis is the guy's name. He deals drugs in Manchester. I hardly know him. He was introduced to me about eight months ago by Natasha and Annabel, who had been buying stuff from him occasionally before that. I didn't like him from the moment I set eyes on him, and I don't suppose he thinks much of me either. I've probably met him about five times in my life, and we've never spoken for more than five minutes – got nothing to talk about. As far as I was concerned he was just a transaction man, nothing more. We had nothing in common, except…"

"Except what?"

Malthorpe mumbled, "Except nothing."

"Did you talk with Davis at the Sublime party?"

No answer was forthcoming from the sullen youth across the table.

"Did the girls talk with Davis? Did you all spend time together there?" McCann tapped his pen on the table for a few moments. A couple nearby gathered up their belongings and left the café. McCann looked at his watch. "So, are you going to tell me or not?"

"Tell you what?"

"I think I might be able to guess the details, but it'd be a whole lot easier if you explained everything clearly."

"What?"

"What Davis was doing at the same party as you, what it is that you have 'in common' with him, and most importantly, why his name never came up during the police investigation. It looks kind of … suspicious, don't you think?"

"Well, I mean, he was there with his mates. He's a drug dealer, it was a big outdoor party, it would be stranger for him not to…"

McCann cut him off, "Why did this guy's name not come up in the inquiry? Why has he been erased from the story?"

"Well, it's kind of … complicated."

"Yeah? I bet it's a lot less complicated than getting a bunch of rich uni kids back to the station to explain why they misled a police investigation by leaving out potentially important evidence. I don't think they've got squash courts in the jail, Conrad. Mind you, it would be a great experience for your law studies. Seeing how the court system operates? Looking at things from the other side of the fence? Only downer is, a criminal record isn't the best way to start a career in the law, is it?"

McCann had seen the expression on Malthorpe's face before. Disgusted, like he had just stepped in dog shit; clearly a good sign for McCann.

Malthorpe rolled his eyes. "Because as well as being the guy she bought drugs from, Davis was Natasha's ex-boyfriend, that's why. It was a … problem. A big problem."

"Mmmm."

"Well, I say ex-boyfriend. Not really, actually. Actually I don't really know what the deal was, but I know they were kind of together. Had been. In the past."

"This was a problem because…?"

"Mr. Philips hated Davis on sight. Really hated him. I thought Natasha was trying to keep her dad from knowing anything about Davis but they did meet, at some party in their house. Why she invited that scumbag to her parents' house is beyond me. She told me later that after the party they had had a huge bust-up. Mr. Philips went crazy, throwing things around the room, smashing stuff, apparently. He ordered her never to hang around with riffraff like that again. I think he guessed she was sleeping with him. I'm not surprised he hated Davis, actually. He's a horrible little shit, a snide little wide boy, thinks he's a big shot."

"Do I detect a little … jealousy, Conrad?"

Malthorpe looked young, confused and angry. "God, I do not know what she saw in him. I suppose she liked the idea of hanging out with a street-smart wheeler-dealer."

"Okay, so Natasha is dating a bit of rough – Swanny, otherwise known as Charlie the Charlie dealer. Mr. Philips doesn't like that. So she hides it from Daddy that she's bangin' a guy he wouldn't even employ to wash his car."

Malthorpe's face darkened.

"Sorry, I should have said cars." McCann carried on, "I'm not seeing anything here that would require all four of you witnesses to 'forget' that this Charlie Davis was at the party the night Natasha died. Pretty serious stuff, to obliterate a potentially important piece of information from a police investigation into a death."

"You don't know Natasha's dad. He's a bit of a maniac, actually. Got a terrible temper on him. He finds out she's with Davis, goes absolutely mental. I'm not kidding, the guy is dangerous…"

"To a drug dealer in Manchester? Surely not, Conrad. I've met Mr. Philips, seen his little tantrums. He's all twisted out of shape about the death of his daughter, which is understandable. Maybe he's twisted out of shape all the time, I don't know, but I can't picture this Charlie Davis quaking in his boots, somehow."

"Well, I don't know about that either. To Natasha, maybe…"

"Dangerous to Natasha? Interesting… but Conrad, Natasha's dead. So what have you got to lose by talking about Davis to the police? What's really going on?"

"That's all. I told you it all already."

McCann sat back in his chair again. It's going to be a good day's work, this, he thought, better than he could have possibly imagined. He went back to tapping the pen on the table. "Conrad, Conrad. You've let slip something very interesting, but you've told me nothing. You think I'm going to believe you? That a bunch of middle class kids who've probably never been in trouble with the police their whole lives are suddenly going to do what you, Annabel, Haley and Ivor have all done? If it would help you put this in perspective, I could reel off some examples of time served by people who've been caught lying – or being economical with the truth – to the police. Don't really make the papers, those cases. Except the really big ones, the Jeffrey Archers. But there's enough of them, believe you me."

He finished what was left of his coffee, then coughed and rearranged himself on his chair. They sat in silence for a few moments.

"Let me tell you a little bit about what I do. People think being a private investigator is like in the films, don't they? Guns, dead bodies, girls in lingerie. But trust me, it's not glamorous. Long hours, ropey pay, no pension. Really, most of the time a job like mine is about putting things together, like a jigsaw puzzle. I sift through stuff, look for inconsistencies. And I talk to people. Loads and loads of people, and all different sorts. If you can't talk to people, you're nothing in this line of business. Once you've done it for a few years, you start to get a kind of sixth sense for it. Especially for people. Knowing people. In your case, I can see, as clear as I can see my own hand, that there's a big hole in your story. To tell you the truth, I've got no idea how you managed to get through a police interview without fucking it all up, but I suppose the situation then was a bit different to this one."

He couldn't resist a grin. "No caffé breve, for a start. You've dropped your guard, Conrad. Big time. Now, I'm sure you're right that Mr. Philips would be raging mad if he found out his little girl was still hanging out with Davis. I'm sure there'd be fallout. I'm also sure that four people all failing to mention Davis' presence at the party cannot be a coincidence, which suggests to me that it was pre-planned by the four of you to keep him out of it. I would also suggest that there's no way – not a chance in hell – that the four of you would do something as risky as that just to… what? To do what? To spare Mr. Philips' feelings? Come on, Conrad. I can see right through you and clean out the other side. What's the real deal? Or do you think it would be better for me to hear it from one of the others? Ivor? Haley? Or maybe I should just go and ask Charlie himself?"

Malthorpe blanched at that comment. "Ah, don't … don't do that, please."

"Because…?"

"Because…" Malthorpe was rubbing his forehead with his left hand. "He's dangerous. Charlie's dangerous, and he threatened us all, and he knows where we live, and he could and *would* do something if he thought we had implicated him in all of this."

116

McCann nodded, then stared hard at Malthorpe. "Details."

Malthorpe spoke quickly. "The morning Natasha died, I got a phone call. I think it came about ten am. I don't know how Davis knew so quickly that Natasha was dead, we had only just found out ourselves. I can't remember exactly what he said, because I'd been up all night. My brain was frazzled, I was coming down, and we'd just been told that Natasha's body had been found down by the river. It was confusing, so very confusing. The call was from Davis. He basically said the accident was nothing to do with him, so he didn't need to be involved. And if his name came up in the police report he'd find us and cut us up…" Malthorpe made a vague gesture with his hand towards his face.

"So what did you do then?"

"I took a few minutes to try to get my head together, but then I got a call from Haley. Davis had phoned her just before me. It turned out he called three of us: Haley, me and Annabel. Said the same thing to everyone, more or less. He didn't have Ivor's mobile number, but he told Haley to make sure he got the message too."

"When Davis said he'd find you and cut you up, did you believe him?"

"I'd heard stories before of fights, violence. Did I believe him? Yes, absolutely. Like I say, I hardly know him. I've only met him a handful of times, and never for more than five minutes. I suppose he can be kind of charming when it suits him. But I've seen a look in his eyes, a really nasty look. People in pubs give him plenty of room. And these are pretty rough pubs, too."

"I don't suppose you have the phone number that Davis called from? Is it in your mobile?"

"No. I checked back later that day, when I was trying to

piece together what the hell was going on. The number he called from had been blocked. We had no way to contact him, either. He didn't give his number out to people like us, and the number Natasha had for him had been disconnected."

"Okay, so what did you do after that?"

"Well, I … I thought that since it wouldn't do anyone any good for Davis's name to come up, we should all agree to not mention his being there to the police. Ivor disagreed; he said we should tell them that we saw him at the party, and that he spoke with the girls. But Ivor's never actually talked to Davis. As you can imagine, for someone in his line of business, Davis is pretty cagey. He doesn't like people he doesn't know being around him. For example, when we got the stuff the night before the party, we left Ivor and Haley in another bar. I don't think Ivor would have been so keen to mention Davis' name to the police if he had met him."

Malthorpe shivered as the sinking sun's rays cut across the table. He carried on, "I don't know, you're probably thinking this is pretty stupid, it doesn't add up. But he knew a lot about us. About me, Haley and Annabel at least. He could find us. Or his mates could… We were scared, we didn't know what to do, and since Davis had nothing to do with it, it seemed simpler and safer just to keep him out of it."

"Actually, it doesn't surprise me at all. If I were in your shoes, I'd maybe do the same thing myself. One last question, if you don't mind, Conrad, then I'll be out of your hair for good. You said you saw Davis at the party. What exactly went on there? Were you all there together, or did you meet by chance, or what?"

"It was really innocuous. Quite early in the evening all five of us were walking together when someone called

Natasha's name. She turned around, well, we all did, and saw Davis, standing there with a big plastic cup of beer and the biggest smile on his face. Natasha went over to him with the other two girls. Ivor and I kept our distance. They talked for a few minutes, said goodbye and came back to us. They mentioned he seemed to be in a really good mood, and that was it."

"Did Natasha say anything more about him?"

"No, nothing. Later on Haley just said they had chatted about which DJs they were going to see, and hoped to all have a good night."

"And do you know if Natasha was still sleeping with Davis at this point?"

Malthorpe sighed. "I'm not really sure. She didn't talk about him to me much."

"Well, thanks for that, Conrad. Oh, and by the way, I'd appreciate it if you didn't mention this conversation to the other three. We'll keep it to ourselves, okay? Like I said, it would be a shame to have to come back down here with the police."

McCann took the bill for the coffees; Malthorpe didn't offer to pay, and anyway, it was Philips' money.

The braying cackle of the alarm roused him and he lifted himself off the bed, his body feeling like a sack of rubble. After ducking his head under the shower – what an effort to turn off the weak stream of delicious hot water and step back into reality – he threw on some clothes, grabbed the wig and moustache and, quietly cursing to himself, headed out once more into the insomniac city.

PART 2-XANADU

WELCOME TO THE PLEASURE DOME

The door to the nightclub was willfully obscure, with only a small silver plate to the left hand side indicating the name. Beef spoke with the gigantic black-clad bouncer for a few minutes, who murmured into his mini-microphone and put a gloved hand to his earpiece to hear the reply from inside. At the same time, he eyed the group up and down, taking the most time with McCann, for whom he reserved a scathing look.

McCann had ditched the wig and moustache after meeting the others, who had their obligatory prepubescent piss-take of him for being the only one 'in costume'. Beef alone had said nothing, remaining aloof and untouched by the feeble rituals of these pathetic creatures. Davis had laughed at McCann too, but said nothing about the night before. McCann was itching to bring things to a head with Davis but ran with the vibe for the moment, contenting himself with a quiet aside, "We'll see who's laughing at the end of the night, you little shit."

The door opened, and they were inside.

The music was loud and it took a few moments for McCann's eyes to adjust to the darkness. The first thing he glimpsed was a perfect set of teeth in the laughing mouth of a tall, striking girl dressed as Cleopatra. She was arm-in-arm with a tanned, short, rotund man in an expensive sports jacket, who was ostentatiously waving his cigarette as he told her a story, the subject of her uncontrollable mirth. Even in the murky light of the club McCann could see that this girl was different from the beauties he had been ogling in the Tokyo streets for the last couple of days. She had the magic dust of the Beautiful People. It dripped off her like the gold bangles on her lithe arm.

"The force is strong with this one," he muttered to himself, affecting a smile that he didn't feel but which nonetheless instantly upped his mood. Cleopatra and her dwarf Anthony drifted out of view, and McCann turned to his colleagues.

Beef had already disappeared, and McCann could see Davis gliding through the crowd, already halfway to the bar. Twilly grinned, raised his eyebrows and jutted his chin to McCann's left. He turned. Walking past him were another three lovelies: one dressed like the stereotypical librarian in a porno flick, lingerie under blouse, short, tight skirt, heels, and huge glasses that filled her face; the second in a black leather catsuit complete with a Venetian masquerade ball mask and a whip; the third ponytailed and mini-skirted in a schoolgirl's uniform. McCann's eyes ogled and goggled and he remembered what Davis had said the day before, "Welcome to the blazing temptations of hell…"

Right on cue, the DJ switched the nondescript club music to Frankie Goes To Hollywood, and the picture was complete. McCann turned wide-eyed back to Twilly, who merely shrugged, leaned towards him and shouted over the pounding beat, "Nah, mate, I ain't never been 'ere before either. It's Beef that's got the entertainment world connections. He's told me some stories would make yer hair stand on end. Said this one ain't the biggest or best party, but apparently some kinda famous media people are showin' up here, and it should be a good one 'cos it's a Halloween bash, so all the girls are in costume, as you can see…"

124

He waved a pudgy hand across the darkened room. There were over a hundred people in the club, and at a glance they could very easily be spilt into three categories. The majority were young women dressed up for dreams, of whom the four McCann had just seen were representative. There weren't many women over the age of twenty-five, but there were a few older ladies, probably in their sixties. They were dressed not in costume, but in ostentatious bad taste: leopard skin blouses, bright orange tailored trousers, gigantic diamond-studded Chanel glasses on their hard faces, gold everywhere. The men, considerably less in number, were almost universally balding, well-fed, over fifty and cocky. They had also evidently not felt it necessary to dress up in Halloween costumes. Davis, Twilly and McCann appeared to be the only foreigners in the room although, with some of the girls wearing masks, it was hard to be sure.

McCann raised his hand to his mouth in a drinking motion and indicated the bar. Twilly confirmed with his wife, nodded, and for the next twenty minutes they knocked back beer in silence and watched the party unfold before them.

The girls were chattering and fluttering and preening like birds of paradise; the older women talked in small groups or conspiratorially with the girls; the men seemed for the most part to be content to ignore the women, smoking and drinking complacently, guffawing heartily but occasionally motioning to the girls and chatting with them when their fellow male company ran out of anecdotes. The girls seemed more than happy to oblige.

McCann tried to make sense of what he was seeing. Logic suggested they were simply high-class hookers invited to a rich businessmen's party, but something about the vibe didn't click. He was constantly trying to assess what he was seeing, but his twenty years of experience observing people as a private investigator seemed to be almost worthless in this idiosyncratic society. He couldn't grasp any clues about who these people were, what their values might be, what they were doing, or why. It was like trying to grab hold of a vapour in the air.

After a while the familiar tingling sensation of alcohol running through his blood calmed him and he started to feel more relaxed in the bizarre surroundings. Twilly's wife had strutted off somewhere, her husband ambling behind. McCann looked around for an innocuous space and found himself carrying two bottles of ice-cold Corona towards a corner sofa where a girl was playing with her mobile phone. He sat down at the other end of the leather sofa and she looked up, smiling with the effortless dazzle of youth. Her straight black hair, parted in the middle, framed a heart-shaped face; long fake lashes highlighted large, dark almond eyes.

"You, umm, want a beer?"

It was noisy with the music. Blank look. He pointed to the beer, motioned to her.

"Oh! Thank you."

"Cheers!" Clink.

"Are you Chinese, or is the dress just for Halloween?"

"Oh! Yes, Halloween. China dress. You like it?"

"It's fantastic. Suits you very well."

She shook her head sadly in confusion.

He moved closer. "I said you look great in the Chinese dress."

"Thank you!" She put her hand over her mouth and giggled exaggeratedly.

"I'm George Peters, nice to meet you."

"I am Mai Takahashi."

"Well, Mai, this is an interesting party, alright. Do you know a lot of people here?"

"A lot of people?"

"Yeah. Your friends?"

"Some are over there," she pointed towards a group of young women who were standing with three of the older men, moving around them and leaning forward like insects to the light. The party was heating up and people were becoming more and more animated. "Some of my friends come later. Maybe the boys come later."

McCann nodded, neither understanding nor worrying about anything anymore. "So, what do you do, Mai?"

"My job? Mmmm, this year I am in TV drama."

"TV drama? You're an actress on TV?"

"Of course. But only small part this year. I need a chance to speak on the TV show. Maybe Kudo-san will give me a chance next time. He said before to me maybe I will have that chance this year, or next."

"Well, I hope so too. You speak good English."

"Oh! Thank you! I studied in California. Six months. Very fun."

"Are you a full-time actress now?"

She leaned towards him. "I'm sorry. Again slowly please?"

McCann looked into her pretty, open face. It looked like a blank slate, one you could write anything on given the chance. He blinked once.

"Are you working only as an actress? Or do you have another job?"

"Oh! Yes, another job, *arubaito*, but I hope next year I can get good acting job, be a TV actress. You? Are you agent?"

"Agent? Ah, yeah, actually I am an agent – a secret agent. International espionage, CIA, that kind of thing."

"Eh? Agent which company?"

"No, I'm just joking. Sort of. I, emm, I just started a job as an English teacher. In Yamato. You know it?"

"English teacher? Not agent?"

Mai's whole attitude, body language, glittering personality, folded right there. McCann could feel the sudden cold formality in her as she moved slightly away from him on the sofa.

"Oh…" was all she could manage.

McCann felt her dark eyes suddenly appraising him differently and the magic show was over; he was stripped back to a middle-aged, slightly scruffy nobody, sitting too close to a petite twenty-year-old girl at a party where his only companions were people he didn't much like and had only met two days before.

Mai made her excuses, smiled too politely at him and glided away from the sofa towards her group. McCann downed the remnants of his lager and put a hand through his hair, ruffling up what was left of it.

He stared blankly into space for a minute or two, then slapped his hands on his knees, stood up and walked back to the bar. As he crossed the dark, open space, right on the edge of his field of vision and through a throng of people, he snatched a glimpse of Davis on the other side of the club, talking: animated, laughing, pushing the tumbling hair away from his face. From where he was, McCann couldn't see who the interlocutor was. He ordered another Corona and steadily worked his way through the increasingly rowdy guests, round the edge of the dance floor to the other side, but Davis was gone.

All round McCann there was the bad dancing, the sexy dancing, the struts, squawks and screeches of a drunken menagerie. He edged back to the wall, vacantly looking towards the dance floor but his eyes darting around the room, searching for the man he had travelled half way across the world to find. It was the walk that he recognised first, that same loose-limbed saunter, a gallous swagger, swaying through the crowd, leading his bounty in his left hand and his beer in his right, towards the steel spiral staircase and up to the second floor, the mezzanine. The girl with Davis wore some kind of casual *kimono*, and McCann felt something, a confusion of emotions, as he watched her laughing, trying to keep up with Davis, lifting the hem of her red and white robe, taking three baby steps for every one of Davis's. McCann followed them with his eyes up the stairs and towards the bar, where they disappeared into the mob.

He waited a few moments then followed them. They were sitting on a sofa similar to the one McCann had just vacated. Davis had his arm round the girl. McCann found himself a suitable vantage point and observed the scene as they did the time-honoured dance, the one that never grows old or boring no matter how many times it is repeated over the centuries.

Davis was playing with the *obi* of the girl's *kimono*, and she was laughingly trying to stop him from touching it, and while she made her half-hearted attempts to block him, she slid closer to him on the sofa. Davis was talking a lot and she was looking at his face with intensity. The scene made McCann suddenly feel old and isolated from everything that was happening around him, and when Davis kissed the girl and she responded to him McCann continued to watch, feeling like a dirty old voyeur. As he swigged his beer he recalled one New Year long ago, alone, drunk, and miserable in a club in Coventry, watching couples French-kissing on stairs moist and sticky with spilled beer and covered in cigarette butts.

'I hate New Year,' he thought to himself. 'And I am a stupid old twat.' He looked away, casting his eyes around the room, thinking nothing, but seeing everything and trying to take in all the clues automatically, like a Pavlov's dog; twenty-odd years of doing this, sizing up the relationships, moods and atmospheres of all those around him – but not his own.

MINDER

He knocked back the remains of yet another beer. It was very clear that things were becoming more and more riotous as the night wore on. There was a toilet marked with a disabled sign to McCann's right, and a procession of people had gone in and come out in twos, threes and fours, some of them laughing and wiping their noses. The men were openly touching the girls now. Hands were up short skirts; drinks, laughter and forgetting were flowing.

A man lurched into view beside McCann and leaned on the bar, ordered something, turned and looked at him with dilated eyes. He was sweaty and grinding his teeth, but smiling, or perhaps leering. He spoke for some minutes, an impossible garble. Eventually McCann realised the man was speaking some kind of English, but the only words he could make out were "Good drugs."

It was impossible to tell if he was offering them, asking for them or merely making a statement of fact for McCann's consideration. The man cackled, shook his head like a wet dog, tutted, possibly in frustration, then whooped and wheeled away from the bar and scrambled down the stairway, staggering into some people on his way. McCann's eyes followed him down.

In the main dance area people were shouting, laughing, grabbing each other in jest, holding each other up, pulling each other down. One man was howling like a wolf in the corner, inaudible above the music, another was wearing a leather face mask and being slapped hard on the head gleefully by three of his colleagues. McCann caught sight of Mai in her Chinese dress with her arms around one of the portly fifty-year-olds. He turned away just in time to see a muscular silver-haired man in a polo shirt approach the sofa where Davis and the *kimono*-girl were making out. Two no-nonsense younger men dressed all in black followed behind.

"Interesting." McCann pushed himself off the bar but by the time he reached the sofa the girl had seen the older man, jumped to her feet and moved towards him, looking embarrassed and shocked as she tried to put back together her spoiled *kimono*. The man ignored her and was calmly saying a few short words to Davis, who was smiling darkly and starting to rise from the sofa. He looked relaxed and in control but McCann could see from the extraordinary expression on his face that Davis was sizing all three of them up as he rose. It was a sinister, street-nasty look, eyes little black dots and sharp on the three men in front of him. Things were happening very quickly:

McCann had half a second. He sluiced between the two groups, doing just enough to unbalance the situation before it kicked off. Davis blinked and jerked his head to the side just as he started to move up and forward. McCann, nervous and half-cut, faked drunken buffoonery and grabbed Davis with a laugh and a hearty hail. The power of Davis' light frame moving forward, the potential energy of his youth and street fighting poise shocked McCann and they almost collapsed to the ground, but instead they slithered into a kind of comical bear hug.

Davis was angrily saying something, but in the noise and confusion of the moment it was lost. Then they did lose balance and the two of them flopped down on the sofa. By the time they had disentangled themselves, the others, the three men and the girl, were all gone.

Adrenalin was flowing through Davis. He grabbed McCann's shirt. "What the fuck, Grampa? What you playin' at, eh? You cut in on my business again I'll fuckin' smash you into little pieces." His expression was twisted into an ugly rage that the watercress and tarot man would find hard to justify. With some difficulty McCann ripped Davis's hands away from him. Conrad Malthorpe's face flashed through his mind, that look of almost terror when he first told McCann about Davis. 'So this is Swanny the big city dealer … I wondered where he was hiding,' he thought.

"Don't know much about Japan, but I'd say in any country three against one ain't good odds, Swanny," he gasped, bobbing out of Davis' immediate range. At the mention of the name Davis's face cleared in surprise. "Happened to be on the way to the bar and I saw those guys coming up to you and it looked like trouble. Thought it would be better to jump in before things got nasty."

Now Davis was smiling, half a sneer, half an understanding that the game was beginning again.

"You are full of shit, George. And yer too old for this game. I could rip you to shreds if I wanted to."

"Maybe you could, kidder. And maybe you couldn't. Wanna give it a shot, Swanny?"

Davis burst into a belly laugh as booming as it was surprising. "You're a fuckin' fanny, mate, but I kinda like you all the same. How long you been spyin' on me?"

"About ten minutes. Want a beer?"

"Fuckin' right I do."

"Coming right up. I'll get them. That way I know you ain't spiking mine with something. Try not to get in any fights while I'm at the bar, eh?"

133

"So what's the fuckin' deal? You sent to me from God as my secret minder or summat? I'd a thought he might've sent somebody younger."

"Gotta keep you outta trouble, Charlie. Gotta get some answers from you, pal. And a mashed up Charlie Davis is no good at talking."

Davis looked away. "Fuckin' jokin', ain't ya? Don't need your help, old man. An' I got nothin' to talk with you about. Nothin' at all. You're fuckin' lucky I don't put this beer bottle right between your eyes. Coulda done it about twenty times already. It ain't like I haven't had the chance."

"No bother. Just as well we're such good mates, eh? Plenty of time, I've got."

They both took a long swig of beer.

In the silence between them McCann took a deep breath, looked around the room. "So, you got any idea what this party is all about? My eyes just about popped out my head when we walked in here. It's like a lap dancing bar for rich old guys and supermodels. Without the lap dancing."

Davis turned away with a sneer. Whether it was the comment itself, or simply the feeble attempt to change the mood, it was impossible to say. "Like I said, you're too old for this shit. Or maybe you're too conventional, I dunno. Just go with the flow, Grampa."

"What exactly do you think the flow here is?"

"Christ, you are a miserable old bore. All I know is what Beef told Olly and me. It's an entertainment business party. I think the guys are mostly producers, agents, scriptwriters – movers and shakers in the business. Fuck knows. All three chicks I've spoke to give the same line – they want a career in entertainment, wanna get in the TV business or the movies or some shit, and I suppose this is where they get the chance to meet the guys who can give them a break."

"Just so happens, the up-and-coming actresses are all twenty years old, gorgeous, and dressed in sexy costumes, then?"

Davis gave him a withering look. "What's your problem? Your puritanical sensibility offended by what you see? You know where the door is. Don't come peddlin' your hypocritical pseudo morality to me. It is what it is, George, or whatever your fuckin' name is." He flicked his jaw forward. "Here comes Beef. Why don't you tell him yourself about your moral concerns?"

McCann glanced to his right and saw Beef strolling towards them, a stick-thin, silver-and-black super-human in his ubiquitous Aviator shades. As he turned McCann felt a hard but open-handed glancing blow across his left cheek and eye. He bobbed and moved forward but Davis was already off the sofa and on his feet, out of range.

There was real scorn in the comment that followed. "Too slow, old man. Too easily distracted. Fuckin' have you for breakfast." McCann's face smarted, but he wasn't sure if it was from the clip or the embarrassment.

"Alright, Beef? George the pro-wrestling champ here wants a word with you. Ain't happy about the party, mate."

It wasn't clear how much of that information had registered with Beef. It wasn't clear at all which planet Beef was from; but he was pretty fucking cool, McCann had to give him that. Beef looked down at him. There was something of The Terminator about his other-worldliness, the way he blandly examined McCann, who immediately stood up.

"Hi, Beef. Ignore what Charlie just said. Talking shit as usual." No reaction. "I was just wondering what the deal with this party is. It's kind of … interesting." Silence.

Then Beef spoke directly to McCann for the first time. "Tequila?"

McCann nodded.

Beef nodded. "Bar."

Beef ordered two tequilas for himself and McCann. Davis had disappeared again.

"*Kanpai*."

Salt. Tequila. Bam. Lemon. Same again. The second drink went down like a bag of nails. McCann felt smashed. Beef lit a cigarette with a silver Zippo and placed the lighter and pack carefully on the counter. They sat in silence while he smoked. He ignored McCann, looking straight ahead at the bar, still in his silver shades. McCann was tired. Objects in the room were beginning to swim and shimmer.

'Is this all some kind of a joke?' he wondered lazily.

Beef started nodding, apparently in silent symphony with McCann's thoughts.

"When we make contact, they will be telepathic," McCann mumbled to himself.

Then Beef started to speak. "This party? Mmmm. These girls want to be in entertainment. On *terebi*." He was still nodding to himself. "Difficult. To get in entertainment. In Japan, connections are everything. Everything. To get a break … tough. But they like it. Dressing up, being sexy. Fun. Sexy is fun, and they are young. They want to meet some famous guys. Maybe Noda, or even Murasaki Ryo."

"Who are they?"

Beef turned like a Gary Numan robot and looked at McCann. "They are here tonight. Murasaki Ryo and Hiromasa Noda. You don't know?"

A shake of the head.

Beef shrugged. "Famous guys. Murasaki Ryo is a *tarento*. In the nineties, in a boy band. Now too old for that. He is in *terebi* dramas, food shows. Lots of food shows. Fat little face, he like food shows. Noda is his *kohai* in Taimou Entertainment. Most people here are in Taimou Entertainment."

"What's *kohai*?"

Beef simply said, "*Sempai. Kohai,*" as if no further explanation were necessary, and turned away from McCann again, back towards his own reflection nestling between the bottles of gin and Cointreau in the bar mirror. Again there was a silence, in which he appeared to be processing McCann's failure to comprehend the most basic of information. He continued to talk to the fragmented mirror façade of himself. "*Sempai* is older. *Kohai* is younger. *Kohai* does what *sempai* says. *Sempai* is like boss. *Kohai* learn from him. Very important. Japanese system."

McCann nodded as Beef continued. "Noda is in a band, Tokoro Times. Taimou's big new band. You can see everywhere. Advertising mobile phones, beer, shampoo. Tokoro Times, next big thing, and Noda is … how you say … pretty boy in Tokoro Times. Very popular. These guys here tonight, somewhere. Private room, maybe. The girls, want to meet famous guys, right? And they want to be famous too. To get here, to this party, must be beautiful and have connections. One step..." He waved his hand in a bored manner, "...on the way up. But you can see, there is lot of competition. Lots of pretty young girls. So they have to do something, *eto*, special, make themselves special. To get their break."

"I think I see where you are going with this."

They were silent again. Beef blasted through another Camel. He smoked like a jet engine gulping in the air.

"What do you do here, Beef? You got us all in here. What's your connection with this party?"

137

"I fuck the girls, sometimes. It is my pleasure. And they like me." He looked at McCann again with the huge, mirrored insect eyes. "Your round?"

TITANIC

In McCann's Japan world it was three am eternally. Time had been battered around something awful in the last five days. Brutal jet-lag, all-night drinking, drugs administered to induce a comatose state: his body clock, his brain and his liver had all more or less given up. He looked at his watch. It was indeed three am. A few minutes earlier he had woken up under a table on the mezzanine floor. He'd been fast asleep in spite of the thumping music and the madness all around. He had no idea how long he'd been out, but it certainly wasn't long enough. He lurched back to the bar and got a double vodka and Red Bull, thinking, 'Need the energy to get out of here; need to rest.' Quickly knocking the drink back, he crunched the ice cubes, shivered, and made his way down the stairs again to the main floor.

It was much less crowded than it had been an hour or two before. With the numbers having declined, the fevered antics of the mass had subsided and people were clustered around the room in twos, threes and fours. Everyone still seemed drunk or wasted, but it was quieter now, and the music was deeper and darker for the remnants who were still dancing. He wandered round, squinting at the shapes like a shortsighted doctor surveying the dead and wounded on a battlefield.

In a while he came upon Davis again, sitting cross-legged on the floor in the corner, looking like an indolent, skinny Buddha with his eyes wide open, huge and unblinking.

McCann mumbled something. Without moving his head, Davis's eyeballs rolled up and observed McCann in silence for a few long moments. In the dark club the whites of his eyes shone like two peeled, hard-boiled eggs. It was a weirdly ethereal vision; he looked simultaneously ascetic yet self-indulgent. Then, in one smooth, swift movement he was on his feet again and the spell, whatever it was, had been broken.

"Charlie, I'm about to take off. Need to get some sleep. Starting to float and sway like I'm on a boat. Feeling a bit messed up. Like you said, too old for this shit, I am. But before I go, there's a couple of things I need to talk to you about. Got a minute or two?"

Davis gave a glacial smile. "Couple of minutes? For you? Sure, daddy-o. You're doin' okay. Work through it with me. Couple of minutes … yeah, you're right. I think now is the time for beginning."

"Beginning what?"

But Davis just looked at him in silence.

McCann shook his head, partly out of confusion, partly to clear his own thoughts. "Bit noisy here. Let's find a corner somewhere."

Davis suddenly brightened up, like he'd just remembered the answer to an unasked question. "Saw Beef a while ago. He said a lotta people've moved on to another place, the second party. Twilly went to a love hotel with his missus. Beef … might be at the next party, I dunno. He could be anywhere, doing anything. It don't matter. A quiet corner? Aye, come on then, let's do a bit of investigating." He started giggling. "Sure we can find what we're looking for with a bit of investigation. Don't you think?"

"Better be careful what you wish for, sonny. It's a bit too late for Enid Blyton tonight, Charles."

"VIP party room. Popped me head round the door an hour or so ago. Beef tell you about these pop star blokes at this party? Apparently they're famous. Never heard of them meself, but we should check it out. Might be quiet. Might be fun."

McCann was well on the way to fully-fledged memory-blank drunkenness. It took a lot to put him down, but he was on the ropes now. He was here to get answers and with Davis apparently knowing his purpose this might be his only chance to question him in something resembling an open state. He had no idea how drunk Davis was or whether he had taken anything else besides lots of alcohol, but now, in spite of his need for rest, for silence and for sleep, he knew that come what may, he had to stick with Davis from here on in, and force the issue of Natasha's death. He had had enough of the preliminaries, enough of the game. Time for action and results, for good or ill.

Once again they ordered bottled beer from the bar, and Davis led the way across the dance floor, along a short corridor and into another area separated by a heavy velvet curtain. There was another small bar through here and fancier sofas and chandeliers. No-one stopped them as they made their way in, and no-one paid any attention to their presence.

There were about fifteen people in the room, all on the opposite side, away from the doorway. Ten or eleven of them were girls, there were a couple of older men, and in the middle of the group were the obvious stars of the show.

The older of the two *tarento* had a blubbery, sunbed-orange tanned face like an overripe persimmon. In the middle of his oily visage his eyes, two tiny darts of silver, gleamed malevolently. His laugh, too, was overripe, like a nasty little bully's. At the precise moment McCann and Davis shambled into the room, he was kissing one young girl on the neck while his right hand was high up the mini-skirted thigh of another. Both girls were giggling and pushing him away and simpering, "*Yada!*"

The other *tarento* was tall, slim and androgynously good-looking, almost beautiful. He had an elaborately gelled mane of dark brown hair, doe eyes and big, sensual lips, the overall femininity counterbalanced partially by a large, square jaw. He didn't seem to have the debased decay that was writ large on the face of his sempai yet, but he was very young, perhaps only twenty or twenty-one. There was still plenty of time. Two girls were vying for his affection, one in the uniform of a high school girl, blouse half-unbuttoned, the other in a crop top, exposing generous amounts of svelte midriff and a navel piercing. He looked to be enjoying the attention but slightly embarrassed by the scene before him.

McCann and Davis flopped down on a sofa, Davis nearest the wall, McCann with his back to the room. Something flickered in McCann's head, a dull warning light. 'You're fucking this up, George. Must be really smashed. Not thinking. You don't sit with your back to a room. Never know who might be behind you.' He ignored the thought. His tongue seemed to have become an oversized flopping fish in his mouth, too big for its cavity. His sight was wavering. His eyes were smarting and puffy: they felt raw, like they'd been sandpapered. A half-finished magnum of Tattinger sat on the table between them, a dark lump angled in a silver bucket of icy water.

He mumbled, "And the band played on…"

Davis was looking towards the ceiling. Thousand yard stare. "Whaa's that?"

"Said, the band played on … you know … Titanic." He pointed at the bucket.

"Eh?"

"The ... emm … champagne … ice … water … sinking bottle. Titanic."

"Yeah, you're right, we better knock this back while no other cunt's around to neck it, eh?"

They picked up the discarded flutes and shared out what was left of the bottle, bubbles gallivanting over the side and across the table like escaping passengers. Davis sank his glass in a second and grinned an inane smile, nodding his head back and forward slightly.

"Fancy a tab, old man?"

"Is that a ciggie or an acid?"

Davis giggled and spluttered. The veins on his temples and in his neck throbbed. He seemed to be making a great effort to control inner convulsions. He sat forward, smacked his chops and looked around exaggeratedly, a hallucinatory Jack Nicholson with a wicked smile playing on his lips, hunched up and channeling energy like an ancient shaman.

"Nothin' like that feelin' thirty minutes after you pop a good one with friends and the whole room is on fire with human electricity, know-what-I-mean? It's in the air, you can almost see it. You're all just sparking, firing the energy off each other. Raw, unadulterated energy…" He looked around again and leered. "Not that I got any friends in *this* fuckin' room, mind, but it don't matter…"

McCann tried to assess the condition of the younger man. His tousled hair was a mess. There were dark purple bags under his eyes. He seemed distracted. It was hard to tell which of the two of them was in a worse state. Yet, even now, there was something simultaneously disturbing but intriguing about Davis, almost childlike, which made it hard for McCann not to grudgingly give him the benefit of some esoteric doubt. Even as these thoughts blundered through his brain he disappointed himself with his own lack of professionalism. He tried to focus.

"So … what's the story?"

"Just goin' with the flow. You want one or not? Fuckin' good quality… Them chandeliers are lookin' fantastic, man."

McCann was sinking into the sofa and it was taking him a long time to gather his thoughts. Images of *Rocky II* slipped into his head, the sweat-lashed fighters in slow motion, simultaneously trying to make the final count, staggering up the ropes, sliding down them. Ludicrous. Or was that *Rocky III*…?

"Natasha, Swanny. What's the story, tough man?"

Davis was looking past him. His eyes were following something. McCann sensed some of the VIP party group talking louder than before, moving around and being ushered out of the room behind him. He didn't want to take his eyes off Davis, but from the distortion of the light on the semi-mirrored wall behind Davis' head, without turning around he could guess that about nine or ten of them had left the room. The right side of Davis' face twitched. He laughed a half-dog growl, fangs protruding, which strangled itself in mid-utterance. He gazed back at McCann. "What. Is. The. Story. What do you want it to be?"

McCann felt a surge of lucidity. A brief burst of focus. Better make this count before the Venetian blinds come down on this endless, senseless night. He struggled to get the words out. "The truth: the Sublime party, Natasha Philips, the cocaine that she never took but was in her body, the river, the corpse. It's time for you to start talking, sonny. I'm an old, fucked-up, drunk wreck, but you're worse, and I got experience on my side. You speak, I listen."

He was aware that there was some sort of disturbance going on in the far corner of the room. He was also aware that this exact moment was not the time to be distracted by anything whatsoever. Shouts and shrieks and furniture being knocked over drifted above the vibrating bass from the main room's dance floor.

"Got no idea what you're on about, mate." Davis was looking across the room towards the ruckus with his nose in the air, as a wine connoisseur might observe a sommelier pouring a nice burgundy into someone else's glass: interested but detached.

The rage of exhaustion and impotence welled up in McCann. He knew that ever since he'd arrived in Japan he'd acted like a miserable amateur: thrown by the strangeness of everything around him he had made one mistake after another. He'd lost his self-respect and felt like he'd been pushed around by a bunch of two-bit wide boys. Inspired by the commotion and the crashes from the other side of the room he launched himself across the table at Davis's neck. No time for words. Waste of breath.

He thudded into Davis like a bull, smashing the back of the young man's head against the wall and lumbering a couple of drunken body punches at him. He knew he wasn't catching much, but the state they were both in, he wouldn't need to. Davis slid onto the floor and McCann went with him, but Davis managed a sharp retort, forcing McCann's head back, which smacked hard off the corner of the table. Black and yellow dots exploded across his eyes. For the second time that night, the two of them ended up a stunned, crumpled mess on the floor.

The grim comedy punch-up would have continued but for an inhuman wailing and screeching from across the room which had become impossible to ignore. They could hear what was going on now. Even above the thumping bass line next door, the wasted mess of their own senses, and the raging blood of violence roaring in their ears, it was obvious. The two semi-comatose men, lying dazed on the rich carpet, covered in the broken glass of the champagne flutes, froze and looked at each other, saying nothing in mute, mutual understanding. They temporarily abandoned hostilities and looked through the table legs towards the new horror show across the room.

GUERNICA

The older of the two *tarento*, Murasaki Ryo, had his jacket off and his sleeves rolled up. He was holding down the arms of one of the young sycophantic groupies who was lying across two tables, her legs opened and blouse ripped. The younger *tarento*, Hiromasa Noda, was holding her legs apart and attempting to enter her. There was a curiously abstract expression on his face, like this was something outwith his control and he just happened to be an actor in the drama. No such detachment from Murasaki Ryo, who was sweating profusely and cajoling more effort from his young protégé, like a jockey in the final straight, shouting at both him and the girl and applying fearsome levels of physical power to the occasion, in marked contrast to Noda's rather half-hearted attempts at penetration.

In his shirt sleeves and with his meaty arms pulling and pinning the girl to the table, Murasaki Ryo looked like a butcher who had just lugged a bovine carcass onto a cleaving table, except that this piece of meat was human and alive. By unhappy chance McCann and Davis had a clear view of her face as they peered round the sofa. She was looking directly towards them, head upside-down in her own private Guernica, abject terror in her rolling eyes and mascara streaked across her cheeks and the bridge of her nose, running up her forehead towards her hair: a macabre Halloween moment indeed. She arched her back and tried to twist out of the iron grip of the monster and it seemed that her limbs would break right out of their sockets such was the contortion.

It was a sickening sight, and as McCann lurched into horrified action between the tables on the other side of the room, she jerked her head and bit into the left arm of Murasaki Ryo, who responded with a bellow, grabbed her head and smashed it down hard on the amphetamine-covered glass table. The table shattered with the impact, so it was impossible to tell whether it was only the glass breaking, or something more precious. The girl, Ryo and Noda fell heavily to the floor in a tangle of limbs and confusion.

The three older men who rushed into the VIP room stopped abruptly when they saw the carnage in front of them: Davis standing impassive in the corner, impossible to read what was going through his mind, if anything; McCann, in the middle of the room, eyes wide, looking towards the girl with the twisted head; the two *tarento* in the process of rolling out of the debris and wobbling to their feet.

Noda scrambled to pull his trousers up from round his ankles, and for a few long seconds time stood still. When the shouting started it was impossible for McCann to understand anything other than that there was an immediate threat of extreme violence to his person. Out of the corner of his eye he could see Murasaki Ryo, forehead ruffled up like a rug, eyes bulging, pointing and screaming at him like a despot. The three men jumped at McCann and, in spite of everything, somewhere a small part of his brain remained detached from the alcohol and the emotion of this situation as he assessed the age and quality of the opposition between him and the velvet-draped doorway. He battered through the first two, felt a hammer blow on his right arm and ribcage from the third who came from behind him, and responded with a stony elbow whipped backwards at the man's unprotected head. The man staggered away from him and he rushed out the doorway without looking back, through the murky club, past the remaining partygoers, up the stairs and out into the dark night.

He fled to the left for two, three blocks, aware that someone was with him, close behind, and he suddenly heard shrieks of wild, pagan laughter: Davis, hooting and howling at the starless neon night sky. Davis, on fire, fierce-eyed, feral, unknowable.

⛓

Once again, McCann looked at his watch. Almost 5am. Staff from the nightclubs, *izakaya* and 24-hour cafés were putting out the night's rubbish for early morning collection. The human detritus, too, was clearing itself off the streets, staggering homewards, the survivors holding each other up as they meandered towards taxis or a watery early-morning McDonald's coffee, like the remnants of Napoleon's army, routed by Russians and disease.

He had no idea where they were. Once away from the club they had carried on running for about two minutes then slowed and tried to take stock. Davis had stopped shouting now, but still looked wild and malevolent. McCann was in a state of shock and, though the events of the last hour had partially sobered him up, he knew he was far from clear-headed. They barely spoke to each other as they half-jogged towards Roppongi Dori. McCann's head was bursting with a barrage of questions and the ribs on his right side hurt. He was nodding and muttering to himself, "Gotta work out what to do here. We gotta go to the police. This is all fucked up."

Davis, still wide-eyed, darted mockingly, like a will-o'-the-wisp, in front of McCann as he walked. "Aw, boo-hoo, the flowers of the forest, now they are fled and fled far away…"

He looked like a riddler with answers but no questions, a satanic Pied Piper leading lemmings to cliffs. And suddenly, with a throaty cackle, he faked a jab then punched with his left and pushed McCann hard, catching him off balance. The punch barely connected but McCann fell backwards onto a huge pile of rubbish bags and Davis was gone in an instant, the automatic door of the taxi closing and Davis waving at him through the back window. The taxi slipped round a corner just as the lights were changing to red. Surrounded on his temporary beanbags by the smell of rotting vegetables, fish bones and cigarette butts, and oblivious to the large rat nosing through the garbage behind him, McCann put his head in his hands and swore, before hauling himself up and staggering on down the street.

✿

Thankful that he had survived the chaos of the night, he paid his taxi driver, entered the hotel and collected his room key from a clearly worried receptionist who, in spite of his professionalism, couldn't hide the surprise in his eyes as McCann shambled up to the front desk. The lift stopped on the fourth floor, and with blood throbbing in his ears through the silence, McCann entered room 437 and collapsed onto his bed, fully clothed, in a concussed sleep.

MASSIVE ATTACK

Nine hours later at the 'Let's Kiosk' in Shinjuku station he picked up a Snickers bar, a bottle of Pocari Sweat (still half-cut, he read the bizarre name of the sports drink and immediately bought it), and a late edition of *The Japan Times*. He also asked for a pack of Marlboro Lights, then changed his mind and cancelled, deciding there had been too much bad stuff already. Time to start cleaning up his act.

His eyes skated over the front page and national news headlines like an insect across a still pond. Corruption and backhanders linking politicians and business contracts; a territorial dispute with China, the Emperor in hospital for a check-up, worries about the Japanese economy. Nothing. The same on the second, third page. What had he expected? Too early for news? He had no idea what had actually happened to the girl, or how severe her injuries were.

Anyway, time was the crucial element now. The situation was becoming complicated. He considered emailing Philips but decided against it until it was clearer what the hell was going on. He recognised that he was taking a huge risk; morally his behaviour was reprehensible, and probably indefensible, and he was quite possibly facing a jail sentence for not going to the police, but for McCann, getting to Davis ASAP was all that mattered right now. Afterwards, he would have to report what he had seen the night before, but who knew what would happen after that? He didn't want to think about it. Take a few hours first, find Davis, get some answers about Natasha Philips. Not for the first time he thought to himself, 'No more fucking about...'

With some difficulty he managed to find his way back to Davis's apartment in Yamato; once again the lack of street names and the dreary functional repetitiveness of the architecture made it almost impossible to get his bearings as the dusk fell, even for someone with a well-honed internal radar like McCann. Once he was in the vicinity he was careful in his approach, walking round the building and peering in at the dark windows. Sensing the interior lifeless, he turned the door handle – unlocked, as Davis always seemed to leave it – and crept inside.

The room was in the same gentle state of disorder as it had been in on his first visit, a couple of days before. A couple of days! An eternity. The dilapidated guitar and the cheap stereo system, the futon still in the corner, thin duvet thrown to one side. There was nothing to see here. The room was barely furnished, so it was impossible to say if Davis had been back or not. Even if he had abandoned the place and moved on, the difference would have been marginal. Remembering the expression on Davis's face as he had sat on the grubby cushion drinking *shochu* – what you can't fit in a rucksack ain't worth having – he left silently and made his way back to the Hunky Dory English Club.

There was a light on in the waiting area, but the classrooms were all dark. He had been given a key to the school by Twilly and clearly someone was there, so he made no effort at concealment and walked straight in.

"Ah, the wanderer returns! Just the man we're lookin' for!"

Davis was sitting behind the reception desk, a bottle

of Jack Daniel's beside him. He looked grotesque, but in tautly high spirits. There were three Japanese men that McCann had never seen before in the room, all in suits, one by the door and two sitting on the other side of the table from Davis with their backs to the entrance. Their heads swivelled round when McCann entered the room.

Quick appraisal. One big meaty guy, scrubby facial hair, toothpick flicking in his mouth, thick neck, wrestler's ears, a large diamond stud in one of them. One smaller man – nasty-looking, glasses. McCann didn't want to turn his head and stare at the one by the door, but from the corner of his eye he seemed big. Problems here. He remembered seeing two dark-coloured cars parked a block down the street on his way in, maybe a Mercedes and a Lexus, tinted windows, wide radial tyres.

Heart rate through the roof, McCann tried to stay cool. "You're looking rougher every time I see you, sonny, and I've only been here for four days. You oughta look after yourself better."

Davis laughed, "You're not lookin' too hot yourself, smudger." It wasn't a nervous laugh, but not a natural one either. 'Highly strung, poised for… what?' More crossed wires for McCann. 'Keep thinking; stay on your toes here.' He could feel the bruise from the guy in the club on his ribcage now.

Davis gestured to a magazine on the table beside him. "Been catchin' up on me reading while we was waiting for you. Did you know that the white guy in Massive Attack is a Napoli fan? Did ye know that? His dad's a Neapolitan. And Bristol City, of course. Ship shape an' Bristol fashion. Just like you, you old cunt. It's all right here, in the mag."

He flipped the open football magazine towards McCann.

The Japanese men were talking with each other in short grunt-like sentences and nodding. Their mouths barely moved as they spoke. McCann's eyes darted around.

He clenched his hands. "Where's Twilly? Students?"

"No classes today, gumshoe. Bit late for work anyway, ain't ya?"

"*Dozo*. A chair. Sit please." The small man was not smiling and spoke in heavily accented English, motioning to McCann to sit beside Davis. McCann stayed standing. The man's face darkened: an explosion of angry Japanese, two or three sentences, short and stunningly powerful. Before the man had finished the first sentence the bruiser at the door had grabbed McCann from behind and hurled him towards the chair. McCann bounced noisily off a filing cabinet and turned. The two big men were standing forward, ready. The small one with glasses stayed seated. McCann looked from one to the other and sat.

Davis hadn't moved. "We was just talkin' about you, George. Good timing. These nice lads want a chat with us, apparently."

The two men at the table settled themselves in their chairs again. The toothpick resumed its erratic motion in the corner of the bruiser's mouth. The man at the door stepped back to his post, crossing his hands in front of him.

The small man spoke again. "I am Takano. We come here on business. Last night happening. Regrettable incident, is it?"

McCann looked at Davis, who said, "I've been over all this before you got here. It's a bit confused and me head's still a bit fucked up, but I think these lads must have had a word with Beef and got the address of this school. Don't think they're the police, like."

Takano pointed at McCann. "You. What happen party

154

yesterday night? Speak slowly please." In spite of his faltering English there was no mistaking the presence of the man.

"I don't know."

"You don't know? *Fuzaken janae zo*. You try to remember?"

A long silence. The small man, Takano, was not pleased. Not at all.

"*Temaera, ore no koto o nameteru noka?*"

A short discussion followed, and there was a silence as Takano appeared to be contemplating options. Finally, he gestured and spoke to the bruiser with the earring, who produced a large leather briefcase and placed it on the table. Takano pulled out a very neatly tied bundle of 10,000 yen notes. And another. Lots and lots of them. He placed them one after the other on the desk. From his suit jacket he took out some papers. They looked like tickets. His face was grim and he pronounced every word deliberately.

"This is 2,000,000 yen. It is first payment for you. Split even. These are airplane ticket. One for you. One for you. You leave Japan tomorrow. Fly to London." Then he pulled two classy-looking silver-plated pens and two sheets of cream stationery, folded in thirds, from the briefcase and pushed them across the desk, one set each to Davis and McCann. "Now write living address in your country, bank information. You go home, we *furikomi* … *furikomi* … transfer? Transfer second payment to bank of you. And you never speak us again. It is finish. Otherwise…"

He sat back. The meeting was over.

"Otherwise what?"

Takano stared straight at McCann, saying nothing.

Davis picked up the pen and twirled it, looking at McCann. McCann turned to the unreadable face beside him and was again struck by its elemental energy. Something drew him in, some mad Billy the Kid sparkle in Davis' eye that was the essence of an unquenchable life force. And bucket-loads of trouble. In that moment he knew the game was up, because he realised that Davis didn't play by the accepted rules of others but by his own warped sense of ethics. As this thought flashed through his head, McCann knew Davis was the only threat to a man like Philips, could understand why Philips must hate him so, because he was the only thing that Philips could not be. Not some bastion of a moral benediction, but simply living, dynamic matter.

Davis, almost smiling, looked at Takano. The tension in the room ratcheted up a few notches.

"Two questions, mate. One, what's this money for? Two, if there is more, how do we know you'll pay into our bank accounts?"

"Question one is stupid question. You know what for. Last night trouble is no comment. To anyone. Ever. It is not your business. You intrude on private party. Your mistake. Some people very, very angry with you and you." He pointed at each of

them in turn as he spoke. "It is troublesome but you are no comment, leave country, is settled. You are lucky. This payment, for your … inconvenient. Question two…" Takano suddenly gave a surprisingly warm smile. "If you know Japanese people, you trust us. We are not always so nice people, I know, but we say we will pay, we always pay. That is our rule. And anyway," he said a little sadly, "You do not have the choice but to trust us."

"This plane ticket. We have to leave tomorrow? Part of the deal?"

"As you say, tomorrow, part of the deal. For us, time very important. *Moshiwakenai kedo*, you stay in Japan, maybe trouble happen again. For you. But yesterday, trouble also. We do not like. Too much trouble bad for business. More trouble bad for us, bad for our bosses. Very, very bad for you. We take you Narita Airport, so there is no more trouble."

Davis listened to this explanation, motioned at the paper and repeated "Name, address, bank account you said?"

"Yes."

He nodded thoughtfully and started writing on the fancy cream paper. He grunted once to himself in satisfaction as he wrote. McCann leaned forward to his own sheet of paper and, like a fourteen-year-old in a maths test he hadn't studied for, stretched his eyeballs to his left to see what Davis was writing. His shoulders were tense, his head didn't move, and the corners of his eyes hurt where they were almost popping out of their sockets. He read Davis's paper:

Name: Charlie Boy
Address: No fixed abode, 90210
Bank Account: Suck it and see
Message: Sorry, not ready to leave Japan yet. Like it here. I got the earring, lad. You take the other 2.

When he had finished writing, Davis moved the paper imperceptibly towards McCann, who scratched his head and made a non-committal sound. His ribs were sore. Davis stood up and with a disarming smile walked round the table carrying the paper and pen towards the bruiser with the diamond earring. The toothpick stopped moving. The big man seemed slightly surprised by the approach, but his look at Davis was quizzical, not hostile. McCann could almost see the question mark hovering in the air above the man's head, like a cartoon. And McCann noticed one thing – Davis was holding the pen the wrong way round, point out. He was holding it tightly enough that his knuckles were white, but the rest of his body was relaxed and calm. Everything was happening like a slow-motion car crash: it seemed to take an age for Davis to negotiate the table, and then he was beside the earringed man and McCann had time for one last thought: 'Hope the guy at the door doesn't have a gun, or we're toast.'

Davis leaned over the man almost paternalistically, a smile playing on his lips, one hand lightly on his shoulder as he showed him the paper, apparently pointing something out to him. As he did so McCann, getting ready for whatever might happen next, moved his chair back a few inches. The chair squeaked loudly and everyone glanced at him.

Just at that moment Davis viciously smashed the point of the pen straight and hard into the left eyeball of the earringed man. In one fluid movement, with the pen sticking horizontally out of the socket, the man's mouth dropping open to release a scream, Davis grabbed the back of his head with both hands and slammed it down on the desk with a sickening crunch. The head bounced off the table, a lymph, plasma and blood broth flowing from the gouged crater, and the man rolled off his chair to the left. The pen was so deep into the socket that only half of it remained visible.

By this time McCann was already on his feet, loudly cursing Davis, picking up his chair and swatting it across Takano's temple as he barged past him to the man at the door, who was on his way just as quickly towards him. They met in the middle, and as McCann faked a left and caught his adversary with a solid right he felt a double crack, one after the other in quick succession, a kick on his left side so hard that it simultaneously winded him and partially lifted him off his feet, and a karate punch that would have taken his head off had his right arm and shoulder not borne the brunt of it. He could hear his iPhone clatter to the floor and the crash it made sounded terminal. Adrenalin was rushing through him and as his momentum continued forward, he pushed off his leading foot into a short, thumping left uppercut at the man's jaw. As he made contact he could feel the man's head wobble slightly and knew it had found its mark. The brute spat blood and luckily the punch temporarily stunned him, giving McCann the chance to head-butt him hard, right on the bridge of the nose. The man fell away clutching his head and stumbled against the far wall, sliding down it.

There was a sharp noise behind him and McCann turned around. The far door at the back of the school, the one which had been locked when McCann had been snooping around a couple of days before, had been thrown open and a fourth Japanese man was in the room. He was pulling something from his jacket as he came in, but Davis was up and already on him with animal speed, the two battering into the table and sending the piles of money flying in all directions like confetti.

There was movement in front of McCann; his man was coming at him again, but a bit slower now, and as he crashed into McCann he received two or three hard blows around the head and neck for his troubles.

The man landed on top of McCann but was no more than a dead weight lying on him. Managing to heave the stunned lump away and pull himself out from the tangle of limbs, McCann got to his feet again, but Davis had already taken care of the fourth man and had moved back to the man with the earring, who was now on the floor, one leg folded awkwardly under him, head pitched forward, gurgling and making inhuman noises while his right side twitched. Davis was kicking and stamping on his head again and again, jumping on the prostrated body with brutal hooliganism. McCann screamed something at him, a kind of proto-human communication, his voice breaking as he did so. Davis looked up and briefly flashed a proud grin at McCann, defiant, merciless and bitter, as if to say "So I finally got under your skin, eh?" Then he raced through the open back door and was gone.

Pain was now flowing into McCann's right shoulder. It felt like a dead arm: he could hardly lift it. The man he had taken out was slumped on the floor, holding his head in his hands, scarlet blood covering his white shirt and dark suit. Incredibly, he was starting to show signs of recovering his orientation again. Takano, still dazed from the chair that had been rattled across his face, was trying to get up from the floor and reaching out for a mobile phone that had fallen onto on the floor, a line of blood running down the side of his face. The earring man was moving but in unnatural ways. The fourth man was crumpled in a corner. Money was scattered everywhere.

Time to leave. McCann dashed towards the same door Davis had escaped through, then remembering his iPhone, went back, scrambling across the floor for it. He found it in two pieces with the screen smashed, stuffed it into his pocket and ran for it. For the second night in a row, he was fleeing for his life from a room full of horrors.

STOCKTAKING

Outside, the cool air hit him and after running for a few minutes he realised it was very quiet in the suburb. To avoid extra attention, he tempered the adrenalin and his natural desire to flee and slowed to a brisk walk. A long way off a dog was barking. There were only a few streetlights and the night was again moonless. Hugging the shadows, he passed enviously by the light emanating from houses and apartment buildings, curtains hiding domestic scenes of kids watching cartoons on TV, the sounds of dishes being washed in the kitchen and the smell of grilled fish, soy sauce and *miso* soup. He was more scared than he could remember ever being before: lost, alone and anchorless in a foreign country and probably now quite high on the wish list of some influential gangster who had plenty of good reasons to want his head on a platter like John the Baptist's.

As he walked, thoughts flitted through his troubled, jumbled mind. In no particular order, he thought about possible connections between Takano and the entertainment industry, who Takano's bosses might be, what had happened to the girl at the party, the potential repercussions of Davis's refusal to cooperate with the heavy brigade, and the chances of Davis doing a runner and his trail going cold. Right now, of course, finding answers about the Philips girl was the least of his worries. Davis had disappeared into the night and, fearful of another meeting with the goon squad, McCann was loath to go back to the apartment a second time to look for him. As he worked his way back towards Yamato station, expecting any minute to see the Lexus or the Benz roll round a corner with four desperadoes in it, McCann promised himself that he would not forget this feeling he had right now, and that he would make Davis regret forcing him into this situation. Davis: the man burned too many bridges, and he had just burned one that he was going to regret.

On the approach to Yamato station he jumped in a taxi and after some considerable confusion managed to be taken a couple of stops up the line, to a place called Minami Rinkan. He checked the timetable for the next train to Shinjuku then locked himself in a cubicle in the toilet for a few minutes, both to pull himself together and for safety. Finally, he edged onto the narrow platform feeling like a condemned man, sweat on his forehead and running down the small of his back. Now his arm and shoulder were aching so much that he had more or less forgotten about the pain in both sides of his ribcage. A train slid to a halt and the passengers milled around. He stayed out of sight behind a pillar at the back of the platform until the station guard whistled for the doors to close, then he joined the end of the nearest line and boarded the packed train, squeezing in at the door. At every station he followed the same process, getting off as the tidal wave of commuters poured from the carriages, moving randomly up or down the platform and jumping back on at the last moment before the doors closed. It was an exhausting journey back to Shinjuku.

First things first: make yourself safe, worry about the rest later. He had checked into his hotel using his real name, but had given the name of a hotel in another part of Tokyo when Twilly had asked for an address in the interview. Everyone in Yamato knew him only as George Peters so he was fairly sure his hotel was safe, but he wasn't going to take any chances of a rude awakening in the middle of the night. Once out of Shinjuku station, he made his way through the crowds, half-expecting a knife in his kidneys at any minute. After walking around for about ten minutes he found a hotel near the station that looked of a similar standard to the 'Happy Sunshine Hotel', walked in and reserved a room. Then he returned to his original hotel and, saying he was expecting a message from a business partner, asked if there had been any messages, calls or visitors.

"No messages or guests, Mr. McCann."

He went upstairs, quietly unlocked the door, collected his things and checked out, paying for an extra night on account of the short notice. Exhausted and desperate for sleep, but too wired and nervous to relax, he needed to talk to someone. He found a public phone in the lobby of his new hotel, pulled a battered coaster from his pocket and dialed the number scribbled on the back.

THAT'S ENTERTAINMENT

Kyle had clearly been at the bar for some time. His head was propped heavily on his left arm. "Hey! Good to see ya! How was Yamato, man? Live up to expectations?"

For the first time in what seemed like an age, a smile broke across McCann's face. He could feel the weight lifting. He let out a sigh, a release of tension and relief. "Yeah, I suppose so. Everything was exactly as I'd expected, more or less…"

"Did ya notice the traffic signals?"

McCann plonked himself down on the barstool and faced the American with a blank look. "Traffic signals, Kyle?"

"Yeah. The traffic signals. Did ya notice 'em?"

"Umm, can't say I did, to be honest. There was quite a lot going on while I was down there … What was it about them that you thought might be interesting?"

"There's a lot of 'em."

"Yeah…"

"Georgie, boy … one day I'm gonna write a book."

"Yeah? About traffic lights?"

"Yeah, absolutely. About the roads … the road behaviour of different countries, an' like, what it means about, y'know, their … psyche…" There was a brief, lopsided silence: two heads full of feathers.

"A drink for you, Kyle? My round, I think. Not that you necessarily need another one, but I could do with a couple after the day I've had. Beer and whisky chasers okay with you?"

"Sure, but go easy there, slugger. Already ten o'clock and some of us have to work tomorrow, y'know."

"Yeah, me too. And if tomorrow's anything like the last two days have been, I'm going to need all the sleep I can get."

"Gonna be busy, huh? Well, don't forget to check the traffic signals in Yamato if you're back there again. Or anywhere, for that matter. It won't be hard – they're all over the place. An' the pedestrians. Ever see them jaywalkin' in Japan? It just don't happen, man."

"Well, like I say, I've had quite a lot on my mind the last couple of days, but you might be right. I have noticed that when the light's red, even when the road's empty, most people don't move until it goes green."

"That's my book right there. Or maybe, like, a scientific paper or somethin'. Now, you take a country like Vietnam. It's like, the opposite. Over there, it's an organic mass of people and scooters and pedestrians, movin' like a… I dunno, like a livin', breathin' organism. Or a school of silver fish, all movin' together like they have some kind of psychic power. That's what crossin' the road in Vietnam is like. You gotta just step out there. Put your faith in the natural rhythm of the system, the people, the scooters, the cars. Go with the flow…"

As he explained this Kyle's hands were twisting like a ballerina. For a big man, his movements could be surprisingly agile and light. "They all move around you. It's a beautiful thing to be part of, man, a human school of fish. Now that's the absolute opposite to what they got here in Japan. Instead of a system of perfect intuition, here they got a system of perfect organisation." He considered McCann for a minute. "You ever been to Vietnam?"

"Nope. Actually this is the first time I've been in Asia."

"Japan ain't exactly Asia, man. It's Japan. Island

mentality. Not a continental mentality. You should understand that, bein' a Brit. In the States, man, we're this big … continental island. From Mount McKinley to Key West, that's a lotta land, man. I dunno what that makes us. Confused, I guess! Japan, is this … floatin' land…" Kyle rolled his right hand in gentle arcs expressively.

McCann slapped his left hand on the counter. "Drinks!"

He returned with two lagers and two Ballantines, no water, no ice, and they sipped their drinks contemplatively for a while, allowing the warm ambience of the bar to fill the space. But behind the silence, wheels were turning in McCann's head.

"What do you think about the popular entertainment in this country, Kyle? The pop bands, TV shows. What's it all like?"

"TV? Aw, man, I dunno. Pretty bad, I'd say. I can only understand about half of what they're sayin' but even I can see you'd need to have a lobotomy to think it was good. I spend most of my time downloading stuff from home, y'know? TV in the States has just taken off in the last 10 years. I love all those shows with a bit of intrigue, bit of gritty real life, bit of violence. I've watched The Sopranos more times than I can remember. And I love all those police investigation dramas, man."

McCann was drinking with his left hand. His right arm hung painfully at his side. "Yeah … I'm, aah, not so keen on that kind of stuff actually. I just ask 'cos I was talking with some of the people I'm working with down in Yamato and they were telling me about the TV shows, the famous people, the way the entertainment business works here, stuff like that. Pretty interesting. The way they were talking, I got the impression the mass market entertainment here, the big companies, they're really powerful organisations. Is that true?"

166

Kyle laughed. "Absolutely, dude! It's a closed shop. Actually, everything in Japan is a closed shop. Yeah, those entertainment groups are powerful, alright. I dunno how many of them there are, but there can't be more than about five that more or less control the whole business in Japan. They got these rosters of young dudes and chicks: singers, dancers, actors. Course none of 'em can sing, dance or act … Actually, I take that back, some of them can dance. But basically they're just like fuckin' ciphers, interchangeable pretty boys and girls who do whatever they're told to do. An' what they're told to do is make shitloads of money for their company."

"A group called Taimou Entertainment is one of them?"

"Hell, yeah. One of the biggest."

"You said they have, like, a stable of stars…"

"Well, I wouldn't call them stars exactly. Mannequins, maybe. They look good. Must spend hours preening in front of a mirror, doin' their hair an' pluckin' their eyebrows. An' that's just the guys. What they do got is energy, I'll give 'em that. No talent whatsoever, but lots of energy, an' lots of the fakest smiles you ever saw in your life, man."

"Does anyone keep close tabs on these people? I mean, any famous scandals over here like there are back home? Y'know, like, 'Cleancut Dave the kid's TV presenter actually spends his weekends snorting coke off a whore's tits', stuff like that?"

"Oh, yeah! 'Specially recently. I guess it all used to be hushed up, no-one knew what those big-wigs were up to. Now, there's a lotta that shit goin' down. Pop stars, TV stars, guys getting caught with their pants down, takin' drugs, girls too, people goin' to jail for tax evasion, dudes getting chucked off their TV shows 'cos of alleged connections with *yakuza*, all sorts of stuff is comin' out now. I guess it used to be swept under the carpet."

McCann felt sweat in the palms of his hands again. "Umm, you said alleged *yakuza* entertainment connections. Any truth in them?"

"Bound to be, man. The *yakuza* are into everything that makes money in Japan. Politics, construction, logistics, they got their fingers in every pie. So entertainment, TV shows, bands, all that stuff, sure, I'd say they're gonna be into that. Listen, there's 125 million people in this country and when they come home from a hard day's work – an' I'm talkin' at like 9, 10 or 11 at night here, not 5:30 – what they gonna do? Switch on the dream box in the corner, crack open a beer and forget about stuff for an hour. They're too tired to do anythin' else. Lotta money to be made in 125 million heads all tuned in to your shit."

"How much money we talking about? Say, a famous guy in Japan. How much does he make a year?"

"No idea. Depends on the guy, I guess. But it's big business. Some of the dudes at the very top'll be makin' hundreds of millions of yen a year for sure."

"So what you're saying is, when a big scandal about some famous entertainer kicks off, a lot of people stand to lose a lot of money, right?"

Kyle's eyes narrowed. "What I'm sayin' is, what's with the twenty questions, anyway? What you snoopin' around for? You doin' some kind of media work over here or somethin'?"

"Sorry, yeah. I, umm, do have a bit of an interest in the entertainment industry, yeah. Not professional, really. More like … social."

McCann toyed briefly with the idea of explaining some of the events of the previous day to Kyle, and almost immediately decided against it. But it would be stupid to pass up this opportunity to get as much information as he could: or as much as Kyle would allow before he got pissed off.

"You heard of a guy called Noda? Hiromasa Noda?"

Kyle slugged his beer. "Nope."

"In some boy band. Tokoro Times, I think they're called. Supposed to be the next big thing."

"Oh, yeah, I heard of *them* all right. Dunno the names of any of the guys in these bands, they're all interchangeable, y'know? But Tokoro Times, yeah, they're big, and getting bigger. What about them? You attracted to young dudes with faggotty hairstyles or somethin'?"

"Not exactly. Gotta niece. Into the whole 'Cool Japan' thing. *Manga* an' that. I got an email from her when she heard I was coming to Japan, asked me to get information, pictures, magazines, anything unique I can get here about some J-Pop guys she likes. This Noda bloke was one of them. And someone called Murasaki Ryo was another. Apparently they're both contracted to Taimou Entertainment, so I just wondered about the whole scene. That's why I ask."

Kyle raised his eyebrows. "Murasaki Ryo? How old is your niece, man? That guy is old school now. And you wanna tell her to get better taste in guys, George. Murasaki Ryo is totally shady. An' he's a fuckin' disgusting-lookin' dude."

"How come? What does he look like?"

Kyle smiled his big, easy smile and glugged some more beer. "What does he look like? Just turn around. He's right behind you, man."

McCann's eyes widened and he slowly swivelled round on the stool, scanning the pub's clientele. A few weeknight drinkers, a couple of bar staff. No crazed orange fat-face rapist to be seen. He turned back to Kyle with a confused look.

169

"Right there, dude. On the TV!"

He turned again and looked up at the screen on the far wall. He watched for a few seconds and sure enough, there he was. The man who just two days ago had instigated a serious sexual assault, and perhaps even worse, there he was on TV, eating some kind of meat dumplings dipped in soy sauce, and, with the TV's sound down, roaring in silent laughter. As Murasaki Ryo joked with the other guests and the obviously straight-laced presenter, in his mind McCann heard that nasty little laugh from two nights before. Murasaki Ryo's face filled the screen as he bit into the food, his head nodding in mute pleasure as he devoured the morsel. He was the life and soul of the party. The sight of him turned McCann cold, but he watched for a few moments, seeing the same mannerisms, the same gestures, and above all, that same horrible laugh, silent on the screen but unpleasantly clear in McCann's head. He looked back at Kyle, unable to disguise the disgust on his face.

"Yeah, dude! Your niece got the hots for that fuckin' slimy piece of shit. Actually he's one of the few Japanese *tarento* whose name I do know, only 'cos Toshiko is always going on about how much he gives her the creeps. She hates the guy. And you know, I don't blame her. Everything about him looks fake – fake tan, fake hair, fake laugh, totally fake name."

"Fake name?"

"Stage name. Murasaki means purple in Japanese. Purple Ryo. What a shit name! What a loser!"

McCann turned again to the screen. He was repulsively fascinated by the ostentatious overacting; every gesture and facial movement obviously drawing the expected and equally fake mirth from the other guests and, presumably, the voiceless studio audience. In the light of his only

170

previous experience of this grotesque man, to McCann the exaggerated devouring of the fried pastry dumpling took on an obscene, rapacious hue, and the two processes, the feasting on the food and the feasting on the woman, became melded in his mind; the perpetrator consuming them both purely as objects for his sensual pleasure. As he looked into the cold little eyes, shining silver in the studio lights, McCann felt a new level of revulsion. He turned back to Kyle again.

"Yo, dude, you alright? Lookin' a bit green round the gills, man!"

"Jesus, that guy is really hideous. You're telling me he's famous here? People like him?"

Kyle flipped a peanut into his mouth and shrugged. "Have you watched much TV at home lately? I dunno about where you're from, but in the States, apart from those great dramas it's a hundred channels of pure shit, twenty-four-hours a day. You gotta filter out what you want. A decent show, you're talkin' maybe two a decade. The rest? Forget it." His face brightened. "Hey, you wanna borrow some dvds? If you're gonna be here for a while, I can burn some stuff for ya, so you can watch somethin' good for a change."

McCann downed his whisky and glanced at the TV on the far wall again. "Thanks for the offer, Kyle, but I think for the next few days, watching TV is going to be the last thing on my mind."

COMMUTERS

It was 6:45am when McCann located the building. Now electronically blind without his smartphone, he was completely at the mercy of the bizarre postal system of Japanese suburbia: not street names, but a series of three numbers that were apparently organised in some kind of logical manner, but not one that McCann could figure out. The maps of the area he had printed out at a 24-hour internet café had helped, but, not for the first time since he had arrived, he was hitting a lot of dead ends. The address he was looking for was coded 3-12-12, and although the three stayed constant, he had spent thirty minutes wandering around aimlessly in the semi-dark, reading the numbers attached to the streetlamps as they randomly increased and decreased like a warped bingo game. Finally, the digits had started to close in on the magic combination, and from then on, as well as searching for the address, he had begun to look out for angry, dangerous people sitting in cars who might be waiting for him. He didn't see any.

The building was a fairly dilapidated, cheap, wooden apartment block, probably put up in the early 70's. It could have done with a fresh coat of paint, looked like it would struggle to keep out a strong wind and could perhaps collapse in a storm. There were eight flats on two floors, uniform brown doors and a simple iron stairway running along the outside. At some of the back windows, above the air conditioner units and the miniscule dirt squares that would perhaps pass as back gardens, a few worn clothes hung limply, waiting hangdog for their owners to fill them and start what surely promised to be a long, hard day.

He knew from the address on the postcard he'd found at Twilly's school that the place he was looking for was on the ground floor, the far left flat. He surreptitiously checked the postbox outside the door: there were two names written on it, one in Japanese which he couldn't read, and *'Twilly'*. He had the right house.

He was fully awake now, in spite of the lager and whisky still in his system from the night before. His ribs on both sides still hurt a little, but after stretching and working the muscles in a hot shower at 4:30am, the pain in his right arm was more or less gone. He was aware that it was risky to come back to this area from the relative safety of central Tokyo after what had happened the previous day; riskier still to be at an address that may well be known to some very unpleasant people. But he had a job to do, and if he wasn't going to lose Davis altogether, he would need to work fast and take a few calculated risks. He wanted to observe things from a secure location to check that Twilly was actually at home, whether he was alone or not, and to see if any *yakuza* showed up looking for Davis and him. He glanced at his watch as he took in the surroundings. 6:50am.

There were a couple of small, scrubby trees, their leaves almost black; some freestanding houses of various shapes and sizes placed higgledy-piggledy and demarked by tiny walls; a cramped car park on the other side of the narrow road. As seemed to be typical in Japan, there was no pavement to speak of and barely enough room for two cars to pass. There were only eight spaces in the parking area. Six of them were filled. He glanced over the vehicles and saw that the end car, a white Toyota saloon, was fairly grimy with a layer of dried-in dirt, partially covering the

173

windows. The car clearly hadn't been moved recently; unnatural inertia hung over it like a pall. The space beside it was empty. He slid between the Toyota and the four-foot wall surrounding the parking lot, hunkered down and looked around with satisfaction. He had a perfect view of the whole building and of Twilly's end flat in particular. He felt fairly sure that he was out of view of just about anyone.

Although it was early in the morning and almost November, it didn't feel cold at all as he watched the autumnal sun climb up the sliver of bleached-out sky between a thirty storey concrete apartment block and a cheap-looking *pachinko* parlour. The golden radiance rose and touched the dull leaves of the scrappy trees, transforming them, even here in this tawdry corner, into something beautiful and precious. Despite the concrete vista and the stunted vegetation there were small citrus fruit of some kind on the trees and the tang of lemon peel in the morning air.

McCann watched the light creep upwards and realised that this sky and these trees, some quality of the light's refraction, lent a completely different hue and atmosphere to the land than he was used to. Gradually, indistinctly illuminated at first, in the distance and caged between the buildings, a huge incongruous cone appeared: Mount Fuji. Still stripped of its iconic snow, it looked like a giant slagheap on the horizon. He thought about Lancashire, about Pendle Hill and the old canal by his childhood home where he had walked so many years ago. Then for the first time in what seemed like ages, he remembered Marvin, and recognised with a shock that he was missing the dog with the delinquent smile.

He was shuddered out of his reverie by a door opening on the second floor. McCann observed the young guy on his way to work with interest. It was obvious from the tool belt slung on his hip, like a gunslinger's in a Western, that he was a builder of some kind. He sauntered down the metal stairway and as he got closer McCann could see his skin was swarthy and sun-baked brown, enhancing the cowboy feel. But his clothes were far from Texan. He wore a towel wrapped tight around his head like a turban, a cropped work jacket and gigantic dark blue trousers, baggier even than anything from an early 90's MC Hammer video. The ensemble seemed to be rounded off with rubber-soled thick socks, but cleft after the big toe, like mittens for feet. The man went over to the vending machine at the other end of the car park, bought what looked like a small can of hot coffee, jumped into a Suzuki minivan and was away. It was 7:05am.

In quick succession over the next 15 minutes a variety of people left the building; a middle-aged *salaryman* in a shapeless grey suit, shiny at the elbows and the seat of the trousers; a woman, also in a suit, checking her watch and rushing towards the train station; another man, this one in casual clothes, getting into a metallic blue Subaru sports car and rumbling away, the engine growling. By 7:40am the flurry of activity was over and the building was peaceful again.

♒

McCann rubbed his face and scratched his head. He fancied a coffee from that drinks machine at the far end of the car park. His legs were cramping from squatting behind the Toyota for too long. He was getting cold feet. He started weighing up the odds of going over to the house. At least he knew most of the other flats in the building were now probably empty, including the one next door to Twilly's.

Then a light went on in the back room.

He perked up immediately and noticed a movement at the drawn curtains. The large back window opened and he saw Maki Twilly, incongruous in a dark, sexy business suit and pink, plastic toilet slippers, take a bag of rubbish out to the bins at the bottom of the tiny garden area. She was animated, talking over her shoulder in a loud voice to someone, who McCann assumed was Olly, and though he couldn't make out what she was saying, it seemed to be English and she appeared to be angry. She returned to the house, slammed the window shut again, then a few minutes later the front door opened and she emerged again, and this time McCann could clearly hear her say "… stupid, dangerous friends…"

Now that the pink toilet slippers had been ditched for dark high heels, Maki Twilly's ensemble was complete. With every piano-black hair on her head shining gloriously in the morning sun, her movement, clothes, makeup, and long nails all exuded sexual energy, the more so in her pouty anger. McCann watched her greedily as she finished talking to the person inside, slung her Prada handbag onto her shoulder, banged the door closed and turned to leave. He realised that he had a gigantic erection, solid as a piece of wood, the likes of which he hadn't experienced in years, and he had to fight off a crazy desire to follow her beautiful little rear end as she strutted down the lane in the direction of the train station.

In spite of himself and his situation, he almost laughed like a schoolboy as he jogged over to the side of the house and sneaked into the little garden, hiding against the wall beside the large window. He slipped on a thin pair of leather gloves. Now he had a huge grin to go with the huge erection and he suddenly remembered letting down tyres on cars as a thirteen-year-old. It was exciting and he was having fun.

With his head against the wall he could hear the person inside moving around, placing dishes in the sink, turning the tap on and off, then moving to another room. And then he distinctly heard a door close and a lock click shut.

Toilet.

He listened some more, but heard nothing. Gently, he tried to slide open the walk-in French window. Bingo. He sneaked into the *tatami*-mat room and could see that the light in the bathroom was on. He stopped and listened. It didn't seem like anyone else was in the house. Standing in the middle of the room, he quickly took in the surroundings. Huge flat-screen TV, far too big for the tiny space, a small sofa and coffee table with a laptop on it, two plants, tatty-looking kitchen units on the far side and a rudimentary cooker, some magazines scattered on the floor.

SQUATTER

He sat himself down on the cheap sofa and crossed his legs, enjoying the warmth of the morning sun through the window. He stretched like a cat, and then felt the last of his hard-on slink down in his trousers.

The walls of the building seemed paper-thin. Even sitting more than ten feet away, McCann could hear the person in the toilet grunt and sigh, then the turn of the roll holder and the rip of the paper. Then he heard the man mumble a few indistinguishable words to himself, stand up, do the belt of his trousers and flush the toilet. The door opened, and Olly Twilly stepped out. McCann stood up.

"I hope you washed your hands, Olly."

Twilly started in shock and squinted at the shape standing in his living room. It was hard for him to make out who was there, with the sun shining directly behind McCann and Twilly in the darkness of the tiny, gloomy hallway. He cupped his hand above his eyes.

"Who the fuck is that?" It was challenging, defensive, a little scared. "How'd you get into my house?"

"It's me, George Peters. Need to have a wee chat with you, Olly."

Twilly's attitude changed. He became suddenly aggressive, angrily moving towards McCann. "I'll fuckin' have you!"

But as he got closer, Twilly saw a slightly different man to the one who had been fumbling around at the Hunky Dory English School. This George Peters seemed much bigger, tougher, more confident. As he covered the ground between them, suddenly he wasn't so sure of himself. He stopped a few feet away from McCann.

"What the fuck are you doin' in my house?"

McCann motioned behind him. "Window was open. Sorry about that. Don't worry, I won't stay long. Wanted a private chat. And I need to talk with Charlie. He's not here, is he?"

Until he had taken on this job for Philips, there hadn't been much call in the last twenty years for McCann to use his boxing skills but, as he'd found out in the last couple of weeks, they were still there when needed. He was a bit slower now, of course, a bit rusty maybe. Pounder had been a tough nut, alright, a real boxer and a street fighter. Although he'd been embarrassed by Davis a couple of times, which annoyed and worried him, he had done fine with the dangerous but low-level *yakuza* boys the day before, and Twilly was a much less intimidating proposition than any of them. McCann could see through the Twilly bravado, knew there wasn't anything behind it other than a big mouth and a bit of street swagger. McCann wasn't a champ in anyone's book, just a guy who'd done some middleweight sparring as a young man.

But that was more than enough for this situation.

The look on Twilly's face told McCann that the lunge was coming. He was ready for it and as Twilly stepped forward and threw a heavy, wild haymaker he simply bobbed out of reach and countered with a fast, light combination to Twilly's open head. He didn't want to hurt him, but he wanted it to be clear who was in control here. Twilly stumbled backwards, hitting the coffee table, but he managed to right himself. He had a slightly glazed look in his eyes, but advanced again, although clearly less sure of himself.

179

McCann stepped forward, faked a right, and clocked Twilly just above the eye with a left cruncher. This time Twilly fell back and didn't get up. He landed on the sofa with a thump. McCann was on top of him quickly; a cut was bleeding at Twilly's eyebrow.

It must have hurt a bit, but the tears in the corners of his eyes were probably from shock as much as pain.

McCann realised guiltily that he was still quite enjoying himself. He grinned again. "Sorry, Olly. Self-defence an' that. Don't struggle. Where's Davis?"

Twilly, still slightly dazed, squirmed on the sofa under McCann and tried to gain leverage by flipping his leg round him. McCann easily countered by adjusting his position slightly.

"I don't have time for this, Twilly. I'm not here to get at you. Where's Davis?"

"Fuck you, cunt."

"Bad answer." McCann playfully bonked him a half-cocked right in the centre of his face.

"Get outta my fuckin' house," was the weak reply.

McCann looked up. The door of the toilet had been left open and an eggy flatulence was pervading the small living room. "Jesus, Olly, that was a hell of a shit you must have had just now. It stinks in here. And I wasn't joking when I said I hope you washed your hands… Now look, I need to speak to Davis. It's kind of important. For him and for me. I'm thinkin' you know where he is. So how about it?"

Silence.

McCann sighed. "Olly, Davis is in trouble. He's done a runner. Where has he gone? I saw Mrs. Twilly looking well-agitated just now, talking about dangerous friends an' that. So I'm betting Davis has contacted you, right? I know the effect he has on people."

Twilly's eyes, which had been vacantly drifting at the ceiling, cleared and focused. He came round. Now he looked genuinely scared of McCann, but there was still hostility in his expression. "Davis is a cunt, an' so are you."

"Have the *yakuza* been round here to speak to you?"

"Charlie Davis is an ungrateful cunt. He ain't got a fuckin' clue how to treat a mate that's stuck his neck out for him. I gave that guy a helpin' hand when he really needed one, for old time's sake, an' he just spits right back in my face, causes me all sorts a trouble. He's gettin' no help from me again. Selfish prick."

"Why did Charlie come to Japan, Olly?"

"What's it the fuck to you why he came here? Who the fuck you think you are, breakin' into my house? I'll have you fuckin' arrested!"

McCann gave Twilly a couple of gentle slaps. "Don't be such a bad sport. A bit of cotton wool, a good wash and it'll not even look like a bad bicycle crash. Yet. There's still plenty of time to really get me in a fighting mood though. An' the way you're going, it's gonna be sooner rather than later."

He delved into his pocket and pulled out his wallet. Holding Twilly down with one hand while trying to work the wallet open with the other he said, "Listen, I'll tell you what. I got 70,000 yen on me at the moment. For emergencies. 70,000 yen. Yours. Just answer a few questions, that's all."

Twilly looked sullen. "What you wanna know?"

"Better! Question one. Where's Davis?"

"Dunno."

McCann's face darkened. "Think carefully before you answer this one, Twilly, you really don't want to piss me off. Has he contacted you?"

Twilly hesitated for a few seconds, then, seemingly having made a decision, said, "Yeah. Phoned me late last night. Left a message. Said he's on the way to Havana. He's gonna join a band an' play at the Copacabana. That's all I know."

McCann nodded. "Funny man. You like your face scrambled or fried in the mornings?"

"Aw, fuck you, man."

McCann punched him again, neatly, sharply, hard, right on the spot where the eye was cut. It opened a little more. Twilly groaned.

"Olly, I gotta tell ya mate, I'm under a bit of pressure here. And my behaviour gets erratic when I'm stressed out. Like now. There's money in your pocket for answers, more punches in the face for nowt."

"Why should I tell you where he is? You want some information that badly, gimme more cash."

"You're not exactly in a strong negotiating position here, you know."

"Neither are you. The *yakuza* are lookin' for you and they know where you're stayin'. You're headin' for a doin', chump. Big time."

McCann reflected on that for a minute. It was just as well he had relocated when he did. He would probably have been okay in the 'Happy Sunshine Hotel' but you couldn't be too safe. He smiled at Twilly. "A doin', eh? Thanks for the concern, but I ain't too worried about the *yakuza* finding me."

This wasn't the answer Twilly was expecting and it visibly shook him, but McCann knew that in another sense Twilly had a point. He had no idea where Davis was, couldn't be sure Twilly would talk, didn't particularly want to cause serious damage to Twilly, and didn't want to stick around in this house for too long. He was thinking about what to do next, what leverage he could force on Twilly, short of panning his face in, which could lead to complications. Then he looked to his left and saw the iPad on a low stool set between the toilet and the kitchen. He had an idea. McCann stood up and with his right hand grabbed Twilly's sweater and yanked him off the sofa towards the bathroom, picking up the iPad on the way.

Twilly was a big lad and hauling him across the floor hurt his shoulder again. The smell from the toilet was disgusting. Twilly was croaking expletives and complaints. McCann threw him down on the floor at the toilet doorway like a sack of potatoes. Twilly's head cracked off the bottom of the wooden doorframe.

"Right, Twilly. See this iPad? Your precious iPad? It's getting smashed and going straight down the shitter if I don't get answers, right now."

As he spoke he looked into the pan. Remnants of sticky dark brown excrement were still attached to the porcelain.

The tears were running down Twilly's face freely now. "Aw, not me fuckin' iPad, man. Gimme a break, you prick…"

McCann held the iPad over the toilet. "All your work files, all those photos, all your beautiful memories, all the trashy potboilers you downloaded for the train, all the other pointless shit you got on this thing. The whole lot is going down this toilet. And your head is going in straight after it. An' neither of them'll come back out the same shape they went in, I guarantee it. So, the question is, is Charlie Davis worth that much to you? 'Cos I don't think he is, Olly. He doesn't give a shit about you. He uses you when he needs you.

"You think he'd protect you if it was his neck on the line? I know for a fact he wouldn't, 'cos what he did yesterday has just put you in a very difficult situation with some powerful people who are pissed off, and no doubt know where you live. But I don't see Charlie boy over here with the cavalry to help you out. Do you? I got no gripe with you … apart from the two days' unpaid work I did for you, if you can call it that. I'm willing to forget about that right now if you tell me what I want to know. So. Where is Davis? Is he going somewhere? And how can I get to him? Answers in five seconds, or it's down the pan for the iPad and you. Trust me, I'll do it."

There was a brief silence. McCann knew the cogs in Twilly's brain were turning, weighing up options, possibilities and odds. Twilly touched his cut eye, which, although starting to coagulate, was still bleeding. He looked up at McCann sullenly.

"Think he's goin' to Hokkaido. I dunno what Charlie's got into; I dunno what the fuck's goin' on anymore."

Still holding the iPad over the toilet, McCann pulled two 10,000 yen notes out of his wallet and dropped them on Twilly's belly. "Go back to the start. What's happened to you since the party in Roppongi a couple of days ago?"

"You're mixed up in all this as well, ain't cha? You turn up here like some total loser and two days later all hell breaks loose. Who are you?" He had a frenetic and confused expression, like a pool player who realises too late that he's being hit by a big money sting.

"I'm George Peters, Olly. Now tell me what's been going on."

Twilly shook his head mournfully. "Fucked if I know. School's been closed the last two days. I been away with the missus. Last night I come back here an' there's six fuckin' *yakuza* waitin' in a couple of cars for me. They say there's been some kinda problem at the school, an' where are the two of you? They're lookin' for Charlie an' you. Maki had to translate all this, they was all speakin'

Japanese, I had no idea what was goin' on. Proper fuckin' *yakuza*. I been around plenty of wide boys in me time, but these guys scared the shit out of me. Like I says, I been away the last two days, I dunno what the hell they're talkin' about, an' I said so. So they threatened me an' Maki, said if I don't watch out the school might have a nasty accident.

"They come into the house, look around, tryin' to see if Charlie's here. Course he ain't. I see there's a couple of messages flashin' on the answer machine. I'm thinking, bet this is from Charlie, just like the fuckin' guy to phone and leave a message just to get me in even bigger shit, but they don't check the phone. So they says to me, where do Charlie an' you live, an I'm thinkin' I'll pretend I dunno, but right away I can see it's a bad fuckin' idea, so I tell them Charlie's address, an' say you're in some hotel in Tokyo an' I can't get the address till I go to the school tomorrow. So what do the fuckers go and do? Put me in the back of the friggin' Lexus an' drive me off to the school, at 10 o'clock at night. I thought me number was up right then an' there. The goon beside me, he can speak a few words of English. He says to me they know where Charlie lives, been there already lookin' for him but the place was empty. Says it's just as well I told them the right address 'cos if I hadn't they'd have beat me to pulp with a baseball bat. An' the guy fuckin' grins at me an' points at the bleedin' bat, lyin' there between the front seats.

"I'm thinkin' this must be a bad dream. I got no idea what's goin' on. They drive me up to the school, I go to open up an' get out the files an' find your hotel address – no offence, like, but I had no choice – an' when I get in there the school looks like a fuckin' war zone. I says to the guy, what the fuck happened to me school? An' they say *sho ga nai*. My Japanese is shit but even I know what that means: it can't be helped! Can't be bleedin' helped! So you tell me. What happened to me fuckin' school?"

McCann considered Twilly's story. It sounded extremely plausible. He was even starting to feel a bit sorry for Twilly, this smalltime streetwise motormouth who was suddenly hopelessly out of his league. But he thought, 'We're all out of our league now, especially me. Time for some strategic economy of truth.'

"I'm sorry about the school, Olly. You probably don't want to know all the details 'cos the more you know, the more trouble you might get into with the lads who paid you a visit last night. All I can say is Charlie had an argument with some *yakuza* and gouged one boy's eye out with a pen, and his mates weren't too happy about it."

"Do what? You havin' me on?"

McCann shook his head. "'Fraid not. They're after him big time. They're after me 'cos I was there and so I'm implicated, and if your mate Charles and I don't sort this out with them, you can be sure they're gonna take it out on the next best thing – you. So for both your sake and mine, I need to get to Charlie, we need to fix this situation and then maybe your life can get back to some sort of normality. If I don't get to Charlie, we don't get this problem sorted out. Consequences for you – not good. Which is why I'm standing in your toilet at eight in the morning."

Twilly looked at McCann with renewed distaste. "So why the fuck does this all kick off two days after you show up? Charlie's a mate. I've known the guy for years. For all I know, you're the twat causin' all this trouble, not him."

McCann could see Twilly was wavering. He was obviously angry and scared and was maybe ready to give up on Davis for all the mayhem he'd brought into his life, but it was touch and go. McCann leaned a little towards him and held his eye. He spoke quietly but with as much confidence as he could muster.

"Well now, Olly, you can say what you like but I think both you and I know that Charlie Davis is a fucking one man Demolition Derby. Everything the guy touches turns to dust, one way or another. Isn't that right? He's just got the knack. I think you know exactly what I'm talking about. He's a black hole, that boy. Everything around him is drawn into him and destroyed by him. That's just the way he is. You know it, and so do I. Right now, you and I are on the brink of getting sucked into that black hole. And I'm the only guy who can stop it from happening. We can sort this out but I need to find him and speak to him. To do that, you need to tell me where he is."

McCann paused and took a deep breath. "Two more things for you to consider, Olly. One – remember, if you don't tell me where he is, or if I think you might be lying, like I say, this iPad and your head are both going straight down this toilet. Right now. Don't make the mistake of thinking I won't do it. You're scared of the *yakuza*. I get that. But you should be just as scared of me right now, as well.

"Two, and much more importantly for you, the *yakuza* may well have paid me a visit at that hotel last night. I wouldn't know, because I'm not staying there, never was. I'm somewhere else. In fact, if I wanted to I could be on a plane right now, flying back to rainy old England without a care in the world. I've got no stake in this country. At the end of the day, if it gets too hot, I'm outta here. I've got that choice. Unlike you. But I'm not on that plane yet, I'm here. You know why? Because I've got unfinished business I should take care of. And it wouldn't be right if I just walked away and left you with a big fucking headache that you can't even begin to know how to fix. So, again, for the last time – details of where Charlie is and how I can get to him."

Blood was half-caked on one side of Twilly's face. He looked tired. Then he gestured with his head and waved a weary arm. "Answer machine."

"What?"

"Play the answer machine. He left a message last night. That's all I know about where he is. Listen to it first, an' then I'll tell you what he's talkin' about."

McCann nodded. "You do it."

Twilly looked shiftily at McCann as he got up off the floor and moved across to the landline. McCann was watching, braced for something. It didn't happen. Twilly pressed the 'play' button and heard Davis speak.

"Alright, mate? You there? Pick up the phone, Olly, it's important." Pause. "Listen man, gotta bit of a problem here. I gotta split outta town. Probably goin' up to Fuso's place, lie low for a bit. Hope it don't cause you any trouble. I'll be in touch. Cheers, mate."

McCann asked Twilly to play the message again, which he did.

"So who is Fuso?"

"Fuso Tochimoto. She's a student at the school, about 45. Took a shine to Charlie, like a lotta women do. Charlie might have shagged her, I dunno. She comes from Hokkaido. Up north, the north island of Japan. Sounds like he's goin' there."

"How far away is Hokkaido?"

Twilly shrugged. "'Bout a two hour flight from Narita."

"What's a woman who lives in Hokkaido taking English lessons here for?"

"Her family gotta bit of money. House down here, another one up there. And a log cabin somewhere way up north, in the middle of nowhere. Was her brother's, but he died. It's hers now. Charlie's been goin' on about how much he wants to go up there an' get away from it all, away from the big city an into the countryside. He's obsessed with the idea."

"So how can I get in touch with her?"

"Give her a phone."

"And the number is?"

"In me iPad."

McCann burst into laughter: long, loud and relieved.

PART 3-
HOKKAIDO

DAY TWO – NOVEMBER 1st

*S*tillness over the water today. Brace of goldeneye *floated by and a group of slaty-backed gulls squabbled by cliff base. Wildlife abundant here. Tempted to try to bring something down by shotgun but prob. messy & noise might bring unwanted attention. Fog came early afternoon and covered the sea. Sat by beach and tried to meditate, counting my breathing until the numbers vanished and I was just a thing breathing, inhaling and exhaling mist.*

4pm – before dusk fell checked the snares and traps set up yesterday. One strangled rabbit!!

Skinned and cleaned it as the old man had taught me. Fried it in oil and garlic powder (plenty of condiments in cupboards here – thank you Brother Tochimoto), added water, let it simmer. With a can of kidney beans went down well – my first animal meat for many a year, and didn't even give it a second thought.

No tobacco or alcohol in cabin. Fuso said the old boy had liked both. Maybe he supped and puffed all up before leaving? Down to my last ten fags. Saving them – 1 per evening. Could murder a joint or two right now. Made green tea and began to prepare the fire – kindling and an old yellowed newspaper. Simple tasks, keep busy, don't think too much. Whistled as I worked. Started with some oldies – stuff from Up The Bracket and some Smiths. Ended up with Oliver! Christ knows why. Only know about three of the songs. These days can't decide if feeling Dodger-ish or Fagin-ish.

Fire is beautiful – truly a gift from the gods. Look into it, smoke my one smoke. Never been happier. End of the day – nowt to do once it gets dark except sleep. And plan.

PANTIES & FISH NETS

McCann left Twilly to his trouble and wife and got as far away from the residence as possible, commuting to the inner city heaving with *salarymen* and the general haste that constitutes normal life in central Tokyo. His first stop was a phone shop; it started positively, descended quickly into Charlie Chaplin and was resolved after a change of staff to an English speaker. Replacing his smartphone seemed inexplicably complicated and time-consuming so in the end he reluctantly settled for what was called a PHS phone, a dinosaur from a previous epoch, which he would be able to hand in at the airport when he left the country.

Next he went to Kinokuniya bookshop and bought an English travel guide about Hokkaido, then found a place nearby where ordering lunch wouldn't present too many problems and sat himself down. The restaurant was named for the Kirin beer company and he felt the right to order one, along with a tuna sandwich. He had two numbers, a mobile and a landline. Although not yet lunchtime, it was noisy and hot in the eatery and he wasn't sure about the Japanese etiquette of calling from a restaurant so he stepped outside and dialed the mobile number. A click and a lady's voice answered saying something in Japanese. He waited for it to stop and left a short, simple message: "This is urgent and concerns Charlie Davis. I will call again in fifteen minutes."

The landline number was equally unresponsive.

McCann returned to his seat and drank his beer slowly,

195

leafing through the Hokkaido guide. Already it would be cold there and he would need warmer clothes. The photos showed a beautiful landscape sporting flowers of the fairest in summer and ski slopes in winter. There were bears and deer deep in the wooded slopes of the mountains, and the body of water to the north bore the name the Sea of Okhotsk, which McCann thought had a chilly, desolate ring about it. As he scoured the map of the diamond-shaped island he wondered where Davis's middle of nowhere might be, and what the chances of finding him there would be. The northernmost point was a place called Wakkanai, and the guidebook said that on a clear day it was possible to see Sakhalin Island. Russia.

He checked his watch and went outside to call again, putting a finger in his right ear to shut out the bumble and drone of the people and vehicles. This time he called the numbers repeatedly, but there was still no response so he left a more forceful message and added that Davis's life could be in danger.

He returned to the café, ordered coffee and another sandwich, this time cheese and ham, and noticed that three high school girls were sitting opposite him, all gazing at the screen of a smartphone and squealing with excitement. He wished he had one too, rather than the Neolithic object he now carried.

His phone rang. He answered and someone spoke in Japanese, but he couldn't hear clearly and spoke over the voice on the other end, "Are you Fuso Tochimoto?"

The voice continued to speak Japanese. He heard the woman say, "McCann-san?" and he asked again if she was Fuso Tochimoto, but he was getting nowhere so he hung up. When he looked up the girls had abandoned the smartphone and were tucking into slices of pizza contentedly.

The phone rang again. Again a Japanese voice. He asked if she spoke English. There was a pause and then, "Just a moment please."

He waited and then a different voice said, "Good morning, sir."

It was a courtesy call from the phone company to a new customer. After thanking her he hung up. He was losing patience and weighing options; he needed an address to follow up, and quickly. Return to Twilly? Not the wisest move. Get into the school and go through the files, at night if necessary? Again, probably unwise, but perhaps imperative. He had come to a dead end and if there was no progress from these phone calls, calculated risks would be required.

The girls at the table across from him stood up to leave, still chattering excitedly. He needed a slash and the beer had made him tired. He had the phone in his hand and on the way to the toilet it began to vibrate in his palm. He turned back and answered as he walked outside.

The voice was deep for a woman and she spoke slowly, "Who are you?"

"A friend of Charlie's, who needs my help."

"Charlie doesn't have friends."

"He has me. Listen Ms Tochimoto, he is in grave danger. Some very violent people are after him and they know where he is. I have to get to him first. If I don't he could lose his life. It's that simple."

He heard a laugh followed by, "He doesn't mind losing his life maybe, or taking one that tries to take his."

McCann rolled his eyes to himself. "Very noble and very absurd. Look, take this seriously please."

There was a pause. "What is your name, please?"

He gave it.

"I can meet you in Sapporo but I must travel far to get there. Can you pay train?"

McCann immediately agreed.

"Well, then. You come to Sapporo. I meet you at lunch the day after tomorrow. I will tell you place when you arrive. Call you then."

The line went dead.

Davis emerged from beneath the bearskin and arose in the dark. He lit the lamps and threw tinder and wood on the fire, then stripped naked and washed in cold water from head to toe and dressed, shivering. He took his tea to the hearth, got back into his sleeping bag and thought over the day. He needed a plan to get moving. He could return here later, when the heat was off. Fuso had no use for the cabin and had told him he could stay here as long as he liked if he kept a low profile. But he had been stupid to mention this place to Olly. If the *yakuza* gave Olly the fear, he would squeal. He had thought of hiding out in the forest, finding somewhere to pitch his tent, but in reality it was getting too cold for camping. So he had had to think of something else.

He warmed his hands by the orange flames as they licked and danced above the wood. The previous owner of the cabin had cut perfectly-sized cylindrical blocks and stored them for a future that he wouldn't have; they burned well and produced little smoke. Davis added the driftwood he had gathered the previous night; each piece burned differently and gave off a distinctive light and scent.

He would need to cross soon, before the ice came and blocked the Nemuro Strait. Then he would need to stay on the other side until the sun returned. He knew it was a dangerous journey and that a trial of nerve and strength lay ahead, then caught himself, laughed and said aloud, "Isn't that what we're here for?"

He thought back to Philips' house with its plush, pompous furnishings, sterile bathrooms and books displayed for view as cultural trophies, not dynamic ideas; a place of living death. Here in the cabin all was cut down to the minimum: a battered sofa, several futons and *zabuton* cushions, a gas cooker, a makeshift sink, and a good sturdy table with two chairs. He had everything he needed: the tarot pack that he had laid out in Arcana on the wooden floor; his Zeiss Victory binoculars, the only expensive thing he owned; the fire in front of him; and the weaponry that the dead man had left and that Davis had polished, sharpened and blessed. The harpoon was heavy and viciously sharp, it must have belonged to a whaler once. With a little practice he had learnt to make her sail well, and if nothing else maybe it would be a protection against wild animals. The man had also left a shotgun and an ample supply of ammunition: these would be vital for his survival when he took passage and wintered on Kunashiri Island.

Two knives gleamed in the firelight. One was a pocket knife that Davis had made razor-sharp, the other a utility knife for fishing and seafaring activities. He planned to put to sea at night for caution's sake, and the man had left a good torch and a supply of batteries. Where he was going food would be an issue. This cabin was well stocked with canned, pickled, dried and salted stores but he could only take a small portion of them with him. He intended to pack food as best he could and carry it both in the kayak and in floating bags that he would trail behind him. They would probably hinder his movement, but he hoped not excessively, and if the weather turned bad he could cut them off and let them drift away.

Once he got to Kunashiri Island he had vague hopes of hunting animal flesh and storing it in the ice; he wasn't sure exactly how he would do this, but he would. He just needed to put his mind to it. Finally, the fishing equipment: rod and reels designed for the sea, and nets too, which he would need if he were to survive the winter. He was unclear about what living quarters he might find but had heard that there were huts and cottages that were uninhabited in winter. He felt buoyant inside at last, as if he had been unchained from a lunatic.

Early that morning he had watched the pirate birds high above the waters, waiting to steal from the labour of others. For the first time he had seen a pomarine skua and it was a majestic sight, soaring on its long scimitar wings that flashed white as they twitched and sailed, carrying the broad body and alert head over tundra and icy waters. Then its bewitching call had descended like the harsh chattering of the unfairly condemned, or the unhinged condemning; the kleptoparasites of the sky. Davis had laughed; he felt alive and happy, free of the traffic of the city, both on the streets and in his head.

But later in the morning, out in Tochimoto's kayak, with paddles at rest and a hand trailing idly in the frigid water, he was sure he had felt a brush of scales under the furl of waves. Unnerved, he had hastened back to the shore, then laughed at himself. He would have to be steelier than that. After a short break he had sailed back out again and paddled hard, keeping a watchful eye on the compass needle as he did so. A trial run of five kilometres showed that the water suddenly became rougher out of the shelter of the point, although in good weather it was unlikely to raise serious problems. He had only been here a couple of days but he was already learning to handle the craft well and was drilling himself incessantly. He would need to work the rougher water from tomorrow.

Now it was night and the cabin was radiant with warmth and a holy light. Davis stretched and roused himself. Taking the harpoon and flashlight he left the cabin and took the path to the sea's edge. A thin sleet fell through the path of light cast by the torch: the night was icy. He raised the harpoon and cast it with all his might into the black water. The splash echoed in the silence with an explosive menace, as if a sea beast had jumped. On hauling it in he found the weapon as clean as on throwing. Not yet then, he thought, but soon enough.

He returned up the incline to the cabin, dimly aglow with fire and lamplight through the sleet-drizzle and looking, he thought, like a scene from a Christmas card.

He entered the warmth and put water on to boil. He recalled the waders that had sailed over the banks on tipped wings and how the previous night he had heard owls in the dark glade as he took his evening walk. He could find a pattern to this life in the wilds, one he knew he would find pleasing. If he was going to be governed, it would be by the solitude he had found here and by the geography of the wilderness.

The water boiled, beginning to bubble and hiss. He stood and watched it for a while, letting the steam soothe the skin on his face, then made a brew, delighting in the simplicity of this night.

The dead man had left a small stock of books but they were all in Japanese. Hidden amongst them Davis had found a suede-bound notebook. He had taken it to the hearth and studied it. It made little sense to him but was very beautiful, like a parchment of hieroglyphs. He decided he would take it with him and, one day, work out what they meant. For now, the only thing he could make sense of was that it was punctuated by dates and that the entries gradually became shorter and the writing less precise. Sitting by the firelight as it rippled over the pages, Davis wondered what enlightenment, if any, the diary might contain. After a while he drew a line under the place where the now deceased man had left off and wrote a new date in a different language, beginning a new thread where the old one had unwound.

THESE GODS

McCann took an instant dislike to the bland, clean buildings in square blocks and the American deal; the soulless malls, the locked windows and lack of any ventilation. Even the hotel lounge was stifling and he chose to sit on a stool at the bar rather than roasting on the plush chairs, which seemed to envelop him in heat when he sat in them. Nevertheless, McCann was feeling much better for a day of rest – he had slept, booked his plane ticket, bought some warmer clothes then slept again – and he ordered a beer, comforting himself with the thought of a second early night before meeting Fuso Tochimoto the next day for lunch.

As he sipped the light, refreshing lager he became aware of a presence by his right side and turned. The man standing next to him was a neat-looking individual of stocky stature who held a glass in a veined, muscular hand. The man dipped his head slightly.

"It would be great pleasure if you gave me the honour of a perch beside you."

McCann almost laughed. "Sure. Grab a pew."

"Let me introduce myself. My name is Sekiguchi."

McCann gave his pseudonym without really thinking about it – force of habit. It seemed to have almost become his real name, here in Japan.

The man took a seat and placed his whisky on the counter. He motioned delicately at McCann's beer. "Another, sir?"

"Alright for now."

"Where are you from, sir?"

"England."

"Ah," the man smiled broadly. McCann got ready for the expected follow-up questions, but the other continued his enquiries along different lines. "What do you say of our northern treasure, the city of Sapporo?"

"Well frankly, so far, not a lot. Modern, sterile, overheated. A soulless kind of city. But I must say, the ladies are immaculate." He looked over at the barmaid who had given him another smile, professional, no doubt, but a heart ticker all the same. She was slim and lithe and it was all cased where it went best, in a skin-tight purple cocktail dress.

"*So, ne*. Our city is a little soulless. Artificial. But then, does the opposite exist? Can there be an organic city?"

The man's expression was friendly; this was not a challenge but an invitation.

McCann smiled back at him, "Perhaps not, no. But some cities have a soul, and others don't."

"You might say the same about people. And modern people … most modern Japanese people lack the soul."

The two men paused, appraising each other.

"It was the money, sir. Corrupted us. May I smoke, sir?"

"Sure, mate, if I may." McCann took a good look at the man. Hair more pepper than salt was combed back over a narrow, deeply-lined forehead, below which the eyes shone blackly; they were still and unchanging whether he laughed or frowned.

"You can leave out the 'sir'. I have yet to be knighted. Call me George."

A pause. The smoke the man was exhaling was thick and acrid. "Okay, George. I am Tatsuo Sekiguchi. Please call me Tatsuo. But … maybe a little tricky for you to pronounce?"

"Tatuo? Like Tattoo-o?" McCann smiled but the man didn't.

"It is easy, George, if you make a little effort. Tat-su-o."

"Tatsuo?"

"Good, George."

McCann watched the man finish then light up another of his cigarettes. It was short and stubby, like him. "Well, what can I get you, Tatsuo?"

"No, no. You are guest, so please let me buy. It is our way." He motioned to the barmaid.

"Do you know *shouchu*?"

"I believe I do. It's the sweet cocktail that comes in cans and gives you brain damage, right?"

Tatsuo raised his eyebrows in dismay. "You mean the *Chu-hi*? No, no, George. That is what you say, hooch, not real *shouchu*. Please indulge me to treat you to a real *shouchu*. On the rocks."

The barmaid came over, he ordered and she asked him something.

He answered, "*Imo*," turned to McCann and leaned back on his stool. "Sweet potato, the best *shouchu*. It summons the scents of old Japan. One can feel the armour of the warrior moving through the marshes."

There was a brief silence, then the man burst out laughing and McCann laughed with him, though he wasn't entirely sure why. The drinks arrived.

"Well, I don't know about modern Japan, but I suppose old Japan had lots of soul. Tell me about old Japan, Tatsuo." McCann felt good: the barmaid was regarding him, and he liked this oddball in the elegant suit and the hard eyes that shone from the bronze-skinned face, creased in all the right places.

"Please wait. I am not yet finished on our modern Japan, George. Patience is what the English call a virtue, true? We Japanese believe we still have it, but we are mistaken. What we have is deadness. Patience is a virtue of life, not death. Patience is watching and waiting for opportunity, deadness is just waiting for oblivion. It is all part of the sterility that is spreading its germless, infertile plain across Japan." He paused, looking pleased with his words. "And our religion."

"Your religion? What religion do you mean?"

Tatsuo looked sternly at him. "Our Japanese religion, George. Our gods are animals transformed into mythical figures."

"Ah, I've heard of that," said McCann. "It's called Shinto, isn't it?"

"No, George, not Shinto." He paused and looked forlornly at McCann. "It is called Disneyland." He exploded into laughter again and it was almost maniacal, expressing itself as a wicked accusation, a curse on stupidity. "Soon Japan will be just a shopping mall, and not Japan at all."

"You could say the same about any country. Nothing stands still, change gradually comes."

Sekiguchi ignored McCann's platitude, rolling the ice gently round in his glass, exuding a kind of power and control over the conversation. "Everything dies, but there is a right way and a feeble way to live, is there not? Take my hand, for example. This is a dying hand and a living hand, George."

He called to the barmaid and she came over, clattering along, doll-like in her heels. He asked for her hand and placed it beside his own. The creature watched with a nervy, puzzled expression but she didn't resist.

"Look you, George, at the difference. This is the hand

206

of a living doll that does all it can to hide its essence. Look at the nails, shaped and painted, touch the skin softened by cream, protected from elements by gloves."

He placed McCann's hand on top of the girl's. She looked with growing dismay at Sekiguchi. "Now, note my own hand once again." His eyes were shining with a benign, jovial madness, and he broke the spell with a gesture to the girl, who slipped her hand out from underneath McCann's. McCann, bewildered, switched his attention to the watch on Sekiguchi's wrist, a bulky Bulgari, the pendant of a wealthy man.

"This hand is alive, George, but I do not hide that it is dying. These days, everybody is trying to live forever and in doing so, not really living at all. Happy families, safety lives, this comfort zone…"

"My uncle would agree with you."

Tatsuo looked closely at McCann. "Agree with what?"

"My Uncle Ricky used to say that. A safe life is a life not lived."

Sekiguchi nodded, "A wise man. I want to meet him."

"Bit difficult, Tatsuo. He's dead. Didn't even make it to fifty, actually."

"Dead is okay, George. Good. All life is transient. Accept death, we can live. Life is sad, but beautiful sad."

He looked at his glass, swirling the ice a little. "*Wabi* is needing little, a contentment with aloneness. *Sabi* is the completeness of the incomplete, the perfection of the imperfect. These ideas are old Japan. But modern Japan is not worth the shit, George. Not worth the shit… Toilet time." He stood up and walked stiff-backed to the bathroom. The barmaid and McCann exchanged glances. McCann shrugged and smiled. He knew which hands he would rather hold, not to mention be held by.

When Sekiguchi returned he looked hard at his watch.

"The night is running down. Are you in the city long, George?"

"I'm really not sure. I'm … it depends on a few things. I may be leaving tomorrow. Or maybe the day after."

"You are going to…?"

"Like I say, I'm not actually sure at this point. Meeting a friend and then…" He shrugged his shoulders.

Tatsuo looked concerned. "But if you do not stay in Sapporo you will need more pleasant entertaining to make better memories than this. Have you heard of Susukino?"

"Yeah, in the guidebook."

"I will take you. My treat. It is fun time."

Sekiguchi paid for the drinks before McCann had a chance to offer and led him out of the hotel. "We go to The Princess' Slipper. This is kind of gentleman's club. You have this in England, I think, for smoking the cigar, talking to the sexy lady and discussion of the world topic?"

McCann blinked at the man. He had no idea how to respond, but Sekiguchi was chattering away happily, occasionally touching McCann lightly on the arm as he led him through another neon-lit city, the tree-lined streets this time wider and straighter than he had experienced in Tokyo and embellished with row upon row of parked bicycles. After a few turns they came upon a discreet entrance and Sekiguchi led the way upstairs, where they were greeted by a smiling, older lady in a resplendent midnight blue *kimono*, then led to a table by a man in a tuxedo. The lighting was of fractured crystal and kept enough of the shadows safe while illuminating what shone to full effect. McCann caught glimpses of eyes enhanced with make-up, high heels, propped-up cleavages and lean but perfect curves.

Sekiguchi flopped down casually and smiled, "The nice place, the relax time. We will drink Hibiki, George.

You know this? I think the best whisky in Japan." He raised a finger to emphasise the point, "It wins many awards now."

Immediately they were joined by two ladies; the one next to Sekiguchi, a young and very dumb-looking girl attired in a party dress, with a mane of dyed bronze hair, knotted and waved into a kind of Japanese beehive; the one beside McCann looked a few years older, just as alluring and a few brain cells better off.

Sekiguchi spoke to the girls; there were precise smiles and formalities and soon the whisky bottle was on the table, with glasses and an ice bucket. The women made great play of pouring for the two men, politely accepting the drinks Sekiguchi offered them and then each turning to focus attention on their designated companion. McCann's company, who introduced herself as Aoi as she flicked her hair away and pursed her lips, had a smattering of English and manfully led the conversation, albeit down familiar alleyways.

Introductions and pleasantries exhausted, she rubbed his knee and told him confidentially, "I will have new job soon. I open fashion shop for hostess wear. Just like Yuri Saki. You know her?"

McCann nodded, "Yeah, I know her." Wasn't hard to imagine who she was.

"Now huge rich. Five million dollars a year. How many dollars do you make?"

"I make pounds."

"Pounds? What mean?"

"Money. Different kind of money."

"They are better than dollars?"

"Oh, yeah."

Aoi let out a throaty laugh. Not much of a princess really, thought McCann. He asked her how she had got into the hostess business.

"Well, men treat you like princess and you dress every night for the ball. They buy you present. Like this." She pointed to a shining three stone diamond on her long middle finger. "So nice isn't it? Can you buy me present and make me your princess?"

The conversation rumbled on for a few minutes more but they were interrupted by Sekiguchi's authoritative voice. Immediately the girls rose, bowed in a docile fashion and moved away as he beckoned to the man in the tuxedo and spoke quietly with him, then turned back to McCann.

"Rotation style, George." Then he leant across the table conspiratorially, "And those girls were not interesting. It is most important that the girls understand the art of make conversation. Those two…" he shook his head like an emperor passing judgment. "I have explained that we are gentlemen and you are an important guest in our city of Sapporo. I think maybe he understand my point of view now."

This time three girls attended to them. They were all introduced and immediately more whisky appeared in large, crystal tumblers. Two of them, Mizuki and Risa, paired off with Sekiguchi while the third, Nami, a plumpish but very pretty girl, sat beside McCann and started talking with him. He found his eyes irresistibly wandering from her beautiful neckline to the low cut of her dress and the pendular breasts under it, and back up again.

Like Sekiguchi, she spoke English very well and something about her unaffected manner attracted him. When she said she was an artist he encouraged her to tell him more. She talked about her own painting first, then said her favourite painter was Frank Auerbach. McCann had never heard of him, so she talked about Lucian Freud instead, and he had heard of him. She said she admired his theories about painting but was not so taken with his actual work; it was slightly tiresome and repetitive. He didn't know much about art but thought the Lucian Freud nudes he had seen were ugly. She smiled he was probably right, told him he looked a bit like Jackson Pollock and asked him which painters he liked.

"Oh, you know, I don't know much. Probably traditional stuff like Cézanne and van Gogh. Not very interesting, I'm afraid."

She looked tenderly at him and said there couldn't be a less traditional or more interesting painter than van Gogh. She was holding his hand and massaging it in a very sensual way. "Next time I'll bring some photos of paintings and show them to you, and we can talk about them. Maybe you'll find something you like…"

He smiled radiantly at her. "I'm sure I'll find something I like…"

The conversation continued effortlessly for fifteen minutes. He was relaxed and enjoying himself but eventually felt compelled to ask, "Nami, forgive me for saying so, but isn't this a strange job for an artist to be doing? Working here?"

"Not at all. It is a perfect *arubaito* for an artist. I cannot eat my paints. I need money to be able to continue with my work and this job is perfect. I spend a lot of time by myself when I am painting, but I like people. Here I can talk with people, enjoy their company, hear about many experiences and interesting stories. It is fun."

McCann didn't know what to say. Somehow he couldn't bring himself to broach the subject of the elephant in the room – what this job actually entailed – without destroying the edifice of the delicate, dreamy artificial wonderland that had been created. Not for the first time he was struck by what seemed to be a deeply confusing

211

ambiguity that wouldn't make sense in a Western country, but that appeared to be quite natural here. Eventually he couldn't resist digging a little deeper. "So you ... talk with the customers, and…"

Her eyes sparkled playfully. "… and …?"

He smiled. At himself, at his own embarrassment and at the bizarre situation he found himself in. "And what happens after you finish talking?"

Nami gave his hand a tight little squeeze then let go of it and threw her head back in obvious glee. "George! You naughty boy! Mmmm, there are many things about Japan that you don't yet understand."

His head was spinning. He was being given the runaround, he knew it, and he was loving every minute of it. His crotch ached gently and he felt a hole in the pit of his stomach.

Just then the other two girls got up and left and Sekiguchi's voice broke in again, first in Japanese then in English, addressing McCann, "Okay, it getting late. Time for the main event! Mizuki and Risa have gone to get ready."

Sekiguchi spoke briefly with Nami, who also stood up. She leaned over McCann, who raised his head and started to lift himself off the leather sofa towards the contour and swerve of her luxurious body, but she motioned to him to stay seated and squeezed him by the hand again, whispering, "So, enjoy your night." She turned and slipped out of the room.

Then McCann was being led out the door and down the steps again. The cold air hit him and he was walking with Sekiguchi, Mizuki and Risa. He tried to offer Sekiguchi money to settle the bill in The Princess' Slipper but the other seemed offended, almost embarrassed, and was so insistent in his refusal that McCann quickly abandoned his efforts.

212

"Next place not far, George. Just two blocks." He giggled and nudged McCann in the ribs. It was a surprisingly hard dig. "Funny chatting with Mizuki and Risa, George! I talk about my favourite kinky thing. I am secretary-type with spanker. How about you?"

McCann felt himself blush in the chill night and thought sadly of Nami. What the hell was going on here? He felt his morality slip anchor and drift freely in an unknown sea. What was he supposed to say? What was he supposed to expect would happen next?

"Ummm, I suppose I'm a heels and stockings man. Without the spanker."

Sekiguchi, in upbeat mood, motioned at the girls walking in front of them. "It's fun, with the girls, is it? Ah, okay, we are here! Time for the big event – climax! Let's sing karaoke together!"

THE EMPTY ORCHESTRA

They stood in the lobby waiting for Risa to organize the karaoke box. She led them up to the second floor and along a corridor punctuated on both sides by grey frosted glass doors through which an aggregation of sounds emanated: melancholy folk songs, floating ballads, energetic shouting, occasional bursts of cheering and clapping. Eventually she showed them into a small, square, windowless room that had a large video screen on the far wall, tables set in a semi-circle and cushion-covered seats laid out round them. On the tables were three large books like telephone directories, a drinks menu, and four microphones.

McCann, still unsure of what exactly was about to happen and what he wanted to happen, saw the mics and decided he would need more alcoholic support to handle this. The girls busied themselves and seemed ready to get started immediately, but Sekiguchi held up his hand. "Wait. Let me explain George the system."

He turned to McCann, "Okay, George, this is your first time to sing the song with friends and ladies. I explain it all to you."

McCann's whole body was tingling with frustration and confusion. "Can we order drinks first, Tatsuo?"

"Of course! Pardon me."

They decided on their cups and Mizuki ordered for them from a phone attached to the wall. Sekiguchi picked up one of the telephone directories, turned it towards

214

McCann and leafed through it, stopping randomly at various points that he indicated with those large, powerful hands of his. "This is the English menu and it is Alpha-based. Many of the songs of the English canon are here: all the greats, George! Please watching: Aerosmith, Backstreet Boys, Clapton, Kenny Rogers and so on. Who do you like to sing?"

As Sekiguchi handed the songbook to McCann the room suddenly filled with music and he looked up. Mizuki and Risa stood side by side and began a duet, a high-tempo J-Pop number with a saccharine-laced nursery rhyme melody. On the screen the lyrics danced across footage of a couple walking hand-in-hand in a picturesque park raining with cherry blossoms. Swaying together in time and pitch perfect, the girls made an alluring sight as the tune weaved merrily along its insignificant path. When the number was over, some kind of score, a rating of how well they had sung, appeared on screen, and the girls chirped and giggled, pronouncing their own satisfaction with their efforts.

"Nice, isn't it, George-san? It is their *juhachiban*, their speciality song… Okay, attention please. This is the English menu. It is Alpha-based. Who do you sing?"

McCann shrugged uncomfortably and took another slug on his drink, "I don't have much of a voice. Can't I just listen to you?"

The grip he felt on his wrist was over-firm. "George, we all must sing. It is a modern Japanese tradition. One that I care for. It is like a refresh button. Look, the Beatles. How you say about *Hey Jude* or *The Garden Undersea with Octopus?*"

Smiling and nodding, McCann considered the latter; Ringo singing a simple tune in the narrowest of note ranges – he could probably manage that. More drinks came: the room filled with sound again and the screen showed a group of young people leaping around, manifesting happiness under a snow-capped Mount Fuji. This time Risa sang alone and her voice rang with assonance and melody as she moved gently to some anodyne pop ballad. Sekiguchi, his eyes closed, quietly sang along at times. At the end of the song Risa bowed and everyone clapped.

"Nice performance, is it, George? Do the girls in England make the song so sweet?"

McCann mumbled something clichéd in reply; he was preoccupied, flicking through the lists of English songs, looking for something that wouldn't entirely embarrass him. He saw *If* by Telly Savalas and briefly considered it. A talkie might be the answer. He turned back looking for *Wandering Star* by Lee Marvin, but it wasn't listed. Then he saw something: Gerry Rafferty, *Get it Right Next Time*. He used to sing that one in the shower, and sometimes while walking along the side of the old canal by his house, donkey's years ago.

He took a good slug of whatever was in his glass and prepared for his debut. Laying the songbook aside and looking up, he saw that Mizuki and Tatsuo were holding their mikes and gazing at each other with a mimed tenderness. A title appeared, and the screen switched to a silver-haired Japanese couple walking along a Hawaiian beach at sunset, gesturing at the sky and the waves. They were dressed in matching aloha shirts. The tune this time wasn't poppy but something more melodramatic. Sekiguchi had a powerful voice and, like the girls, he could more than hold a note. He was also quite a performer, at times pressing his fist against his heart and looking at Mizuki as if he was about to break down sobbing. As the song came to an end McCann realized that his own knees

216

were trembling. He clapped enthusiastically along with Risa and then felt all three sets of eyes fall on him.

He explained to Mizuki what song he had chosen and stood up, like one waiting to be executed, as she punched in the number and it popped up on the screen. When the hail of bullets came he began to sing along to their tune, the lyrics about a man confused by life seeming more apt to him now than ever. The first verse finished and he felt his body gently responding to the rhythm. He looked at his audience and it was a happy one. Sekiguchi seemed a little bemused but was clapping along with the girls. Buoyed by the smiles he continued and realised he was beginning to enjoy himself.

Now, for each chorus of 'Next time' McCann pointed his index finger individually at the audience, and Sekiguchi and the girls laughed and raised their glasses. The song continued and he really allowed himself to relax, dancing round the little room as the saxophone played, even hauling Mizuki onto her feet for a quick tango. As his confidence grew the clapping of the other two became stronger. When the song was over he was sorry to put down the mic, but bounced back to his seat and grabbed the book again, flicking through its bizarre alphabetical snapshot history of Western pop music: good, bad and very ugly. Between the Righteous Brothers and Right Said Fred he turned to Sekiguchi and grinned, "Jesus, I enjoyed that, Tatsuo!"

"I can see that, George. Sing the song! It is good for the soul!"

And for the next forty-five minutes all four of them took it in turns to get up and perform; sometimes solos, sometimes duets, the girls and Sekiguchi doing Japanese songs, McCann becoming gradually more self-assured with the Western numbers.

Finally, during a brief lull Sekiguchi looked at his watch and said something to the girls in Japanese, then addressed McCann with a strangely intense look in his eyes. It was hard to tell what the emotion was, whether sad or happy, but whatever it was McCann felt it. "Next time we might all sing again. But … time is short." There was an unmistakable flicker of desolation in those dark, compelling eyes. McCann looked away.

Risa began searching for a song and Mizuki came over and poured more drinks for the men. McCann thanked her, drank from his and then looked back at Sekiguchi, but the other's face had an inquisitive look now and his mood had instantaneously lightened.

"Do you know Freddie?"

"Freddie?"

"You must know? The tough guy with the hair above his lip, the moustache, and the fur on the chest. He sings of heroic things."

"Freddie Mercury?"

"Precisely, George! A man's man. He sings before death, he sings with death. All Japanese love Freddie and his song of rhapsody. I sing for his memory."

"*Bohemian Rhapsody?*"

"Yes! I sing it for you, for the girls, and for me. It is even better than the Puccini." Sekiguchi took off his jacket and handed it to Mizuki, then removed his tie and threaded it through the lapels of the jacket. All three of them looked on intently, like interested students watching a teacher set up a science experiment, as he placed the jacket over his shoulders, knotted it round his neck with the tie and pronounced boldly, "My cape!" Then, as the song appeared on screen he leapt onto the table, raised his head to the Formica heavens, and with a flourish worthy of an operetta, began to sing of real life and fantasy, landslides

218

and reality. Ignoring the video screen featuring youths riding bicycles down floral country lanes, he dropped to one knee and sang directly to his stunned audience with the same glare of chilling fervour that McCann had witnessed a minute before. For a moment it was possible to believe that Sekiguchi had just pulled his trigger and killed a man.

It was a performance not so much of skillful or even powerful singing as of pure, raw emotion, the very spirit of the man pulling himself and all the others with him, away from this room of artificiality, reducing McCann to slack-jawed wonder. It was like Sekiguchi was speaking in tongues, and the silhouette-o, scaramouche and fandangos rolled through him effortlessly, like he was nothing more than a conductor of sound waves, until he let out a shrill possessed scream of "*Galileo!*" and the other three found themselves joining in, "*Magnifico!*"

Then as the guitars wailed Sekiguchi rose up again and, swinging the mic, broke into a dervish dance, wildly spinning his taut body around the table top and stomping his foot like a furious flamenco dancer, spitting the words and throwing down his cloak. His face gleamed with sweat and passion.

The finale was hushed, post-orgasmic, the little death.

There was silence in the room for a long time, and McCann realised he was swaying with inebriation and emotion. At last, Sekiguchi got up and there was a hesitant, almost embarrassed clapping. He gave a small bow. "Please stop now. Let there be quiet. Silence for Freddie."

Mizuki put the jacket round his shoulders again and handed him his tie, and together they shuffled and tottered out of the room.

THE ROOM AT THE
SHERATON

Fuso Tochimoto permitted herself a suite on the
twentieth floor, overlooking the city and Mount
Moiwa as well as an aerial view of concrete high-rises
leveling to a criss-cross of streets. She could see Orion's
Belt and The Plough above the lights of the city as she
refilled her glass from the small bottle of Riesling in the
ice bucket on the bedside table. The journey to Sapporo
had been delightful; the train had moved through each
segment of the day with a meditative motion.

What to make of this foreigner she would meet
tomorrow? She hadn't decided what to do about him yet.
She had dropped Charlie at the cabin thinking that was
the end of it and he would soon tire of the wilderness,
at least when the cold came. She knew he was in some
kind of trouble and naturally he could hole up with her.
The thought wasn't disagreeable in itself, but if he was
in serious danger, as the man on the phone had said, she
couldn't just leave him out there on his own. For a woman
disinclined to get involved in matters outside of herself,
this was an inconvenience. Over time she had slid away
from concerns, cutting off her emotional links with people
and separating herself from the risks such associations
posed to her equilibrium.

After her divorce her brother had advised her to return
to the family home in Hokkaido. She had also bought a
small apartment near Tokyo with her divorce settlement
and now divided her time between both places. She was

grateful to her brother for suggesting she get away from the increasing madness of a city addicted to sterility and benign, ignorant self-destruction, and to find out if there was anything left of herself that wasn't artificial and expendable.

At first she had been bored, alone in the empty house in Abashiri, smoking too much, unable to cope with time freed from structure, and angry that a vision had again come to nothing. But slowly a rhythm and pattern had taken over without her consciously realising it. In the absence of employment or duty she was able to cast off the clock and develop a routine more akin to how the world really moved. In the pre-morning she would wait for the day to usher out the dark, then she would dress and drive out at first light to the beach, taking in the coastline on the way. She swam regularly in a light wetsuit which cut out the deepest chill but allowed the awakening shock of immersion in a cold sea. Floating on her back below the sky, she felt lifted and carried by life and sensed a distance from the unhappy woman she had once been.

At night, too, she would drive to one cove or another, wrapped up against the cold, and let the sound of the waves fill and inhabit her, clearing away all she had been before, that tense, competitive urbanite. In its place there was repose and something that had been shut out for decades which filled a space with light.

On the wall of her house she hung a poem from *The Pillow Book* that read—

> *The sake is cold*
> *Because my torment*
> *Makes me inefficient.*
> *There is such a thing as grief,*
> *Such a thing as*
> *Being shut in.*

Or such a thing as being shut out. She had flitted between both most of her adult life. A plane passed close to the window. She sat and surveyed the hotel room, pastel walls adorned with two tasteless paintings. She unhooked them and placed them in the wardrobe, then turned on the TV and lit a cigarette.

DAY THREE – Nov. 2ND

*A*pparently there are owls here – Blakiston's fish owl. Most active at dawn and dusk. Have yet to see one. What a place this is! Habitat inland pristine. I feel like a bit of an intruder. So far have kept to the exteriors. Heard there is a real danger from bears in the thicker foliage. (Unlikely?)

Last night slept early but woke early too. In bed snug by the fire embers, warmth lapping over me. But no Yukari to share it. How my daubed lovebird would hate it here! Wish she'd been here last night. Her memory stayed with me all night & all this day.

Morning at dawn watched a sandpiper bobbing its small head in search of invertebrates. It was you, my fine-limbed wader.

You had stayed close to the domains of my tides right enough. Where are you today? Wonder what will become of you when the costume comes off, the exposure begins, the walls start to close in. That is what they do to you. Wall you up and lock the door.

But out here there are no walls.

> Silver maps with wings so sharp on
> delicate swords of silence:
> The sand piper, with a voice of dream;
> curves over darkened water. That senses
> And stops

This place has no distractions. No books, no TV, no twittering.

Just this dead man's journal...

The trick with the harpoon seems to be to swivel it slightly in the palm before throwing and to follow through to the apex. Difficult but getting better at it. A surprisingly sharp and dangerous fucker. Using driftwood as floating targets. Now managing to retrieve most for burning later.

PREY AND MANTIS

He woke with a start to a ringing telephone. Struggling out of the muddled bed he glanced at his watch and realised it was almost midday. It was the Tochimoto woman calling him, but her voice was so indistinct he could barely hear her.

"Sorry, could you speak up a bit, please? I didn't catch that."

Suddenly the voice came through clearly, almost aggressively, "Tobu Hotel. I am in the garden. Waiting."

"Ah, shit. I'm sorry. Give me fifteen minutes."

A pause. "Maybe."

McCann jumped into the shower and was done and dressed in less than ten minutes and checking out five after that. The receptionist hailed him a taxi. It was a short ride and he bustled through the lobby, blundering into the garden in a sweat, already out of kilter for the task ahead.

Nobody was there.

Cursing aloud he rubbed his neck, got his breath back and took a seat, then fumbled for his PHS phone and dialed her number. A waiter appeared and offered him a menu. The phone rang and rang. No answer. He took off his jacket: the midday sun was a little too warm. As he started fanning himself with the large menu, a tall, elegant lady in a lime green summer dress came out of the building and passed him without a look, seating herself at the opposite end of the garden. McCann looked over and smiled, then waved, but to no avail. Tired of feeling like an idiot, he got up and strode over to the table.

"Excuse me, would you be Ms Tochimoto?"

She looked up at him and nodded once in mute confirmation. She was wearing a white surgical mask and all he could see of her face were dark eyes that darted and dashed below pencilled eyebrows.

"I'm George Peters. Sorry I'm a bit late. Hope I didn't keep you waiting too long." He extended his hand, which she ignored, offering instead another nod of acknowledgement. He gestured to the spare seat. "May I?"

She didn't respond to that so he seated himself. Attempting to break the ice he smiled, "You worried about pollution, Ms Tochimoto? I mean the mask and that." She glared at him and in the sunlight he thought there was a blue tint to her eyes, almost Prussian blue, or darker.

"Mainly it is to protect from germs. I do not wish to catch a cold."

He nodded. "I see. Germs. Can't be too careful."

She pulled the mask down from her face and let it rest below her chin. A pink box of cigarettes appeared from her bag and she placed one, long and slim, in her mouth.

"Let me."

She smiled as he leaned over the table, then blew a long plume of blue smoke towards him. It was a dramatic face, with the smooth coating of pale foundation he had seen on many of the women here, although in her case it might have been her natural skin. Her body was lean, well-formed; the way she smoked was mannered and affected. She had an effect on him alright, but it was intimidating as well as interesting and there was something about her that made him feel like an oaf. He stumbled on, a bull in a china shop.

"Thank you for agreeing to see me. You probably have no idea how important this is … Davis, I mean Charlie, is he okay, have you seen him?"

She smiled and then half laughing said, "I'm sure he's the same as ever. Never changes."

"When did you last see him?"

She didn't respond, just sat looking at McCann.

"You've been in touch with Charlie recently, right? That's not necessarily a good idea, Ms Tochimoto. The boy is a danger zone. The sooner we get him away and out of here the safer we will all be. Particularly you."

He was still sweating and repeatedly wiping his brow.

She looked at him with an icy contempt. "Safer? I don't want to be safer."

"Do you want to be hurt?"

She shrugged and smiled, "It depends on how. Right now … I would like a drink." McCann looked around and, seeing no service staff, got up, brought over the menu from his table and gave it to her, then went in to the bar. He returned with a waiter in tow and sat back down. "Are you having something to eat as well?"

"Just a drink for me, thank you." She scanned the menu with her blue-black eyes, her tapered fingers flicking across the wine list then stopping. "A glass of the Roccaperciata." She glanced up at McCann. "Maybe you would like something to make you relax? A whisky perhaps?"

"The same as you will be fine, I think."

She smiled at the waiter and ordered, and he departed with a bow.

"So, how long you have been here in the city?"

"I got here last night."

"You … seem to have had a good night."

McCann felt himself redden before her knowing eyes. "Well, you know, a few too many drinks…"

She looked bored. "Please enjoy our country. There's much to enjoy. These days we cater for foreigners. Even the dumb waiters understand some English."

McCann smiled and rolled up his shirtsleeves. The waiter returned with their drinks. The wine shone like gold in the afternoon sun and they clinked glasses. It would have been nice to relax, to enjoy the presence of an intriguing woman and to let the afternoon languidly roll by in chatter, cultural chatter, any old natter except what had to be done. He quietly cursed his stupidity for having been sucked into yet another boozy night. His brain was fuzzy and knowing he was making a hash of everything he bumbled on like an imbecile.

"Ms Tochimoto … it's very important that I speak with Charlie. I have to tell you that he is in all sorts of trouble, and he may have … killed someone."

Her eyes widened and she beamed at him with obvious pleasure, "Really? How dramatic." McCann let out a sigh of exasperation as she continued, "Well, he is a man. Man should kill." Then she began to laugh. "That is what man used to do."

"Is it? Kill a woman?" He looked hard at her but she gazed steadily back, razor-sharp flint in her eyes.

"If necessary. Maybe … for love? But you know … what's your name again? Billy, isn't it?"

"George."

"You know Billy-George, woman kill man these days by making him not the man. You say … emasculation?" She seemed to smile luxuriously. "Kill with other methods…"

"Ms Tochimoto, we are not talking about social behaviour patterns here. We may be talking about murder."

"What is that? Charlie would only do what he had to for everybody. My antennae show me he is a real man."

"Your what?"

"My antennae. My sense."

"What is that, like a sixth sense? A woman's intuition?"

"Maybe, yes. My animal tuition tells me he would kill man, not woman. I know." "Well, it looks like he killed a woman."

"Looks like? You look like too. Big, old, bitter Billy-George."

She laughed and McCann, despite himself, laughed too. Try another angle, he thought. Take a deep breath, change tact. Rescue the situation; she's making mincemeat of you.

"I bet you could kill a man, Ms Tochimoto. Probably quite sweetly."

"Oh, yes, that is woman duty. But now I am old woman. Past times."

"You are an elegant mature lady and there are future times."

"There are no future times."

McCann laughed. "You could be right there. I sometimes think so too."

"You sometimes think so. Think so. Thinking…" She looked blankly at him. "My brother liked thinking. He worked at Keio."

"Oh? What's Keio?"

"Keio University. Always thinking. Teacher thinking. Finally, he was happy when he stopped thinking."

"How did he do that?"

"By throwing it away. Stop thinking. The mind is not for thinking."

She lit up, herself this time, and dropped the lighter heavily onto the table, gazing through him. "He began to live as he was dying, each day an eternity, every moment a reality. Maybe then he became Japanese."

She looked away for a few seconds, like an animal checking the breeze for scents, then rose from the table, silently mouthed 'rest room' and walked across the patio into the hotel, leaving her Gucci bag languishing on the table alongside her phone and wallet. He couldn't help but notice the grace of her movements and the confidence of her elegance as she drifted away in that cotton dress. She certainly was a head spinner, a right unnecessary distraction.

While she was gone he took the opportunity to tidy himself up a bit and try to regain some poise. You couldn't have started off worse; you're all twisted up like a pretzel, so now all you can do is just give her the story. Leave out the girl at the club maybe, think of another excuse for the trouble, but mention the *yakuza*. He thought of them again and broke out in a new sweat. Just get this done with and get out of here. She came back with the waiter and a different vibe; he knew she could turn it on and off like a tap.

"Billy, I ordered a bottle of champagne. My treat. Let's both relax a little. I am so happy you paid for my trip to Sapporo. I had a lovely journey. Thank you so much."

"My pleasure, Ms Tochimoto."

"Please call me Fuso. We do not need to be too formal, do we, Billy-George?" Champagne: just what he needed. Sitting in a hotel garden sipping bubbly on an empty stomach as the clock ticked, trying to forget what happened the last time he drank a glass of champagne... The waiter uncorked the bottle and poured a little in each glass, but Fuso took the bottle from him, waved him away and liberally topped them up.

"A second cheers. *Salut.*"

"Yeah, bottoms up. Look, Fuso, I realise I haven't made the best of first impressions, and I haven't explained myself at all clearly. So please just let me fill you in on what's happened before you make your conclusions."

She looked hard at him. "Yes, why don't you? Who are you? And what do you want with me?"

230

"I am in Japan because of a job," McCann began, "A job that started off problematically enough, but is now an absolute nightmare. Charlie may be implicated in the death of a girl back in England. How much he is implicated, I'm not sure. That's what I'm here to find out. I need to talk with him. He may be completely innocent, then again he may not. But if you care about him, if you are interested in his welfare, you need to trust me and take me to him, because now he's in some serious trouble here in Japan, different trouble. There are some people who are looking for him and if they find him – and I think they will – I have no idea what they will do to him. But it won't be nice."

"What is this Japan trouble that you think he is in?"

"Not think. Know. He contacted you a few days ago, asked you to help him get away from Tokyo, didn't he?"

She didn't say anything.

"That's because – and I know this will probably sound ridiculous to you – he beat up a gangster, beat him up bad, and that gangster's friends are looking for him. And when they find him…" McCann paused, "So forgive me for my persistence and lack of charm, Ms Tochimoto, but time is not on our side. Please tell me how to find Charlie. Where is he?"

She was trying to appear unconcerned, but he knew she was listening and thinking seriously. "In his heart."

"Where's that?"

Her eyes narrowed. "What are you going to do? Do you want to kill him?"

He spluttered back, "Don't be ridiculous! Do I look like a hitman to you? I need to find him to talk to him. Just talk, that's all. There was a young woman back in England whose future was taken from her. Maybe it was just an accident. Maybe it was a bit more than that. I need to find out what Charlie knows about it. Or at least... Are you listening?"

Something had moved on the ground beside the table and Fuso leaned over to pick it up, cradling it in her hand like a delicate *origami* crane. "In Japanese we say *kamakiri*. In English?"

McCann stared at her. "A praying mantis. It's called a praying mantis."

"Interesting. What is it praying for?"

"Probably something to eat."

"Or to screw. Charlie taught me that word. I like it. Direct. He said making love was nonsense, not the real word."

The mantis moved across her hand, edging over the ledge of her crimson nail, then scurried back, assuming a fighting stance. Fuso examined it silently and then looked up, straight into McCann's eyes. There was a standoff for a few seconds.

"So ... what are you trying to tell me? That you and Charlie are some sort of item? You don't believe me when I say his life is in danger, and you're not willing to take me to him?"

She looked at him the way a cat regards a half-mangled mouse it has grown bored of. "Why, Mr. Peters, you ask such dull questions."

She deftly placed the insect back on the edge of the flower bed. He was about to speak but she cut him off with a sweep of a hand. "I am not an old lady yet, Mr. Peters. I like Charlie because he entertained me. In the French they say *divertissement*. I did not go to the English school for the language instruction. I did not go for cheap play with some handsome foreign boy. I go there to lose some time in a way less ... painful than I am losing it now."

"Wouldn't most people say the point of time isn't to

lose it but to preserve it, add meaning to it?"

Again she cut him off. "Time is now, Mr. Peters, and you are wasting mine."

She pulled another cigarette from the pack. He didn't bother offering to light it, but he did refill her glass, then sank back into his chair. He closed his eyes and felt the warm sun soothe him, and he could see nothing but the pink light behind his eyelids. He sat in silent luxury for a few minutes. When he opened his eyes she was staring at him. She uncrossed her legs and leaned forward across the table, placing her face close to his.

"Sin made him, that's why you don't like him. You haven't sinned have you? He is not a moral virgin like you."

McCann took a large glug of champagne. "What you mean is I have a moral compass and he doesn't. Not quite the same thing."

"You don't know the first thing about him. Not one thing."

He wondered about the bravado of her attitude and decided to call her bluff. There was something in her excessively aggressive attitude that suggested a kind of desperation.

"Fuso, I don't have time for this anymore. Either you are going to tell me where he is or you're not, and if you're not, then we have no reason to continue this conversation."

"Who do you think you are, coming here and making these demands of me? Charlie is my friend, you are here to cause him trouble, and yet you speak to me like I must take you to him, as if he needs your help."

'Roll the dice, George,' McCann thought to himself. 'Let's see how good your game is.'

"Well, you might be right there. I suppose it all comes

down to this – do you believe me when I say Charlie's in trouble, here in Japan? I would have thought that if he hasn't told you directly, his behaviour in the last few days would have made it pretty obvious that what I say is true. And then, if you do accept that, you have to ask yourself who would you rather found Charlie first – you and me, or an angry bunch of gangsters?"

She sighed and looked down at her watch. McCann admired the top of her head, the perfectly styled hair, thick and shining in the midday sun. Then she lifted her face and it was as if she had taken off a mask; the game was over.

"I told you about my brother. He had a cabin, log cabin, in the hills of Rasu. He died there. He stopped thinking about the logic and the pointless word tricks he did in the university. He refused all the medication but morphine, and went to that cabin to … meditate. Meditate on time left. I mean, he went into the moment. And he died there.

"I told this story to Charlie before, about a month ago. Charlie was deeply moved. A few days ago he came to me and says he has some trouble, and ask if he can use the cabin as a hide place, a refuge. I ask him what his trouble is, because he act very strange. He doesn't tell me, tries to play funny as he always does. But this is different, I know. I can tell. And he just says he needs to go to my brother's cabin, to stay for a while. We talk a little; he tells me he has trouble. So I agree that he can stay at the cabin. I took him there."

McCann nodded, trying to keep his expression neutral, and probably failing. "Now you need to take me there."

Fuso finished her champagne and replaced the mask over the bridge of her nose. Her face was hidden behind the veil once more but the eyes remained unmasked. "If he is in danger, we will go there today. I have booked the train to Abashiri. We have one hour and then we leave."

McCann was flabbergasted. He nodded, understanding nothing of this woman. "I understand. But you understand this. Your brother's cabin may not be a refuge anymore. I don't know. I do know I must see Davis."

Fuso nodded and rose from the table. "So. Please get your bags."

THE ART OF SHEDDING

Tatsuo Sekiguchi took breakfast at a small eatery, fifteen minutes walk from his hotel. The morning meal was important to him and he chose this location with care after rejecting many more convenient options for being, variously: too modern, too Western, too vulgar or too clean. He had a nose for what was just right, and although he had never entered this particular restaurant he slid open the old wooden door and stepped into the *genkan* confident of what he would find inside. He greeted his hosts with a quiet nod. The proprietors were older – a good sign – and the wife in particular was stooped, probably from years of manual field labour, but they seemed hale and sturdy like the traditional Japanese, not like the new finicky types with their fancy hair, toy dogs and plastic spouses.

The simplicity and authenticity of the restaurant reminded him of his childhood in the 50's, a time of great change and furious progress, an accelerated intravenous injection: frantic rebuilding and snowballing American influence. Japan and the West; such a complicated relationship! Like a teenage love affair: convoluted, heady, exhausting and impossible to ignore. Not that he minded the amalgamation *per se*. One couldn't live forever in the old ways. Life moved on, he accepted that. There was much to learn from other cultures. But the fundamentals mattered, should not be trifled with, have to be observed, or all will become meaningless.

He sat down at one of the functional tables and had the

briefest of dialogues with the wizened husband, who, he noted with satisfaction, knew almost instinctively what was required. He could already smell the fish cooking: *aji* – horse mackerel – split open and cleaned then grilled, served with boiled white rice, dried seaweed cut in easy-to-use square sheets, home-made pickles to bring out the flavor of the rice, and miso soup to finalize the subtle piquancy of the dish. On the side, a portion of *natto* – fermented soy beans.

His meal was brought on an old lacquered wooden tray and he ate it slowly, concentrating on the food and its simple but deep taste. Not for him the distractions of TV or newspaper while eating: one thing at a time and focus on it completely, no matter how simple the operation. This is the Japanese way; or at least, it used to be. A single brushstroke on *shodo* paper; a perfect form in *kendo*; the presentation of the *chawan* in the tea ceremony: such simple actions, yet so elusive to perfect when the spirit drifts and fails to focus on the empty purity of the moment. Sekiguchi smiled to himself as he chewed and thought about this focus – the clear, meditative concentration on absolute perfection of the simplest form, which is the mainstay of all the Japanese arts – and the fundamental, irrefutable truth of it. And now? In modern Japan? A world full of interruptions and disturbances; a world full of feeble, restless minds.

The food was served with good, earthy Japanese tea and he drank it in the same deliberate manner as he had eaten. In thirty minutes he was finished, and sat back as he lit up a cigarette, satisfied and replete. Almost ready for the day: just his toilet to attend to now. He finished smoking and stubbed the cigarette out, pursing his mouth distastefully as he thought of modern Japanese toilets: such a disappointment, a scandal; the full realization of

237

flabby Western aspirations – the lazy shit. Men no longer squatted on strong haunches to relieve the body into a clean hole in the ground, framed by stone or porcelain. No, they would be pampered like cripples: a button here, a knob there, press, stop, press, hot spray.

The imbecility of it; even turning on a tap to wash the hands was impossible now. Everything was controlled and done for you. But Sekiguchi was a man who liked to attend to matters directly with his hands. He scowled to himself again at the thought. Washlets! What has become of us, now softer than the Westerners? He stood up and headed towards the bathroom, observing with approval the ancient poster on the wall of a very young Masako Natsume, advertising soap. A real beauty, and – though no-one would dare say such a crass thing aloud – a beauty all the more appealing to the Japanese sensibility for the tragedy of her story.

He made to enter the toilet, but on dragging the venerable door open his heart sank. Smack in the middle of an otherwise dark and tastefully aesthetic bathroom, like an insolent gaudy god, pristine, gleaming and covered in buttons, the lavatory of the future faced him down with utter contempt. Growling to himself he clenched his buttocks, turned on his heel, paid for breakfast and marched back to his hotel.

🔣

Sekiguchi's was largely a spare, purgative existence. A typical evening was spent sitting on his *zabuton* cushion, chewing dried squid, complementing the taste with a glass of *nihonshu* from Niigata or Nagano, and punctuated by an occasional look out the window. He lived in a single, six *tatami* room that had a one-ring cooker and a small sink. It was enough: generally, indigence was his preferred state.

He had begun the art of shedding shortly after his dismissal from the Special Security Branch in Osaka. First, a paring of the flesh, cutting his weight to nothing but muscle; next, of his possessions; finally, of his wife and family. It wasn't a conscious decision to dissolve his old identity. It came like a command and he accepted it. After this process of reverse acquisition was complete, he had moved north to Tokyo and stayed there for so long that the years meant little. He lived alone and earned enough to meet his needs, as a part-time English teacher in a cram school, supplemented by the odd big assignment: the links with the underworld that had been established through his former job had been maintained and had kept him comfortably solvent over the years. He took few holidays and saw to his carnal needs through occasional transactions of commerce.

He was as self-contained as a clam inhaling and exhaling in his shell, pulsing steadily, needing little to distract him. The outside eye never bothered him, and this was his idea of luxury. His mother had bequeathed to him the property in which he had been brought up, a big house on a small island in the Inland Sea, between Honshu and Shikoku, and he went back on occasion to access himself, but never came to a conclusion. The large house made him feel vulnerable and after two days by the beach, nature wore him down. He had a limited tolerance for the pristine beauty of the place. It seemed to contain gods, and he wasn't in favour with them. On the other hand, he felt something more palatable wandering the streets of what was left of old Tokyo: Yotsuya, Asakusa, Kanda. The city was all about ghosts, and ghosts are different from gods. There he felt peace, in all its delicate simplicity.

Sekiguchi had an admiration for Japanese classical literature and a love of the philosophers of single-handed warfare. The greatest of these, Musashi Miyamoto, he admired the most. Of course Miyamoto's legacy had been disgracefully marred by idiotic TV dramas, and worst of all, had undergone a thorough and sacrilegious bastardising through the infantile form of the *manga* comic. Such is the state of the modern world. Miyamoto had been an expert in the use of throwing weapons, and in one or two of his early jobs Sekiguchi had even tried the same method, but had soon switched to the gun, being cleaner and more efficient, given the environs of his work.

Miyamoto's most famous manual, a beautiful and meditative work on the art of swordsmanship, *The Book Of Five Rings*, was indeed excellent, but Sekiguchi's favourite Miyamoto text, the *Dokkodo*, was less well known. *Dokkodo – The Way of Self Reliance*, or *The Way of Walking Alone*; somewhat out of kilter with the current crop of lame Japanese who couldn't do anything – including wiping their own arses – by themselves. He sighed quietly to himself; his country was literally going down the toilet.

⚏

Back at the hotel he grudgingly made use of its Western style latrine: at least it hadn't been fitted with a washlet. A nice start to the day had been hampered slightly and his mood had a dent in it now, an intrusion. He opened his attaché case and pulled out a genki drink from a side pocket, downing the small bottle in one, anticipating the mild buzz from the caffeine and ginger cocktail and feeling good about it. Then he lifted out a hard plastic case, opened it and picked out the Beretta.

He had been using the same model for over a decade and knew her like a lover.

He had honed his skills by taking gunmanship courses in the States. He had already been very handy from the Special Security Branch training but had wanted to learn more: a different environment, an alternative perspective. Those courses had been mere case studies; he had needed to extend his range on living matter. Hiring a camper van, he had headed off to the Rockies and perfected his skills there. First he had netted small game with the pistol, waiting at first light for the crepuscular fauna to reveal themselves. He had blown the heads off several rabbits, learnt to drop a variety of birds both on the wing and on the branch, and had once taken down a fox at run. Then he had moved on to more serious animals with more serious weapons; his greatest prize a moose, hit as it drank by the river, unaware of the assassin's presence, and shot accurately through the head from a distance of twenty metres. Over time, he discovered that he was marginally more comfortable killing people than animals.

He moved the Beretta around in his hands and worked the mechanism: click went the gun, satisfying his Japanese appreciation of precision manufacturing.

He felt more relaxed now and decided to perform a dress rehearsal. He prided himself on a clean job and his résumé was impeccable. The irresistible accumulation of details is what is important: the mental preparation, an essential part of the process. One of his favorite things about this occupation was the presentation and his only concession to luxury was in his work clothes, which were all of the finest quality and cut. To be sure, his footwear, a leather sports-type walking shoe, acquiesced style to practicality. It wasn't important for the feet to look elegant in his job, but it was vital that they were equipped to make a swift and silent departure. He liked what he saw when he dressed and stalked around the room practicing moves. It felt right, almost right, but something was off balance. He checked the gun and then felt a lightness to his left; too much lightness. He smiled and tutted to himself, walking to the bedside table. Picking up his Bulgari he attached it to his wrist and at once everything was in place. He was ready now. After visualising various gruesome scenarios, he undressed again, laid the outfit on the bed and smiled, replacing the gun in its container and then back in the attaché case. Satisfied, he decided it was time for ablutions and marched to the bathroom.

Removing the bristles from his face was a ritual and barely a day had gone by since his teenage years without him doing so. He used an old-style razor but had bowed to the superior quality of Braun shaving foam over soap and water. It left a smooth finish without chafing the skin. He shaved slowly and never hurried. Next, he attended to his fingers and palms, scrubbing them first and then soaking them in an alcohol solution, which he made himself, until they were as pure and sterile as a surgeon's. In a way that was what he was, a surgeon, but in reverse, taking away rather than giving life. Done, he turned on the shower and stepped in, closing the curtain with a sharp swish.

When the phone rang thirty-five minutes later he was ready for it, sitting straight-backed on the bed, staring silently through a fixed point on the far wall. He let it bark at him twice, then leant across and lifted the receiver on the third ring. "*Hai? Hai ... eh ... ii desu ... eh ... eh ... wakarimashita. Hai.*"

Replacing the handset very carefully, he closed his eyes and returned to his semi-meditative pose for a few minutes. Then he lifted himself from the bed, delved into the bag and pulled out a large, brown envelope. He

242

reacquainted himself with the contents: photos of the two men that his employer had given him. This young one he didn't like; clearly a punk who fancied himself. George … well, he would like to spare George but he couldn't. This job wasn't for the sentimental. They would both have to go, but he would make it clean and fast for George. At least Sekiguchi had presented him with a good time, had shown him a modicum of respect. The kid wouldn't have that. This Davis boy would hear the *Diamond Cutter Sutra* before his heart was blown away. He would hear his master's voice before departing.

Sekiguchi wondered about this hit. Highly unusual to be dealing with foreigners: from the first it had seemed like a very bad idea and potentially problematic. Etiquette demanded that Japanese relations with outsiders should be of extreme politeness, a deferential, surface friendliness, yet almost complete detachment on any deeper level. Everyone knew this; it was simply commonsense. A stranger is an unknown quantity and so must be respected but kept at arms' length. So Sekiguchi had initially tried to turn down this job, something he had never done before, and had only reluctantly accepted as a courtesy to his oldest and most senior contact man – in fact, he *couldn't* refuse. As usual, his background knowledge of the situation was very sketchy indeed, which was normally the way he liked it, but this time the exceptional nature of the case had compelled him to ask for at least some kind of basic outline of the problem.

He knew that the two had been in the wrong to begin with, being party to events that were entirely of a private nature and absolutely none of their business; that their presence had considerably complicated a delicate matter; that despite these indiscretions they had been made an extremely generous – not to mention unusually trusting

– offer as a solution, which had been refused in the most egregious fashion; and that neither would probably be missed. So much so, that if they were disappeared in a suitable manner there would be no more than a cursory investigation, a flapping of arms, a chasing of fireflies with a stick. Given all that, and the apparent urgency of the situation, he felt he couldn't very well refuse his sempai's request to deal with the situation.

The contacts at McCann's hotel had been very professional, as he had known they would be. The receptionist would inform Sekiguchi when McCann left, and the young lad would follow him and pass on updates on progress. He knew the Davis one was somewhere in the Hokkaido mountains and he knew George would lead him there. Then there was the woman. Unfortunate. She could complicate matters a little: but just a little.

SNAKEY

The train was half empty, the seats comfortable with ample legroom. They sat opposite each other, gazing across the space, smiling awkwardly. She seemed less assured now than she had been in the garden, but no less elegant. He said she looked great but had expected her to change into more practical clothes for a trip into a wintery landscape. She responded with a wintery smile, "Ladies in Japan do not often dress down in public."

McCann was invigorated by the prospect of the journey. He was on his way somewhere again, at least. No place certain, but he was getting used to that. He checked the map in the guidebook as the train pulled out of the station and made a soft sound to himself.

"So you live in this place, Shiretoko, then?"

"No, I live in Abashiri. This train's last stop."

He found it on the map.

"Famous for prison."

McCann laughed. "So you're a prisoner. That explains a lot!"

Her gaze was unblinking. "Not now. Yes, I knew prison. But not that one. Maybe worse."

He was still smiling, waiting for the punch line. "What kind of a prison was that then?"

"Arranged marriage, Billy-George."

For the first time he could see her vulnerability; see that she was at the turn which was taking her towards old age. Though beautiful, hers was not the brilliant glow of youth, more a gossamer spun of spirits and experiences that she would keep to herself and, in time, take into oblivion. When animated, her face was alight with mystery but when still, almost a death mask.

Some nervous reaction compelled him to ask a further question, which he immediately regretted. "That's surprising. So there is forced marriage in Japan?"

"No force. I was weak. That is all. It is past now, dead. All ashes."

She looked out of the window and he let the topic drop. McCann also fell into introspection. The train passed though the bland cityscape and into the countryside, more magnificent with every additional kilometre they progressed away from human habitation. They drank coffee from paper cups and as the remnants of the champagne wore off, sobriety kicked in.

"This cabin of your brother's. Did he live there all the time?"

She allowed herself a wistful smile. "No, no. He lived in Tokyo, surrounded by... busy life. Then he got a one-way ticket. From the doctor. But when he was told the news it seemed more like a prize than damnation. He threw away the nonsense that filled his life and focused on the essential."

She pointed at the landscape sweeping past in verdant greens, browns and blues.

"And he took himself to the wilderness. Without other people, naturally."

McCann nodded. "What about his job, family? The practical stuff. How did he deal with that?"

Fuso looked displeased and waved a hand as if dispelling some annoying flying insect. "Practicalities are the first thing the Japanese attend to. What do you say – from the cradle to the pyre, George? He fixed this

246

practical stuff, as you call it, and when he was done with that he could focus on..." she shrugged, "the end of his life." McCann looked down at his paper cup. One of his father's old adages popped into his head – 'Life is short; move slow.' They both looked out the window in silence, the pleasing rhythm of the train removing the need to fill the space with empty words. After a while Fuso spoke again. "At the end of the year he went up to the cabin for good. The coldest months were coming but he insisted that was the place he had to be. I was told I would know when to collect him. And there he was, on the bed."

"Was he … serene?"

"Serene? I do not know this word."

"Peaceful. Was he in peace?"

"Not at all. He looked puzzled."

"Puzzled?"

"Yes, like he had died with a complex thought."

"Death?"

"Death is not a complex thought."

The train was arriving at a small station. It came to a halt and she looked at him. "Ten minute stop. I smoke."

He went outside with her and the cold hit him, fresh and clean. It seemed almost obscene to smoke in it and he replaced his pack in his pocket. Instead, he walked back and forth along the platform, eyeing her as she stood wrapped in a mist of blue smoke in the mid-afternoon light and yet on the fringe of the twilight.

The woman pushing the refreshments trolley bowed as she entered the carriage, excused herself politely for troubling the passengers, and began to make her way down the aisle. Tatsuo Sekiguchi was relaxed, enjoying the pleasant journey. He smiled to himself as the train moved out of the station and back into the wild. When she came to him he ordered a small can of beer and a packet of dried squid, then pulled a baseball cap down low over his face, put in his earphones and closed his eyes, delighting in the voice of Hibari Misora singing *Kawa no Nagare no yo ni*. He began to tap his foot.

The woman continued down the train with the refreshments trolley. McCann ordered some snacks and another coffee. Fuso had mentioned a few things about her brother's funeral ceremony but McCann got confused about Buddhist and Shinto and it became complicated. He was trying to follow her but couldn't pin down exactly what she wanted to say.

"Maybe for you, our Shinto spirituality is confusing. Perhaps it is easiest for you to think of it as being like your country before the Christians came, a kind of paganism. Of course, your Christians came to Japan. They went everywhere, didn't they? But it was … a little difficult for them. They caused trouble for the *kampaku*, Toyotomi Hideyoshi."

"*Kampaku?*"

Fuso waved her hand impatiently again, "The ruler of Japan, under the Emperor. So those troublesome Christians, they were killed in the style of their Jesus. How do you say? On the cross."

"Crucified?"

"Certainly. Crucified. Perhaps it was good for them, to go with their leader that way.

An honour?"

McCann nodded uncertainly. "Mmmm. Perhaps."

He took another sip of his sugary coffee as Fuso continued. "Japanese spirituality is not like the Christian. There are gods in everything: in rocks, rivers, trees, animals. Everything. But these gods do not necessarily represent good things and bad things. They are not ... absolute like in your culture."

"So what do they represent then?"

"Only themselves."

"They don't have any moral substance? But there must be some kind of meaning. If you have a Shinto religion, it must have values."

"Shinto is not religion. It is more like a ... system of rituals. In Japan, our rituals are very important. Maybe the rituals are more important than the ideas behind them."

"But you pray to these Shinto gods for ... what, some kind of purification?"

"Mmmm, there is some truth in that, but not exactly. Sorry, my English is not clear. I think it is difficult to explain. Shinto is both more and less than a religion."

McCann laughed. "More and less! That's a good one – very mysterious."

She looked a little hurt. "I think it is very difficult to explain to you."

They were silent for a few minutes. McCann, used to knowing when to speak and when not to, left her alone with her thoughts; he felt she wasn't finished yet.

"When I was around five or six years old, I remember playing one day, with my brother Shinichi, near the river where we used to live. I remember it was a beautiful day in early summer, when the leaves have just opened. They are a wonderful, bright, lime green colour. You should come to Hokkaido in early summer, Billy George, it is good for you. So beautiful. This green colour I remember clearly. I was playing with some small stones, trying to put them on top of each other." She laughed, "My world was very small then! Shinichi shouted at me to come quickly, see what he had found. I ran over to him. He had a strange, bright look in his eyes. He was holding a big stone. I was a little scared, but he whispered just one word: 'Look!' and I followed his eyes and there I saw a snake, a brown-coloured snake."

McCann raised his eyebrows. "Poisonous?"

Fuso shook her head. "No, not poisonous. In Japanese we call it *shimahebi*. I do not know the English word. It was not so big, and it was warming up in the sun. We moved towards it, it sensed something and suddenly moved away quickly. Slathered, is that the word?"

"Slithered."

"So. Slithered. Anyway, I screamed and my brother dropped the heavy stone on its head. In fact the stone did not hit its head, but it died just the same." She stopped, seemed to be recalling the incident in her mind. "I still do not understand why he did that. It seemed to me so pointless and destructive. Little boys trying to be big men can be so stupid. Pathetic little bullies…" her voice trailed off. Again McCann said nothing, waiting.

"I was scared and he was maybe scared too. We ran home and found our mother; I remember it clearly. She was washing dishes in the kitchen. She had her back to us, of course, and the sun was shining straight in the window. It was so beautiful. Of course she immediately knew something had happened because of our strange actions. When we told her our story, that we had found a snake and killed it, she was furious. Her face went completely white; even at five years old I could see she was very angry and trying to control herself. Of course she smacked my brother on the behind, very hard. He started crying and tried to move away, but she grabbed him by the arm. Then I started crying also, but she didn't seem to care that we were upset. She was very, very angry. She took us outside and told us that snakes are gods; it is wrong to kill a snake.

And she ordered us to go back to it, bury it properly and pray. And we did. We were scared to go back there, and we both cried a lot, all the way there and most of the way back, but we went there anyway, dug a grave, buried the snake and made a shrine of stones. And we prayed to the snake."

McCann nodded, unsure exactly what this story was supposed to illuminate. She continued, "I used to go back to that little shrine of stones sometimes. It was always there. Many, many years later, after I was married, I happened to be in the area again, near the little river, and I returned to the spot. The stones were there, covered in … *koke*. *Koke*. It's green, on trees and rocks."

She looked questioningly at McCann.

"Moss?"

"Moss! Yes. With the moss, they had become a natural part of the landscape. And of course again I prayed for the snake. It was the right thing to do."

McCann considered this story for a few minutes. He was still waiting for the punch line. They were speaking the same language but he could feel that there was something wedged between them that was elusive, something missing that refused a clear definition. It was simultaneously interesting and frustrating. Talking with her excited him, and not only because of her good looks. After a few minutes, perhaps as a way to try to bridge the gap, he took a gulp of coffee and launched into a story of his own.

"When I was about eight I saw a kid a year or so older than me crouching over something in my local park by the swings. He was so involved with whatever he was doing that he didn't notice me at all. As I came towards him I realised what he was doing; pulling the legs off a daddy-longlegs, one by one."

"Daddy what?"

"Daddy-longlegs, a kind of …ummm … insect, I suppose. About this big. Got really long legs. Hence the name."

"Yes. But why did he do that?"

"Because he was a nasty little prick, that's why. So I stayed fairly close to him and watched him, and when he had pulled off all the legs and squashed its body under his shoe, he stood up and realised I was there, watching him. And without saying a word, I stepped up to him and wellied him right in the face. And when he fell onto the ground, I got on top of him and punched him a few more times. His nose was bleeding, and I said to him, 'If I ever see you kill little insects again, I'll kill you,' and then I walked away. It made me so angry. Like you say, a little boy trying to be a man."

Fuso's eyebrows knitted together. She looked perplexed. "Why did you do that to him?"

This was not the reaction he had expected. "Eh? What do you mean, 'why'? He kills a poor little insect, I teach him a lesson. Pretty obvious, I think."

She sighed and looked around the train carriage, then turned back to him with a stony stare. "I think I will find the bathroom on this train now," and he heard the slide of her tights as she unfolded her legs and moved past him and down the aisle. The hint of her perfume lingered behind her.

McCann rolled his eyes and shook his head, muttering to himself, "Jesus Christ…"

PARLOUR GAMES

Fuso returned from the toilet. Her vibe had changed; she looked completely relaxed and she sat down smiling. The train continued on past pristine forest that seemed to echo with light as it surged past them.

"Do you like trains, George?" She didn't wait for his answer. "One of the reasons I agreed to meet you was so that I could take this journey. Your offer to pay for the ticket was irresistible. I have a lust for trains." She looked at him, smiling, "Is it okay to say that, a lust? It is the only gentle form of travel we have left."

"Lust! You mean trains make you horny?"

She laughed teasingly. "They wake me up and arouse a desire again for life.

Sometimes I find this desire absent when I am in less … what word did you say? Serene? Less serene places than this one." She leaned forward and whispered, "Soon this land will be covered in snow like … a bride of death."

As she mouthed the words her face lit up. She enjoyed playing with English; it freed her from the shackles of expectation that she felt with her native language. She could try out new phrases, put on different hats, throw careless words in every direction. It gave her an opportunity to be someone else. "Charlie liked my clichés. It was the only time he took a real interest in me, that his eyes truly shone."

McCann felt a pang of jealousy but put it to the back of his mind and instead tried to work out how much of what she said was for real and how much was masquerade. He was enjoying trying. She cocked her head to one side playfully and carried on talking. "I love winter. But winter is in retreat everywhere. Without winter we are without mystery, don't you think? Here in Hokkaido winter is the season of dark nights where even the moon is snow-white. Here, it is still mysterious. But in other places, not any more, I think. So I stay away from humans, and all their shitty global warming up. And in winter this is what I do. Train journeying."

"To where?"

"From one station to another station. Isn't life this? One station after another, a short stop and then again motion. From place to place. I told Charlie this and he understood. He said that motion is beauty, stopping is death. He said that he would always keep moving, never stopping or glancing behind. Never really arriving, just passing by."

McCann shook his head and laughed lightly. "You don't much rate normality, do you? Or is this all just talk and bluster?"

She pushed back a stray lock of hair that had fallen across her slim forehead. "No, once things are normal we are dead. How about you Billy-George? Are you a practical type or a fucked-up dreamer like me?"

He baulked at her language. Obviously a gift from all-knowing Charlie.

"I liked to think I was an existentialist once. But I lost my beret in a fight."

She didn't get the joke: he wasn't sure if he did either. He thought for a second. "Practical enough to live in days and dreamer enough to wish I didn't."

Time passed; the train continued onwards. They looked out at the sleet that had begun to drift past in streamers of delicate, iced lace. The train slowed down and came to another halt. Fuso got off and went to the smoking area again. McCann had lost the desire for nicotine, but he went outside and stretched, enjoying the freshness but feeling the weariness of continual travel. There were four smokers: Fuso, a young couple, and a stocky, middle-aged man hunched up far down the platform. He had a baseball cap pulled down over his eyes and even though the awning did not extend to where he was the man seemed disinclined to join the others, preferring to smoke by himself in the sleet. The other passengers remained aboard the train.

McCann re-embarked and looked at his guidebook. It didn't look too far now. Fuso entered smelling of smoke and wind.

"How far do we have to go?"

She looked at him as she reapplied her lipstick. "To death, not very far. Both of us near."

He laughed, "No, to Abashiri."

She shrugged. "Maybe an hour. Please get me my bag."

McCann stood up and brought down her Gucci holdall from the rail above the seats.

She was looking at him. "You are strong Mr. Peters. Powerful. I don't like these new types, these flowerstalk boys. In Japan we call them *soushoku danshi*. Herbivores, grass eaters. They have no contact with the physical world and live inside the brain of a computer." She opened the holdall and began scratching around until she found what she was looking for: a bottle of Remy Martin and – more miraculously – a brandy glass. "We have to share the glass. Okay?"

"I'll get a paper cup."

She looked through him. "Are you afraid of my lips?"

"No, just … Nothing." He felt himself blushing; at his age and with his experience he felt very foolish indeed.

"Besides, we don't put quality liquor into paper cups, do we, Billy-George?" She poured out a hearty measure with a playful grin, diluted it slightly from an Evian bottle and took a sip, leaving her lip print on the tip of the glass. "Mmmm, good. Your turn."

He drank and it warmed him. He passed the glass back and she had some more. She sipped it like they were taking part in some kind of ritual. Her eyes had grown merry and softly mischievous and now she was flirting with him. "Misery, George, so much misery. And why? Timelessness in which we hardly register a speck, in which we seem to spend all our days clinging like a baby to its mother's breast. Hiding from the dark, cleaning our plastic boxes and gazing more and more into other plastic boxes."

She began to laugh. "What happened to us all, George?"

The train lady came by again with her impeccable smile and her perfect service but Fuso waved her on.

"Faking happiness – or truly dumb. Is this the substance of life? This show of masks?" She edged her elbows into the middle of the table and was cradling her head to one side in her sparkling nailed hands. "How about you? You don't seem to have this spiritual cancer, big George."

"Me? I'm just a regular guy, you know…" He gazed back at her. She dropped her eyes momentarily and then they flashed back.

"Well, you don't show the symptoms. You're not married are you?"

"No."

"I'm sure you are very keen to talk about other people and their private lives, but I bet you don't like it when the spotlight is turned on yourself, do you, Billy-George?"

McCann shrugged uncomfortably. "That comes with the territory, I suppose."

She looked down again, smiling. "Talking to you is like talking with a Japanese man. You are like a shellfish."

"Selfish?"

"No! Shell fish! Closed. You say nothing about yourself. This is a bit unusual, I think? I had foreign boyfriend once. He told me everything that was in his head all the time. He said in his country it was normal. People talk about their feelings and their problems, he said. His constant talking about how much he loved me, or him being tired, or him being so happy – round and round in circles – drives me crazy. In Japan, love between man and woman is not so ... noisy."

"It didn't work out then?"

"Questions, George, always you ask questions. How about you? Don't you have a private life? Or have you left this material world of merchants, slaves and bosses?" Her eyes were sparkling and she raised her eyebrows suggestively. "Those doing the whipping and those who are whipped. But not you? Do you live like a monk?"

McCann raised his head in mock nobility and clasped his hands together in prayer.

"Yes, I dream of it."

"Monk gets no play. I talked with Charlie about this. He said one day he will forget girls – maybe he would say pussy, not girls? So, forget this pussy and go into the wild."

"He's there now."

"Yes, but not through choice. I'm sure he goes crazy up there. He said sex is a spell and we are all hypnotized but he doesn't want to wake up just yet."

McCann felt like he was being hypnotized himself. She attracted him, attracted him and almost scared him. He looked her in the eyes and they looked back brazenly, dark black-blue. He had never seen such eyes, they made him dizzy.

"So, Billy-George with all the secrets. Let's play a game. I ask you questions and you must answer truthfully. Okay? So first, an easy one. Do you have a TV in your house in England?"

"I do. How about you?"

She clapped her hands in unaffected delight. "One question and you already ask me something back!"

She looked at him for a long time and he felt like she was appraising something, that whether she answered this question or not would have some kind of significance beyond itself. "No, I don't have a TV Just a big bed with a nice view."

"Not a futon?"

"Oh, no. A big bed. I spend a lot of time in bed. I am not a busy woman." She poured another hearty shot and he could smell the booze on her breath. "I miss my bed. It is the only thing I miss when I am away."

McCann smiled and felt the verve of the drink on his tongue. "Is there room for me in that bed?"

He immediately regretted saying it, but Fuso kept smiling and remained silent, looking at him with a combination of merriment and inchoate affection.

"Naughty, naughty George. But I like your nerve. Here, for courage, drink more." The glass's rim was completely smudged with lipstick and he felt she was deliberately staining it. He raised the glass, ready to drink.

"Oh, wait, George. It is dirty. Here, let me clean it."

She had taken out a handkerchief and was waving it in front of his eyes like a conjurer.

He smiled, "It's fine just as it is." And drained it in one.

"Next question. A more interesting one. Do you have a lover?"

"No, I haven't had a partner for a couple of years."

"I did not ask you if you have a partner, George. I said do you have a lover?"

He laughed, embarrassed again. "I ... have my moments, I suppose."

She pursed her lips. "I'm not convinced by this answer. Are you sure you are telling the truth? Remember, it is against the rules to lie to me, George."

"What do you want, secret diary entries or something?"

"Do boys keep such secret diaries?"

"I have no idea. But I don't."

She considered this for a moment. "Children?"

McCann wasn't sure about kids. Anyway, it was probably too late in life now to be worried about them. "No children. You?"

"Another question from you. I do not need to answer this."

Some emotion passed through her face, but he could not determine what it was. He was starting to feel dizzy with tiredness, seeing double. He relaxed back into the seat, aware of her hand on his brow and heard her voice as he felt himself slip nicely towards the border of sleep and then through it to the other side.

She wiped her lipstick off the wine glass and replaced it back in the holdall with the almost empty bottle. He was out clean and sleeping happily, a small grin on his face. She wondered where he was and with whom. Was he with her now, playing with her mirage in the dreamtime? Creating realities that waking dissolves? She looked at the fur on his arms and stroked it very softly. She liked his big sad brown eyes and his big body. He was funny, too. Not dynamic like Charlie, not that type at all, but strong in different ways, and better really. A better man. He seemed younger than Charlie, somehow.

She was a little drunk and looked at the sleeping man with desire. A longing for companionship filled her. She would take him to Charlie but when they had finished whatever had to be done she might take him somewhere else. She believed in chance and this one had come. As the train rolled on she sat in silence for some time, thinking over a multitude of things, smiling to herself as she thought – life these days doesn't involve many people. Eventually she looked at her watch and checked her face quickly in her hand mirror. They would arrive soon.

A hand shook him awake.
"We are almost there, George."

She had cleaned up the table and removed the glass, and seemed sober. McCann still felt half-cut and sleepy and through the window the land was mystical in the closing light. In due course an announcement came over the tannoy and the train started slowing down. She looked perfect and the force and challenge of reality hit him on the chin. He excused himself, went to the toilet and took a leak. In the mirror he looked far from perfect and his nails were dirty. His everything was dirty.

When he returned the train was pulling into the station and she was all business again, readying herself for the next stage.

"So, tonight you will book into a hotel here in Abashiri. I will pick up my car, and go to my house. Tomorrow morning, I will drive back to town and will wait for you here at the station at 8:30. Then we will go to Charlie. For better or worse, we will go to Charlie."

GYPSY MOTH

Davis had made his final preparations and – weather permitting – would leave late at night. He packed his rations in ziploc bags. They consisted mainly of dried food: mushrooms, fish, seaweed, and a stock of jerky which Fuso said her brother had enjoyed chewing as he drank and waited by the water's edge. Davis would attempt to transport some tinned food too. He had improvised floats and they seemed to work adequately. Everything was ready. He did a card reading and noted the spread laid before him on the floor: The Fool, a good card for him, a symbol of rejection of the wisdom of others and the search for one's own; The High Priestess in reverse; a worry, that one, could be seen as a warning. Davis grimaced to himself. Then The Star, a card of light that pleased him, followed by The Hierophant, one that didn't at all. Finally, The Lovers. It was a peculiar set that darkened his mood slightly, but like all Tarot he needed to wait for its message, if there ever was one.

Before leaving he wanted one more go at finding the Blakiston's fish owl, so he filled a water bottle and tooled up. He headed for the small *beyul* he had found the day before, a fifteen-minute walk away and jealously guarded by a peculiar cluster of trees. It proved difficult to find, as if it moved location at will, but at last he emptied his mind, followed his nose and there it was, bathed in moonlight, a clearing as if man-made, but too beautiful for man; more God-made.

"Niklas would like this one," he murmured to himself, squatting on his haunches by the edge of the grove.

⚏

He had been alone in a bar, in the Thamel area of Kathmandu, when the German entered and sat at his table without invitation. The man had extended a hand and Davis, liking the cheek of him, took it. It was hard to guess the man's age but he was over fifty, tanned and lined, with a tobacco-stained goatee and sparkling eyes. Niklas pulled out a green silk wrap and opened it to reveal a set of Tarot cards. He did a reading for Davis, one that was disturbingly accurate. Charlie wasn't a person who liked others to know a lot about him, but this man did and they had only just met. They drank together that night and Niklas told him more about the *beyul*, paradises on earth that could only be discovered by the initiated and learned. Places where the world of the spirit and the flesh merged.

He remembered Niklas saying, "The *beyul* are not on maps, friend. Don't look there, look here," and he pointed two reefer-filled fingers at his chest.

Davis laughed, "Like a trip without the drugs then, mate. Is that it?"

The other shrugged, "Well, I think with the drugs they are much better." Then Niklas taught him the basics of the Tarot and he decided he liked this way of seeing things, instantly judging destiny: intuition over intellect and courage over caution.

When he returned to England the first thing he did was procure a pack from some burnt out hippy vendor in Hebden Bridge. He smiled, looking back on the memory fondly. "Crazy old nut that guy, Niklas, but he was the one who got me into the Tarot." Despite the lateness of the hour a half-soft light gradually began to permeate the *beyul* and Davis decided to cut the torch. There was an absolute stillness and a force of silence that seemed almost conscious of itself: a feeling that something was coming, beckoning him. He took a deep breath and closed his eyes.

On opening them he saw that there was a creature on the torch, smooth white and resplendent, with wings of silken fur. It was a gypsy moth in form, but in spirit he knew who it was, for this was a *beyul*, a place of metamorphosis where death has no meaning. At least, he let himself believe it was. He spoke softly, peering at the moth. "Well, well. After all, you have come back. I thought you might. The cards told me I would be visited. I was worried who was coming, but it's you."

He blew soft breaths onto her wings for she seemed weak. "We're a long way from Manchester now, eh, Natasha? I'm happy to see you in this holy place."

He touched her, but the moth was still. The wings and heart had both stopped beating.

The light faded and he looked up, noting that the weather had turned for the worse. He cursed his luck. A miasma was falling across the sea making his plans to decamp look forlorn: the plangent waters resounded as if angry. He gently placed the dead moth on the ground and headed back for the cabin.

DRIFT ICE

The Okhotsk Limited Express pulled into Abashiri bang on time, five and a half hours after leaving Sapporo. Any vague ideas he had had of a fantastic night in Fuso's big bed left him as suddenly as she did, and McCann had a night in a town that was desolation itself, scattered with forlorn cube-like buildings laid out with no apparent evidence of design beyond the strictly utilitarian. The air was crisp and smelled of fish entrails and clean seawater.

He stood in the middle of absolutely nowhere, holding the city map he had cut out from the guidebook. In front of him was the Heartland Hotel, an uninspired construction that in its appearance bore none of the swagger of its name.

He entered and found the reception unmanned. There was a small gold bell by the desk. Ringing it lightly, he waited as a faint echo of the bell murmured back. Nobody came. He tentatively called out, "*Sumimasen*", but heard neither footfall nor answer. Perhaps it's condemned, he thought to himself. Well, better let the ghosts know you are here. He tried again, this time both in Japanese and English, and heard a scurry from the far corner and a door opening.

The lady who shuffled towards him was tiny and wore her hair up in a bun. She was dressed in a dark *kimono* of indeterminate colour and she was bowing and smiling nervously in apology. She looked about a hundred years old. McCann bowed back and, aware that he towered above the lady, attempted to reduce his height by bending his knees. She indicated to him with hand gestures that English wasn't spoken but McCann opened his guide book at the 'useful phrases' section and showed her the highlighted

Japanese for 'Do you have a room for the night?'

She shook her head in an ambivalent gesture and with a wave of the hand directed him to the reception desk, where she opened a drawer, found her glasses and put them on. She smiled and seemed more at ease once she saw the Japanese writing. She wrote down the price for a room on a piece of paper, looked up and smiled, "Okay?"

McCann nodded back. He liked her smile; it seemed guileless – but then, sometimes he was a sucker for smiles.

She gave him the key. "Big man. Japan okay?"

McCann laughed, "Yeah, all okay."

He took the stairs to the second floor. The room was adequate. He ran the tap in the bathroom for a few seconds before filling a glass and downing it. It was 8pm and once again he was too tired from journeying to sleep. Now that he was alone and more or less sober, in the silence and the middle of nowhere, the events of the past few days began to cascade through his head. He looked out the window onto the street. It was truly quiet; the odd car passed but there was very little going on down there in the street or up here in the hotel. He sat on the edge of the bed and thought of what he had been through and the pace and the oddness of those events, the intensity of them. He got up again and paced the room. Guiltily, with a fistful of half-truths that he knew were not really true, he tried to push the thoughts of the girl at the party in Roppongi as far from his mind as possible; under the circumstances, how could he have been expected to do anything? Then the toothpick man with that pen sticking out of his eye socket... But these memories oppressed him and he consciously moved to other things. That Sekiguchi: what a nutter he had been, but what a time he'd had with him and the girls. A night out here was something else. He thought of his stodgy local back home, pints of bitter and games of darts. And then there was Fuso Tochimoto: a beguiling woman and a baffling one. So here he was, a private detective after a solution, collecting his new puzzles one by one.

He suddenly felt exhausted and cramped, needed to walk, get some air and clear his head. He put on his coat and studied the map; the harbour wasn't far and could be reached by following the river.

Down in reception the desk was vacant again so he pocketed the key and went outside. The air was keen but not too cold and he walked down Chuo Dori, a solitary pedestrian enjoying the space and the quiet, stopping at intervals to check his map. It told him he had reached Jonishi and it seemed that if he went more or less straight he would end up at the harbour. He looked up from the map, then up further still, and for the first time noticed the stars that glittered graphically in the grey-blue dark. He was beginning to like

Abashiri and he suddenly thought, Marvin would like it too. But what would he do here?

Watch the stars and walk the dog. Wouldn't that be enough? Dream on, old man, maybe one day.

He walked through the area called Johigashi, the air thickening with the scent of the sea and the fishing trade. He could hear the gulls too, as he turned right a little and finally saw the sea. It felt colder by the water and an onshore wind blew. McCann shivered, cursing himself for leaving his hat back at the hotel. It seemed he was alone here, for no lights shone inside the lines of bobbing fishing boats on the water. His only company were the seabirds;

gulls, of what type he didn't know, but big and strong in flight, turning on the wind, riding its strength and force. He kept on walking to the end of the breakwater but there was nobody around and he found himself at the far end of the town, facing seaward and watching the waves coming to shore.

The sound of the water filled him as he looked above the waves to the starry sky, throbbing with the lights from a distance he would never travel to. Looking down again, the waves seemed somehow hindered, and despite the onshore wind they fell and splattered back against some unseen force in the water. The moon struck light onto the sea and McCann climbed down a metal ladder attached to the wall to get nearer to it. He huddled against the concrete, closer than before. The wind blew against his face and it was cold but bracing. He wrapped his scarf around his head, pulled it down to eyebrow level and watched. The waves were smacking ice shards that were drifting in the sea of Okhotsk.

He had read about this in the guidebook, how in winter it was a frozen sea. The winter hadn't really hit yet, but it was coming. All common rhythm was disturbed and broken, the movement of the tide tamed. He felt he could see ice slowly forming below the waves, or rising to meet them. It was like a slow motion fight; something thrown, something blocked. Then there was a breakthrough as a clean wave broke slickly over the hidden ice and ran to shore. McCann was transfixed as he watched it. He was nearing something like this: he had to get this case sorted before it froze over. As he climbed up the ladder and back over the wall he felt dazed and cold, but he was smiling. He retrieved his bag and found his miniature bottle of rum and, removing the scarf from his head, he took nips from the bottle as he made his way back from the end of the breakwater towards the anchorage and the nodding ships.

A cloud of birds was milling around above the fishing boats and as he got closer he noticed there was a solitary light on one of them. A squat man was unloading something into the water, via crates, and the birds were fighting for position both on land and sea. As McCann got closer he saw that the man was throwing entrails into the water. The other stopped briefly and looked at McCann as he approached, then wordlessly went back to what he was doing. It was sending the birds wild. McCann stopped and looked up at the whirring phalanx of bird life that hovered, dove, dropped, then rose again.

It was dizzying to be below the frenzy, radiant with life, pulsing with raw natural energy. He felt like he was witnessing a prayer that had no object of worship. He opened his mouth to express some wordless praise when it hit him: a hot, fresh spray of seagull shit right between the eyes. Then, as he bent in shock and defence, another volley straight onto the top of his head.

Embarrassed and quietly cursing, he departed quickly without looking back. At the corner of the street he wiped off what he could of the excrement with his hand and his scarf. It was viscid, acrid stuff and he needed to find a place to properly wash. It was some way to the hotel and he was feeling cold, besmirched and hungry. He couldn't remember seeing anything resembling an eatery open on the way down, but now as he retraced his steps he checked the side streets. At first they yielded nothing, and then he spotted a red lantern and moved towards the light. Hesitating outside, he counted to ten, drew a deep breath, opened the door and went in.

The heat, the smells of cooking and oil, and the astonished eyes of the proprietress who quickly disappeared and returned with a man, a towel wrapped around his head, all hit him on entry. The man was smiling and speaking in Japanese whilst pointing at a picture menu, "*Irashimase! Dozo, okyakusan, suki na seki dozo.*"

McCann smiled back and raised his thumb then asked for the toilet. The man seemed to understand and indicated the way. It was tiny, a squat type, but McCann was only after the sink. He washed off the bird shit with cold water, first from his hair then from his face. The simple bar of soap smelled good on his hands. When he returned to the counter, a steaming bowl of noodles was waiting for him with a drink. The lady explained in halting English that it was hot *shouchu*. McCann tucked into the noodles and drank down the broth, emboldening it with sips of the sweet potato spirit. He paid, bowed and thanked the staff and decided that he rather liked this town. The woman managed to explain that they were a couple and business was almost non-existent at this time of year; some locals came, but rarely this late at night. McCann checked his watch: it was 11pm. She spoke again, "They come here for the drift ice, all country, even Europa. But not yet." Her husband smiled and nodded and served him another hot *shouchu*. McCann liked them both very much.

 ♊

The alarm woke him from a dreamless sleep. He showered but didn't bother to shave. At the reception desk the old lady was waiting and he returned the key and paid in cash. She smiled and McCann returned it with one of his own. Outside, a Nissan saloon car was waiting with Fuso masked again and at the wheel. McCann had no idea whether she was smiling or not.

DAY 4 – NOV. 3RD

I marvel at my bed. Two futons, my sleeping bag, some kind of army issue blankets and a fucking bear skin!

Tried fishing with line from kayak this morning. Wanted to take harpoon but not enough hands. Need to be a Hindu goddess for that. Jesus, what I would do right now for a day & a night with a Hindu goddess...

In spring killer whales frequent this sea along w/ various other sea monsters. Makes you think when out on the water alone. So far, have seen a few dolphin only. Cast my line through the fog and waited in the silence. Bob, bob, bob. Voila! Caught my first fish. A Japanese mackerel, called hokke in these parts. One is enough for Charlie boy.

Back to the cabin, had a nap. Woken by a strange dream. Saw the Voodoo Man. Was leaving the old terraced house in Montague Gardens but as turned to close the door he appeared behind me, already inside. Big tall guy. Don't really remember his face – might have been like the Voodoo Man in Live & Let Die. Or maybe had a big mop of curly hair like the guitarist in Guns 'n' Roses, or perhaps he was a skeleton. Or maybe all three.

Don't remember now. He had a monkey on his shoulder dressed in a little black suit and a top hat. The monkey pointed at me and grinned. Maybe the Tokoloshe Man did too. The door closed and I was locked out my own house and the Voodoo Man was inside.

If this is a premonition it is fucked up shit. The Moth

*in the beyul too, the card reading, and then the weather
going bad ... should be out of here already. Gotta leave
tomorrow night. Got up, drank tea @ 5pm. Before it got
dark took the gun & went to search for owls in the depths
of the forest. Had flashlight ready and harpoon slung over
my shoulder. Eerie when the light dims and it becomes
even quieter as night descends.*

*Taptap of the woodpecker has ceased and birds are
at roost. Followed the stream, stepping slowly, carefully,
watching for... something. Nothing. Cast my light across
the trees and banks but not a thing moved. Will return
tomorrow morning. The dawn is less spooky!*

JOUSTING

It was almost the end of the road, almost the end of the world, as the Ainu name for Shiretoko implies, 'Land Thrusts Out'. They passed one hot spring lodging house, then another and then there was no more road. The car juddered onto an unmarked, rutted farm track, better suited to a 4x4 than Fuso's functional saloon. At the start of the journey their conversation had consisted mostly of the practicalities of getting to the cabin and what they might find when they got there.

"I am worried because when I left him Charlie told me he will go to Russia."

"Eh? How's that possible then?"

"From Shiretoko to Kunashiri Island. Kunashiri used to be Japanese but is now part of Russia. Only about 30 kilometres across the sea. It is not so far, but it is dangerous to go, I think."

"What's he going to do, swim it or something?"

"My brother's kayak."

The wipers swept back and forth rhythmically across the windscreen, pushing the unconvincing splattering of rain and sleet away, but helpless against the mist that swirled around, teasing them by occasionally revealing then hiding the virgin surroundings. They fell silent, lost in their own thoughts and the uncompromising landscape.

After thirty minutes of painfully slow progress, some worryingly jarring potholes and sump-scraping rocks, Fuso announced, "We will be there in five minutes."

McCann peered expectantly out the window, unable to see much through the swirling white vapour.

Soon she cut the engine and pointed, "The cabin is just down there." Her voice was neutral; her face had become an unreadable mask again.

Though they were now stationary McCann felt like he was still in jerky motion. As the mist cleared temporarily, he saw the roof of the cabin, a short, steep walk down from the dirt road, perched on a fairly flat, nondescript piece of land, a mixture of slate, stone and grass. The beach itself was only about another thirty metres away from the building: pebbled and dark with rain and sea spray; in every direction a palette of a thousand colours, all of them shades of grey. The haar closed in again and the shapes deconstructed, shifted. McCann's extremities were cold and he felt a sniffle in his nose. Clapping his hands together and rubbing them, he grabbed his luggage from the back seat, grunting as he stretched for the handles.

"Right then, let's see what grand thoughts Charlie's brought us from the end of the earth…"

Visibility was somewhat better outside the car and the cabin remained discernible, even as the cloud thickened. They made their way down the path, McCann grabbing Fuso's hand as she slithered off balance. They both shouted and laughed; it seemed a rare, unscripted, unguarded moment that morning. The wind came in gusts, buffeting their ears then dropping suddenly, replaced by the rumble of the sea.

"Your brother had a great sense of humour, building a holiday home here!"

"Not a holiday home, I told you. A place to find … something that was lost." Her hair tumbled across her face. He looked at her.

"If I had lost something, I think I'd start looking for

273

it in Okinawa, not Shiretoko!" She smiled warmly at this inane comment; ten minutes earlier she would certainly have snarled.

McCann was feeling good, like the search was almost over, that there was nowhere left to go. He had surprised himself. In the last few weeks the search for an answer to Natasha Philips' death, which had started out so mechanically, methodically, like a search for a missing piece of jigsaw under the sofa and then behind the bookcase, had become something much more all-encompassing than he could have possibly expected.

McCann was less than five feet from the door of the cabin when it burst open and Charlie Davis rushed out like a medieval swordsman, a kayak paddle raised above his head, his breastplate a grubby yellow lifejacket. Before there was any time to react, the hard plastic edge of the paddle came down on McCann's skull and then he was on the ground, blood covering his cold hands and a hundred little fireworks bursting through his brain. He could hear Davis shouting something, and Fuso too, but when he opened his eyes and tried to stand up he was surprised to find that his legs refused to budge. A high-pitched noise was singing in his ears.

The door of the cabin hung forlornly on its hinges like the swing door of a saloon in a ghost town. A few seconds passed. Fuso had crouched down and was looking into his eyes, talking to him in an incomprehensible jumble of Japanese and English and pointing at the shore, but although she was right beside him, her words seemed to come from a distance. He followed her finger through the swirling mist to the waterline where he could see a

274

brightly-coloured object slowly moving into the open water. After what seemed like a long time, he rose to his feet and made his way towards the shoreline. Now he was aware that the object was an orange kayak, and as it pushed away from the shore, through the mist and into the sea, he realised the seriousness of the situation. 30km across the Nemuro Strait. For an experienced seaman in decent weather, it was quite manageable. For a man in desperation on a heavy sea, was it even possible?

Fuso was guiding his arm away from the view of Davis' disappearing kayak towards another object pulled up on the beach; a wooden rowing boat with spindly oars sticking out askew from under a hap cover, like the legs of a newborn deer. There was blood on McCann's collar; it was trickling down his neck, he could feel it sticky in his hair. He bent down beside the boat and put his hands in the water: the inky liquid was too dark to know if the blood had washed off them. His hands stung for a second then became numb. He covered his head and face with the freezing water, lightly touching the cut and the swollen, sensitive lump on his crown as he did so, and felt a shiver all the way down his back and through his very soul; he was alert now. He stood up, not too quickly, and helped Fuso, who was struggling to pull the heavy canvas cover off the boat.

In a couple of minutes the dinghy was at the edge of the water, the stern moving with the waves, the bow still touching the land but threatening to bob into the sea. McCann was dazed and things were happening too quickly for him, before he had a chance to think or form ideas. His feet were soaked and already felt like two dauds of unresponsive wood as he jumped into the vessel and used the oars to turn its bow out towards the water. Fuso was speaking to him, but with the wind, the rumble of the sea and the rush to prepare the dinghy he had no idea what she was talking about. Now that he was facing the land and pulling on the oars he realised that she had been trying to get into the boat too. She was in the water up to her knees, her face crumpled in an anguished expression, but he didn't want to waste any more time, and anyway, he didn't want her with him.

He started to row away from the shore and quickly understood the difficulty of the task. Screwing his head round towards the open water, the kayak appeared and disappeared through the white-tipped waves and the haar, already some way ahead of him. The wind was fierce and the tide was coming in, sending him halfway back towards land for every pull on the oars. His frozen feet slithered on the rain-soaked lip of the bulkhead as he tried to get purchase to pull through the water; one oar slipped out of its rowlock and almost sent both him and the oar tumbling into the sea. The waves came in surges, briefly calm between the ridges of water, then raising the boat even higher before dropping into another trough, the hull slapping noisily off the water. Everything inside the dinghy was soaking wet and McCann knew he would drown if he ventured further in this weather.

Once again he turned to look for the kayak; once again he had the feeling that, in Davis, he was dealing with someone operating outwith the bounds of regular perceived wisdom, someone who cared nothing for the primal animal instinct of self preservation. He muttered petrified curses to himself as a gigantic wave pulled him upwards, the boat hanging in that moment of perfect balance between skyward and earthward movement, before the rollercoaster dips, the stomach follows a second later and fifty kids and adults scream in unison; a man-made exultation, boxed in, controlled, to be followed by ice cream and pizza. But not here in the Sea of Okhotsk. He looked again for Davis, now believing it was suicide to follow much further. For the first time he noticed that the kayak was no longer pulling away from him, that the distance between them was constant, or perhaps even reducing. He could also see, when the swell and the mist allowed, that where Davis was, perhaps sixty metres away, the waves were almost double in size to the ones McCann was still struggling through. He mumbled another agnostic prayer. To what, and for what, he did not know.

LEVIATHAN

Heaving through the frigid ocean as best he could, for an unknowable amount of time, McCann followed the progress of Davis' kayak staggering up a series of seemingly vertical walls of water and disappearing, only to materialise a few seconds later, having been thrown ten metres or more to port or starboard like a plastic bag in the wind. It amazed him and seemed incredible that the tiny vessel was still afloat. Yet, although not quite foundering, the inevitable was happening; the kayak was gradually being beaten back by the onslaught of wave and wind. As McCann pulled hard on the oars just to maintain his position against the force of the tide, his shoulders and back now groaning in complaint at the workload, the garish orange object was gradually being blown back towards him. Through the sea spray and mist he could see Davis more clearly now and it appeared that his energy was spent. He was paddling unevenly, like a drowning rat, full of lactic acid and bile, missing the heaving surface of the water as often as he dug the paddle into it. McCann pulled into the wind again, his head twisted over his shoulder towards Davis' location. He merely had to hold his position as well as his nerve, and eventually the kayak would come back to him.

When the boats were around fifteen metres apart, a huge surge of water lifted Davis's kayak beyond McCann's line of vision. He felt the energy starting to swell up underneath his tiny dinghy, much bigger than any wave that had hit him so far. For a second he looked up as it threatened to throw his boat bow over stern and send him crashing to his death – a pointless death, he thought, in a strangely abstract snippet of time.

There was wild movement, confusion, a crashing roar as the wave stumbled over itself. He was thrown off his bench seat; the oars were out of his hands. He felt the small of his back batter against wood; the invisible hand threw him forward and then his head was in the bottom of the boat, coughing up seawater, salt taste in his mouth, blood on his hands and on his face again, whether from Davis' previous attack or a new assault from the more formidable energy source, he could not say.

He was lying in fifteen centimetres of water. The wooden deck planking was floating loose, as was one oar. The other oar was gone. The dinghy continued to toss and turn in a whirling dervish dance. Struggling onto his knees, he grabbed the gunwale with numb, bloody hands, looking around, hardly able to breathe.

⚓

It was difficult to say exactly what had happened or how far the boat had been thrown by the wave, but his instincts told him he was now much closer to the shore and had been pushed to starboard. The dinghy didn't seem to be sinking, although it was half-full of water, and the ferocity of the waves had reduced somewhat. About twenty metres away, the scraped and battered underside of the kayak moved erratically on top of the still considerable swell. The mist lifted again, partially, and to his right McCann could see the shore: grey and angular like a battleship. It was surprisingly close, which perhaps explained the slight drop in the intensity and size of the waves.

He grabbed the one remaining oar in his iced, cut-knuckle hands and paddled over to the kayak. As he got close another wave lifted his boat almost over the top of the capsized hull, before the clattering of wood on fibreglass threw the two vessels together.

Even before the wave drove him into the helpless kayak McCann knew that Davis wasn't in it. A yellow object bobbed and rolled a few feet away, and he knew that if Davis wasn't already dead, in these circumstances he had a matter of minutes to get him into the boat or the guy was fish food.

With only one oar and the sea still heaving and dropping a metre or more every few seconds, it was difficult to get to any one particular point on the water, let alone stay in position. More by luck than design he maneuvered the dinghy beside the inert body and tried to grab the lifejacket, but his hands were so frozen that he couldn't grasp it with any power. His unresponsive fingers slipped uselessly across the material like fingernails down a blackboard, flailed at an arm, but could hold nothing. For a second he had the lifejacket straps round his wrist and was pulling Davis towards the boat, but another big wave once again knocked the precious cargo away from him. Using the oar he moved back into position to try again, knowing that Davis' life was on the line and time was very short. Kneeling in the boat, his knees locked solid in twenty centimetres of glacial arctic sea, he got close enough to risk his own life again by delving his hands into the dark water.

The swell knocked the dinghy against Davis's body, clattering his unconscious head against the clinker's hull. McCann felt everything was slipping away from him. He leaned over the side, dangerously close to tipping into the water himself, and summoned from somewhere the anger and energy to wrench Davis by the neck into a brutal head-lock. He began to pull him out of the water and as he did so he could feel Davis' legs follow the contour of the hull and his body almost slide right underneath the boat. Unbalanced, the boat lurched further over on its side.

McCann roared at the sea in impotent rage, no longer caring if Davis was alive or dead; a strangled, crippled bellow of tears and phlegm and caustic hate directed at the windblown nothingness, and with a series of irate lunges, a herculean effort, twisting Davis's limbs in unimaginable directions, he ripped the prostrated lump out of the grasp of the waves and into the boat.

He lay gasping for a few moments in the bottom of the dinghy, but in the freezing water and with the heavy mass of Davis's body almost on top of him he wasn't encouraged to remain there, despite his feelings of exhaustion. He was shaking uncontrollably and so cold that he could hardly pick up the oar again, but the tide was bringing the dinghy back towards land and he forced himself to poke the oar feebly at the water. They had drifted a hundred metres or so down the coast and he didn't think Fuso could have possibly followed the progress of the two boats, given the mist, the rain and their distance from the shore. Approaching land, the boat smacked against some jagged rocks, splintering the gunwale and rattling the occupants once again, then finally came to rest on the coarse sand. McCann threw himself over the side into the knee-deep water, hauled the boat up as best he could and grabbed Davis once again, pulling him roughly back onto the land. Waves broke on the stony beach like millions of little fingers trying to grab hold of his legs, always slipping back but never tiring, then coming back again to slither over the smooth, dark stones for all eternity.

He staggered towards the cabin through what was

again becoming sleet, dragging Davis' immobile body behind him like a carcass. He had barely gone twenty metres when he saw Fuso running towards him. She covered the ground amazingly quickly and as she came to him McCann could see that she was also soaking wet, and he knew from her puffy, red eyes that some of the salt water was from her tear ducts, not the sea. She ran straight to him and put her hands to his face, a sculptor of emotion. There were words, things said and things not said, and in his hazy comprehension of the next few minutes he felt that something fundamental had changed between them, a barrier smashed, an intensity of mutual understanding created through the ferocity of the moment. Then there was the cabin, some kind of respite, some kind of release, some kind of unconsciousness.

LOCH RANNOCH

❝The sun's going down now. Midgies'll be out soon and feasting on us, son. Better get inside."

He smiled and lit a Benson and Hedges. A plume of blue smoke rose into the sky. "These bloody things'll be the death of me. They're good for nothing, except keeping those midgies away."

The tang of the phosphorous; always followed by the smell of the cigarette. Like the reek of petrol or the odour of sunflowers, never forgotten. The way he always held it in his left hand, despite being right-handed. That smile. The timbre of his voice.

Another draw on the cigarette.

"I like it here, Dad. I'd like it a lot more if it didn't rain so much, though!" That smile again.

Displaced words from inside the cabin floated out to him randomly, the voice comforting, like an old friend. 'Prime Minister Heath … when the Senate Committee meets again as the scandal continues to grip America … after the shocking death of the actor, and martial arts superstar, Bruce Lee…' Then another more familiar voice, calling out from the kitchen, "Steve, Colin, dinner's ready! Honey, do you know where Josie is? See if you can find her and tell her dinner's on the table and getting cold."

"Right then, Colin. You heard the boss. We'll get our dinner but the midgies won't get theirs. At least not from us."

Sitting on the wooden steps of the cabin – he'd never

stayed in one before – looking across at the loch and the mountains beyond, as the setting sun blazed salmon-pink and peach across the clouds, he felt the need to say something. He knew the moment demanded it but didn't know what he wanted to say. Perhaps too complex a feeling for an eight year-old to put into words, perhaps an early premonition of *saudade*. So as he stood up to go inside, he simply asked, "What are we doing tomorrow, Dad?"

"Thought we might drive through Glencoe tomorrow. It's beautiful there, you know. The most beautiful road in the whole world. And we should try to go when we can actually see something; the forecast says tomorrow will be okay, but from Thursday it's back to the rain, I'm afraid."

"If it rains on Thursday we'll have to play *Uno* all day again, right?"

"Then we'll have to play *Uno* again, correct."

"Don't worry, Dad, with all the practice you're getting this week, you're bound to win one day…"

His father put an arm round his shoulder and they stepped into the cabin, leaving the midgies to search out some other prey. And the dying embers of the sun touched the edges of the cloudbank with fire for an appreciative gallery of insects.

⚓

Something was wrong. The smell should be meatballs, mashed potatoes and Heinz baked beans, but it was … curry? Some weird kind of curry, not like what you get in Sparkhill. He tried to listen for an intimate voice: his mother or father, his sister. The sounds were a strange mix of the familiar and the not so: the quiet clink of dishes, movement in the kitchen; a softly crackling fire, a wood fire; a hissing sound like that of air being released from a bicycle tyre. His body ached all over, especially the ever-increasing number of bashes, bruises and scrapes that seemed to be multiplying daily.

He opened his eyes.

He was lying on a roughly made-up futon, his nose barely three inches from the wooden floor of the cabin. The bed was warm and enclosed him, womb-like; he never wanted to leave it. He could see Fuso's back as she moved around in the rudimentary kitchen area. On the sturdy, wooden table in the middle of the square room, a Tilley lamp gave out a beautiful, yellow glow and hissed merrily. There was food on the table but he couldn't see what. He smiled to himself and went back to sleep.

THAWING OUT

❝Is there a selection of starters, or is it the chef's choice?"

Fuso jumped at the voice behind her and laughed. "Oh, Moby Dick is awake! How are you feeling?" There was playfulness, but also a genuine concern on her face.

McCann liked the look.

"Ishmael, please. Moby Dick is the name of the whale."

"Whales don't have names."

"That one did."

A wave of desire to grab her, hold her, came over him, but he restrained himself. Her eyes flashed across his face; in the soft light of the paraffin lamp they sparkled like dark gemstones.

"For starter we have miso soup straight from a pack," she waved the plastic pouch in front of his face, "and for main course we have curry rice, the curry also straight from a pack." Smiling broadly, she showed him the metallic packet of rue bubbling in a pan of boiling water. "The only thing that isn't from a pack is the rice. It is from a bag. If I don't bring the rice, there is no real food in the whole cabin."

"No problem. This food'll taste better than a five-star restaurant 'cos today we have bucket loads of mountain magic."

"Mountain magic? What is that?"

"It's the taste of hot food after a long day out in the fresh air. Any food. You know what the best thing I've ever eaten is? A cup noodle at the end of a fifteen-mile hike. Tomato flavour. I'll never forget it, and that was when I was 21. That's called mountain magic, because a mountain can make any food, even bad food, taste great."

"I understand. You mean it is not the taste that is so important but the desire to eat?"

"Exactly. The desire to eat. The appetite."

They looked at each other for a few seconds, both acutely aware of what was happening. The only sounds were the hissing Tilley lamp and the bubbling water in the pan. Fuso turned back to the stove with a smile. McCann felt simultaneously exhausted and acutely alert, tense in a satisfying way, like tired but taut muscles after a gym workout.

Fuso spoke with her back to him but he knew by the tone of her voice that she was still smiling. "Does your mountain magic include drinks as well as food?"

He rubbed his hands together expectantly. "Absolutely! What have you got for us?" "Do not be too excited, Moby Dick. I don't think it's very good, but in the desert any water will do, right?"

She bent down to open a cabinet by her knees, produced a bottle of brandy and passed it to him. He took it from her, reading the label aloud, laughing.

"Suntory V.O. brandy! This is just what we need – for cleaning the cooker." She came close to him, looking at the label over his shoulder. The contours of her face showed up in the lamplight, and he was struck by a kind of tremendous beauty.

Not an easy, radiant beauty, but a more internal, self-contained allure.

"Is it so bad, Billy-George?"

"Actually, do you know what? This bottle of brandy will be perfect mountain magic."

The seal was still unbroken. "You haven't had any of this yet?"

"Yes."

"Yes? You have? Or yes, you haven't?" She smiled uncertainly as he pointed an accusing finger at her playfully. "You drank a whole bottle of this by yourself earlier, didn't you?"

"No!" she laughed, "Just open the bottle, Billy-George, and let's try it!"

She produced two teacups from the cupboard and rinsed them. "You are a gentleman, so you can have the broken one. I am a lady, so I deserve the good cup."

McCann bowed elaborately. "Just as your ladyship requires. Cheers."

"*Kampai.*"

He looked at her, basking in the warmth that had come over their relationship.

"*Kampai.*"

They both drained their teacups in one gulp. Fuso finished first and poured out a second for them both. "Well?"

The amber liquid melted deep into McCann. He shivered then sighed and smiled with pleasure, drunk on positive vitality. "Best brandy I ever tasted. And the chipped cup adds a little something to the flavour."

She put the bottle down and looked at him, her face sensuous and serious. "You are really okay? This afternoon, I thought you would be dead…"

"I'm okay, yes. And I thought I might be dead too, but I'm not."

"It is incredible, what you do today. It is brave. I do not really understand it, but I think it is fantastic." She leaned towards him and touched his torso lightly. A buzz of static energy pulsed through his body as she kissed him lightly on the mouth, as soft and fresh as spring rain. It was a light touch, but one that promised much more, and McCann

288

felt a luring incitement as he pulled her towards him. He kissed her mouth, her neck and her ear and she purred but quickly slipped out of his arms and backed away towards the stove. McCann tried to interpret the look on her face – it seemed serious and perhaps confused, but alive and full of possibilities. She poured another brandy for herself and held the bottle out to him, but her movements were self-conscious and awkward.

"Drink?" She almost pleaded.

He took the brandy from her, nodding silently. He was confused but not surprised. Just another crossed wire to add to the collection he had compiled over the week. But this one was different; there was an honesty in this confusion that was the delicate birth of something, and that made him want to be cautious, not to crush it with the heavy hand of an over-urgent move. So he forced himself to bide his time, and pulled out a chair at the big table with the Tilley lamp. Sitting down, he poured a cupful, sipped carefully from it, and took in the whole room for the first time over the brim of the cup. His face fell; a dark, brooding, wild, storm cloud lay immobile in a camp bed by the window, neatly tucked inside sheets and warm blankets. He set down the chipped cup of brandy. His positivity was evaporating like snow in the sun.

"How is Davis?"

Even as he said the words he knew he should have stayed silent, and before the utterance had left his lips he silently cursed his own stupidity. He had tried to keep the jealousy from his voice but obviously he had failed. Fuso turned quickly from the stove. He looked up at her and, just as his relaxed mood had been erased by the sight of Davis, so her face changed too as she looked from the flawed man to the flawed man-boy and understood, and her guard was up once again, the mask back in place, at least partially. It was why she was here; it was why they were both here. She shrugged her shoulders and sighed. It seemed to be the exhalation of a hope.

"He is alive, thanks to you. To be honest, I do not know how he is; I am not a professional nurse. But I know his pulse is okay, he is breathing, I think normally. He is resting. That's all I can say."

He sniffed and nodded, took a large swig of brandy and looked down at the table. But the damage was done.

"Why can't you let him go? Do you not see that he will get away from you eventually? Why is it that you are chasing him down like, like … an animal?"

"I've told you a million times, it's my job. I have questions and he knows the answers. Call me old fashioned but if I start something, I see it out, and especially in this case. That's the way it is. It's the way it has to be."

She said nothing but he knew his response had not impressed her. He was angry with himself for letting Davis get to him again. He was angrier still with Davis for… what? For being Davis? Like a man slipping into quicksand, McCann couldn't help but flail and squirm further. But he was also angry and felt no compunction about justifying himself, even to his own detriment.

"Fuso, I've been around for a while and I've seen all kinds of people, and most of them don't impress me one little bit. This guy's got something alright, he's a Pied Piper. He could get people jumping through hoops of fire for him, no bother. He even gets me going sometimes when he starts playing his tunes. Maybe he should start a cult, collect some fucked-up, disappointed, confused, weak people and bring them here. Preach the end of the world to them.

"It shouldn't be too hard. There are always plenty of takers around who want a band leader to help them beat

290

that kind of drum." The look of disdain returned to Fuso's face. Everything positive that had happened over the last few hours was unravelling. "You are a strange man, Mr. Peters. You are a brave man but I think sometimes you are not smart. Or are you just bitter that you cannot be free, like him?"

McCann sneered, "Yeah? Thanks for your insight. Very deep. You're right, I wish I could've been a drug dealer, a charlatan, a cock-and-bull peddler, maybe a murderer. It's easy to be impressed by the Charles Manson bollocks when you're looking from a distance." He looked straight at Fuso, "Or when you act like a star-struck teenager. I am being paid to investigate a highly suspicious death in which that man," he stood and pointed at Davis, his voice much louder than he would have liked, "has a starring role. There's nothing romantic about that, Fuso. He's just a streetwise chancer with the gift of the gab, looking for a good time. And I've been employed to call his number in, which is exactly what I'm going to do."

She looked glum. "You say things which I think you do not believe yourself." It was a quietly angry response, resigned to disappointment, and cut McCann to the quick. She turned back to the stove, "You must be very hungry. There is nothing more than this to eat, but it is hot food."

She noisily dished out the meal and artlessly put it in front of him. He mumbled thanks but she ignored it and before he could say anything salutary she was across the room, kneeling over Davis again, checking him, tucking the sheets carefully around him, with her back to the table. McCann, famished and defensive, wolfed the food down in silence. The moment of mountain magic had gone, frozen like the Hokkaido night.

UNDER THE DIAMOND SKY

Cradling the shotgun in the crook of his arm, McCann unlocks the back door and steps into the sharp, pure air. Shivering, he walks twenty or thirty yards towards the beach, at times silver and white, then blue-black in the variable moonlight. The squall has passed and it is much calmer now, the sea breathing like a sleeping animal. Laying the gun down he sits on the edge of the shingle, occasionally picking up pebbles and throwing them at the water. He doesn't know what to think about the events of that afternoon, about how close his sentience had come to being erased from the earth.

He mumbles something to himself, perhaps "Fuck you, friend", or maybe it's "Fuck you, Freud"? Perhaps he doesn't even know himself. He cradles a smooth, black pebble in the palm of his hand, judging the weight of it, then hurls it at the breaking waves. The air is clear but his head is fuzzy. Perhaps he is still in some kind of shock? Ideas and feelings, for Fuso and about Davis, slither and slip around without taking shape, like serpents in dark dreams. The back of his head is numb; the front throbs slightly. He closes his eyes and runs his hands over the contours of his face as Fuso had done when he had staggered out of the water with Davis. But his hands continue to move up over his forehead to the deeply receding hairline. He feels the short hairs and the follicles, a few less than last year; the inexorable advance of the desert. He yawns so deeply that tears come to his eyes. His begins to shiver.

Why had he risked himself to pull that kid out of the sea? Just for a paycheck? It is unfathomable. He looks again at the sky; diamonds occasionally shimmering through a dark feather boa. Everything is incomprehensible: this sky; his pitiful, meandering passage through his own tiny window of consciousness; his understanding that he could have been dead now, at this very instant. And yet he can't seem to grasp the enormity of his continued existence, like his brain is shutting it out from him. Perhaps understanding it would just be too much, he ponders.

He sits in silence for a few more minutes, looking at the waves and the bashful stars, before eventually standing up stiffly, stretching, and turning towards the cabin, windows blazing warmth in the black night like an old-time homestead. One window is visible to him; one window and a sliver of light from the back door that he has deliberately left ever so slightly open for re-entry.

He bends down to pick up the shotgun but as he does so he freezes in mid-motion. Why? He does not know. Blood throbs in his temples. The waves break on the beach, hissing, rhythmical, endless. The moon has floated into cloud again and it is pitch black. He slowly adjusts his position, squatting and quietly collecting the old shotgun, cold in the palm of his hand.

Something.

What? Like everyone else, he has seen the nature programmes; the gazelle pauses in mid-graze, ears and nose twitching, head raised, assessing the danger. The lionesses lie watchful in the scrub, lightly panting, almost smiling. He has seen this programme, but he is not thinking about it now. He is not thinking about anything. He is just listening and looking, stock-still, peering into the darkness. A shape suddenly appears at the back door, a figure. It is silhouetted briefly against the glowing yellow light as the door slides open and it slips noiselessly into the cabin like a snake.

SILENCER

McCann is running. He is thirty yards away. He will be there in seconds. He knows the figure must be Fuso, because aside from himself she is the only person here apart from Davis, who cannot even stand up yet, never mind move around. But he knows that this figure is not Fuso. He stumbles and falls, twisting his ankle on a hard divot, drops the gun, curses. A sharp pain shoots through his body, but as he is getting to his feet again he hears a high-pitched scream, a clatter, the discord of violence and confusion. At the sound of the shriek he goes cold; a wave of goose pimples swim across his skin, followed by the hot rush of adrenalin, which blocks out any discomfort from his ankle, and he is dashing to the cabin again.

He makes it to the back door almost immediately, but the terrible noises have abruptly stopped. Too abruptly. As he breenges into the cabin shoulder-first, slamming the door against its hinges, he knows that there should be a clear view into the main room, provided the connecting door is not closed. It is open, and as the intruder turns at the unexpected commotion, he is astonished to see that it is Tatsuo Sekiguchi.

It is undoubtedly Sekiguchi, standing in the middle of the bigger room beside the wooden table; and yet it is not in any way the same man McCann met in Sapporo. His face shows a kind of surprise at McCann's sudden appearance, but not really a human surprise, for it is not a human face; it is as hard as antimony, emotionally detached – a death mask. Even with the distance of a room between them, even with the blurring of motion, he is shocked at the coldness of this face. Sekiguchi is dressed all in black, and in his gloved hand there is some kind of long-barrelled pistol, which is now raised and pointed at McCann. There is also a metallic, smoky smell in the air on top of the ligneous scent of the dying fire.

All this has happened in a split-second.

Without a break in motion McCann continues his forward movement, throwing himself down behind a wooden counter as he hears a dull double crack and pieces of wood splinter and shatter on the wall behind him. He curses and fumbles with the shotgun, trying to pull two cartridges from his right-hand pocket. Strangely, as he does this, his first thought is, 'The pistol has a silencer,' then, 'I have seconds to live.'

He doesn't understand anything except that he must load and fire the shotgun before Sekiguchi's pistol appears over the top of the counter and McCann's skull and brains are exploded all across the back wall.

Fumbling, he pulls the two cartridges from his trouser pocket, tilts them up, slides them into the barrels and closes the weapon, wishing he knew if he had forgotten a safety catch, a hammer. Too late to worry now. Three seconds have passed since Sekiguchi's first salvo; time is up. He has not fired a gun in years; he dare not try to control the kick of the discharge, or even aim, but simply pokes half a head round the side of the cabinet, points at the open doorway and pulls the trigger.

The noise is deafening and a huge chunk of the doorframe disintegrates, sending bits of wood spiralling into the other room, and a plume of blue smoke towards the roof. His ears are ringing, he is temporarily stunned by the noise, but dimly he hears a surprised exclamation, a

Japanese man's voice, and the sound of someone jumping for cover.

The big table crashes over and the paraffin lamp goes with it too. The golden light flickers wildly through the cabin for a second, like a struggle between Nephthys and Isis, before night inevitably wins and the cabin is shrouded in semi-darkness. Now there is only a soft, almost insignificant reddy glow from the embers of the wood fire and a small camping light hanging in a corner of the main room, which throws a weak, blue-white luminosity and many shadows. Its power is so meagre that McCann hadn't even noticed it until now. It creates a strange eeriness in the cabin, like a scene from an old black and white film, hiding as much in darkness as it illuminates.

McCann has bought himself some time. But how much? He had four shotgun cartridges in his pocket; now there are two plus the one left in the gun. The box of shells is in a cupboard in the bigger room. He hears Sekiguchi, probably behind the overturned dining table, reloading his pistol. Has the paraffin lamp not caught fire? What has happened to Fuso and Davis? Muffled noises are coming from the room, but he does not know if they are from Sekiguchi, Fuso, Davis or all three of them. Of course he fears the worst.

Crouched behind the wooden counter, he waits for a few seconds, listening. What happens now? He is very scared. He is disorientated by the noise of the shotgun and the smoke, and the shadows that the ethereal, cold light of the lamp throws.

The sounds from the other room continue. McCann realises the front door is being unlocked and opened. "Oh fuck…" he whispers to himself. Maybe he panics. He bobs up just above the edge of the counter and fires another deafening volley, obliterating most of the front door, which sags drunkenly off its hinges. But he knows he has missed his target and that Sekiguchi is already somewhere outside the cabin, probably moving towards the back door or one of the windows.

Conscious that he needs to move to stay alive, McCann stumbles blindly into the bigger room and slumps down in a dark corner, trying to keep his breathing under control and his hands from shaking. He struggles with his last two cartridges, opening the breech, carefully and quietly removing the empty shells before inserting the new ones.

In the almost malevolent light, like the fuzzy screen of a TV in a dark room late at night, he realises with a start that he can make out Davis by the far wall still lying in his cot, but the sheets are disheveled and one arm is hanging limply. Davis's face is hidden from McCann's view; he also cannot see Fuso. McCann is swearing to himself over and over again. His mind has frozen; he cannot think what to do. All this has come as too much of a surprise, too quickly; in a day that has been full of surprises already, this is the deadliest.

Although he is straining his ears, he cannot hear any kind of movement, only the high-pitched ringing caused by the shotgun and the absurdly loud sound of his own breathing. He can't tell if he is panting like a jogger after a tough run, or if he merely imagines his breathing is so loud. He reminds himself again: he needs more cartridges and the ammunition box is in a cupboard only about twenty feet away. Stooping like a simian prehistoric, eyes glued now at the windows, now at the gaping hole in the front of the cabin where the door used to be, he lopes silently across the shadows towards the homemade cupboards in the kitchen area – silent, at least, until he thumps into something hard, shrouded in the gloom, and loses his balance. His hands reach to the floor to break his fall, the shotgun clatters on the wood, and he slides in a warm, viscous fluid. He is appalled and involuntarily lets a miserable, pitiful wail slip from his lips.

It is Fuso.

No time to digest this; there is a crash of glass behind him. Sekiguchi is at the side window and has heard his clumsy movements. A short, crisp burst of bullets zips and pings round the room through the broken pane. As McCann scrambles behind the upturned table he hears the bullets chasing him, waspish insects searching out death in the coffin-cabin.

Crouching behind the makeshift barricade, in the spectral light he seems to see ghosts; hollow-cheeked icons flit before him for a millisecond in the dark night outside. Another flash of a face – his mother? McCann screws his eyes shut in fearful horror. He knows that this is the inevitable endgame of everything that has happened since the party in Roppongi; or maybe that he has been out of his depth and followed by an ill-fated star from the moment he took this job. He cannot help himself any longer. Fists crunched into impotent white-knuckle epilepsy, he breaks into a ghastly, sub-human groan, a pitch as grim and hideous as his gothic surroundings. Gradually, the grotesque teeth-grinding noise morphs into one word: "Sekiguchi!"

THE UNDEAD

Eyes wide, lips curled in unbridled hate, jerkily stepping up from behind the table, he is too angry to be afraid, too lost to be careful. Uncaring of his vulnerability he puts the shotgun to his shoulder, takes deliberate aim and blasts straight back at the broken window, punching a gaping hole in the wall, utterly pulverising the remaining three panes. Bits of wood and window frame disappear into the night like debris being sucked out the fuselage of a disintegrating jumbo jet in a disaster movie.

Has McCann realised that Sekiguchi is no longer there? The killer waits for his moment, shoots and instantly moves on. By the time McCann knows where he is, Sekiguchi is already somewhere else. The gazelle is not equipped to face the lioness; it must escape or be killed. Anger cannot change this law of nature, nor brash bravery. But McCann is like a reckless chess player who has made one bad move and has lost his concentration, exposing himself to his opponent. That he is no longer thinking clearly is evidenced by his stepping out from behind the protection of the table and pulling the trigger a fourth, final time. Another pointless explosion of energy as the last precious cartridge thumps into the wall near where the window was, blasting apart another piece of wall, but the sound and fury signify nothing.

In the deafening aftermath his teeth grate together again; his jaw clicks unnaturally; he blinks twice and staggers back a couple of steps towards the sanctuary of the table, but he is still almost in the middle of the room and he knows he has regained his composure too late.

From the cavity of the front door, he perceives a miniscule, devastating movement, and he understands what is coming. From the side, too, out of the corner of his eye, he can see some strange motion, slow but unbearably menacing, as inevitable as the turning of the gun turret on a tank. The entire room seems to be alive, revolving towards him; or perhaps it is just his head that is spinning. He is suddenly pinioned by the light of a torch from the front door, so bright after the half-light of the camping lamp that he temporarily sees nothing but the veins inside his own eyes, blood red on citron-gold. In the centre, nothing but a blinding brilliance and dark dots, black holes. In his peripheral vision, a figure takes one step into the doorway and something moves further over on his left side. He knows Sekiguchi is in front of him, although he cannot see anything other than the outline of his adversary. The shadow seems to shrug almost apologetically, as if to say "Sorry, but…"

Another movement: it must be the pistol raised to end this struggle. The impotent shotgun is limp by McCann's side: perhaps he can use it as a club; perhaps there is a chance. How long will it take him to cross the room to Sekiguchi? Can his momentum get him there before the bullets take him down? But even as these ideas pass through his head he teeters backwards. It is impossible; he knows it is over.

The undead rises up to meet him, to keep him company on his journey to the River Styx. The ferryman Charon is waiting. A coin to pay the ferryman, he thinks. Do I have one? This undead in the margin of his vision: tousled hair suggesting an odd vigour that the caved-in face denies, knots itself in a supernatural energy as its torso rises from the cot, a literal and deadly Lazarus.

The torch suddenly wavers slightly, as if something has attracted the holder's attention, but it is already too late; the harpoon has been launched from a practiced arm.

McCann cannot see the arc of the ancient weapon on its short, final journey, because the torch has lurched away from his eyes towards something in the corner of the room, and the dazzling light is replaced by blinding darkness. He cannot hear the spear thump solidly into the torso of its prey for the rush of blood in his ears, pounding like the rapids of a river. He cannot imagine the shock and incomprehension on Sekiguchi's face as it registers the impossible truth – that a long, slim harpoon has passed straight through his sternum and he is falling backwards, forever – because

McCann's own mind is frozen in confusion.

Then there is the unmistakable sound of another shot from the muffled pistol, a final random expiration, and the Beretta and the body simultaneously hit the floor. Murky green darkness gives way to night shapes. McCann floats forward towards the prostrate assassin; have his legs carried him? Some force compels him. As he leans over the Japanese man lying on his back with the hideous projection sticking through his body, Sekiguchi raises an arm; a mute, imperial gesture that is as eloquent and futile as the shrug had been a few seconds before; the entire landscape has changed in the time it takes to throw a pebble at the waves. Sekiguchi is still breathing, but very slowly and with a quiet, deadly asthmatic rattle. He does not register McCann's approach and although his eyes are fixed at a point on the ceiling when McCann stoops over him, they quickly drift away into infinity. There is a deep intake of breath and then nothing. Not a murmur has crossed his lips in his passing.

302

THE DIMMING LIGHT OF
THE FIRE

Then the silence, or the almost silence, is ushered in. It is a charged lull and contains a discord of struggling breath, a hiss of sizzling embers and the thump of McCann's own heart. There is a smell too, one he can't define, but that sickens him. It has a sweet scent and reminds him of something past, gone but alive in the chambers of memory, a ghost carrying an ashen lamp in a maze of dead trees. He approaches the light and the visage of Davis comes into view just as McCann's fractured sense of perception begins to clear and he can discern the outlines of the horror.

Davis is smiling a crimson smile and McCann notices that the boy is also weeping, though not out of sorrow it seems, for he wears an expression of some macabre merriment. McCann kneels beside him and he whispers an entreaty, "Wood, George. I am cold."

McCann reels out of the cabin back into the night, benumbed with shock, overwhelmed by events he cannot handle. The night is a firmament of stars and iced rain stinging his cheeks and bringing him back to a kind of consciousness. He collects a bundle of dry wood and makes his way up towards the cabin, the place that not long before had been full of possibilities, perhaps answers, perhaps something more than just answers. He returns to where the door used to be and passes over the threshold: entering the home of the dead and dying. He replenishes the fire with shaking hands and finds a blanket.

"Can you stand?"

Davis grins again but then splutters and coughs up a mixture of bile and blood. "Nice one, mate. Help me, George."

He wraps Davis in a blanket and offers him brandy, which he takes.

⚏

They are seated by the fire now, side by side, and Davis seems stable. McCann has no idea how many times Davis was shot by Sekiguchi, but there are two obvious wounds, oozing blood, and he wraps them in towels. He knows that the boy is gravely injured and bleeding to death. He must get an ambulance, but how? He can't speak the language and is in a place without an address, in a wilderness whose name he has forgotten.

The mobile phone. He grabs for his jacket, crumpled on the floor by the overturned chair, and with agitated hands pulls it from the pocket. He can barely hold it and cannot push the buttons. Finally, he manages to switch it on. There is, of course, no reception. It takes McCann quite a few minutes to understand that he is in a truly primeval world: they have left all the succour of modernity far behind.

Except one: the car. He can carry Davis up to the car and drive to a town. There's still a chance. "We're going, Charlie. We have to get you to a hospital. You can live through this."

McCann stands and bends over to lift Davis up and is greeted with a spit of blood.

Davis tries to rise, but fails and falls by the grate, then somehow twists himself back into a squat, grabbing the poker and speaking quietly with halting breaths. "You touch me and I will kill you, George. I don't die in fucking hospitals."

McCann tries to fight this. He reaches for Davis again, grabs him under the arms, but is met with a crazed kind of resistance, and anyway, he knows deep somewhere inside himself that Davis is right. Helplessly, wordlessly, he sinks back down. He looks at his hands that are gloved in blood and gleaming in the playful, yellow dancing flames. Davis has found the bottle and is drinking.

"Give me my cards, George. The deal is almost done."

McCann picks up the silk wrap and notices for the first time that it is patterned with small dragons: childish, almost cute ones; cuddly dragons of fairytales, friends of children and bedtime stories by fires, just like the one that is blazing now. He hands the package to Davis. With difficulty the boy opens the bundle and takes out the cards. He then drops them onto the floor, laughs a wheezy, dying laugh, and speaks again. At that moment McCann stands up and steps to the window, where he wipes blood and sticky tears from his face. In a sudden stasis of mood, a stop in time, he can see that a soft snow is falling like a warning, or an invitation.

"Sorry? I missed that, Charlie."

Davis smiles, "I said, I won't be needing these anymore."

The boy is throwing the cards onto the fire and haltingly humming a tune as McCann comes closer. The cards dull the flames and the light darkens, covered as it is by the ever-increasing steps of the arcana, major and minor, glowing in their last act, finally meaning something. "That's that. And this is for you."

The boy hands the man the wrap. There are still objects in it.

"Go on, open it."

Inside there are some envelopes addressed to Charlie Davis, and others addressed to Natasha Philips. McCann opens one and finds a plain postcard. Holding it in the dimming light of the fire, he reads: '*Charlie, this is a union of dreams, an absolution.*' The card is signed with an imprint of a lipsticked kiss and she has etched her name into the rouge in tiny writing: '*Natasha.*'

The boy pulls McCann close to him and whispers some words in his ear. Then he moves away again and is talking, but not to anyone that McCann can see. Charlie has found a shell that he turns around and around in his hands. He puts the shell to his ear and smiles. "George, she wants me to go now."

McCann has settled into something approaching a dark tranquility and knows the boy is in the final chapter of his story. It is with a soft voice that he answers, "Who is it Charlie? Who wants you to go?"

Davis has stopped grinning and is looking at McCann with an expression he hasn't seen before. He seems ready for what is to come and a truce is in his eyes. It no longer matters to McCann who has done what and to whom; he has had enough of judgment, of right and wrong, of everything.

"George, will you sing with us?"

McCann smiles, "Yes, Charlie. I will sing with you."

Davis slumps forward and drops the shell. His attempt to pick it up fails. "Please,

George, give it to me."

McCann obliges. Davis sits straight and with jerks of affliction manages to coerce his failing body back to its familiar cross-legged position. Then he begins to sing into the shell. McCann knows the song from his own childhood, and a lost world sweeps him back there and he sings along, with the boy before him and in him. The song enters him and clears him of all thought as he looks at Fuso, then at Davis, and then finally he just sings:

'Puff the Magic Dragon lived by the sea,
And frolicked in the autumn mist in a land called Honalee.'

Davis is smiling now and looking at McCann as he interrupts the song to say something, but the words are garbled and unclear. They begin to sing again and this time Davis is singing himself to death, but as each note gets lower and weaker McCann covers for him; one voice slipping away, the other singing out with more gusto:

'Little Jackie Paper loved that rascal Puff,
And brought him strings and sealing wax and other fancy stuff.
Puff the Magic Dragon lived by the sea,
And frolicked in the autumn mist in a land called Honalee...'

The fire casts a luminous light over the funereal scene: the man and the boy; the beautiful dead woman lying on the floor, eyes open and present at the ceremony; another impaled on a harpoon, stiffening in rigor mortis and firelight.

McCann takes Davis's hand and Charlie presses it. He is going now and his voice is fading, but he holds eye contact and there is nothing hard about those eyes anymore; he is done with the acts of the world and pretence, and slips away with the song as his eyes close forever and his grip ceases. McCann sings:

*'One grey night it happened, Jackie Paper came no
more,
And Puff the Mighty Dragon, he ceased his fearless
roar.
His head was bent in sorrow, green scales fell like rain,
Puff no longer went to play along the cherry lane.
Without his lifelong friend, Puff could not be brave,
So, Puff that mighty Dragon sadly slipped into his
cave.'*

Afterwards, he may have slept. He remembers getting up and covering Davis with the blanket. Later still, he goes outside again and watches a thin snow fade into the waters of the sea. A curlew calls from the distance and he knows that he is alive and he has things to do.

PART 4 -
COSMOS

HIERONYMOUS BOSCH

McCann floats out of the cabin, carried by the same mysterious propulsion that had taken him towards the dying Sekiguchi. He is operating entirely on autopilot; his memory is fragmented like a drunken man who wakes up in his bed with no idea how he got home. While his sentient processes have been stunted and warped by the dreadful night he has just endured, his subconscious knows what must be done and goes about it in a surprisingly efficient manner.

He is back at the dinghy, a hundred metres or so down the beach from the cabin. With a shock, he realises that he is wearing Sekiguchi's black leather killing gloves, stretched tightly over his great muckle hands. A shiver runs down his spine. He feels like he has put his hands in a bag of snakes, but he does not remove the gloves. His conscious mind does not know why; perhaps his innate intelligence does. Perhaps he won't even remember wearing them at all when this grisly business is done. In the incomplete darkness he once again sets foot in the boat, mechanically bales out most of the ice-cold bilge water sloshing around in the bottom of it, and uses the one oar to paddle back up to the scene of rotten carnage.

As he pulls the dinghy back down the beach, the pebbles clack together under keel and foot like marbles. Yet again on this long and difficult day, a memory from the past rises to the surface, as vivid as a lazy Sunday morning dream: he is rolling marbles at toy American soldiers his father has set up in the hall, then his dad is rolling them back at Colin's German soldiers, each of them knocking the miniature infantrymen down like it's the Battle of the Bulge, last man standing is the winner. Last man standing … but his intuition has no time for dazed meandering. It is a practical beast and with scalpel-like precision cuts the useless remembrance from him.

He bumps into a dark metal object and realises he is now looking for something in the outhouse; a small shed of fishing equipment, old skis and rusty pulleys. He doesn't think he's been in here before, but he could be wrong; at this point it's hard to know what is a real memory and what is not. Whatever he was looking for, he must have found it, because the next thing he is aware of, he is back in the boat, clamping a small Yamaha outboard motor to the transom. Fiddly, with those too-small leather gloves on. But they stay on.

He checks the petrol, opens the choke, pulls again and again on the starter cord until eventually it splutters into life like a consumptive old man gasping on a cigarette. He runs the engine for a while until the croaks become more energetic phut-phuts and he is confident that the motor is in a good enough condition to take him on this last journey.

Faced with death, McCann thought he had seen a vision of the ferryman on the River Styx coming for him. Now it seems he himself is the ferryman, transporting the dead to the afterlife. The bodies are heavy, heavier even than their lifeless density. He has weighed them down with large rocks in the pockets of their bloody clothes, although he has no recollection of doing this. As he drags the miserable corpse of Fuso Tochimoto over the stony beach he considers his handiwork critically. He knows that these rudimentary weights will not keep the bodies

314

on the seabed for long, but he is beyond caring and hopes that, provided they are not discovered too soon, it won't be his concern when they do wash up somewhere, bloated, half-eaten, warped by nature, bullet-ridden.

He stacks the three bodies on top of each other in the dinghy, trying to think of them as inanimate cargo. But looking down at them, mouths and eyes open, their limbs splayed awkwardly, he is repulsed and disgusted. Weird paintings come unbidden to his mind: heads placed backwards on stunted torsos, ghoulish dismembered body parts, fish coming out the mouths of bigger fish, coming out the mouths of bigger fish, coming out the mouths of bigger fish...

The cold water he delves his face into brings him briefly to his senses. He looks up at the sky and it is as unchanging as it was a few hours ago, when he sat on the beach and the three corpses were alive.

Certainly, some time has passed. He is sitting on the beach, his head in his hands and he has dreadful pins and needles running all the way down his legs from his knees to his feet. It is time. He must do this, quickly and competently. Manoeuvering the dinghy, jumping in as a gentle wave breaks over his ankles and the freezing water rushes into his shoes for the umpteenth time, he pushes off from the shore, sits on the wooden bench at the stern and with a couple of heaves at the cord, starts the outboard again, pointing the bow at the darkness of the sea.

Although the storm has passed and the weather is calm, as McCann travels away from the shore he looks fearfully at the purple-black water, which rises and falls with the easy omnipotence of the giant sleeping ogre as Jack tiptoes towards the beanstalk. Further and further he progresses into the sea, as far as he dares, until his nerve goes and he can bear neither the silent orgy of death before him nor the continued stretching of his umbilical cord to the land any longer.

Terrified that if he turns off the engine he will not be able to start it again, he leaves it running and moves gingerly to the body on top of the pile: Tatsuo Sekiguchi. Strangely, he does not seem to feel much real anger at this man who brought such a chaotic and miserable conclusion to the episode; but nor does he feel the need to make any kind of spiritual offering to the stars over the man's dead soul. He can think of nothing to say or do other than roll the body over the side, but with the dinghy pitching and yawing in the water and the considerable weight of the dead Sekiguchi, this act is not as easy as he had hoped. With an ugly lunge and a collision of insensible flesh on wood, he eventually manages to send the carcass over the side and into the sea. As he watches the body descend swiftly into the darkness, luminous white where the skin shows, its hands and black hair lifting back towards the surface of the water even as it drifts deeper, he knows that he will never forget this moment, that it will haunt his nights for many years.

He slumps back at the tiller and opens the throttle, and for ten minutes he sails away from both the shore and Sekiguchi's final resting place.

Fuso is next. This time he does switch off the engine, lifts her cold, inert body and holds her briefly, closing his eyes but thinking nothing at all. The sound of the waves lapping against the clinker hull in the night is complex and intimate, a million different tones for a million different wave shapes, each as unique and ephemeral as a snowflake. When he opens his eyes again the night sky is blurry and he realises he has been crying. He mumbles an inadequate prayer for this person he could not really know, kisses the quiescent object on the forehead and rolls her into the water. As her centre of gravity shifts and she tips over the gunwale, the horror of having watched Sekiguchi sink into the deep is vivid in his mind and he closes his eyes again. He hears the gulp of the water as it swallows Fuso, and then he sits for a long time looking up at the clouds and occasional stars. He decides not to move the boat again, realising that he is not concerned with possible discovery of the corpses together, or, for that matter, apart, but is instead preoccupied with making sure that Fuso and Davis are not enshrined alongside Sekiguchi. And it seems fitting to him that Fuso and Davis are laid to rest side by side.

He sighs deeply and looks at Davis. Even in death he is a force of nature, dynamic, indestructible. It does not matter that the face is slightly thrawn, the supple limbs of youth are hardening, the hair is plastered down dully on the forehead. Encased in this body is something untouchable, something beyond life and death, or right and wrong. McCann feels the closeness of a cosmic enigma, the biggest unknown of all, and as he looks at Davis he is aware that even now there is more than just a shell here, that the energy which was contained in it will simply be redirected, pulsing through the seas and up into the night sky and beyond. He moves stiffly to the middle seat in the boat and, sitting down beside Davis, pats his shoulder familiarly, before quietly addressing the corpse.

❧

❝Charles, when I was sixteen my Uncle Ricky – that's my dad's youngest brother – gave me a book. He was a funny one, Uncle Ricky, bit of a character. Great storyteller. But you never quite knew where you stood with him. Of course, I realise now a lot of that was because of my age.

I was just a kid at the time. He emigrated to Australia before I was twenty, and about five years after that he died in a car crash, so I never really got the chance to talk to him as an adult. Somehow, you knew he wasn't going to end up at ninety in an old folks' home. With some people you can just tell. They have something about them." He pauses, looks down at the handsome, twisted face.

"Ricky was a big Jimi Hendrix fan. Used to laugh at my Sex Pistols singles and say, 'Yeah, not bad. You think you lot invented rock 'n' roll, eh? Bollocks!' And I laughed at him and gave him the vikkies and said, 'Never mind the bollocks, Uncle Ricky. You don't know nothing!' And then he used to laugh and cuff me on the side of the head – hard. Every so often he'd give me something; a tape he'd made up, a book of poetry. Never said much about them, just, 'Give this a go, lad. Might turn your head.' And I'd go home and try to make sense of whatever it was. Maybe Tangerine Dream, or Herman Hesse or something. This book he gave me once, it was tremendous. It was called *On the Shortness of Life*, by Seneca. Roman philosopher.

"'Colin,' says Ricky…"

Breaking off suddenly, McCann turns to look at the corpse beside him. And for the first time in a long, long time, he does not really know why, his face bursts into an unaffected grin. "That's my real name, by the way. Colin. Colin McCann. Sorry I never told you that before, Charlie."

He pauses for a long time, looking at the firmament and listening to the sounds the boat makes in the water. Then he clears his voice and continues.

"So Uncle Ricky says, 'Colin, get this down your gullet, young man. You think you're a smartarse, eh? You've read nothing till you've read this.' And he gives me this book On the Shortness of Life. You would love it,

318

Charlie. It's right up your street, pal. I remember opening it and reading the first page. Still remember the shock of it now, realising that this guy was writing two thousand years ago, and every word jumped right out the page at me. Most people complain because life is so short, that just as we're getting the hang of it, it's over. But in fact, it's not that we have a short time to live, but that most of us waste the precious time that we do have. That's how it starts. That was it, right there, got me hooked. Somewhere along the way, though, I think I forgot that. Lost the fundamental truth of it. And I need to get that back again."

He nods to himself, aware that a subtle change is coming over the night sky. It is still nowhere near morning, but something in the hue of the darkness tells him that in a couple of hours the dawn will break over this vast sea. He inhales deeply; his whole body shifts as he breathes out; a huge plume of condensed breath issues from his mouth into the sharp sky like a ghost.

"Time to say goodbye, Charlie."

As he moves his position the boat rocks to and fro gently, a tiny insignificant cork trembling on the now impassive sea. He lifts the body to the edge of the boat and reverses his actions of just a few hours previously, easing him back into the deep once again.

DRIFTING

The sky imperceptibly lightens from tar-pitch towards neutral grey. Shoeless, pressing gently down on the accelerator, feeling the shape of the pedal grooves through a pair of cold, wet socks, he decides he doesn't like automatics. His sodden footwear lies on the floor of the empty passenger seat. Sure, in a big city changing gears up and down as you inch along can be a pain, but rural Hokkaido is sparsely populated and Route 39 is almost empty at 6am this dull morning. As he drives away from Abashiri towards a place called Kitami, he wishes he had the control and enjoyment of a manual gear change.

His mind is clear: perhaps a little too clear. He needs to be careful; he knows he is in a state of utter nervous exhaustion. An accident in a car that is not his, that belongs to a dead woman who may or may not wash up one day on an unsuspecting beach, could comprehensively topple his house of cards. Keep it simple: stop if you need to, don't drift into fatigued hallucinations; don't blow it now.

Even as he thinks this, his mind is wandering. For the third time he ticks off a checklist of all that he has done, uselessly trying to close loopholes in his mind, when he should just be focusing on staying in the left lane and driving straight. His jumbled, hyperactive mind bounces from the three on the seabed, to Twilly, to the *yakuza* and Murasaki Ryo, to the compulsory fingerprinting at Narita Airport when he arrived all of ten days ago. There are huge complications that he has absolutely no control over, but given all that has happened these risks are inevitable. He knows that his best option is to tidy things up as best he can, try to erase his fingerprints and his presence from the cabin where possible, do something with the car that Sekiguchi came in, and get the hell out of Dodge City. At some point the missing people will be noted, the cars will eventually be found and traced, the bodies might appear one day, but the most important thing is that by then he will be long gone and disassociated from it all.

The shroud continues to lift as the morning gradually brightens. He gazes blankly out the window for a while. Although the scenery is quite different, memories of that childhood family touring holiday in Scotland float back again.

Returning to the present, or at least the recent past, he nods to himself, lightheaded but pleased he had the presence of mind to keep both Fuso's and Sekiguchi's car keys. He disposed of the killer's vehicle in woodland half an hour from the cabin. For the first ten minutes it was a darkly slapstick one-man tag-team car relay, and he giggles indulgently at the recollection of running back and forth from car to car before he realised he hadn't even checked for a tow rope.

He amuses himself, like someone with a hangover recalling the events of the night before. Then his head jerks and he wakes with the realisation that he had lost consciousness and the Nissan is sliding across lanes, in danger of slipping off the road altogether. With a sudden adrenalin spike he swerves back to the correct lane and, taking the hint, pulls over for a break at the next opportunity. He sleeps for fifteen twitchy minutes then drinks from the flask of strong coffee he made before leaving the cabin. After that he massages his temples with his still-gloved hands; when that seems to have no effect, he starts slapping himself around, which helps, and grins stupidly in the rear-view mirror. He looks like shit.

He stops for breaks three or four times before arriving at his destination, the small town of Iwamizawa. He drives around assessing the lie of the land, but resists the urge to eat despite his desperate hunger; a frayed foreigner in this town on a grey November morning would certainly be remembered. Leaving the car in the corner of an unobtrusive piece of spare land on the edge of town, he collects his small rucksack and suitcase from the back seat, shudders as he slips into his still-saturated shoes, and squelches the twenty-five minutes back to the train station, shivering with cold and passing nary a soul on the way.

Inside the station, an incongruous ultra-modern glass-and-brick affair, he sneaks around, struggling with the ticket machine, desperate to attract neither the attention of benevolent locals nor the equally helpful train staff. Sweating profusely, hunched deeply into his jacket, he tries to make sense of the route map, inserts some money, pushes some buttons and somehow manages to procure a ticket for Sapporo, where he will be able to merge into the busyness of the big city. Having looked at the atlas in the cabin and considered his options, he has decided that his least easily traceable route is not to fly from Sapporo, but rather, to take another train to the port of Otaru, then a ferry back to Honshu and finally, he hopes, a plane from Tokyo to London.

᛭

He is clocked by the passengers as he makes his way down the aisle to his numbered seat on the Sapporo train. He catches the eye of some of them and their stares dart away, back to newspapers or smartphones. Thankfully the seat next to him is empty. Depositing his gear and pulling a small white towel from his holdall he heads instantly for the toilet. It is occupied so he waits, looking blankly out the window at the landscape that sweeps by in sliding pictures of wild majesty.

In the washroom he gazes at his reflection; it looks back at him as if not sure who he is. He strips off his sweat-scented clothes and washes himself as best as he can before putting them back on. As he cleans his arms and hands he notices specks of the dark sand of Shiretoko run in soapy rivulets down the plug hole. He ruffles his hands through his hair, then there is a cough outside so he squeezes out of the tiny space, bowing slightly to the man who is waiting. The man returns the gesture with an apology.

Sitting at last, he runs through a series of options. Ideally he should book into a hotel for a short time, change clothes and assess the situation. His stomach groans again; he also needs to eat. Presently the carriage door opens and a young girl comes out wheeling a trolley full of goodies – almost as if she is cognisant of his complaining belly.

McCann orders a cold rice lunch box, a container of something that looks like crisps, and a bottle of green tea. He demolishes the food, then falls into a disturbed slumber, waking at intervals, frightened by the images he sees behind his eyes and the echoes of voices both whispering and shouting. The train begins to fill up and at length a lady sits beside him, staring straight ahead and holding the handles of her branded bag as if she is riding a bicycle. For a second he gapes at the woman. She looks like Fuso and suddenly McCann feels the horror return: he pictures her dead body and imagines the thump of it hitting the floor. He fights back the temptation to speak to her. He is alone in the world, condemned to be a silent witness.

SEA CHANGE

It is a substantial ship that waits on the dark water of Otaru and a jittery McCann who boards it. During this long day of travel his head continues to churn, full of questions and doubts. He has bolted from three crime scenes and is carrying a bag containing belongings of those slain, aware that he is a man on the reverse side of the law he professed to uphold. As he embarks he looks back over his shoulder at the purser, but the uniformed man is standing by the gangway in a halo of sickly yellow electric light, staring straight ahead into the darkness. Is McCann starting to lose his grip on reality? His berth is compact and the bunk just long enough to lie on without being cramped, but he is restless and agitated and knows he won't be able to sleep. When he arrives home he will have to face Philips, who will be expecting answers. Does he have any? He opens his suitcase and, for the first time since packing, he looks at the items he took from the cabin.

Somewhere deep down below the engines rumble and the ship begins to leave port and move out towards the open water. It gives him some relief to feel unlocked from stasis and moving again. He goes up on deck to watch the departure, picking up a few beers from a vending machine on the way. There are very few people about, no doubt deterred by both the lateness of the hour and the weather; the air is clean and bracing but icy cold. Retrieving his hat and gloves from his pocket he opens a beer and stands watching the lights of Otaru fade into the distance towards the vanishing point, then walks around the deck from starboard to port, trying to clear his mind and to dim the recurring fear that somehow he won't make it back and will instead be caught by the police and tried for the murder of three people, framed by the *yakuza*. They will be waiting for confirmation of a successful job from Sekiguchi and when they don't receive it, presumably they will be on their way to find out why. He shivers, not with cold but fear, then gives himself a talking to and hurls the empty can into the clean water, watching it fall from the third tier of the deck and hit the calm sea, bobbing for a moment before disappearing beneath the waves. He immediately regrets his action.

Opening up a second beer he gulps down a draught, talking loudly to himself. "Should just have taken a flight from Sapporo. This is a time waster and time is what I do not have."

Within him a darkness of memories brews, fresh, vivid and scarlet: of survival and death amidst butchery. A sense of guilt builds too, as it occurs to him that without this prying mission perhaps Fuso and Davis would be alive now. He trembles as a mist comes over the sea, enveloping the ship and clearing the decks of the few souls remaining on it, but McCann is frozen to the spot, arrested by the trauma of what he has seen and the dread of what might await him. He looks down at the sea, more ruffed now, and at the white wake left by the ship. How easy it would be to disappear, put this and all else behind him. The drop to the water is mesmerizing. It wouldn't take long; the cold would kill in minutes. What does a life add up to anyway? A gentle breeze comes over the sea, bringing further, denser mists that glow ghostly in the ship's deck lights. He recalls snapshots: of Tokyo and its neon fantasiascapes; drunk Kyle and his quirky theories; Davis with his impish seductive grin; then to Sapporo, and Fuso with her cryptic comments and mischievous eyes; even the crazed Sekiguchi on stage with Freddie somewhere in a karaoke box in the sky. He is almost knocked reeling by the intensity of the memories but somehow finds himself smiling, tearfully but not without joy, and he feels buoyed and heightened. He begins to laugh out loud, then notices a couple walking along the deck through the mist towards him. He realises he is almost howling and tries to muffle the shrieks but cannot and cracks up even more as they do a swift about turn and retreat.

"I'd probably do the same if I saw a crazy geezer laughing in the mist at midnight," he mumbles to himself. The fit eventually passes and he quickly makes his way below deck.

The cabin is warm and womb-like but claustrophobic too; he can't stay here, so he gathers the letters and postcards that Davis gave him and a small torch that belonged to Sekiguchi, puts them in his leather day bag along with the remaining can of lager, and goes back on deck.

Stars are faintly glittering over the Sea of Japan. The fog has mostly dissipated now and visibility is fair, but a wind has risen so he goes to the leeward side, finds a bench on the lower deck, switches on the torch and takes out a letter postmarked the previous January. Clenching the torch between his teeth he begins to read the flapping epistle.

Nothing much here, just a regular love letter from Natasha to Davis – '...*thought I'd write to you in the 19th Century way ... it was a wicked gig ... awesome place.*' He reads through it again, but in his excitement and exhaustion his eyes are jumping all over the page. He knows he should just go back to the cabin, sift through the letters properly and read them in order but he's not yet ready for the enclosed space or the possibility of meeting other people.

As he browses through the papers it's clear that while most of them are from Natasha to Davis, some of them are Davis's own musings; indeed, there is also a small diary, mostly written by someone in Japanese, but containing a few entries by Davis near the end. He leafs through it briefly and his attention is caught by a single loose sheet signed 'C Davis'. It is a poem and McCann finds that unlike with the diary and letters he is able to focus and read it carefully:

When death is a sin
The living are only masks.
If fear is an alien
And hospitals cathedrals
The soul is history.

When life is not life
The inhabitants are ghosts
And there's only a place
For them left
A cliff edge with a cushion
In a fake spun tapestry
Of
What one was known
To fear
Become normal.

Humanity doesn't shudder
Anymore
About a thing.
It is lost and done.

And who wants that!
Who?

Certainly not Davis; normality was the last thing he wanted. McCann smiles and raises the last can to Charlie. He pockets the poem.

Even at this time of night and this far from the shore gulls are spinning in the sky, following the ferry, screeching shrilly and without apparent reason. He remembers the tattoo of a seabird on Davis's inner wrist and hails them, "Here's to seabirds everywhere! Those that shit on me in Roppongi, those that shit on me in Abashiri, those that lie at the bottom of the sea, and those that follow me here."

He empties the last can, pulls out a long letter from Natasha to Charlie and starts to read. The tone is sombre and disturbing. She lays into her family, her university life and also, in a swathe of curses, Davis for not showing up for a meeting. The wind is getting up now and McCann shifts his position to lessen its impact. He is having a hard time reading in the buffeting wind and with the mad squall of birds overhead. A sudden voice startles him, and as he shifts round to meet it a mighty gust of wind rips the letter from his hand.

"*Sumimasen!*" The ship's crewman holds a torch and gazes nervously at McCann.

"Danger, sir. Please come."

McCann stiffens and thinks *yakuza*, then notices the man pointing out to sea.

"Big water sir, danger. Come."

McCann stares at the crewman, then at his empty hand and out to sea where the letter is forever gone, flying free with the seabirds.

THE LETTERS

"Davis is dead."

He didn't say anything else at first, just those three words for them to digest. Harold Philips' eyes bulged. Sitting once more at his big mahogany desk, he looked down at his hands then looked up again, made a noise that was halfway between a glottal stop and an uncomprehending grunt.

The clock in the corner continued its methodical demarcation as if nothing in the previous two weeks had changed. Rather than soothing the quiet space it seemed to be slicing up the time, rushing the three in the room towards oblivion; or at least, that was how McCann felt. Philips still said nothing, looked unsure how to react to this opening bombshell.

His wife cleared her throat. "So … what happened to him?"

McCann opened his bag and placed the bundle of what remained of Charlie Davis on the table. "I have to tell you, Mr. and Mrs. Philips, that I am not prepared to say anything at all about what happened to him, except that he is dead. And that I … did not kill him, but I was with him when he died."

As he spoke he was aware of the high-pitched buzz of blood in his head, a tinnitus of emotion, but he had decided what he was going to say and knew this was the only way.

"As he was dying he said a few words. And he gave me

this." He motioned to the bundle of letters wrapped in the dragon cloth, opening it and carefully pulling some out with the tips of his fingers.

"These are letters from your daughter to him. And there are these also." He placed two of Davis's rings on the table. He had felt like a robber scouring a battlefield when he had pulled them off Davis's gelid hand, but he had known it would be necessary to have something corporeal, something substantial to show for his efforts. One ring was large and distinctive, a chunky piece of dull silver with a Celtic spiral design. The other was tiny – Davis had worn it on his pinky – and somewhat effeminate, a small ruby heart set flush in a simple gold band. At the time McCann had thought it a strange piece for Davis to wear, but then Davis was a strange young man.

When he put the jewellery down Harold Philips' face drained of all colour. Barbara stood up, putting her hand to her mouth and letting out a small involuntary cry. "But … that's Natasha's ring! We gave it to her for her birthday, years ago…" There wasn't much to say. "I know. It was on Davis's pinky in Japan. He wore it all the time."

Mrs. Philips struggled to keep her emotions under control.

Her husband was surprisingly quiet; he was thrown again and looked a bit lost. "It wasn't an expensive ring…" he mumbled.

The unhappy hopelessness of the comment hung for a couple of seconds; the clock took the opportunity to cut a few more off what remained. Harold's eyes narrowed then were distracted by a languid-looking bluebottle that landed on the corner of his desk. It seemed gorged and sanguine, like a fat hideous emperor from some ancient past returning to his chambers after a feast. Harold made a half-hearted attempt to swat it away and the fly limped into the air, landing this time right on top of Natasha's letters. It stopped then moved again, altering position, squatting and rubbing its front legs together. All three of them were transfixed by it; there was something almost sacrilegious about the way it sat there, a dark affliction on the pearl-white epistles of the lost one.

It was too much for Harold, who rolled up his Daily Telegraph and whacked down hard on the table, missing the fly and scattering the letters onto the floor. McCann and Mrs. Philips found themselves on their hands and knees collecting envelopes and papers while Harold bumbled and muttered apologies and curses. The fly meandered over to the globe in the corner of the room, settling somewhere between Madras and Rangoon.

McCann stood up, his hands full of letters. "By the way, I talked with Annabel Hollis again yesterday."

✂

She had been outside the cafe and rolling a cigarette when McCann and Marvin reached the corner. He stopped and muttered, "Belle of the café alright. What do you think, Marv?"

The dog looked up with an approving friendly growl. They walked on towards the table.

"Hello again."

She looked up at McCann and down at the dog, who gave his usual friendly throaty rumble at seeing a friend not yet met. McCann could see Marvin had scored again.

"Wow, I love dogs. Especially little tough guys like him."

The approval was mutual and soon Marvin was sitting contentedly beside her.

McCann wearily took stock. She looked at least

as beautiful as the first time he had met her: a girl for whom uncertainty was an antique idea. On the table lay her tablet of technology, her network of links and tags; she was checking a message with her right hand on her smartphone whilst petting Marvin with the left. McCann took a seat and ordered a pot of Earl Grey.

"Sorry, just a friend mailing about tonight. We've booked a table at 'Sherbert's'. You know the place? Just soooo lucky."

"Yeah. Thanks for coming. You okay for a drink?"

"Okay for now. Gotta white wine. Aussie Chardonnay. Really mad into it at the mo."

McCann realized that despite the time she was slightly tipsy. "Bit early to be on the sauce, Annabel." As soon as he said it he thought of his own previous twelve days' experience.

She giggled lightly. "Yeah, loving it!"

The tea arrived and McCann poured himself a cup.

"Just before you came there was a song playing and it reminded me of Natasha. She liked the bit in it when he goes 'shoot it all up' or something."

"Song about drugs?"

"Nah. Some old song. 'I wanna shoo-oo-oo-oot the whole day up'. Or 'down', one or the other. We used to hear it on the radio sometimes."

McCann nodded. He quite liked the song too: but not that much. He liked less and less lately.

Annabel was smiling. "So, do you shoot people or just hassle them?"

"Neither. As you know this is very important. Something that has to be cleared up and concluded."

She laughed as Marvin nuzzled closer beside her. "He's just tough cute. Can I have him?"

"It's about Charlie Davis, Annabel."

332

"I know. You told me on the phone. Him again. The Swan, I call him. Charlie the

Swan. He likes that. He hasn't been around lately."

"You missing him?"

"Oh, sure. Ha. He'll turn up eventually. Always does. Pond life."

She took a sip of wine. Her eyes shone and her hair gleamed. Prime time. She was there and knew it. "He's got a bit of grace, Charlie has, though. Not like the usual rough trade."

"Your type?"

"In the party world he's a lot of girls' type. Outside of it he's a nobody. You shouldn't take him so seriously, Mr. McCann. Nobody else does."

"Apart from Natasha."

She put her lips near to Marvin's snout, smooched with him for a while and murmured a couple of sweet nothings. It was a while before she quietly addressed his comment.

"Yeah, that surprised a few people. That they hooked up."

McCann could see she was about to say more but then changed her mind and held back.

"Did you hook up with Charlie too?"

She rolled her eyes. "Can't remember, really. Did you hook up with someone in your time before you started, like, the inquisition?"

"That wasn't actually a serious question. But you never know. Stranger things have happened."

She grinned. "I think you could be right about that. Could I have another wine?" He ordered, opened his small bag and started taking out the items that Davis had given him.

"Hey, I just got to nip across the road and get a new lighter. This one's buggered. You ain't got one have you?"

McCann shook his head. He had decided to give up smoking.

"Can I take him?"

"Sure."

"What's his name again?" She ruffled the dog's neck.

"Marvin. Marvin the Brave. Not quite Charlie the Swan, but close."

She laughed. McCann rather liked her and the irritating sparkle of her youth. She took off with Marvin across the pedestrian walkway towards the shops. McCann had a sip of her wine and wondered how she would react to the news she was about to receive. He stared into space for a while until they made their way back. It was a pleasure to watch the way she moved as she crossed the street towards him. The dog looked sprightly too.

She sat down and Marvin again took the seat beside her. They were both having a good time. She looked at the rings and the bundle on the table and began to roll a cigarette.

"Do you recognize these, Annabel?"

She carried on rolling until she had completed the job and then lit up. "Let me see."

Recognition was kindled. She picked up one of the rings. "These belong to Charlie. How did you get this ring? Natasha gave it to him. He never took it off."

"I pulled it off his hand."

"You've seen him?" She looked at McCann with a puzzled expression, knowing more was coming.

"Charlie's dead, Annabel."

She lowered her head again, pushing the rings and the letters around on the table. Sensing a change in the vibe, Marvin's glaikit, joyful smile was reduced to a mournful, unsure look. Marvin wasn't big on tragedy.

"I think you know he went to Japan, right?"

No reaction.

"I followed him there. He got into trouble. Gangster trouble. I tried to help him because I needed to talk with him about Natasha. But I was too late. I found him and I was with him when he died. He gave me the letters from Natasha and directed me to you. He said only you could tell me what happened to her. The real story. Actually what he said was, 'Read the letters then ask Annabel if she'll join the dots for you.' It was just about the last thing he said. I've read the letters. So can you?"

She started to cry a little, then let out a large sigh. She looked at McCann through smudged, swollen eyes and ran a hand through her hair, then petted Marvin's head again.

"I loved Natasha, Mr. McCann. More than anyone else I've ever known. I couldn't say I was a close friend of Charlie's. We were chalk and cheese, really. But him and Natasha together were…" She shrugged. "Do you mind if I take him for a short walk? To clear my head. If you have the time."

"Sure. I'll wait for you here. Got plenty of time." Plenty of time: he remembered saying the same thing to Charlie at the party in Roppongi, before everything got messed up for good.

Annabel stood and picked up Marvin's lead for a second time. The dog glanced at McCann with an inquisitive look, then at Annabel. He seemed almost contented as she led him off, but as they approached the corner he looked back once. McCann smiled at the two of them, then finished his tea and ordered an espresso.

Half an hour later the sound of a friendly bark aroused him from his reverie. They were returning the other way, across the cobbled courtyard. He waved to the girl but got no response. Annabel sat down and dropped her head, muttering, "I need another wine. I have something to tell you."

McCann ordered and waited. When it came she took a large gulp and looked straight at him.

"I saw the body."

"Natasha's body."

She nodded. "Yes. By the river bank. A couple of hours before she was found by… whoever it was. The way that night panned out, I had a feeling she might be there. She was so still. And I felt so guilty about it. I can't have left her for more than five

minutes…"

McCann waited. The girl seemed to be reliving the moment and her eyes filled with tears. "I went down to her and said some last things. Whispered our secret things and I pushed her from the bank back into the open river. The water took her and carried her downstream."

"Secret things?"

"We had a sacred promise. We were blood sisters."

"You were what?"

"We were related."

McCann froze. Philips was this girl's father?

"We entered our blood into each other. It was an oath."

She grew silent and McCann waited, exhaled. He looked at Marvin who sat respectfully with a look of concern on his face.

"When we were thirteen our parents let us go on a camping trip together. Our first one. Well, actually, we stayed at Dad's caravan near Conwy. We went up to the castle and waited for it to get dark. We hid from the security guard and when he closed the place up we were all alone. Natasha had brought a bottle of wine and a knife. So, we became sisters that summer night." She lifted her right thumb and he could see a slim white scar almost an inch in length down the middle of it.

"I see. A ritual. Blood brothers."

"Not brothers. Sisters. It's different. When the light came up and we walked down from the castle we were different."

He nodded. "Okay. But what has this got to do with Natasha's death?"

"I knew her, Mr. McCann. Better than anyone. We told each other stuff, stuff we promised that would remain secret, no matter what. 'Never tell them anything.' I promised I would accept whatever she did and remain silent and Natasha never forgot our promise. She always said we were outside this world looking in. It was sacrosanct to her. When I saw the body in the water I couldn't betray her. It was to be our secret."

"You expected her to do this, didn't you Annabel?"

"Do what?"

"Kill herself. You lied before."

"I misled you. I couldn't tell the truth, you see. It was a promise. Natasha hated the word 'suicide'. She thought it belonged to the authorities and the truly dead. She liked the idea of euthanasia, the good death. She hated the fear of death that prevails now. That was a belief she and Charlie shared. One of many, actually. She hated all those old people hanging on in front of television screens: the timidity of our age. I understood her and she trusted me. I respect Natasha."

They sat in silence for a while.

"But now I have broken our trust. So you see, I the flip little tart you take me for after all."

McCann shook his head and smiled at her.

"I don't know if the verdict – misadventure – was correct. Probably was. But I wasn't saying anything. What was secret between me and Natasha was for us only, and still is. Mr. Philips didn't like the verdict, of course, but he's her Dad. I am her best friend. I didn't want to say anything. That verdict seemed the ideal solution. Until you came clattering around, turning over the graves."

She attempted to roll a cigarette with shaking fingers but failed. McCann retrieved the fallen tobacco and paper from the table and rolled one for her, surprised at his dexterity.

"I had forgotten I could do that. Bloody better than you at it."

She looked at him, calmer now, and smiled wanly as she lit up and exhaled, "Yeah, that's a great rollie."

LIFT UP YOUR HEADS, O YE GATES

McCann took a gulp of the Philips' coffee and looked once more out the window at the trees, now almost entirely bare. A couple of tired leaves still clung obstinately to their branches. The sky was turning autumn pink and McCann could almost smell the Benson & Hedges in his father's left hand once again. When all was said and done, he had only experienced the relationship from one side, and he had no real way of evaluating the Philips' feelings from their point of view, as parents: he knew neither the joy nor the burden. He nudged the parcel towards Harold.

"Mr. Philips, Mrs. Philips, I think you need to read these letters from Natasha to Charlie Davis. It is her writing, isn't it? I mean, there's no question that she wrote them?"

He already knew the answer to that one, so carried on. "I read them, as Davis suggested. If you want to know the truth, I think you ought to as well. They … show a side to Natasha that perhaps she was very good at keeping hidden. I think the only person who knew about that side of her was Annabel. Until Davis came along, that is. She opened that part of herself up to him. It comes through very clearly in the letters. I need to tell you that some of what she has written will be painful for you to read. Some of it will, unquestionably, be hurtful to you. But if you want to really know what happened to her, I think the answer, basically, is there."

Mrs. Philips was silent and poised, on the edge of her seat.

Her husband looked grim. "Why don't you carry on with your story, Mr. McCann? We will read these at a more … suitable time."

"Okay, well, let's put it this way. I don't think your daughter was of the right kind of emotional make-up to be taking drugs at a music festival. Or anywhere else for that matter. Especially not after she got freaked out at the party – I don't know if they still call it a 'bad trip' or not – and had an argument with her boyfriend. I'm not a psychologist, but it looks like your daughter…"

"Had suffered from very acute depression for a number of years."

McCann's eyebrows lifted as his head swivelled round to Barbara Philips.

Her husband blurted out, "What nonsense is this?"

"Harold, forgive me. It's high time I said something. Mr. McCann, do not think that as a mother I walk around with my head completely in the sand about my children. It's true that Natasha hid her illness from us – especially from you, dear. But I did know she suffered. I just didn't know how much. Until the night she … took the overdose of sleeping pills. That was no trifling matter, I'm afraid. I tried to talk with her after that, but I think she was already too far from us by then. I don't know … I suppose I'd thought making a big deal of it would have been counter-productive, make things harder for her. Now I know I was wrong. Very wrong."

Harold looked from his wife to McCann and back again like a double-crossed bank robber. His reality was collapsing around him. "But … what are you saying? What do you mean 'too far from us'? What is it you are insinuating?"

"Our daughter was sick, Harold. Very sick. She managed to hide it from us. Or maybe it was more that we just didn't want to see it."

"Like I say, Mr. Philips, I'm no expert on mental health. Perhaps she would have been diagnosed as bipolar, I don't know. But if you read her letters to Davis, you'll see that it probably wouldn't have taken much for her to... go over the edge. What I do know is that the night she died, she took some drugs – a mix actually – that had a very bad effect on her, and quite early in the night she had an argument with Charlie Davis then stormed off. Davis went to Annabel – the only other person who really knew about Natasha's condition – and told her what had happened. Annabel found Natasha and looked after her for the next few hours, but Annabel told me she went to the bathroom at about two in the morning and when she returned five minutes later, Natasha was gone. By the time she found her, down by the river... well, you know the rest, I think."

Apart from the ticking clock the house was unnaturally silent, mothballed, a structure that seemed to have lost its purpose. Harold, dejected, put down his cup and saucer, folded his hands together and started silently at the table.

Barbara touched her forehead as if she felt a migraine coming on. "So, why the deception, Mr. McCann? Why did the Davis boy disappear? And why did Natasha's friends all lie when, in fact, there was nothing to lie about?"

"Davis did phone them all, that was true. I'm not sure how threatening he was – Annabel told me he was more persuasive than he was sinister – but with Davis you never knew exactly where you stood. He was capable of a lot of things, some of them very unpleasant. Davis never did show much faith in the institutions of the establishment.

He told Annabel that morning that he knew he would be a scapegoat for Natasha's death and didn't expect a fair hearing. It was easier for him just to disappear. That suited Annabel. She had her oath to Natasha; she felt very guilty about what had happened, the two of them had their secrets and she wasn't inclined to divulge them to anyone, no matter what happened. The others were easily persuaded. So Davis' name was erased from the story. And when I started looking into it, things worked out exactly as Davis had said: all the fingers pointed at him, all the more so, of course, because he did a runner."

Harold's eyes were still fixed on the letters and rings in the middle of the table, his voice hushed, like someone making small talk at a funeral. "I remember it clear as a bell. It was her thirteenth birthday. We gave her that ring."

Mrs. Philips shook his hand, thanked him, and closed the front door behind him. McCann walked back down the path and the tree-lined suburban streets towards the golf course and the train station, back towards the less salubrious part of town. He had nothing to do for a while: a thought both pleasing and disturbing. He put his hand in his overcoat pocket and felt Marvin's lead. Perhaps that was enough.